Sir John's Companie

Trade & Treachery in Medieval Yorkshire

by Frank D. Macaulay

DORRANCE
PUBLISHING CO
EST. 1920
PITTSBURGH, PENNSYLVANIA 15238

Dorrance Publishing Co
585 Alpha Drive
Suite 103
Pittsburgh, PA 15238
Visit our website at *www.dorrancebookstore.com*

ISBN: 978-1-6461-0597-7
eISBN: 978-1-6461-0043-9

Prologue

Nájera, Spain – April 3, 1367

"Keep up!" James shouts hoarsely. "Stay together and keep it tight!" Won't they ever learn he fumes? If his Companie lags and lets Sir John's flank be exposed, the rebuke will be swift and harsh. He sweeps his view back and forth, turning his head to the right and then to the left. Finally, in frustration, he flips his helmet visor up to see what is going on. The Castilian cavalry is forming for another charge. "Aarchers!"

"Hugh, William, Tenebro, make ready!" He points vigorously at the Castilian horsemen. James' eighty long bowmen are divided into three sections. It is up to his lieutenants to keep them concentrated on the right target. "Here they come; wait on my command." He can hardly be heard over the heavy fighting to their left where Chandos and Lancaster press the outnumbered enemy vanguard. "Now!" he hollers, bringing his mace down in a chopping motion.

Their arrows fall thick as rain into the lightly armored men and horses, bringing them down and destroying their charge. They will not be able to rescue their trapped comrades and withdraw for the second time.

"Sir James!"

Virgil points left where the brutal fight is suddenly surging towards them. "Clyde, get your men reformed!" James lowers his visor and moves quickly to the front of his heavies as the Spaniards break through a gap in an attempt to escape their predicament. "Stay together!"

A sword slashes down towards his head. James parries it with the mace in his left hand and brings the spike of his war hammer in his right hand, viciously into the side of the man's helmet. The slender spike punches through; he tears it free and then slams his shoulder into the man's crumbling body to avoid a spear thrust from the side – just in time. He squeezes the spear shaft under his right arm and brings his mace down on the extended wrist, smashing it into broken bones. Don't stand there looking at him scream! Keep your feet moving! Keep your eyes moving! The endless lessons are pounding in his brain.

He swings the mace again as a man staggers past, clips his shoulder, and then rushes forward towards a big man swinging a two-handed sword. The Spaniard clangs it hard against a raised shield, knocking James' man to his knees. James leaps in close, swinging the war hammer against the man's forearms to stymie the man's backswing and swings the mace as hard as he can at the man's belly. Its sharp flanges bite, and he screams in rage, spinning James off his feet, as the dark brute finally gets the big sword back around. Roll and back to your feet, James, in one motion! The voices are there again.

He lands back upright as the big sword again whirls towards him. It never gets there as Clyde's halberd nearly takes the Spaniard's head off with a blood spraying thaw-ump. Their eyes meet, but there is no recognition from Clyde's wild-eyed frenzy. The enemy falls back; their surge expended.

"James, the bridge!"

What bridge? Sir John Chandos is trying to get his attention. "We have them here, James. They are trying to retreat across the river." He is pointing back over his shoulder.

James throws up his visor, nodding. "To me! Form on me! Virgil get Clyde!" Yelling at each face he recognizes, he reforms the Companie to pursue the retreating main body of Don Enrique's army. When he gets to the front, he can finally see what Sir John was telling him. The Spaniards are running to escape across the Najerilla River back into the town of Nájera.

"Stay together! Reform on the march! William, get your men moving!" The lanky archer is forming his men up like it is a damn parade. As the confused and panicked enemy mobs the narrow entrance to the bridge, they quickly close in on them. A Spanish knight attempts to form a defense but is having little success. The men's only thought is to get to safety, and they will not turn and form up.

"Archers, make ready." James calmly brings the company to a halt with his arm in the air. "Let loose!" he yells, bringing his mace down. "Hugh, concentrate on the men on the bridge." Hugh nods and gets his men shooting, not at the mob fighting to get on the bridge, but at the men already trying to get across into the town. James wants to clog the bridge with fallen bodies to slow them down. His archers are slaughtering the packed soldiers. Some jump into the river gorge, which is deep and rapid, trying to escape, but only drown instead.

"Forward!" Virgil and Clyde lead the heavily armored foot soldiers into the melee. "Keep it tight!" When the men stay in an organized front, each supports the man next to them. As they begin to slaughter the Spaniards at the back, their panic only increases the disarray of them all in their haste to get away. Finally, James' Companie reaches the bridge on the heels of the retreating army.

"Forward!" They clamor over the dead bodies sprawling on the bridge, and James rushes towards the front, spurring his men onward. He does not want the city gate to close before they can get across. He swings both mace and hammer at the backs and heads of the running, panicked enemy and then stumbles himself in his rush to reach the gate. Then they are through and into the town, right on their heels.

James follows two Spanish knights and their men towards a large stone house, but gets the door slammed in his face. Virgil points to an open window on the second floor, and James goes back to get a running start into the big man's cupped hands. He is literally thrown up the wall to the window. His elbows on the sill, he pulls himself up and into the room. He hears men running up the stairs from the inside and quickly turns to pull the spry little Tenebroides in through behind him.

James hears Clyde outside the door on the street, with his men hacking away at it with axes. He turns to face the men coming up the stairs inside, and they quickly retreat back down them. Surrounded from above and the door splintering below, the Spaniards soon surrender.

The knights are the Grand Prior of St. Jago and the Grand Master of the Order of Calatrava. They will bring a fine ransom. The house had clearly been used as a residence for Don Enrique himself or one of his high-ranking followers. It has many chests of plate, jewels, and other riches. Outside the army of Prince Edward is now entering the town in mass. James can hear the screams as they slaughter or capture everyone they find and loot the town.

All the English mercenary companies of Prince Edward are currently in the employ of Pedro the Cruel and will be scrambling for spoils now. James pulls his Companie in and around the stone house to hold tight to what they already have in their possession. Even after turning over a third of the treasure to Prince Edward, he will be set for life if he can get back to England with it.

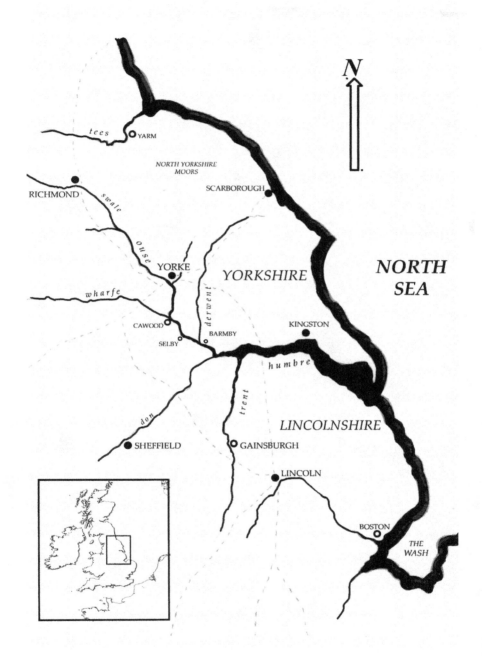

Chapter 1

The Dairy

The Birkdale Beck and Great Sleddale Beck tumble down their respective valleys to join and form the River Swale. After the falls below Richmond Castle, the Swale meanders gently another forty miles south, all the while collecting a little more flow from various side streams until it becomes the Ouse, which passes through the City of Yorke and continues until it empties into the broad Humbre estuary. Kingston-upon-Hull sits on the north shore a few miles before the Humbre reaches the North Sea. Starting below Richmond, with wares for commerce, you can be at the seaport of Kingston in less than a fortnight. From there all the world is your market.

It would be a simple journey, except for low water in the summer and the flooding after heavy spring rains. These rains can cause the Swale to quickly rise as much as fifteen feet and spill up over its banks. Fifty-four miles south of Richmond, when the Ouse reaches the city of Yorke, it becomes tidal. Sea-going ships of shallower draft may sail up to Yorke, provided the water is not unusually low and the tide is in their favor. Deeper drafted vessels typically make port nearer to the mouth of the Humbre estuary at Kingston and sell to merchants there or transfer their cargo onto barges that then travel upriver to the market in Yorke.

The barge *Marie* was built at a boatyard in Yorke specifically to ply the river between Yorke, the second largest city in England, and north to Richmond. She is thirty-two feet long, has a beam of eight, and her draft to the bottom of her keel when fully loaded is just two feet. She is decked flush with the top of the thwarts fore and aft but open to ribs and lapped planking over most of her length. There are tholes for twelve oarsmen, but typically her crew is eight, plus Virgil at the steering oar. At the moment, her triangular lateen sail is furled and tied to the spar as the sky is cloudless on this breezeless afternoon. The riverbanks just below Richmond are empty of folks as they stroke their way past the Abbey of Saint Agatha to the gravel beach below the Dairy.

It is harvest time; everyone is in the fields. Since it has been dry, the grain is in the barn, but the pease, vetches, and beans are yet to be harvested. Folks are tired but also jubilant – it has been a good year. The barge crew considers Richmond their home as it is where they spend the winter. Some have families in the city, which is just a half mile or less farther up the Swale. Virgil doesn't have a family, and so he just stays at the Dairy in the house. It is not actually a dairy any longer as the family died, and it had been left vacant. Sir James d'Arzhon was granted the property rights as a reward for service along with other lands from the Earl of Richmond, who is also the king's son, John of Gaunt – the powerful Duke of Lancaster. It was after the Battle of Auray; the same time as when he was knighted by Sir John Chandos, may he rest in peace. All an agreement between Sir James, Chandos, Lancaster, and the Duke of Brittany over the ransoms of high-ranking French prisoners. In battle the poorly armored soldiers may be slaughtered, but generally, high-ranking nobles are captured and then ransomed to gain their release. The higher the noble the higher the ransom and James had captured Bertrand du Guesclin, the Seneschal of France. Only a squire, then, he had to turn du Guesclin over to Sir John, but whatever the terms, Sir James came out of it with the knighthood, property, and considerable wealth.

The Dairy is made up of several low grey stone buildings that surround a courtyard. They were once whitewashed but most of that is gone. It had been a dismal place when Joel first arrived. All the existing buildings required new rafters and thatched roofs. The largest building was recently built with a slate roof. It is a warehouse on the ground floor, a large workroom on the next, and additional storage in the loft above that. The next largest building is the barn where the milking had been done; it is now a dormitory on the second floor and various workshops below.

Joel, Sir James' steward, meets the barge at the bank. "Tough pull?"

"Not bad; too many shallows," Virgil replies as the crew ties up to the large willow. If it got any drier the Swale will be unnavigable for the boat, even lightly as she is built. They needed to all get out and haul the boat across some spots. The *Marie* is the only river barge that comes up all the way to Richmond. Those that hired someone else to transport their goods needed to haul them south by wagon first. It was an advantage for Virgil when he bargained to secure a shipping consignment.

"Did you bring the millstones?" Joel peeks under the tarp. The grist mill was almost ready for the stones and he wanted it in operation as the harvests came in. Sir James wants to see a steady income stream in Richmond and the mill will help. He has been spending a lot of money here and it has yet to pay out.

Virgil nods and announces, "Let's take a break and get some supper. Then we will all get the stones out together." The crew moan in the reluctant understanding that wives, children, and, in some cases, girlfriends will have to wait until the boat is unloaded. "If we drop them, it will shatter the boat."

You would think a pair of millstones could be acquired locally; in Virgil's mind hauling them all the way up here was just lunacy. Master Tenebroides just said that it was a particular 'buhrstone' that was required and Gainsburgh was where we had our source. That meant that Thomas had brought it north down the Trent on his barge and then to Barmby; Tenebroides brought it up the Ouse to Yorke, and from there it had been Virgil's 'stone to bear.'

By the time they had eaten and re-assembled back above the beach, there is an audience. Word got around quickly that they were back and loved ones, workers here at the dairy, and folks anxious for items ordered from Yorke are showing up. Everything else is unloaded and the tarp and its frame removed. The eight oarsmen, formerly long-bowmen, are big fellows. The water is only thigh deep on a firm gravel bed as they wade in on both sides of the barge. "We're going to work it up to thwart height and then to these long beams… stop waving at her and pay attention, you bloody knave. Drop this through the boat, and I'll find out how long you can hold your breath!"

"Right you are, Master Virgil, right you are."

"We'll get the small one first." First one side of the round flat 'running,' or upper, millstone is lifted and a stubby timber slipped under, and then the other side is lifted. The process is repeated four times until the stone lay on the crisscrossed stack of timbers even with the sides of the boat. "On my signal, we will lift it clear of the boat, get one end of the beams on the bank, and then tump it out on to the gravel."

"Well, that wasn't too bad. Joel, do you have a stout fence post that will fit through here?" The millstone has a convenient hole right through the middle just like a wagon wheel, except the hole is square, and Virgil intends to use it. "Bertrand, the big rope up and around the oak for me, if you please," he said, pointing to the large tree at the top of the slope. "Let's rig a parbuckle."

Joel returns with the fence post, which fit nicely through the stone like an axle. The mid-point of the rope went up around the oak and the ends are brought down and wrapped around each side of the fence post several times and then run back up the hill. "Starboard oars," he said, pointing to the right end of the rope. "Larboard oars," he said, pointing to the left. The eight big oarsmen clamored up the bank to their assigned rope.

"Ease the slack out now, stay even with each other, and walk up the hill on my signal. Easy as she goes – now." The crew walks easily up the gentle slope at the top of the bank. The rope winds off each side of the 'axle' as they walk up and winds on each side at the same time from the ever-shortening length of rope that went up around the oak. Soon the stone has rolled up the bank and reached the tree. A short time later, the first stone is through the gate and sitting on edge in the courtyard of the dairy.

The second stone is twice the thickness, and therefore weight, of the first one. It is raised to thwart height and onto the long beams. With the stone on the bank, the parbuckle and fence post is re-rigged and once again, this time with more brute effort, the big stone reaches the oak tree. "Let's get it unrigged and rolled up through the gate; then we are done."

Everyone relaxes as the rope is unwound and coiled. Some gentle nudging between the oarsmen and banter with the women watching and they get careless. Mark starts to slip down the slope and steadies himself by pushing against the stone. This results in the millstone starting to slowly roll back down the hill towards the river and gather speed before anyone realizes what is happening. The chase is on, but the stone reaches the edge of the slope first and disappears down the bank heading for *Marie*. The stone tips as it hits the gravel bed, one end of the 'axle' digs into the beach, spinning the rolling stone downstream and splashing into the Swale just behind the barge. The initial horror gives way to guffaws and then open laughter

Virgil is red-faced and furious! But when he sees that his precious *Marie* is still intact, he starts laughing, too. Anyway, it is better than crying. "Bloody hell!" he shouts. "Roll that damned thing back up here."

"Took you a bit to see the humor there, Virgil," said Mark, grinning. Virgil's reply was an open-handed cuff on the side of his head. As tall as Virgil, but not nearly as heavily built, Mark goes down in a heap.

Virgil leans down until he is nearly nose-to-nose. "I was imagining myself explaining a shattered barge to Master Tenebroides and Sir James, enduring the tongue lashing that would surely follow, and convincing them that we could all be productive workers until it was repaired." The barge is essential in their work. The realization that there might be no need for them until the boat was replaced or repaired is a sobering one.

"Not a conversation I would want you to be having Master Virgil," Mark said quietly. Tenebroides may be small, but he was tough, wiry, and when crossed cruel and unforgiving. As for Sir James, if you were not up to the task, he would find someone that was. You would end up with more menial work. He takes Virgil's hand and is helped back to his feet.

In the evening, Virgil begins surveying the merchandise for the next trip downstream. "No more sacks of wool?" Wool is his primary cash cargo, but no more sheep will be sheared until spring unless they are also being slaughtered. Usually a good number of ram lambs will be slaughtered on Martinmas at the end of the month. You don't need that many rams. They do produce wool, but no milk for cheese, and obviously no lambs. No point in feeding them over the winter. They will be tethered aboard for the trip to Yorke where they bring a good price.

"None. I need all we have left through the winter to keep our own weavers busy, and you took the last of Simon Quixley's wool last month." The steady click of the shuttles can be heard through the open windows of the new workshop building. "Four Flemish weavers each on their own loom. The captain wants them busy all winter." Sir James had been their captain in of one of the many mercenary companies ravaging France and they had all served with Prince Edward in Spain.

"I well know they are here; I brought them and the looms all the way from Yorke, and Master Tenebroides brought them up the Ouse to Yorke from Kingston. What do I carry to Yorke, then, besides sheepskins and cheese?"

"We will have a good load of grain if I can get it winnowed before you set out…"

"Really? I thought all the demesne harvest was needed here to get us through the winter and to the following harvest." In recent years the lord's harvest, which is Sir James', after the tithe was taken was barely enough from the little villages to support the people that lived at the dairy and provide seed corn for planting.

"We're doing a bit better now, but Flemish cloth is what Sir James wants delivered this month." Joel smiles conspiratorially. "Let me show you."

"These are nice! Our weavers made this?" Rolls of cloth in forest green, rust, dark blue, and beige sit on the table and make for a compact and high value cargo.

"And our new fulling mill finished them. Come with me."

Next to the old walled dairy buildings the Sand Beck had been dammed to create a mill pond. Joel led the way across towards the waterwheel rotating slowly in the sluice. The dam walk continued over the sluice on a bridge and into what turned out to be the second floor of a stone mill.

"Looks like a castle barbican; I did not see it as such before the water filled up behind the dam." Indeed, it did. The lower story of the mill had no windows; the second floor only had them on the sluice side. It stood three floors high below the dam and two above, and the mill pond and the catch area below formed what could have been a moat. In fact, if you add in the last hundred yards of the beck and with the River Swale it 'moated' the dairy on two sides. The third side of the triangular area, to the west, was only protected by a little wall and the buildings. "Is Sir James expecting a siege?"

Joel laughs. "Of course, there is no entry on the far side, so it cannot actually be a gatehouse. It is absolutely our intention to make ourselves less vulnerable over time."

"Well, the bloody Scots raid as far south as Yorke. Usually bypass Richmond because of the castle and the city walls but that doesn't make outlying farms like us at all safe. What's this?"

Joel had led him inside. "This will be the grist mill. Pull this lever and it engages the gears to the water-wheel shaft to turn the stone you brought. The big stone sits here; it doesn't rotate." Down the staircase to the bottom floor and Joel had to shout to make himself heard. "This is the fulling mill." Two timbers went up and down as lever arms beating fabric in a trough of water. "If I pull this lever, it disengages the mechanism." As Joel pulled back the timbers stopped moving and the shaft attached to the center of the waterwheel spun without load. "Not so loud now."

"Seems rather simple. What does it do?"

"It's just like the fullers in Yorke stomping up and down all day in the cloth tubs. It cleans and fills out the wool fibers. This trough refills the tubs with clean water heated as it passes through the burning charcoal trough."

"And this pipe empties the tubs," added the boy, Joel's son, minding the mill.

"You called this Flemish cloth?"

Joel pulled back on the lever to start the beams back up and motioned Virgil upstairs above the grist mill. "Yes, I did. I believe Sir James intends to sell it as such in Yorke. 'Made by Flemish weavers.' The first return on his investment." Virgil nodded with pursed lips. This is interesting as imported Flemish cloth commands a much higher price than English cloth. This is to sell as 'first quality broadcloth' at almost three times the price, and since it is woven here in England there will be no import duty to pay to that vile thief Lord Latimer's customs agents in Kingston. Virgil saw no incongruity with being loyal to the king and detesting the men responsible for collecting the wool subsidy on his behalf. After all, what did they do to tend the sheep and ship the wool? Nothing! And yet they still take a hefty sum from the profits of those that work so hard. It did seem that half the population of the dairy is now Flemish. Four weavers and their families, their apprentices, and the dyer and his family are all Flemish.

"Do you speak Flemish?"

"Just a little but learning more every day." He laughed. "I understand more than they think I do. Oh, and all this is not to be talked about openly; I do not know how we plan to manage potential tax assessments yet. I need to go into Richmond in the morning to deliver some of your consigned cargo and check on the carpenter's progress. Any interest in coming along?"

Virgil shakes his head. "I've got to ride up into Swaledale and arrange a purchase of lead. It is needed for the roof of Saint Peter's – Sir James intends to improve our standing with the archbishop."

"Lead? I also could not help but notice the geese that were herded up from your boat into my courtyard," Joel said with a touch of sarcasm.

"They can be a bit aggressive if you don't show them who is in charge."

"I assume they are not for our Christmas dinner?"

"Ha! We are supposed to fletch arrows through the winter. I think Sir James believes we just sit around during the months we are not on the river."

"Sit around and sometimes get into a bit of trouble with the town bailiff."

"We didn't start that; we just finished it. Anyway, we need to find ash for shafts and set up a forge to make the heads. Ten weeks and two sheaves a week is almost five hundred arrows."

"Those geese will not look the same in March."

"No. But the Crown pays four pence a sheaf."

"Six shillings and change are not much for nine men over ten weeks. But it will cover the fine levied in the wapentake court for the fighting." Joel enjoyed teasing the big man.

"The constable was a fool to try and break it up without identifying himself."

"He learned that lesson the hard way."

"I expect we are to make many more arrows next year if the war continues. The geese can stay in the beck and the mill pond. They have had their wings clipped, but they will still wander off."

"If we feed them, they are more likely to stay. This may be a good winter craft for some of the Companie men up in the Swaledale villages, too."

If you do not have the good sense to be born the son of the king or a duke, then wool is the best way to wealth in England and has been so now for many years. It is English wool that supplies weavers in the low countries; so much so that King Edward cut off wool exports, at times, as a political weapon bringing the economies of these countries to their knees. What Sir James had explained to Virgil was that exporting wool and then importing it back as cloth was not financially wise for the overall English economy: more money going out than coming in. There are English weavers, but they are typically making a poorer quality cloth. King Edward supported bringing Flemish weavers to England and settling them here despite the objections of the English weaving guilds. What his captain had been saying was that quality broadcloth, cloth not wool, is going to be the next source of significant wealth in England. This is particularly true with the cost of the wool subsidy on exports at six shillings eight pence a sack! That so much of the subsidy ends up in Lord William Latimer's pocket must gall Sir James to no end.

The next morning, Joel and his son walk to the market square in Richmond. It is a short walk and, as it is not market day, not very crowded. The bridge across the Swale on the south side of Richmond is very convenient to the dairy and just downstream of the falls and the castle. There is no roar of water over the cascade today as it has been so dry, but when it rains the torrent pours down the valley and thunders over the rocks. The great square Norman keep of Richmond Castle towers over the walled city; it is one hundred feet tall. The rock precipice above the falls made a strong site for fortification and had been used as such since at least Roman times and that is why Richmond exists in this spot. The 'Honor of Richmond' is a lucrative and coveted royal land grant, which is why Lancaster petitioned his father for it and with vast other holdings he is the wealthiest man in England, besides his father, the king, of course.

Joel had not been able to purchase a shop on the market square as those were all prime space and occupied. His best purchase was just one shop off the corner, and he was able secure two more buildings on that block. They would have to do. There are still vacant houses in Richmond as the city was not recovering as quickly as Yorke from the Black Death, but they were not close enough to the market. Richmond had lost almost half its populace from the plague just over twenty years past. The narrow buildings are all three stories plus the garret with about ten foot of frontage on the street.

Sir James' relationship with the Duke of Lancaster is able to make things happen in their favor here in Richmond. That the plague created severe labor shortages and empty streets may have helped, too. Commerce generates tax revenues and the local wapentake bailiff is always anxious to meet the city's financial obligations, the 'farm,' to the Earl of Richmond, who is also the Duke of Lancaster. Joel stepped into the former brewer's shop and home, it is open, and he hears banging upstairs.

"How is progress?"

David, the master carpenter stood and removed his cap. "Almost finished here, Master Joel."

Joel tapped his foot gingerly on the new floor and then more firmly. Then looked up at the new boards in the ceiling, which was the floor of the garret. "The roofing is satisfactory?"

"It seems to be. No leaks last week, and it was raining steady and hard. They are working on the roof down the street today."

"Is the lift working yet?"

The master carpenter nods and leads the way upstairs. From the central roof beam hung a pulley and the rope ran through it to a windlass. "Give 'er a try," he offers.

Joel's son jumps to turn the handle. "Can I do it?" Joel nods and the gear clicked as it went around. Soon the platform rolled up level with the garret floor. "This will work nicely." The attic is going to be used as the malting floor. The barley will be spread and allowed to sprout. The gable windows had been enlarged and replaced with vent louvers to prevent the barley from cooking itself as the process produces heat.

"We can move in tomorrow, then. I need you down at the mill when you are finished here; the stones have arrived. I expect to be able to keep you busy through the winter, and I have a place for you to stay. If that is agreeable to you?"

"Oh, yes, thank you, sir!"

Steady work for craftsmen in one location was very desirable. Otherwise, when one job was done, they packed their tools and searched for more work.

Even the great cathedrals ran out of funds for periods during their decades of construction and had to let their craftsmen go. At the moment, construction on the cathedral in Yorke is busy, indeed. If David went there for work, it might be years before they found another master carpenter.

The brewer had been working in the dairy for several months and seemed to know what she was doing. Her ale was good, very good. Just like the weavers, Virgil brought her up from Yorke with her brother, but Tenebroides said he was not a Companie man. The 'Companie' consists of veterans that fought across the channel with Sir John Chandos. Many returned to England with Sir James after the Battle of Nájera in Spain back in 1367. All of Virgil's barge crew had been in Sir James' Companie as archers.

After getting the millstones rolled to the mill, Virgil rode west up the Swale valley into the rugged region called Swaledale. Seven of the oarsmen loped along on foot. Bernard had begged off due to a 'family matter.' They hardly appeared like a barge crew now. Bows were strung, swords, axes, and daggers belted. They were what they had been for years: English longbow men. They just weren't marching through France on chevauchée.

Lead was the worst cargo of all things. It was heavy, of low value, and was to be transported at this time of year with the water down. Millstones and lead; would this penance for sins unknown never end? Well, Virgil had to admit to himself that some of the sins were certainly known. Soon the rolling hills were dotted with sheep and they were on the hunt for the shepherds.

"Heard ya coming a mile away. All a jingle and a jangle!"

Virgil recognized the shepherd grinning at him from his perch on a rock outcropping: a Companie man. "Walter, I should have been using you as a forward scout today."

"Naw." He gets down and limps towards them. "My scouting days are done. How are you boys?"

"We're still running the barge between Yorke and Richmond. It is mostly peaceful; just battles with toll men and gravel banks."

"How is the captain?"

"Always with plans and schemes."

Walter laughed at a memory. "I remember a time or two when things went bad and I was sure we were gonna all die, but the captain, he had a plan, and we slipped out of the noose."

"Expect something to go wrong and be ready when it does is what he always told me. By the by, I'm supposed to ask you if anyone has been trying to buy your spring fleecing."

"A puffed-up Fleming was by in mid-summer. I told him I wasn't the owner of the sheep and he went on. He got the same answer from all of us."

"Did he ask after the owner?"

"I told him it was the Duke of Lancaster to get him gone."

Virgil wondered if Walter knew that his answer was not entirely incorrect. The duke is James' liege lord for his lands in North Yorkshire. "Good, that should do it! If another foreign wool buyer comes around again, we may need to give him a bit of an education."

The shepherd smiled. "We already came to the same conclusion."

A Flemish buyer this far north might force Joel to pay a higher price for wool. Not all the wool they shipped came from their own flocks. Worse, it could be part of an effort by Lord Latimer and Richard Lyons to get a foothold in the wool trade. Wasn't it bad enough that they farmed the customs revenues on every sack exported! Virgil would need to talk to Sir James; he will want to know. "If I continue up this valley, will I find lead miners?"

"You will, indeed. The free miners are not hard to find; just listen for the 'tink tink' of the digging. Umm…might I ask why yur lookin' for 'em?"

"I need to buy lead for the cathedral roof in Yorke."

"You may want the smelter, not the miners."

"I just might." Virgil was not above a little enlightenment. "Give me the lay of the land."

"The miners dig out lead-rich rocks looking for silver," Walter explains. "The smelter buys that rock, gets the lead out, and pours it into lead ingots."

"Ah, where do I find the smelter?"

"This valley splits up ahead; turn to the right and down. You'll see the smoke."

"Do the miners find much silver?" Mark asks greedily, having suddenly perked up.

"They seem more desperate, hungry, and miserable each time I see them."

"Let's get moving, then, and stop all that damned jingle-jangle."

Many brewers are women, but they would not allow Matilda into the brewers' guild in Yorke, as she wasn't a freeman of the city. She is young, a petite and attractive blonde, with a quick smile and a quicker wit. She may be small, but she sure tells Gus what to do and how. Must have been Sir James that determined she would come to Richmond. The Carmelite Priory in Yorke had a brewery already, but it was not very good. Stocky and bald, Gus said nothing but seemed to work hard and without complaint.

There are guilds in Richmond, but not one of brewers. For an annual fee to the bailiff of the wapentake, rights to make and sell are secured. More money to Lancaster. With the help of the boat crew, when they are in town, they work at whatever needs doing, Matilda is moved into her new shop, brewery, and home in Richmond. A sign with a picture of a frothy tankard is hung, and a fresh keg opened. They all celebrate noisily to attract a bit of attention to the news of a new brewery in the city. She has a few kegs made from her stay at the dairy to serve immediate customers, and the ingredients to start making more.

"How is our brewer doing?"

"She seemed satisfied."

"Joel, do you expect any trouble from other brewers in Richmond?"

"No, I spoke with them, and they sell out every new batch in just a few days. They seem to think there is enough business to go around. Are you concerned?"

"A little, but I've no good reason to be. Why don't you take her around and introduce her to the other brewers, the constable, bailiffs, archdeacon, and some of the other important persons of the city? Have some of my men to carry some modest gifts for her to present to them."

"And show that she is not all alone in this mean world, Virgil?" He teases the big man.

"Something like that. She is one of us now. I want to issue a subtle notification that if you are tempted to try and take advantage of her you should think again. It would be a shame to have to be heavy-handed later, when it could all be avoided."

"Agreed!" Joel did not want to think about Virgil being heavy-handed. That sounds more like Sir James' anticipating trouble than Virgil, thinks Joel, likely to be his suggestion.

"I don't like her helper." The man was furtive and shy. Whenever Virgil had set eyes on him, on the trip upriver, he looked away. In Virgil's experience that meant he had something to hide and that was rarely good.

"You like our pretty little brewer, don't you?" Joel smiled with mischief in his eyes. "Gus has quite a catch, doesn't he?"

"I don't get what she sees in him; a dullard."

"Opposites attract."

"That is certainly the case here!"

"Virgil, he is her older brother."

"Oh! What? Then why is she the brewer and he the assistant?"

Joel responds gently, "He is 'simple,' Virg."

Virgil is stunned and ponders that for a moment. "You mean like an idiot? Possessed?"

"There is no violence in him. In fact, I don't believe there is a mean bone in his body. He just lacks the capacity to manage his own affairs."

"He never says a word."

"He is like a child, and you probably scare the shit out of him." Virgil was a full head taller than most men and could be a hard disciplinarian with his barge crew if required. "He speaks just fine. I don't believe that 'possessed' nonsense, not a word of it, and neither does Sir James. Didn't you read the letter that you brought with him?"

"I've never done a thing to threaten him." Virgil was fine with numbers and a list of goods on his barge, all words he recognized, but not a letter.

"Good, be gentle with him. Coletta found him chained to a wall one night, sobbing at Saint Leonard's, and then met Matilda visiting him the next day.

Then she went to Sir James. Now they are here, and as you said, 'They are ours.' It is hardly surprising he was intimidated."

The following day, Virgil splashes across the shallows of the Swale to call on the White Canons of Saint Agatha's at Easby. The Premonstratensian abbey is just downstream from the dairy.

"I've a delivery for the cellarer." Virgil shows the brother at the gate his canvas bag. This small gate opens into the service yard of the abbey near the kitchens and storerooms. The buildings here are smaller than the main buildings beyond. A cellarer is responsible for the provisions of the abbey, their proper storage, and purchasing what is needed.

The gateman looks the bearded and scarred big man with his bare muscular forearms up and down; Virgil towers over him. "Very well, then," he says as he opens the gate, just wide enough for Virgil to slip through.

A groom steps forward looking to take his mount. "No need, good brother, I walked. But do please direct me to Brother Robert, the cellarer. He has sent for these." Brother Robert was what you might call a difficult customer. He had tried to re-negotiate the agreed price upon delivery once and Virgil had turned and walked out his door. He had to pay half up front now.

"I'll walk you there myself." This brother is irrepressibly cheerful.

"You seem in good spirits."

"Oh, yes, the weather has been perfect for the harvest this year," he said brightly.

Cheerful people always make Virgil suspicious. His memories are anything but pleasant of monastery life. However, it can be a comfortable life and Saint Agatha's appears to be doing well. The huge, soaring church with its beautiful stained-glass windows and stone tracery, as well as the tall refectory, chapter house, dormitories, and main gatehouse of the compound make the recent improvements at the dairy seem quite paltry. The expense of the beautiful and extensive abbey was beyond his grasp. They arrive at Cellarer Robert's door, and Virgil knocks as he enters. "Brother Robert?"

"Yes, yes, what is it?"

"I've brought the spices you ordered from the market in Yorke." Brother Robert closes the ledgers on his table and sets them to the side. Spices are an extravagant purchase, and the cellarer carefully weighs the pepper, cardamom, nutmeg, and other spices to ensure he is getting full measure. He squints in the dim light to count up the weights after setting each one on the scale. "Here is the tally on the balance due." Coming back up the river spices are Virgil's most valuable cargo, and as they do not take up much space or weigh down the boat, they are easily his best goods.

Brother Robert scrutinizes the invoice but can find no fault and slowly counts out the coins. It is more than he liked to part with, but he had placed the order at the abbot's insistence, and the cost is what he had been quoted.

Virgil marks the invoice paid in full. "If you're wanting more salt, I'll need to buy it this trip. There won't be any more that is affordable after that until late April, Brother Robert." Salt in the winter had to be imported. Virgil still did not trust Robert and the feeling was mutual, but the Abbey had more spending ability than anyone else in Richmond. Virgil had access to goods that Robert needed and could not get cheaper elsewhere; he had tried. So, they both make the best of it.

Robert winces at the memory of the price he had to pay last year. "When will you be leaving?"

"In a week; shall I return before I depart to see if you desire anything?"

"That would be helpful. Will this be your last trip of the year?"

"Should certainly be one more after that. Maybe two if the weather holds and we get a little rain."

Chapter 2

Haste for Lincoln

Sir James steps out of The Swan and into the crisp Yorkshire air. It is cooler than usual for the time of year, but there is not a cloud in the sky. The inn is busy this Friday morning as guests hastily depart following market day; most have many miles to travel. He is, as always, elegantly attired for the meeting just concluded with Simon Quixley. Master Quixley and his brother, William, are wool merchants and leading citizens of Yorke. They are customers but also competitors, and it is necessary to maintain good relations as they could make things difficult. This is the first barge load of wool from Richmond since the spring shearing and all of it belongs to the Quixleys. They have additionally paid James for its transport on to Kingston.

The Swan is on the River Foss, just beyond the walls – outside the Monk Bar gate on the north side of the city. It is a good location for an inn, outside a city gate and next to one of the Foss bridges on a main road. Space inside the city walls is crowded and too hard to get, and this allowed enough property to build on stables, barn, and tavern at an affordable price. Sellers at the Thursday market can pull their wagons into the courtyard the night prior where they are secure, so they can get a good night's sleep, and be close enough to Market Square to be there early for the market opening. Being on the Foss allows the Whitefriars to pick up supplies with their boat at The Swan. The friars have a boat quay on the edge of their compound in the city into the Foss at the King's Fishpond. The Church is exempt from city fees paid at the gate, but it makes a convenient back way to get other goods into the city.

"Sir James, Sir James!" Master Tenebroides' son Peter ran up the street dodging people. "Fa, Father has ja-ja-just arrived…"

"Catch your breath, Peter." There was no mistaking the ten-year-old for someone else's son. Peter is small for his age and has a thick mat of red hair, like his father. Hopefully, he will not grow up with his father's famous temper.

"We took aboard some Companie men at Barmby."

Barmby is Sir James' manor on the salt marsh south of here near where the River Ouse joins the Trent to form the Humbre. "How many?"

"Eleven, Sir James. The sheriff in Lincoln has seven more locked up."

"Alright, Peter, ask your father to get them up to the priory in twos and threes. I'll find Prior William." James picks up the pace. What caused them to get locked up and how will he manage to get them released have now completely displaced thoughts of wool shipments.

James heads through the barbican and three-story gate of the Monk Bar and enters the walled city of Yorke. Saint Peter's cathedral dominates this side of the city, and the archbishop is extending the nave east in a massive construction project. The addition will make it larger than the Church of Saint Mary's Abbey just a few streets down towards the River Ouse. The Archbishop of Yorke is spending an enormous amount of money again this year. Carpenters, masons, stonecutters, and unskilled laborers swarm over the site and scaffolding. At first James found their noise irritating, now it has blended into the other sounds of the city; he barely takes notice. James has The Swan making meat pies and selling them to the workers at midday. He is selling as much ale as he can purchase. What he really wants is tavern near the market. The cathedral construction is likely to go on for at least the next decade. Getting part of that spending into the Companie's coffers is often part of his contemplation.

He avoids a swirl of stone dust and the piles of horse dung in the street. A light rain overnight has made for a nice morning. By afternoon, the city stench will return. It is a short walk to his townhouse just past market square. In his upstairs bedroom, James slides the clothes hanging in his wardrobe to the side and pushes open the back of the cabinet to reveal a dark staircase. His fingers graze the stone wall of the passage to guide him down through the back of his house and through the perimeter wall of the priory. The paneling in the dim hallway behind the Prior's study opens to his touch and he emerges.

The prior's lodging is in the west range of buildings of the walled compound of the Carmelites. James knocks as he opens the door and enters the study. "Prior William?"

"Yes, yes, I am here."

"William, a moment of your time." Prior William stands as does Mark, the priory cellarer, with whom he had been talking. "Actually, good to find you both together; Tenebroides is sending eleven Companie men here now. He picked them up in Barmby."

"We will show them the hospitality of our order."

Mark asks, "How long do you think they will be staying?" As cellarer he is responsible for the inventory of foodstuffs at the priory. It is a reasonable question.

"It may be for a week or two. We'll know better when we see what condition they are in. The Sheriff of Lincoln has seven more locked up. I need to ride for Lincoln, but I'll want to speak to them first."

"Yes, of course." William nods. "I'll have all of them assembled in the refectory."

James retraces his steps back up the way he came.

An hour later, dressed in a dove grey doublet quilted in a diamond pattern and grey hose disappearing into thigh-high calfskin riding boots, Sir James d'Arzhon emerges from his townhouse onto Hungate. A matching cloak and broad-brimmed hat with a tuft of silver-grey feathers complete his attire. A fine-jeweled sword hangs from a broad black belt that crosses his chest over his right shoulder. The wealthy French nobleman for whom it had been made would never need it again. Two, tall squires stride behind him to Fossgate and then down to the Whitefriars' entrance.

His gloved hand thumps the knocker on the heavy oaken door, which is immediately answered by the opening of a small window behind iron bars. A face fills the opening. "Captain, welcome!" he says as he unlatches the main door to allow entry.

"Greetings, Brother Michael." Michael is a Companie man.

"Welcome, Sir James. Prior William and our guests are in the refectory. Brother Hugh will escort you there." At the mention of his name, a large man with an infectious smile came forward and led them off in a direction they already know perfectly well.

The prior and several white-robed brothers rise as Sir James enters the hall. Following their example, the eleven ragged guests quickly shuffle to their feet. James looks them over; they may appear worse-for-wear, but these are tough men. Some seem familiar. "Please, please, have a seat, all of you," he said, waving an elegantly gloved hand. "It would appear that you have had a rough journey."

The men nod and sit back down wearily...except for one. "You'll remember me, Sir James?" he said almost pleadingly as he kneaded the hat in his hands.

"Geoffrey." Amazingly, the name came to him. "Fine man with the bow." Geoffrey had served with him at Auray. "You've lost some companions in Lincoln, yes?" They nod. "Tell me."

Geoffrey blurts out, "We ran out of money north of London. Had to get food somewhere."

"I see. So, you stole food." It was a plight all the Companie men could relate to. Armies did not provide adequate food for the men; they were expected to find it themselves on the march. Sometimes that was hard to do in a hostile land and you went without. As a result, most of the Companie men, including James, never had the possibility of hunger far out of mind. Even now, when they were all well provided for and the notion irrational, it was a fear deeply ingrained. "Did you injure anyone?"

"No one."

"Not even the sheriff's party?"

"They found our campsite while we were out foraging. The men we left there were in a bad way. When the sheriff got them, we just went ahead and moved on north. Figured at least they would get something to eat and a dry bed. Attacking the sheriff and his men would just get us hunted as murderers."

"You are right about that." James expressed his thoughts out loud. "Hopefully, the Sheriff of Lincoln doesn't plan to make an example of them as thieves." The men winced at that.

"We have been led to understand that you would help us Sir James; find us work, a place to stay." Geoffrey was desperately pleading.

"I'll need their names, Geoffrey. I want all of you to stay here until I return. Help out as asked. Prior William has graciously agreed to offer you the hospitality of his order. Respect his authority and the routine of the priory. Brother Hugh, please see where some of these men can find useful work."

"Indeed, Captain, The Swan can use some men that are good with horses and wagons."

"I am riding for Lincoln."

James catches Prior William's attention on the sly as he heads out. As the prior joins him, he says, "Please, get word to Master Tenebroides that I need Thomas to meet me in Gainsburgh in four days. Oh, and post this with the sheriff to send on to Prince Edward."

Master Tenebroides gets the big sailing barge cast off from the wharf in Yorke and moving as the tide turns on the Ouse. Running with the outgoing tide and the flow of the river should quickly get him many miles toward Barmby. He will be able to head downstream until the incoming tide completely turns back against him. They should arrive by morning. With luck, he will catch Thomas in Barmby or Blaketofte as the four days specified by Sir James is not much time. Even if Thomas is not near the confluence of the three rivers, it will just be a matter of moving up the Trent until he finds him. The farther up he has to go, the closer he will be to Gainsburgh. The Trent is big enough for his barge, the *Christine*, but he is not nearly as familiar with the sand banks and side channels. It will also mean heading away from Kingston-upon-Hull, but this load of Quixley's wool, some dye, and empty barrels will not spoil.

"I appreciate your seeing me so soon after my arrival, my Lord."

"You appear to have ridden hard, Sir James," Thomas De Fulvetby, the High Sheriff of Lincolnshire, replies slowly, rising from his chair. "Though I know to not what purpose. I was told you wish to succor the thieves I hold in my cells?"

James had, indeed, ridden hard, and his lower back hurt painfully. They had come down the Earninga Straete, the old Roman road, east of the Ouse and crossed the Humbre on the ferry as the tide was in and James did not want to wait for the ford to be passable. "Indeed, they are men that fought with me under the late Sir John Chandos. I hope to relieve you of any difficulties they present."

"Difficulties?" The rotund man smirked. "They are locked up securely and will be duly sentenced – not difficult at all!" The sheriff is the king's justice here and is a man used to exercising authority.

"All well and efficiently done, I am most certain," Sir James purred. "We cannot have lawless bands of men preying on the good people of England, even if they are veterans of our king's campaigns across the channel." He paused and then continued, "Perhaps the victims of their predations would be better soothed by financial compensation for their losses and inconvenience than by the satisfaction of seeing punishment inflicted? Prince Edward has encumbered me, as his man, to pay a reasonable fine and recompense for expenses incurred in instances such as these, my Lord."

"I hardly think that serves as a warning to those that would be tempted by thievery!" But James' shameless mention of the Prince of Wales had given him pause. His complexion was beginning to turn red.

"I do, indeed, understand your most justifiable intent. I only ask you to allow me to serve Prince Edward's interest in this matter." Keep him off balance, and prey on his uncertainties!

The haughty attitude had now vanished entirely from the sheriff and, for the first time, he saw past the languid figure before him to the hard eyes and powerful build of the former mercenary captain. "Is that so, Sir James?" he wavered. "The prince is aware these men are here?"

"On the prince's behalf, allow me to pay restitution to you now for all acts of lawlessness committed. If you could see your way clear to release the men into my custody; as an act of clemency for their service to the Crown… His Highness will be most appreciative. I have been led to believe that they are unwell and have suffered greatly already," James adds gently.

"I hardly see how that demonstrates the authority of the Crown," he sputters. "You will be responsible for their further conduct?"

"Entirely responsible. As you know, the prince and the king are still quite despondent over Sir John's death. I can have the offenders out of Lincolnshire in just a few days, my Lord. If I might have some writing materials, I will directly post a message to the prince to assure him that we were able resolve this difficulty."

"Thomas departed just this morning for Blaketofte with salt and barrels. He left some cargo for you to take up to Yorke as usual, Master Tenebroides. Ya missed him by an hour or so."

"I'll get the cargo on my return, Sig. He is headed back up the Trent?"

Sigismund, Sir James' stocky steward at Barmby Manor, scratched the scar than ran across his bald head and wrinkled his nose. "I guess back up the Trent as far as Gainsburgh."

"I need to see if I can catch him. Shove off fore and aft!" he hollers. "We still have another hour with the outgoing tide and this breeze will serve, as well." Tenebroides shoves the tiller bar over and the big barge moves towards mid-river. "Shake out the reefs. Look alive! You move like fat abbots today." This wind is in their favor for the next several miles until the Ouse curls north briefly and then they will need to rely on the river current to carry them through the slack until the tide turns strong against them. Then anchor and wait. The incoming tide can move as much as eight miles an hour at peak; there is no making progress down river against it.

Ahead is an anchored ship waiting for the tide to continue upriver. She looks Dutch built, shallow drafted, ideal for going as far as Yorke. They are signaling for him to pass to their larboard side, which will briefly take the wind from his sails. But he sails the Ouse every month and agrees there is more room there. They should not have anchored in mid-stream; likely concerned about getting grounded at low tide. She is taller than his *Christine* for sailing on the open sea, has full sides to the top of her rail, and two masts, but she is not much longer. Tenebroides' fifty-foot barge also has two masts, both lateen rigged like the great Venetian trading galleys rather than square sails like the Dutchman. The deck in the waist is below the gunwale just enough to allow the rowers to sit at an optimal level but she has no railings. The Humbre estuary can get riled up and choppy, at times, but the shore is never far. She can sail across the channel in a pinch but pray for fair weather if you choose to attempt that voyage. The six-foot foredeck is flush to the sides and angled up slightly to the stubby bow sprit. The twelve-foot stern deck is raised to allow a cabin below. Between the rowing benches is an open deck with hatches for cargo below and more can be lashed down above. The triangular fore sail shivers followed by the matching one on the main, but they refill quickly as they surge past at a handsome clip.

Thomas and his crew unload the empty barrels next to the communal shelter where the Companie fishermen of Blaketofte gut and clean their catch. Barrels half-filled with salt are rolled to Cnut's house and left with his wife, Freydis. This is one of the larger villages in the area because of its location on the river. Both village and manor are held by Richard Haunsard and have been in his family since the conquest by Duke William. The fishermen must pay a rent to them from their catch.

"Greetings, Freydis! Mending nets, as usual." All the fishing boats are out. He takes care to confirm that all their barrels are branded "Oliver of Yorke." Oliver has the fishmonger rights to sell on the Ouse Bridge, to Saint Mary's Abbey, and the other religious houses in Yorke.

"It is truly a never-ending task, but not an entirely unpleasant one."

"If Cnut would quit tearing them up, you could attend other things," Thomas teases.

Freydis laughs. "We have had that discussion." The older woman smiles. "Cnut insists that it is the fish that tear the nets and not him."

"Well, he would say that. Will you sign for the barrels?"

There is no rush. He will catch the last of the outgoing tide for the remaining half mile downstream and then wait at the mouth of the Trent for the tide to turn and carry them upriver. He turns back to the crew. "Let's get the work done; get some water in these barrels." If they were left empty, they may dry out, the oak shrink, and the ash hoops slip off.

As Thomas walks up the gang plank to go back aboard *Suzanne*, he sees Master Tenebroides' *Christine* taking in sail. He shouts, "What news?" as the white bow wave vanishes. Tenebroides brings her nose around to take the way off her and then around again to ease alongside.

Suzanne could be *Christine's* little sister at nine feet wide and twenty-four feet long. It is clear they had the same builder, and in this case the same owners.

"I've been chasing your wake all this day, Thomas!" Once tied up, the wiry, red-bearded bargeman confides, "I need you to wait on Sir James in Gainsburgh."

In the courtyard of Lincoln Castle, the released prisoners are in a pathetic state. They blink and stagger in the early morning light. Malcolm gives them each a chunk of dark maslin bread and a slab of cheese to eat while their irons are being removed. Maslin is a hearty peasant bread of mixed grains that are often sown together. "They need a good meal, Will," Sir James comments.

One has the shakes, another nurses his arm close against his body, and they all reek of their own filth. Several seem to have a pronounced limp, but that could just be a temporary result of the shackles. Almost all have a cough. "They need more than that," Will mumbles under his breath.

"Picking up more criminals to join your pathetic band, d'Arzhon?" sneers a tall figure emerging into the courtyard from a door at the top of a corner staircase.

"Lord Latimer, I thought you preferred the prostitutes of London. Are you spreading the pox further north?" James replies with contempt. He feels the old fury start to build in his chest.

"Stinking invalids from the reeking privy pit of society; they will fit in perfectly!"

One of the men lunges toward the staircase, but James intercepts him. "This is not the time nor the place!" he hisses and forces him back towards the wagon. He cannot let his anger get the best of him again. He hears Sir John's advice from years ago: 'He is baiting you, James; don't fall for it!'

"I hope our good sheriff has peeled the flesh off their backs with a good whipping. Enough to see the bones of their spines as I have seen yours, d'Arzhon!" Latimer spits out. "Do you still feel the sting of my piss on your back as you crawled?"

"Do not be foolish enough to think I have forgotten." James reply is cold and menacing. *I will kill that slimy whore-son one day and enjoy doing it!*

Latimer laughs with glee at the memory, but he is the only one. Even the men behind him on the stairs avoid James' stare. James sees one of them hide his face; it is his cousin and Lord Latimer's brother-in-law Allan – Lord Yarburgh, but their eyes do meet as the party disappears into the great hall.

Will and Malcolm must assist several of them up into the wagon. "Get moving," James barks irritably. "Right now, I want to get us all out of Lincoln as quickly as possible. Get one of these blankets around you if you are cold." They clearly were cold. "I am Sir James; this is Malcolm, and he is Will. We'll get better acquainted on the journey." *It would be useful to find out what mischief brought Latimer and Yarburgh to Lincoln, but that would have to wait.*

Normally, the majesty of Lincoln Cathedral, reputed to be the tallest building in the world, was an inspiring sight to Sir James. Today he could not get away from it fast enough. Each time he turned in the saddle, the soaring spire of over five hundred feet was still in view up on its hill. As long as he could still see it, he felt he was still within the reach of the sheriff, should he change his mind. Or, if Lord Latimer sought to change it, and the thought made him angry all over again at the exchange in the courtyard. A few hours later, Sir James brings them to a halt where the road ran through a small creek. "Everyone, get down and get a drink. Clean up a bit as best you can."

After a too short wait, the impatient James calls out, "Malcolm, Will, get them up on the back of the wagon one at a time, so we can see if anything is urgent. We will be late getting into Gainsburgh, so we should prepare a hot meal mid-afternoon."

"I'll get them some more bread and cheese to nosh on. There is nothing we can do now other than keep them warm and get more food into them," Malcolm replies.

After about another ten minutes, he says, "Right, then, let's get moving again."

It is several hours after sunset when the wagon pulls through the gate into the courtyard of the manor house in Gainsburgh. What had been a chilly late April day had gotten bitter cold at dark. Not so much for the three riders with the warmth of the horses beneath them, but for the men in the wagon. After the hot stew of mutton and root vegetables in the afternoon, one of the men, Ben, had taken the reins of the wagon team, so all three could ride as escort. Sir James was all keyed up looking for trouble, as was his nature, but no one bothered them.

"Get some more logs on the fire and bring something warm to drink Harold!" James calls out as they enter the courtyard in Gainsburgh. Yeomen emerge from the house and barn to attend to the guests. "Seven Companie men turned over to us from the Sheriff in Lincoln. Give them a hand," he said in answer to the curious looks.

"Yes, Sir James, right away, Sir James" sounds in the cold air as they hustle to do his bidding, get the horses to the barn, and close the gates. Their lord has just materialized from the dark.

"Thomas is tied up on the Trent, Sir James. He pulled up early afternoon and told me you were headed this way," Harold confides as he hands a warm mug over. "Trouble?"

"None yet."

"Expecting any?"

"Maybe; this hot broth does me good. I want a perimeter posted before dawn."

"We've quite a few Companie men here. If the Sheriff of Lincoln tries to get them back, he will have a fight on his hands."

"Good to have them back in the fold. Lord Latimer was in Lincoln. We will get most of them aboard the *Suzanne* tomorrow and head north. I prefer not to have a fight with an appointee of the Crown."

James leans against the door frame, looking out on the courtyard. Hot pease pudding warms his belly as the sun comes up. He slept fitfully. In his dark dreams, he was crawling face down in the mud, trying to get up but being held down with Latimer leering and laughing at him…none of which had ever happened. Such are dreams. Harold has all his people: men, women, and even children up and busy. The men picked up in Lincoln still slept in the gathering room in front of the fire. It had been kept stoked all night.

"Shall I send for Thomas?" Harold asks quietly as he strolls up.

"Show me around first. You have a lot of people here."

"Today is market day, Sir James." Towns typically double or triple their population on market days.

"Our people are in from the farms?"

"Some are and Justin brought in a wagon of wool yesterday; he and Matthew are still here, too."

"I would like a chance to speak with each of them." Justin is his wool buyer for the area. The idea is to secure the shearing from as many flocks from here west to Sheffield as possible. It could be a competitive enterprise. In Sheffield, Justin bought cutlery items, knives, shears, and tools, which are then sold in Yorke. He also purchases iron billets, which are resold to smiths the entire length of the Ouse and Swale system all the way to Richmond. "The new men need clothing, shoes, jerkins; everything they have on is in tatters."

"We have some cloth in from Thomas that I was going to offer for sale today. I'll pull it from the stock and get some of the women busy. I'll speak with the cobbler about shoes; he owes me for skins."

"I bought this wagon and the team in Lincoln. You can keep it if needed or sell it."

"We can surely use it, Sir James."

"What is your name?"

"Paul Fitz-William, sir."

"Let me have a look at that arm." Paul gingerly removes his hood, and Will helps him gently pull off his jerkin. "Looks broken judging from the bruising; how long has it been like this?" James asks.

"I fell in a stream trying to catch a trout. It was the day before the sheriff's men got us. If it hadn't been for that. I would not have been caught."

"Did you get the fish?"

"No, I didn't get the damned fish!"

James' eyes twinkled at his own little joke. "This is going to hurt." He could feel that the small bone in the forearm was broken as Paul gasped in pain but did not pull back. "I'll need some wool for padding and some thick ox hide to make a hard sling." Will left to secure the needed items.

"Where are you from?" Turned out Paul is the son of a marcher lord on the Welsh border. He had joined Sir John's Companie after a dispute with his father sometime after James had already returned to England. When James asked if he wanted to go back there, he said no.

"There is no inheritance for me. That goes to my oldest brother."

"I know how that is; my father is a second son." Fitz-William was of noble birth and literate, though. James might be able to find good employ for him if he was interested.

It could have been worse. The bone is slightly out of alignment but not too bad as the big bone still kept the forearm from compressing. "Bite down on this leather strop and stand behind this post." Fitz-William stood behind the barn post. "Put your chest up against the post. Will is going to pull hard on your wrist, so I can try and get your arm bone lined up right. It is going to hurt like hell." Fitz-William hugged the post with his right arm as Will grasped his left wrist. "Pull slowly and firmly."

James bound the arm snugly by winding a strip of fine cloth around it and then fit it in the hide sling with some thick wool padding. "My purpose is to keep you from moving your elbow or your wrist until the bone heals." James said as he secured the arm in the sling. "Paul, usually when this goes wrong it is because the patient, you, try to do too much too soon. You need to baby this for about five weeks or have a messed-up arm for the rest of your life."

"I've seen enough disfigured soldiers that didn't get the right attention to their wounds." Perspiration beaded on his forehead. "I'll behave. Is it true you captured du Guesclin?" Paul thought better of asking him about the encounter he witnessed with Lord Latimer.

"We were in a melee; he blocked my halberd strike with his mace. The mace broke, and he surrendered. He did not have much of a choice. I am glad he saw it that way as he once beat a man almost to death with just his mailed fists, and I was exhausted."

"So, Francis, how is our farm in Moretun progressing?" Moretun is just north of Gainsburgh on the Trent.

Francis had been one of the few serfs left working the farm after the plague when the land rights with Blanche of Lancaster had been arranged. Harold freed him at Sir James' direction and then employed him as reeve to run the farm. This was the first time he had met James. "The men are working hard on the spring ploughing and of course tending to the sheep. We have increased the herd two-fold, my Lord."

The farm was half arable and also had a lot of moor land. "Well done. And the farming?"

"I have twelve more acres back under tillage: wheat, barley, and rye. We had a good year. It got us through the winter and a bit more for Harold to sell at the market."

"I am sending flax seed to you."

"To make linen?"

"Linen and cordage for fishing nets; it is a good winter activity – retting and scrutching to get the fibers. I understand that you are also making baskets." James believed that every village needed a craft that enabled them to make money through the winter. It just was not always a simple matter of getting that in place.

"Yes, in the winter, we spin yarn and weave baskets for the salt. Thomas takes them. I heard you want us to learn how to fletch arrows."

"For now, grow your gaggle of geese. Your home and the buildings are in good repair?"

"Indeed, your men are very good at building. We put up two new cottages and a granary this summer."

"Harold said your wife died. I am sorry about that. The children are managing?"

"I have a new wife now and things are much better."

James nodded. "That is good. You have three Companie men or four?"

"Five."

"Do they seem content?"

"Well, they do not complain, and they work with a will." Francis paused. "They can leave if they are not happy. They are not bound to the land?"

"No. They are freemen. I worry that they will become restless."

"At the moment, it seems they are glad not to always be marching somewhere, can sleep with a good roof overhead, a sure meal to eat, and not have to keep a nervous eye out for trouble. Or so they say. Most of them have found female companionship."

Justin, James' wool buyer is anxious to speak with him. "Sir James, we've got a busy competitor trying to buy next year's sheering in the area."

"Is he having success?"

"Not with the flocks I've already secured. I've lost a few I was hoping for."

"What do you know about him?"

"I heard he is out of London; the Flemish community there," Justin said with distaste.

"So, he is Flemish. Still around here?"

"Last I heard, he was headed north, toward Wakefield. Most don't trust the foreign buyers."

"Make sure you know what he is offering: letters of credit or payment on receipt and, of course, how much. Keep me informed."

"Certainly, Sir James."

"Thomas, I've four passengers for you to take to Barmby. You will have a full boat with the wool."

"I'm just glad it is not all seven, Sir James."

"One has died and two are still too bad to travel."

"Sorry, I didn't know. Will they make it?"

"It does not look good for them. Same affliction that got so many of us in Spain; just like our prince. One of the ones traveling with you, Paul Fitz-William, has a broken arm; he needs to be careful with it," James said pointedly.

Chapter 3

The Whitefriars

MAY 1372

"I need to pay my respects at the priory."

"Will you be back for supper, Master Virgil?" Ruddy is the usual cook aboard *Marie*.

"I expect we'll join the brothers for the evening meal. I'm takin' Bertrand and Mark along."

"They are, indeed, great sinners, Master, and the visit will do them good."

"Go bugger yourself, Ruddy" is Mark's retort as he comes over the bulwark to join Virgil and Bert on the dock. *Marie* is docked on the west bank of the River Ouse that runs through the city.

The precinct of the Whitefriars is across the Ouse Bridge and in the northeast part of the city. Most of Yorke lies on the east side of the river. It is just a short walk up Ousegate and then a right turn down Fossgate to the priory gatehouse.

Mark raps the knocker, resulting in a friar peering out through the small, barred window. "Hey, Mark!" he says with enthusiasm as he draws back the bolt and opens the door. "I did not know you were here. Yo, Bert, greetings, Master Virgil; everyone is in the chapter room."

Virgil nods. "Merci, Andrew." The three pass under the shields of Neville and Skirlaw, through the door, and into the confines of the Carmelites.

"My apologies for any intrusion, Prior William."

"Oh, Master Virgil," he replies with a start. "We were just finishing."

"Good evening, brothers," Virgil replies. The mischievous smiles around the room tell a different story; they indicate that they are delighted with the early conclusion. The lanky prior could drone on and on. "Tenebroides has some supplies for you. He is moored just below the castle, this bank of the Ouse. These items go to him."

Four friars rise, take Virgil's packages, leave through the door of the chapter room, and head for their boat at the quay on the Foss Pond, which forms the eastern border of the precinct. That the *Christine* is moored below the castle means that she is not yet above the river chain and in the city; Tenebroides has not yet paid the toll.

"Is Master Tenebroides going to join us?" asks Prior William.

"Yes, I am to wait for him here."

"Then you will all be joining us for dinner?"

"I was hoping for your invitation. Thank you."

"You look tired; why don't you wait in my lodgings?"

"We just got in an hour ago, and there is much to do," says Virgil as he joins the prior for the short walk across the courtyard. It is not long before the small, wiry red-bearded man joins them.

"This is ale is new yesterday, and I think it is one of Tufty's better batches." William pours Tenebroides a pewter mug full and two more for himself and Virgil. "You sure look out of sorts; any trouble?"

"The Capetians are advancing across Normandy. The Crown is seeking gold, men, and ships for a new campaign across the channel. It is getting harder for Sir James to avert the pressure; tempers are short including mine. One of the king's men was eyeing my crew this afternoon."

"Surely we have all done enough!"

"This ale is good, indeed. Is Tufty keeping notes, so he knows why one batch is better than another?"

"He has been reminded often." Prior William's frustration is in his voice. "I'll ask why this one is so good and see what he says. It will be good to pass him a compliment...for once."

"Yes, everyone that matters agrees we did enough and more. But that was then, the king is old, and the prince is ill. Desperate times mean a short memory of inconvenient promises."

"You can always put on a white robe," William said with a grin.

Tenebroides shakes his head with a wistful smile. "That is one way out, but nobody would believe me, and it brings certain constraints that I find onerous."

William laughs heartily. "Will you also stay for supper?"

"Not the celibacy, Wills; that can be circumvented. Having to stay cloistered would be make me crazy. Yes, to supper, but I need to make a delivery first."

"We were discussing some issues affecting the order when you came in. Brother Rainer died last week."

"He hung on for a long time."

"I don't know how much pain he was in at the end or how much awareness he had of what was going on around him."

"You took good care of him; God knows you did." Virgil pats the prior on the arm in reassurance. He is the last of the old brothers?"

"Yes, the last. One of the few that didn't succumb to the plague. We're all Companie men now. Something else, Tenebro…we have the opportunity to take on a few novices. Some of the brothers thought Sir James would have a problem with that."

"No, I don't think he will. In fact, I expect he will be most enthused. Not that I speak for him, of course. Well done."

"I was leery of asking him. He becomes wroth with me when I fail to 'understand the broader strategy.' Sometimes I get the feeling he thinks I'm stupid."

"You are not stupid." To himself Tenebroides thinks: all the fasting you do does make you a bit befuddled, at times. "To quote Sir James: 'Understand the role of your men and how it coordinates to the units around you.' Just like in battle. Your problem, and mine, too, is we lack James' imagination and tend to concentrate on our own tasks."

"Novices won't cause…um, difficulties?"

"It may make things better for a number of reasons, including that this is a really big priory for thirteen friars. Property is hard to get here inside the city walls, and there is much resentment at the amount of Church property. Eventually there would be pressure from the town council. We'll need to make a few little changes…that's all."

"How do I explain you and Sir James?"

"To the novices? Just tell them the truth. We are old comrades from the war, and Sir James is a dear essential benefactor to the priory. They do not need to know more than that."

Bertrand peeks in behind the door. "Boat crew is back. Do you want your packages in here?"

Tenebroides stands. "Yes, have Alfred bring them in, please."

Brother Alfred comes in bearing four canvas wrapped packages each the size of a large loaf of bread. "This is what Ben gave me for you."

"Exactly right. What did he have for you here at the priory?"

"Ben gave us six grain sacks, a basket of smoked fish, twenty faggots of wood, two score eggs, a round of cheese, and twelve chickens!" Alfred said with a smile. A rare show of good humor.

"Also, exactly right. No salt?"

"Yes, I forgot; he brought us a bushel of salt and a crock of butter."

"You are spoiled, and I can see that you are going soft."

"Yes, and I thank you most kindly for all that you do on our behalf." Alfred bows and smiles even more broadly as he backs out of the room.

Tenebroides comments to the prior, "He seems to be doing better, doesn't he?"

"He still has nightmares, but it is no longer every night."

"We all have nightmares. Screaming in the middle of the night and waking everyone up is a bit of a problem, though."

"That is fairly infrequent now, Tenebro," Prior William replies softly.

Tenebro heads up the Fossgate towards King's Square, then to Saint Andrewgate and the home and shop of John de Thornton, spicer. "Welcome, Master Tenebroides, Father is not in at the moment. What have you brought us?"

Tenebroides sets the four packages on the counter. "Your order has arrived Richard!"

"Oh, excellent," he says, slitting open the largest package. The powerful smell of black pepper fills the shop. Then package by package a succession of exotic aromas permeates the air: cloves, cardamom, cinnamon, anise, turmeric, and the smallest and costliest package – saffron. In all about fourteen different pouches of varied sizes and pungency are opened and weighed. "These are wonderful; almost every spice we hoped for."

"These come from such a long way off that I always worry Richard."

"We'll regain the position of pre-eminent spicer in Yorke with this selection. I'll be right back with your balance." That John de Thornton and his son Richard were important customers was certainly one of the great ironies in Tenebro's existence. Richard had been wooed by the Carmelite Priory when he was a lad, under the age of fourteen, and had made a profession of faith to the priory, or so they claimed. He then changed his mind about becoming a friar and the priory sought his arrest as an apostate. The King himself stepped in and placed Richard under his protection, had an investigation that determined he was too young to become an apostate and stopped the arrest. Of course, this was many years ago and before Prior William and veterans of the Companie had taken over the plague ravaged brotherhood. Nonetheless, it was prudent to obscure any connection between his spice trade and the current Carmelites!

Richard returns and counts out enough coins to make up the remaining £5 balance. Most workers make perhaps three pence a day, and at 240 pence to the pound, it is more than they would see in an entire year. It is a large order and a lot of money, but he is giddy with delight. The price is better than through his other traders. He is sly enough to never ask why. The discussion turns to a new order.

"I think I can get your next order more quickly. The sailing weather is better from Bruges in the summer."

"That would be very helpful; we often go for weeks and weeks without items."

Master Tenebroides and Virgil sit under the awning on the quarterdeck of Tenebroides' *Christine*. It is the next day and both barges are now at the city docks nearest the warehouse of Simon Quixley in Yorke. This is as far south as Virgil comes and the northernmost stop for Tenebroides. As such merchandise can be transferred directly from barge to barge if they both happen to be in the city at the same time. Otherwise, it needs to be taken to the Quixley's warehouse, where they rent space. They make an odd pair – one so small and the other so large.

"When will all of Quixley's wool be down from Richmond, so you can start moving our own?"

Virgil responds, "The shearing is still going. If we ship the same amount for him as we did last year, then one more load. It is good money. What I need is cargo to take to Richmond; we usually return near empty."

"I am working on that, but there will always be more coming downstream. At least it is easier to pull upstream with a lighter load." Sir James was on him constantly about just that. "I'm not knocking Quixley or Graa, for that matter. Having a business relationship with members of the council has been very good for us. Our wool will wait."

"Why do we need their help?" Virgil replies pugnaciously.

"You are not paying the city river toll because you are bringing lead for the cathedral roof. Ever hear of the city council helping out the Church when it comes to tolls?"

"That does seem odd, but James said he wasn't willing to load down my barge with a break-even cargo."

"Right, and the archbishop got the abbot to free us from Saint Mary's river toll on your entire cargo, but there was no reason for the city to forgive their toll was there? Quixley ships his wool on your barge…"

"He got us the exception, so he doesn't have to pay the toll on his wool!" Virgil slapped his thigh.

"And, getting our people into the guilds with minimal resistance: fellmongers, weavers, fishmongers, butchers… buying property without council objections. Reasonable assessments to our share of the city's farm! There are lots of reasons."

"And a market stall on Thursdays when we want one."

"Exactly; you have no notion of how difficult…I should say impossible… these things are to obtain without the right endorsements. They could also try to compete with our wool suppliers to push us out."

"That might not be so easy." Virgil patted the haft of his dagger.

"No, they wouldn't be able buy out from under us where we own the flocks. That is most of our supply, but not all. Protecting the rest would get messy and we want to increase our share of the wool trade not fight to keep what we've got. When do the new barrels get here?"

"There is a problem with that."

Tenebroides gives Virgil a snarl. "What kind of problem? Are they refusing to sell to us?"

"Nothing like that. The cooper's apprentice is locked up in the tower. They say he tried to murder his master during an argument."

"The cooper is still obligated to get us the casks."

"I think the apprentice did most of the work. Master Jeb is an old, mean drunkard, but Nicholas will hang just the same. Maybe we can break him out Tenebro?"

"This isn't like those other times, and Nicholas is not our responsibility. Even if I wanted to, we wouldn't be able to spring him from Clifford's Tower; too secure."

"Shame, though, not the young man's fault from where I sit."

"Be sure to tell the sheriff your assessment. No doubt he will make things right," Tenebroides replies with more than a touch of sarcasm. "Tell that drunken cooper we expect him to honor our order."

Janice the weaver has a small shop on Saint Andrewgate leased from the Whitefriars. Tenebroides enters to the tinkle of a small bell mounted on the door. "Just a moment!" Janice says through her loom behind the counter. "Oh, Tenebro, it's you," she says with a grin.

"I thought I would check in and see how you are doing. Are Daniel and the children doing well?" There are rolls of woven material in russet, olive, chestnut, grey-blue, and ochre on display. He runs his hands across them and likes what he sees and feels. Some of these were just brought down by Virgil on this last trip.

"Yes, everyone is well. This cloth is very nice. It has been fulled in the new water mill, hasn't it?"

"Yes, that is what I was told. It does seem to do a better job and isn't so tiring. Have you shown them to any of the tailors yet, Janice?"

"Just curious…in case I get questioned, there were no tariffs paid because this was not imported?"

Tenebro nodded. "Correct."

"Did Sir James specify my sell price?"

"You should undercut competitive Flemish cloth venders by just enough to make the sale."

"Do I say it is Flemish cloth?"

"Say it is first quality broadcloth made by Flemish weavers…"

Janice smiled. "I will appear to be cutting profits and so infuriate other merchants …"

"While the reality is that our profits are much higher than theirs, the buyer is happy…we are happy."

"The other merchants will complain. What if they charge me with evading tariffs?"

"Insist that all monies due to the Crown have been paid in full!"

"Do I say it with your indignant tone?" she teases.

"Yes, because you have been unjustly accused, and that tone lets people know it. This has been Sir James' plan all along and why he gave you the money for your guild fee."

"And arranged for the shop with Prior William of the Whitefriars."

"Do you think it will be difficult to get a price like imports for this cloth?"

"No, it is clearly Flemish cloth and as fine as any I've seen. I'll show the tailors tomorrow and ask them to send their customers here. I think I will sell every bit of it this Thursday. The way Sir James tells it, you'd think the king himself had asked him to bring the Flemish weavers to England."

"The king has encouraged Flemish weavers to come here and guaranteed them his protection. So, in a way, he has."

In the late afternoon, Tenebroides heads to tannery row in the west bank side of the city. Summer was just beginning and already the smell is offensive. The tide is in and has yet to turn, which certainly made the stench worse as the river backed up and can't wash the foulness of the city away. The Ouse serves as the sewer for all the city trash, excrement, and waste from butchers and tanners. "Did the load of sheepskins arrive from the barge yet, Judd?"

The fellmonger looks up from the back of his shed where he is defleshing a skin as Tenebroides strides in. Softly, he says, "Ya-ya-ya-you know, they da-da-da-did Master Tenebroides. We got them yesterday." His stutter is worse when something does not make sense to him.

Sitting down close to the quiet, big man in spite of the smell, he said, "Got a little job for you tonight." The stutter, odor, rangy build, and torn work clothing create the impression that Judd is 'simple' to most people. A man easily ignored. Nothing could be further from the truth – he is quite clever, quick, and nimble when he chooses to be. "Jeb the cooper is a drinker."

"So, I am told."

Laying some coins on the bench, he says, "Make sure he is in his cups this evening and does not get home until just before curfew."

Sir James is waiting for the prior in his lodgings when he returns from vespers. "William, I have another potential novice for you."

"Really! Who is it?"

"His name is Nicholas; he was the Jeb the cooper's apprentice. I want you to visit him in Clifford's Tower and then convince the magistrate to release him to you."

"No wonder you are in my room at this early hour. Oh, I heard, so you are not fooling me, tried to murder his master. I don't know…"

"The master cooper is a mean drunkard, and everybody knows it. The magistrate will be relieved to have a way out of hanging the poor lad. He also happens to be damned good at his craft."

"You want a cooper."

"Right, I need a cooper. And I need you to be the indignant prior fighting to right a great injustice. Go save a soul, William…and don't take 'no' for an answer. I need to attend to the archbishop; he has sent for me."

"It has been suggested that you are only bringing small lead shipments to stretch out your river toll exemption as long as possible, Sir James." John de Thoresby, Archbishop of Yorke, is not pleased.

"Not at all, your Grace. I just do not have a source for the quantities you need. I do not own mines or a smelting operation, and I do not want to. I assure you that I am buying everything that this smelter is producing." James answered all the while wondering why he was having a building materials discussion with the archbishop.

"At this rate, it will be three years before the cathedral roof is complete. Not at all satisfactory!"

"It is an unprofitable commodity; lead costs more to mine, smelt, and transport than anyone is willing to pay for it. The king, I am told, has lead mines in Cornwall that he subsidizes. I will happily pay the river tolls again if you choose to get your lead elsewhere. Twenty stone of ingots is the most that is available to me each month for a barge run down from Richmond."

"I have already spoken to His Royal Highness. His chamberlain maintains that all of the production is committed to other projects."

"I did not know that." Mention of the king's chamberlain, Sir William Latimer, always puts James on edge. He took violent exception to James' romantic interest with his much younger sister. This personal animus persists and has been exacerbated through the years since. The mutual contempt makes everyone within earshot uncomfortable if they are in the same room. "The toll exemption does make it worth shipping. Let me look to this personally, then, my Lord Archbishop. Lead mining and smelting is not something I am well versed in. I do understand that the free miners are just barely getting by. Perhaps something as simple as a load of new picks, metal tipped shovels, and a few meat pies will solve the difficulty."

"Those are costs I am all too willing to pay!" the archbishop exclaims.

"I must already ride to North Yorkshire on some other business. I will attend to this directly."

"Another matter is on my mind. Are you familiar with the limestone quarry near Tatecastre?"

"I have not been there. That is where you are getting your building stone?"

"It is and I want to know if you can transport it."

James was familiar with some brewers that he had once hoped to do business with there. "If you can get the stone to the dock below the river ford at Tatecastre, then it should be possible." The River Wharfe is tidal to within four miles of the town and joins the River Ouse at Cawood, south of Yorke. "I will need to build a barge for the purpose and am pleased to do so."

"You do not have a craft available?"

"I do not have one both sturdy enough for the weight of the stone and of shallow enough draft for the River Wharfe, your Grace. Six weeks are needed to build a barge – at most."

"The sooner the better; make it so. God be with you, Sir James."

"And also with you, your Grace."

The High Sheriff of Yorkshire is standing outside with others when James returns home.

"It is late for a social call, Sir William."

The sheriff considers James carefully as he hands him a warrant from the crown. "This is not a request, Sir James, but an order and I am commanded to enforce it if necessary."

James read the warrant. "This is signed by the king's chamberlain, Lord Latimer, on behalf of the Duke of Lancaster." The writ directs him to assemble a company of not less than eighty archers and be in Calais in sixty days. "The duke was merely persistent, but he is now threatening, is he not?" James says, smiling.

"Do you intend to comply?" Then, almost apologetically, he says, "I do realize you spent many years fighting on the continent. Can you raise that many men?" The sheriff was almost at the end of his term in office. He had maintained good relationships with the leading citizens, including James, and did not want to create antagonism now.

"Oh, he can recruit them, alright! See that he does, Sir William."

"Simon, it has been years, but I recognize your foul stench," Tenebroides and several men from the *Christine* have just arrived. Word that the sheriff's party was at the house reached them where they were tied up on the Ouse.

"Why, what is that smell? I remember it now: the stench of cowardice!" Tenebroides wrinkles his nose. The barge crew laughs. "Has something fouled your drawers, Simon?"

"You lying bastards!"

"That wasn't you with Lord Latimer in the reserves at Auray?" Tenebroides goads him further.

"The reserves of the reserves maybe?" someone in the crew suggests.

"Perhaps hiding behind the boys with the baggage train?" The crew is warming to the task.

"I'll kill you for that!"

"That is enough!" the sheriff attempts to take control of the situation as his men shrink back from the big, rowdy oarsmen.

"Indeed, it is, Sir William, why don't you step inside with me." James' mind had been thinking about buying up horses for resale to the Crown at profit; there was going to be a shortage. "Tenebro, take your crew around back. I do not want a confrontation." James opens the door and leads the way upstairs to his study.

"Yes, I suppose I could recruit men if I was willing to pay them enough up front to leave their families. The city seems to have men in from the countryside trying to find work; I would start there. However, I have no desire to do so. I was one of the few that got back from Spain after the last campaign. Many of those that did manage to get back have died or are still sick just like the Prince of Wales. I'll let others serve and I'll pay the taxes. Sixteen years in the saddle is enough for any man and it should cover my service obligations for the rest of my life without paying a farthing!"

"I do not disagree with that statement, but…"

"This is not wholly unexpected, Sir William. Prince Edward granted my plea to be relieved of such future duress in appreciation for past service to the Crown. Please, have a seat while I find his letter."

"Sir William," Malcolm sets a goblet of wine next to the sheriff, and one on the table for James as he went through a leather satchel of correspondence.

"Here it is," he says, handing Sir William a folded parchment document. "Here is Prince Edward's grant and that is his signet seal. More light please, Malcolm." He was already lighting the candles in the chandelier.

The sheriff carefully read the document through and then read it again. "This is but two years old. Lancaster will not be happy with this. He may force you to forfeit your holdings in Richmond."

"To be sure, Lancaster can find ways to make his displeasure known. I have my doubts he even knows this warrant was issued. He was present when Prince Edward granted my request."

"You think Lord Latimer issued this without his knowledge?"

"I feel sure the duke told Latimer to issue warrants to knights of the realm sufficient to assemble an army. What I doubt is that he made a list of those knights." James was actually by no means certain that Lancaster had not specifically mentioned him knowing that James had many veterans of earlier campaigns in his employ. He also had no doubt that the king's chamberlain would cheerfully send him back to the wars hoping he would die in France. No love lost there.

"Some old animosity, or so I have heard? Or an innocent mistake?"

"Ironic that those 'shy' of battle themselves are so willing to compel others to serve."

"Now that is only between you, as this is more than enough to satisfy my obligations!" Sir William said, holding up the prince's grant.

"I heard that Jeb the cooper has now accused his apprentice of robbing him."

"Virgil, where did you hear that?" Tenebroides replies.

"Edward picked it up on the dock this morning. His tools are gone. Odd thing is a crowd was there when the sheriff hauled Nicholas off to prison and some of them say the tools were all there, then."

"So, if he was in the tower how did he also take the tools?"

"That's what's odd," Virgil shook his head.

"Jeb is soft in the skull. I assume we aren't going to have the barrels we ordered."

"No. I'm pushing off after I locate some picks and shovels."

"There are some at the priory to be sold to the cathedral workers when they need more – you can take them; I'll get more in Sheffield. Give my best to Joel. I still have a few things to do before I catch the turn of the tide and head south myself."

Nicholas is quite confused, but glad to be out of the windowless cell in Clifford's Tower. A churchman had visited him and told him to declare his devotion to the Lord and desire to become a Carmelite friar when questioned by his jailers. He had done so and been transported to their priory by boat. Now he was aboard a large river barge watching benches of oarsmen pull on their sweeps from under the overhang of the quarterdeck.

"You'll be taking a turn at the oars ere long Nicholas; no free-loaders here."

"Yes, Master Tenebroides," what else was there to say? Unbeknownst to Nicholas, all his previous master's draw knives, hatchets, mallets, saws, and chisels are also aboard.

Back north in Yorke, James strolls through the boatyards to see if one of the better builders needs work or better yet has something suitable already started without a buyer. Yorke has a thriving ship building trade below the city. Timber is available from the nearby forests; workers can be had in the city, and if the tide and the season are right, then large ships can be launched onto the Ouse.

"Wreck one of your boats, Sir James?"

"Not that I know of Master Swain. I'm looking for a forty-foot barge, built of heavy timbers, and of shallow enough draft for small river work." Swain had built some of James' fishing boats.

"Heavy cargo, eh?"

"Building material – stone. Do you have enough timber on hand?"

"I do or know where I can get it. When are you wanting it?"

"I am willing to pay fourteen pounds and will advance half now if you can launch in no more than four weeks."

Seven pounds sterling in his hands today could not be easily passed up. It would solve some of his problems. "Four weeks?"

"You are to include poles, sweeps, steering oar…"

"Mast and sail?"

"Not a mast but a heavy boom crane; the barge needs to be able to load and unload the stone itself." Paying for use of the city's crane would cut into profits and there was no crane at the ford on the River Wharfe. "I have a drawing." James pulls out a pouch of coins.

The boatwright unrolls the drawing and sets smooth stones at the corners. "Those are large pulley blocks on the crane. Your timing is tight, but as I do not have any payment on this boat I've started here, I will clear it aside and start yours in the morning. The crane may take an additional week, Sir James."

"Agreed, then – five weeks. I require a fast completion and that is why my offer is generous. You must understand that after five weeks my price goes down by a pound every three days."

"I understand."

James borrows quill and ink and writes the agreement in the margin of the boat plans. He pulls out a second copy and repeats the written agreement. "Seven pounds, then?" as he sets down the pouch in the middle of the drawing.

"Agreed." James signs the agreement and that the £7 deposit has been paid; then he hands the quill to Master Swain.

"Always best to have things in writing," Swain says as he adds his signature. "I should start doing this with all my clients; prevents arguments later."

The Humbre quickly widens after the confluence of the River Ouse from the north and the River Trent from the south to become a wide estuary. Cnut guides his fishing boat in the pre-dawn mist towards the anchorage off Kingston-upon-Hull. The outgoing tide is in his favor but will soon be at the ebb. He had left Freydis and his warm bed over two hours earlier in Blaketofte and sailed in the dark through the familiar waters but now is having trouble lighting the candle to put in his lantern. It is too damp. The Humbre is over a mile wide now. He needs to stay nearer to the northern shore. If he passes the River Hull, he has gone too far. There are ships in the anchorage emerging in the fog as he drifts. They are bow on as he approaches; anchor lines taut against the pull of the tide. Avoiding them, struggling with his flint and steel, and searching for the blue lanterns of the *Neuchâtel* makes him frantic. Cnut did not want to drift past and then have to fight his way back against the current.

A blue light emerges through the dark and, thankfully, Cnut alters course and hooks on to the main chains. "Is dit het *Neuchâtel*?"

"Ja, ben jij dat Cnut?"

"Ja, goedemorgan, Master Schiffer. I could not get my bloody lantern lit in this wet!"

"Come aboard I've got warm gruel in my cabin."

Cnut climbs up the wet wooden footholds on the side of the ship to the entry port. Gerhard Schiffer greets him warmly. "I did not know if you would show this morning."

"I got word you were in port just last night. Have you unloaded in Kingston already?"

"Today on the ebb."

With Master Schiffer's warm gruel in his belly, Cnut pulls on his oars to clear the side of the *Neuchâtel* as the dawn breaks over the estuary. He gets his nets in the water and settles down for the rest of the morning. He will fish here and then drift back towards home as the tide turns. Three barrels of salted fish and two wool sacks are now aboard the *Neuchâtel*. A new barrel, which he marked 'Oliver of Yorke,' is lashed into his fishing boat. A boat full of herring would be a marvelous reward for such an early start this far out the estuary, but in truth the biggest 'catch-of-the-day' is already aboard.

Chapter 4

Discovery

"Well, Captain, we pissed on it!"

"Start from the beginning because I am not making any sense of this." Sir James had ridden to the far seacoast of the North Yorkshire moors after receiving an urgent, somewhat cryptic, message from this, the most remote extent of their holdings, with much misgiving.

On the ride he kept dreading whatever bad situation he would find upon his arrival. At least it was so remote here that it was unlikely the Bishop of Durham had learned of it. Whatever the problem he would bury it and cover-up all traces. The Bishopric of Durham owned this land sitting high upon cliffs overlooking the North Sea. It was windswept and good for pasturing sheep; not much else. It had not been hard, with the prince's letter of introduction in hand, to get the bishop to let him have the whole area at a reasonable rent. He had warmed to the elderly bishop immediately. It turned out that Thomas Hatfield had been a royal servant of King Edward charged with the administrative side of conducting the war across the channel many years before James had been born and, of course, many years before his election as bishop. They had talked deep into the evening. This was not his usual experience with princes of the Church.

His discussion with Prince Edward – he needed a place for some men that just could not be trusted back in civilized society. The war had changed them. They could no longer control their passions or their anger. Every good warrior got a certain violent madness in battle. James certainly did and he honestly believed it is what gave him the strength to keep fighting past exhaustion, and what left him so completely spent when the battle was done. These men had simply lost the ability to suppress that violent response in everyday life. So, now they are shepherds out here at the edge of land. He had hoped they would find some sense of inner peace and learn how to control themselves. And that they were far enough away from anyone that might cross them.

He had been blunt. It was this or they would be killed while sleeping in their hammocks and tossed into the sea before they ever reached England. The only reason he didn't was there were just too many times they had won the fight together through the chaos of battle. They were still his comrades: Companie men. They knew. They knew that they had gone too far, too many times in camps and taverns and most recently while aboard that small ship. Now here he was, ready to hear the worst and the six of them were telling him about pissing on rocks?

Clyde, a hairy brute of man, started at the beginning. "We piled up this grey slate to make a wind break and reflect the fire back to us."

"Right. That part I understood. Then the rocks caught fire?"

"Yes, must be some coal or peat in them. Then we piled on more rock to smother it."

"But it kept burning."

"Yup, burned for about a year. Then it stopped burning and just sat there for while getting rained on."

"And we pissed on it during that time," Auggie added with mirth.

"Why wouldn't you?" James said sarcastically. "Then you were shoving each other around…"

"Just playin', Captain, nothin' serious," he spread his arms out in a show of innocence and the rest nodded to confirm his words. "And Harry landed in the pile…"

"And it didn't hurt me, cuz it is soft!"

"The rock pile is soft?"

"And pinkish. And…has these crystals," Clyde said conspiratorially as he poured them out into Sir James' hand with a sly smile. The whole crystals were nearly clear, and diamond shaped. The broken bits were more of a white powder. The grinning Clyde wet his finger, touched the white powder, and put it on his tongue. "Tastes acidic; it is alum, Captain."

"It just looks like alum."

"Nope. I was a dyer before I joined Sir John's Companie. My family has been dyers for generations. The alum is in the shale."

"You are certain?"

"I haven't tried to dye any wool with it, but, yes, I am certain."

"Do your women know?"

"They know we are excited and think it could make us a lot of money."

"How much is there?" Clyde sets a sheepskin bag on the ground in response. James lifts it. "About ten pounds."

"More crystals will form in the pile. I think the rain makes 'em grow."

"First let me take this to our dyer in Richmond. I need to confirm that it is alum and not just something similar. If it is really alum, which I am still having some trouble believing…not that I doubt you Clyde, then we need to figure out how to harvest the alum in a dependable manner. Nobody is getting rich on a ten-pound sack every few years if crystals decide to form."

"And we need to keep it secret," added Clyde.

"Absolutely. Not a word to anyone. If even a rumor gets out the Crown and the bishop will go to war over this sheep pasture, and we'll be brushed over that cliff there and out of their way!"

"Shouldn't be too hard. Nobody comes up here." Clyde gave James an odd look. "I mean, that's why you put us here, didn't ya? We even lower our wool down the cliff to the boat with a rope and just a wave."

"You pick up provisions and your wages from Arthur."

"He doesn't know anything. He's scared of us and isn't friendly."

"What is this sack worth, Captain?" asks Harry, rubbing his hands together.

Harry used to go into battle with a cleaver shaped chopper bigger than any butcher had ever dreamed about. James was not sure why that memory had just come to him; the weapon is probably not far. "The last time I tried to buy alum it was going for over four pounds sterling a bushel. So, your sack would be worth about…a bit over six shillings. But I wasn't actually able to buy it; the cargo was already sold. Alum can be hard to get, even if you're willing to pay for it." The Venetians and the Genoese control almost all the alum, which comes out of the Mediterranean. Then it has to be shipped and the Flemings buy it all up."

"Six shillings is a lot, though." Little Auggie seemed satisfied with that.

"Over two months' wages for a worker in our dye shop at eight pence a week. Not bad at all." James had some thinking to do. "What's for dinner? I'm hungry!"

Well, the men looked like they were doing alright. Normal congenial banter while we were eating dinner. No signs of short tempers at least in his presence. Where did the women come from, he wonders, but they look fine; no visible bruises and they smile easily. He had heard there was a shortage of men after the years of war, perhaps it was true. Someone for everyone, or so they say. The ragout was good, so they could cook; mutton and whatever else they could find to put in the pot. Decent bread just baked that day – they were getting supplied from Joel in Richmond. He turned in early with a lot on his mind.

It is an easy day's ride west to Stockton, which he thought of as a splendid town. Bishop Hatfield had freed all the serfs some years ago; it gave the place a good feeling. Numerous craftsmen make it their home and it has a sizeable fishing community. Stockton is a small port city where the River Tees feeds into the North Sea. A barge can use the tide to go upstream as far as Yarm, which is only a twelve-mile ride to Richmond. Near Yarm lives Otto; he is James' tenant on a small farm, and he has a workshop that makes dyes. He also sells a bit of cloth at the Stockton market. The wool from Clyde and the men on the cliff comes through Stockton to Otto. He takes it on to Richmond.

As he turns upriver toward Yarm, it is not the first time James is thinking about how to increase his business in Stockton. It just does not have the ability to really move merchandise like the Yorke Market; the town is too small and has fewer merchants and buyers coming in. Some instinct breaks him from his inner thoughts...

"Whoa, there, traveler!" A tall man with an axe steps out suddenly from a thicket to the right and reaches towards his mount's bridle. Others are springing out on all sides.

Sir James instantly spurs his big stallion forward past the man's grasp. He pulls his sword singing clear of its scabbard and slashes down. The jarring impact stings in his forearm as the sword bites into flesh and bone and he surges past. The man screams. They have chosen well. The road goes up a rise that would slow any wagon or smaller mount trying to get away. But this big chestnut was born to run, and James looks back from the top of the rise to see the shocked men circled around their fallen leader. It is still broad daylight and just outside Stockton; bold, indeed. He scabbards the sword, and dismounts while grabbing his bow. James slips the loop of his string on the end of the bow and sets the tip on the side of his foot pulling the bow into a curve against his thigh to secure the loop at the other end. The four men standing in the road with clubs and spears have too late realized that he has not fled the scene. He steps from behind his horse and lets a broadhead fly. At this range he rarely misses, and this is no exception as a feathered shaft now sprouts from deep in the man's chest. Lawlessness in the realm is an offense against the king and James has no tolerance for it.

They leap to the brush before he has the bowstring pulled fully back for a second arrow. James remounts; arrow still nocked and gallops on towards the dye farm. He chastises himself: it was foolish to make this trip alone. James clinches his teeth against a pain in his lower backside. The bulge there had not bothered him much this trip until just now.

"In a hurry, Captain?" The chestnut is lathered from the fast four-mile ride to the farm as he pulls up to the gate. "I heard you coming a ways off; like thunder!"

"A bit of trouble just outside Stockton, Otto," he replies in Flemish as he was addressed. The dyer strokes his pointed beard with a blue hand as the story is related.

"I have heard some talk. To be careful. I should report this to the bailiff. Is that alright?"

"They were wearing hoods, of course, but they could be local. It is hard to hide the fact that family members are now missing."

"They could claim you attacked them. Three witnesses against you."

"If you are the one reporting it and there has been trouble recently the bailiff should see through that. He would expect it and hopefully discount it.

In any case, I do not wish to be delayed. They have already paid a dear price for the attempt. I think I prefer to remain unknown if possible."

"Extra oats for my horse. He has earned them today!" he says as Otto's son comes forward to lead his mount to the stable. "They will expect to be hunted and be on the run."

After dinner he and Otto lean on the fence looking over the rows of dye producing plants. "What's that tangle over there?" James asks, pointing towards the back of the plot.

"Madder, it spreads everywhere; I just keep cutting it back and processing the roots." Madder root produces an orangey-red dye.

"Otto, do you ever get used to the stench?" The unmistakable odor of woad processing is thick about the farm today.

"What stench?"

James laughs. "Have you any wool in the barn?"

"Yes, the boat just brought a load in a few days ago. I'll have some more dyes ready tomorrow and I'll take it all to Richmond, then. You can ride escort if you're so minded."

"I want you to try to dye some of the wool tomorrow. I want you to show me the whole process."

"Sure," he says with a surprised look. "Do you have a color in mind?"

"A bright aqua."

"I cannot get a bright color without using alum as the mordant. Ah, you already know that," he says as his eyes meet Sir James.' "I'll send the boy into town for some tartar. Do you plan to get your hands wet?"

He looked at Otto's blue hands and forearms. "No."

Otto howls with laughter. "I don't blame you."

Otto washes about twenty pounds of wool yarn to remove dirt and lanolin. "We'll start with a five-pound batch to make sure I have the quantities right. I'm going to use colder water with a bit of chalk to get as bright a color as I can." James feels the water temperature and makes a note. "Next the alum and the tartar – about a pound of alum for ten pounds of wool."

"How much tartar?" Tartar is a by-product of wine making; a white powder left in the bottom of the barrel. It is inexpensive and readily available.

"About a third the amount of alum," he says as he stirs the trough with a wooden paddle. "Now we'll see." Otto adds the wool, which has been tied in loose hanks. "This will soak until afternoon."

"How do we know if it worked?"

"After we dye it, we'll hang it out to dry, and in the morning, wash it in clean water a few times. If the color stays it worked; if it washes out, then you were hoodwinked on your alum purchase."

"So, far do you like everything you're seeing?"

"I'll have a good idea when we pull it from the dye pot."

James and Otto spend the balance of the morning going through the accounts. He pays the fishermen to bring the wool from the shepherds on the cliff and gets paid when he brings the wool and the dyes to Richmond. James pays the rent on this and the grazing lands to Bishop Thomas in person, once a year.

"Well, I like what I am seeing," Otto says as he smiles with satisfaction at the bright aqua. "This is nice." Other metals can be used as mordants to allow dyes to set. Most commonly James' dyers use iron as it is cheap and easy to get, but it would dull and darken this to a blue-grey color. When Otto is satisfied with the color, he drapes the hanks over wooden rods to drip and dry. "Now we wait. I'd like to get your opinion on this mead I purchased of recent if you're agreeable."

"I do find that I am quite parched and would be happy to render an opinion. I am partial to a nice mead." Ale is more common than this fermented honey drink in Yorke.

"Take the rest of the alum and the aqua yarn straight to Joel. Tell him to put it in a lock chest." As he finishes sewing up the bag of yarn he adds, "Not a word about this to anyone, Otto. When I start selling bright cloth in Yorke it will cause a stir and people may ask questions. I'll leave your pack horse in Richmond and you can take some of the shovels there to replace these. Tell Joel I will be back before the week is out."

The two part ways at mid-morning. Otto goes to Richmond with his wagon of wool and dyes behind a mule team, and James rides back to the cliff edge on the North Sea by another route.

"You were right. It's alum." James shows them the hank of bright aqua yarn. "Otto used your alum to dye this yarn for me."

"I told you!" Clyde shouts and dances with glee. "Just look at that color!" It seems a bit odd to see these grizzled veterans happily stroking a skein of yard, but that just adds to the revelry of the scene.

"Now comes the hard part."

Clyde nodded. "How to get more crystals. I've been thinking about that."

"Good; it has possessed my thoughts the entire ride."

"We're going to need some stuff."

"Picks and shovels to start with. I brought some with me."

"And a barrel to piss in."

"You won't need urine until after the pile has burned for quite a while."

"We'll need to save it up."

"Alright, I'll get you some keg sized barrels."

"We've got another sack of alum for you from going through the pile. Some more crystals formed since last time. Raking the pile to expose more to the rain seems to work a bit. They form where the rain puddles"

"Maybe the crystals form the way salt crystals form in our salterns on the marsh. We need to get the stuff that forms the alum out of the shale and dissolved in water. Then reduce the water to a point where the alum is thick enough to form crystals; just like the salt does," James theorizes.

"I've seen the salteres, as they are called in France, when we were in Brittany. The sun boils off the water and then the salt crystals form and they are raked out."

"Exactly Harry, you grew up in Brittany, so you know."

"Not really, my family is fishermen. I passed by the salteres my whole youth, but I never paid much attention."

"What we need are some big troughs up here. Then we can try a few things. I brought some thick canvas sacks to take some of your burn pile back with me. I'd like to try to take just the best pinkish soft stuff if possible. The burning must consume the coal and plant material in the shale."

"We'll make another pile of the grey shale and get it burning. Where the cliff erodes and falls to the sea it exposes the good stuff. It is just a matter of searching the cliff edge and that saves digging."

The following evening, Sir James is in Richmond at the dairy. He had ridden all day with the pack mule in tow. Everyone else had already eaten, as it was late, but Joel, Virgil, and Otto, who is still here, all join him while he sups. He lays out his plans for the visit.

"As long as the weather permits, I want to ride up the valley tomorrow and see the miners. Virgil, have your men ready for an early start. When we get back, I'll want to see the new mill, the shops in Richmond, and the weavers. Otto, please get with the dyer here and make as much more of the aqua yarn as you can from the alum that I brought."

Joel smiled with sympathy at Virgil; he will have to spend the night here at the dairy instead of in Richmond with Matilda.

In the early morning, James and Virgil, escorted by the oarsmen of the *Marie*, head up the valley of the River Swale into Swaledale to find the free miners. It felt great to be leading a company of men in the open air and rugged, rolling hills once again. And once again the men were back in the garb of stout yeomen bearing long bows. The mules follow with picks, shovels, and food-stuffs. Obviously, no one made excuses to be elsewhere today.

Virgil points ahead. "That's the escarpment where we found our shepherd, Walter, the last time we came up, Sir James. He is a Companie man; was a scout. Bad leg."

"I remember Walter. So, the smelter is not far. I suppose that is the best place to start."

The smelter had located his furnace on a large flat rock face. It was burning when Sir James and his party arrived. Armed parties do not typically pass through and the smelter was immediately on his guard. Virgil and James left the oarsmen up wind, dismounted, and walked towards the fire. "Greetings old friend," Virgil calls out.

"Oh, it's you. I should have realized that!" he said, waving his fire poker towards the group of armed men. "I don't get many visitors such as you."

"I am, Sir James. I am told that you are Paul and that you have been our valued source of lead."

The smelter removed his hat. "You've bought every bit for the last six months."

"Would you join us for a meal and tell me about your work here?"

The rain and streams wash the topsoil away to reveal the silver-metallic ore veins in the limestone of Swaledale. Once the miners discover a vein they pay for a patch of ground and dig out the ore. From there Paul hauls it to a hard rock outcropping next to the stream, breaks it up and dumps it into an open timber-framed box. At that point he diverts part of the stream to wash the ore of impurities by repeatedly flooding the box. The heavier lead remains in the box. Then the smelting can begin. The ore is relatively soft and when James breaks a square chunk it split into small cubes and rectangles.

"If it breaks into curved pieces the miners say it has silver; they keep that."

"How much do they keep, Paul?"

"Not much here. More other places, I'm told."

Smelting is not complicated. Turns out that lead is one of the easiest metals to smelt, perhaps because of the low melt temperature. First Paul piles brush and dried grasses on the rock. Then he piles the broken-up ore on top and lights the fire. Then he piles on more brush. The wind on the ridge makes the fire rage until the sulfur burns away leaving the lead under the ashes. Shovel the ashes away, peel the soft lead up off the rock, melt it again, and let it run into molds and form ingots. The ingots, or pigs, each weigh about five stone and are about seventeen inches long.

The limitations are collecting enough brush, getting enough lead ore from the free-miners, and transporting the ore to the site, James determines. We had already solved the fourth problem for him – transporting the ingots to market. Joel has them picked up once a month before another buyer might show up.

"Virgil, next I would like to find Walter and have him lead us to the nearest miners. Paul obviously needs to stay here with his fire." Pulling his horn from his saddle bag and smiling, he said "do you think this will bring him to us?"

"I do! I'd bet even money he has been watching us since we climbed up the valley."

With that James blew a long and loud blast on the horn. Before long Walter strides up, his limp barely showing, and salutes Sir James.

"Captain!"

"I did not think my best scout would be far. Grab a bite, and then I want you to lead me to the miners that supply Paul here with lead ore." Noticing his hesitation, he says, "We'll move faster if you are willing to ride Virgil's horse."

By early evening, they were back at the camp that had been set up just far enough from the smelting operation to stay well clear of the lingering smoke. "Long day, I thank you for your assistance Walter. Your descriptions of the free-miners' plight were certainly not exaggerated. They live on the hope of finding silver because they certainly hardly take time to find food or attend to personal cleanliness!"

Walter nodded. "They certainly took the time to eat up those fried pork pies you brought, Captain."

"Yes, they did. What would it take to get twice as many lead ingots each month from you Paul?"

"Whew! I just don't see how that is possible," he said, shaking his head back and forth in bewilderment.

"The Archbishop of Yorke is frustrated that I cannot get him enough lead for his cathedral's roof. Would it help if we gave you two of these mules to drag brush and carry ore from the miners to your burn site?"

"Goodness, yes, Sir James! I could carry much, much more each trip."

"Enough to have a burn twice as often?"

"I suppose so, if I could get enough ore."

"I want your commitment to sell all the lead you smelt to me in exchange."

"That's fair enough since you buy all my pigs now and pay in coin…not promises."

"Those miners were using broken tools and fire-hardened sticks. Paul, if you give them these picks and shovels, I am willing to bet they can move twice as much material for you."

"Until they break them."

"There is always that; we'll replace them. Here is what I want to do: first we will leave you these two mules, and the picks and shovels for you to distribute. I'll have Joel send men to pick up your ingots every two weeks and they will bring some food, a solid meal or two, and tools each trip." James paused and looked at each of them. "Virgil, what do you think?"

"I'll need to bring up tools each trip from Yorke."

"The miners may think they are getting into a debt that they cannot repay, and you will own them," Walter warned.

"They became 'free-miners' because they did not want that, eh? Paul, if we say they need to commit all their ore to you and no one else in exchange for the tools and the food… You do pay them for their ore, don't you?"

Paul responds, "Indeed, I do, and in coin, just like you pay me. At least I do now-a-days since you started paying me."

"Is that something easy for them to agree to, and makes them feel they have a deal that doesn't indebt them long term? They can break it any time by refusing our tools and provisions."

"I get all of it now, except the silver-rich ore."

"Well, obviously, I don't mean that."

"So, it should be easy for them to agree! Committing to selling only to me as long as they take the tools is a bargain they can live with."

"I'll tell Master Tenebroides to get more picks and shovels up to Yorke. Let's make this good enough for the miners to pick out more ore. Are there other smelters like you up here?"

"There is another a few miles north."

The next morning is wet and foggy as they move down the valley to the River Swale. The little valley is steep and the beck running down it rock-strewn, so it is slow going. James' horse steps awkwardly, at times, sending a spasm of pain up his spine. Walter and the rest of their shepherds get supplies from James' village of Ghyll at the foot of this valley on the Swale. The Swale is not navigable past Richmond, so he wants the village to retrieve the lead and supply the miners. Then Joel would only have to journey as far as the village. Not surprisingly there is some alarm as the armed party emerges suddenly from the grey mist into the village center.

"You are the reeve here?" James asks of the sturdy man in front of the villagers.

"And who is asking?"

James laughs warmly. You just have to admire an unarmed peasant standing his ground to a mounted man at the head of an armed party. "My name is James, Sir James d'Arzhon, and yours?"

"I am William, my Lord, and I am the reeve here," he said, removing his straw hat and bowing his head.

"If this is Ghyll, then this is my village, and you are my reeve."

"This is, indeed, Ghyll, my Lord; I did not know you were coming." He was now clearly discomfited.

"My apologies," he said, dismounting. "I had not planned on a visit to Ghyll, but I am pleased to meet you William. Joel has spoken highly of you." Joel had not mentioned him as he had not anticipated James paying a visit, but he was anxious to put the man at ease. The villagers slowly emerge and put down their hoes and staves.

"This mist will burn off shortly and then folks will head into the fields, my Lord. I did serve with you in Brittany, my Lord."

"Did you?" He was a Companie man, then.

"Well, not in your command, but with Sir John. Joel recognized me and offered me work on your behalf. I'm indebted to you."

"If you are a Companie man that is good enough for me. I have been up the valley trying to get more lead for the roof of the Archbishop of Yorke's cathedral. I will not be long. While here I would like to greet all the residents of the village."

William nodded and began waving everyone in. "Come greet our Lord James, everyone!" The men remove their hats and edge in nervously towards James and his party. The women hold back with the children but come close enough to satisfy their curiosity. Sir James is the landholder of the village and therefore their lord.

He concludes, "I understand that the shearing and haymaking are going well – so, well done, all of you!" The people look good, but there are too many of them, which has him perplexed. "I won't keep you as I know you have much to do." Quietly, he says, "William, we need to talk."

"Yes, my Lord?"

"Virgil, please water the horses and have everyone take a break for just a bit."

"So, first, you obviously know Walter and the other shepherds up the valley?"

"Yes, one of them comes down each week for foodstuffs. Occasionally, they bring an old ewe for us to slaughter. That stockade is full now with one last flock for spring shearing. They bring the flocks down and then Joel comes here for the wool."

"Exactly. I want you to do the same thing with the lead ingots from the smelter up the valley. His name is Paul. I want you to go buy his ingots every two weeks and bring him some foodstuffs each trip. Joel will then pick up the ingots from you and bring you the funds to pay Paul. Hopefully, he will also bring some mining tools each trip to take up to Paul."

"That seems simple enough. Walter can show me where to find this Paul?"

"Indeed. He knows what we are about. Now I want to understand how a village with six or seven households has more than thirty grown men to greet me."

"Well, my Lord, I don't really know what you mean."

"William, there are well over a hundred people in this village! I know full well that two years ago Joel was talking about moving the few folk here to Kelde, so we would have enough to farm the demesne land."

"Joel has sent us a few Companie men."

"I saw them."

"Many of the lords are not very understanding, Sir James. They work their remaining people so hard on their demesne leaving them no time to work their own. There is much hardship."

"So, what you're saying is that this many people have left their lords and come to us? I said to make them a home here if some came by…."

"I do not know where they came from. I do not ask."

"You did not seek them out, did you?"

"No, no, of course not. I just encouraged the first ones to stay and I guess word got back."

"What have you offered them?"

"We had empty land to give them. More than they had before, and we weren't trying to farm more demesne land than we could reasonably support. Now I'm told Ghyll has more people than we did before the Black Death. All the land is back in tillage."

"What did you give them?"

"We, I mean you…err…we, on your behalf, granted them each a virgate to farm for themselves."

"And in exchange for those thirty acres…"

"Two days labor each week. Actually, ninety days each year and three shillings nine p rent."

"And what is left of my demesne land?"

"You have three times as much back in tillage as you did before, even though I granted some to the newcomers. I hope you are not wroth with me, my Lord."

"You can get my work done with just two days labor, rather than the usual three?

"I believe so."

"Joel knows?"

William nods.

"I have three times more in tillage now than was supportable when Ghyll became my holding?"

William nodded again.

Twenty or so new families meant another 1,800 days of labor and another seventy-five shillings in rent income. "Are they villeins or freemen?"

"I'd say freemen now, my Lord."

"So, they owe service on my demesne land and rent for the land you have granted them but are free to depart if they so choose."

"I'd say that is how it is."

James is starting to get uneasy. Villeins cannot legally leave their lord's land and that is what these people are...or were. If their lord found out they would be branded in punishment and forced to return to his land. He could also take James to court and the penalty would be severe. "Are they all from the same village?"

"I think they are from several."

"Nearby?"

"Not from this wapentake."

So, they were not from this same area, the Wapentake of West Gilling. "Hang West or Hallikeld?"

"No, my Lord. They—we—will not be found out."

Well, that was something. They were not from the North Riding of Yorkshire but farther away. Perhaps they are from over the mountains just west. "It may not be that easy – what about the tithing?"

We take it to Grinton; we haven't had enough for the Church to bother to send someone to our tithe barn in years. We took a good increase down last year.

"Don't give them reason to become suspicious and investigate. If the Church thinks you are cheating them...on the other hand if they get a modest increase each year, they are not likely to want to cut off their own noses. I do not know anything about all of this William."

"That's what Joel said: Sir James doesn't want to know any of this."

"No more, though; enough is enough." James had visions of peasants passing the word of a better life and causing a great migration to his lands. The nobility would draw and quarter him.

"Umm, the same thing has happened in Kelde and Waite, my Lord."

"They well know the punishment if they are found out. No more, though...you understand me? I will disavow all knowledge if it comes to it. Provided no one finds out for the year, this is very well done, William. Very well done, indeed."

"Everyone understands that I assure you, and so do I, my Lord."

"Small game and firewood?"

"The usual…they can take small game and gather dead wood."

"We can do a little better on that. I need white oak for barrel staves. Harvest a few big trees this winter, sled the wood suitable for staves down to Joel for seasoning, and distribute the rest. If my fall harvest is good and you are well satisfied, then Virgil can organize a deer hunt a few times through the winter."

"That is most generous!"

"If a man goes out deer hunting on his own, I still consider that an infringement on my prerogatives."

"Of course."

"And, just as the king does, I expect every man to be skilled with the bow. Make a note of the day when each man left his village. I want to know when they are legally freemen." English common law was that if a man was gone for a year and a day, then he was legally a freeman. Most could never leave because to do so would be to lose the land they had been granted, and they would have no way to support themselves.

Having been granted three nearly deserted and worthless villages that could not even pay for themselves, much less the fifteenth in taxes assessed, that have now become large and productive ones was most satisfactory, indeed. This explained why Joel had been able to send grain to Yorke for sale. Provided he could avoid prosecution for a year, he could start making money on more things than sheep and spices. And James had an idea about the tithing.

Chapter 5

Inferno

LATE JUNE 1372

Master Swain arrives at Sir James' townhouse, looking despondent. "My creditor has taken possession of my boatyard and all my tools, Sir James." Swain nervously wipes his rough hands again and again over his leather apron. "I am embarrassed and most sorry to bear this news."

"Then they have also taken my barge that you have almost completed?"

"They have, and so now, I also owe you the seven pounds that you advanced me." His lips quiver in his distress.

"Master Swain, you have built several boats for me at a fair price, and I have been most satisfied with them. Your yard has always seemed busy; may I ask how you have gotten yourself into this situation?"

"I am still owed the balance on a few craft that I delivered last year, and they have not been able to pay me. I also paid a premium for the boatyard because it is just outside the city walls on the river. I cannot seem get enough money in hand to pay on the loan, and now I have lost everything including your boat."

"Most creditors want their money not tools and the property. How much are you behind on the loan?"

"I paid him four pounds from what you paid me. I thought surely that would please him!"

"How much do you owe them?" James repeated.

"I am a year behind now, which is eight pounds. That is more than the balance you owe on your boat."

"And the total amount of the loan?"

"I borrowed forty pounds sterling, and I still owe Benjamin thirty-two, including the interest."

"The lender by Holy Trinity?" Swain nods. James is surprised. "He generally tries to avoid attention."

"Some say he is a Lollard." The Lollards are a Christian sect that follow the teachings of John Wycliffe. They believe that the Church is guilty of excesses for their own comfort rather than helping the poor and preaching. Another belief is that Church officials should not hold government positions, which is common practice. A third heresy they preach is that tithes are merely alms and should not be compulsory payments. Obviously, the Church seeks their persecution, but they have friends among the nobility, such as the Duke of Lancaster, that believe the Church has become too powerful.

"I will pay a visit to Benjamin. While I do not know him well, I have not thought of him as an unreasonable man. He certainly does not want to be the owner of a boatyard. Of that I feel quite certain."

Holy Trinity Priory is on the west bank near the Micklegate Bar, the main city gate to the west. James takes both squires and rides through the city and across the crowded Ouse Bridge. The tide must be in as the river reeks of sewage. It is at its worst in the heat of the summer.

Malcolm dismounts and knocks on the heavy wooden door of Benjamin the moneylender's home. Even though they are inside the city walls this is not a prominent area. The houses are ramshackle and crowded one upon another. This is the only decent house on the narrow dirt street; piles of refuse and stray dogs seem to be in every corner. James shifts uncomfortably in the saddle; they have begun to gather attention from the residents. The upper floors are built slightly further over the street than the one below. This is to the point that you could almost reach from the third story and open your across-the-street neighbor's window. It makes for a dark and confining place to be caught. A dark-haired woman leans from a second story window. "What d'ya want?" Then, noticing Sir James mounted in the street, hastily adds, "My Lord."

"I wish to speak to Master Benjamin regarding a business matter."

The woman disappears from the window and, shortly afterwards, can be heard unlatching the heavy bolt-studded door. "My father will meet you in his study. May I tell him who is calling?"

"Sir James d'Arzhon."

"Sir James, to what do I owe the honor of your visit?" Benjamin wears a robe with a shawl and has on a hat as he stands behind a well-worn table in the dark room.

"I understand that you needed to call in a loan that is in arrears."

"Might you be referring to Swain's boatyard?"

"Yes, exactly so."

"He is a year behind in his rent payment. May I ask how it is of concern to you, my Lord?"

Clearly Benjamin is disguising the loan as rent to avoid being accused of usury. Since Swain does not own the boatyard until the balance is repaid the interest on the loan is being termed his rent to use the property. Rent is legal but collecting interest payments is a sin. "He is building a barge for me that is almost complete and partially paid for."

"Anything in the yard is an asset against the balance due. I am most sorry about this."

"Surely it is in your interest to allow Master Swain to complete the barge and collect the remainder against the loan, is it not?"

"I have a buyer for the boatyard, and he wishes to take immediate possession."

"Perhaps the barge can be moved to a nearby yard and I can arrange to have Swain complete it there?"

"I apologize for being difficult, but my buyer wants the yard and insists on keeping everything that is in it."

"Master Benjamin, that barge is being built at the request of the archbishop to transport stone for the cathedral construction. I believe it is in everyone's best interest, including yours, for us to find a reasonable accommodation."

"I am in a difficult position, I hope you understand, but that does explain some things to me. The man who wants to buy the yard currently has the contract to transport the stone."

James' agitation gets into his tone. "Having a buyer's offer does not require you to call in the loan or sell to them. I cannot but believe that you are not telling me everything."

"The man has been most threatening."

"I can be threatening, too."

"He has threatened to accuse me of heresy against the Church."

"As a Lollard, a usurer, or a Jew?" James demands angrily.

Benjamin sits back with his fingertips together and considers the man across from him. He knows that Sir James does business with many of the most prominent men of the city, and he has heard rumors that he is not a man to be crossed. "As a Lollard. Please allow me to pour you a glass; I have not been hospitable."

"I see." Calming down a little, he says, "So, he will accuse you of heresy to the Church, which will not renew his contract, unless you prevent the archbishop's new supplier from getting his barge built? Once he has destroyed the barge, you will not get payment for the boatyard. Of that I feel sure!"

"This situation is worse than I supposed. I have no desire to make an enemy of the archbishop, or you, Sir James, for that matter."

"Let me think for a moment. What if I were to pay the balance due? Here is what I propose to you: first I will pay the balance owed on the loan, err rent, to you now and assume responsibility for the remaining payments. I will be the new owner of the boatyard, second, I will speak to Archbishop John about Master Hubert's threats. That is the man we are speaking about, is it not?"

"It is, but…"

"Master Hubert is at odds with the archbishop over his deliveries, and it would be his court that would hear accusations of heresy. I believe I can assure you that no matter the nature of the accusation, the archbishop will turn a deaf ear. You have not been preaching against the Church, have you?"

"Oh, no, of course not." He laughed at the thought. "Nothing could be further from my mind."

"I will also speak to the sheriff and see if he will pay a visit to Hubert regarding blackmail."

"I have concerns for my safety and that of my daughter. He is very menacing, and he has quite a few men."

"Leave that to me. I believe eight pounds makes the rent current," James said as he stacked the money on the table.

"It does."

"Geoffrey is one among your group a talented bowyer?" James asks of the man that led the Companie men back from Normandy that fell afoul of the Sheriff of Lincoln.

"Nathan was a fair hand at one time making long bows, Sir James. He is one of the men you were able to have released from the Sheriff, but was in a bad way; is he still alive?"

"Two of your party have died, but I do not recall Nathan as being one of their names. Perhaps Malcolm will remember Nathan. Malcolm?"

"Sir?"

"A Companie man named Nathan that we got released from the sheriff in Lincoln."

"He is at Barmby minding a salt pan. He lost his foot and then we had to take off his lower leg," he adds with a wince.

"So, he is alive, at least."

"Seems that he will be alright now. Healthy stump and no sign of corruption."

"Sir James, I'm thinking he can make bows with just one leg."

"I am thinking the same. Likely he will enjoy it more than what he is doing now. I'll get the bargemen to bring him some good English Yew from our villages."

"There has been a complaint about our cloth."

"Not totally unexpected, Janice. Who griped and to whom?"

"The master of the weaver's guild complained to the city bailiff. He makes a fine broadcloth and sells in the corner stall."

James smiles. "We undersold him?"

"There is talk that our cloth is of superior quality among the tailors. They used to say he had no equal that was not at an imported price. I am charging more, close to imported prices, but the tailors are influencing their wealthy clients to buy from me. He has had to cut his prices. The bailiff told me about the complaint."

"And?"

"He says I am selling imported cloth below market price and that the only way I could do that is by not paying the tariff. He threatens to take his grievance to the king's customs agents! I assured the bailiff that no tariff had been avoided on my goods as Master Tenebroides told me to."

"Good; somehow I doubt that this will be the end of it. Making legal accusations against a competitor is a risky game to play." While James fully expected a weaver in the city to make a complaint, it still came as an annoyance. Between this and the issue at the boatyard, he could feel himself getting testy and irritable. He had better put his mind in a calmer frame before meeting with the archbishop.

That afternoon James skirts the construction around the cathedral. The stack of stone block is much reduced.

"Your Grace," James says as kneels to kiss the archbishop's ring. Thankfully, he is in the city today.

"How is work on your barge to transport my stone coming along, Sir James?"

"It will be ready shortly; have no concern about that. I have had a run in with Master Hubert, your current contractor, of which I need to make you aware."

"He is a difficult man, at times, which is why I am not renewing his contract."

"Also, a threatening one."

"Oh?" replied the archbishop. "He has threatened you?"

"He tried to buy the boatyard including our barge by threatening the lender. Master Swain, the owner, was behind in his payments. I have bought out the loan, so I am the new owner of the boatyard at this point."

"Then the matter is resolved."

"Almost resolved, your Grace, he threatened to accuse the lender of being a Lollard if he did not foreclose on the loan and sell to him, and, of course, to prevent the construction of our barge."

"I have no sympathy with Lollards. They are heretics."

"No, I am sure you do not. I want you to assure me that you have even less sympathy for a blackmailer trying to force you to keep him as your supplier against your wishes."

"He will not use my own court to manipulate me." John de Thoresby was a crafty old churchman and the most powerful man in Yorke. "That I do assure you."

"Your Grace, I do not want to manipulate you, either. He may intend to accuse Benjamin the moneylender of being a Jew."

"I appreciate your being so forthright. It is certainly possible that Benjamin is a Jew! That would constitute a crime against the King's Law and is far less troubling to the Church than a heretic Lollard."

The Jews were expelled from England almost a hundred years previously in the reign of Edward I. They once had a sizeable community in Yorke. Many practiced money lending because Christians cannot. Accusing Benjamin of being a Jew, because he lends money, would find sympathy in the royal courts even if it was not true. "I take your point. I shall speak with the sheriff." James withdrew hoping he had gained the archbishop's support in whatever might happen next. While the details were not completely clear to James, he had been told that years ago many of the Jews in Yorke had been forced by a mob to take refuge in Clifford's Tower and then burnt to death. The leading nobles responsible for their protection may have instigated the riot as they subsequently broke into the Jews' houses, and destroyed the ledgers that recorded the loans they owed to prevent any heirs from collecting what was due.

"Master Swain I have bought your boatyard."

Swain removes his cap and nods glumly. "I guess that gets you your barge back."

"It does, for now you work for me unless you have an objection. We'll figure out some arrangement on wages, and between us on the boatyard's ownership, later."

"At least I have a job, then, and my men?"

"Get them all back to work. I still need that barge launched!"

Hubert slams his fist on Benjamin's door. "We had an agreement you damned heathen!" The short and stocky stone carter gesticulates angrily with his fat stubby arms.

The second-story window opens and Benjamin replies, "Get yourself gone from here. We had no such agreement – only threats!"

"You would have done well to have minded them you old fool. Mark my words: you will be sorry!"

The raised voices attract attention. The narrow street soon becomes a gauntlet for Hubert as buckets and chamber pots of filth shower down on the carter from the over-hanging upper floor windows of nearly every house. He abandons all pretense of dignity and makes a run for it. When he finally emerges onto Micklegate he is purple with a rage he can scarcely control. Then he sees one of the city bailiffs and his party eyeballing him. Somebody had spoken to the sheriff and Hubert was quite sure he knew whom.

It is past midnight when first the bell of the Franciscan Friary begins to ring, and then the alarm is taken up throughout the city. Just outside the city walls a conflagration is burning along the west side of the river. A few warehouses, boatyards and houses are aflame.

The good fortune is that the fire is confined by the city wall to its north and the river to the east, but the closely packed houses of the poorer neighborhood have thatch or wood shingle roofs and begin to go up in flames quickly as the fire spreads away from the river. It is almost dawn when the fire is brought under control by bringing down houses in its path to keep it from spreading rooftop to rooftop across the streets. A fire threatens everyone, and the entire city seems to be present to fight it.

Smoke hangs thickly over the west side of the city and stings the eyes, mouths, and lungs of the citizens on the bucket lines. The fire is no longer spreading, but it is still burning. If it had been a windy night far more would have been lost. The sheriff, mayor, and a red-eyed and soot covered Sir James end up standing together outside what is left of Master Swain's boatyard. Obscured in the tired crowd is the ring of Companie men determined to assure that James comes to no harm.

Crowds in the dark and insanity of fighting a fire is the sort of confused situation that Brother Hugh fears the most. He exchanges meaningful glances with Malcolm, Will, Geoffrey, and the Whitefriars forming the perimeter. At least it is daylight now.

"When did you get here James?"

"We came across with the Whitefriars in their boat. The fire was already into the houses by then."

John de Gisburn asks, "Does anyone know where the fire started?"

"That is certainly the question my Lord Mayor!" the Sheriff replies.

A badly burned man walks up gingerly to the group. "It may have been started in my shed."

"Master Swain?"

"That squares with where we first spotted the fire." The leader of a city watch group joins in. "Of course, we were across the river, so it is hard to be sure."

"Pitch, rope, turpentine, and wood will get a fire going," James frowns. "Swain you need to get some care!" The boat builder's face was red and blistered; his beard and hair gone to a blackened frizzle. "You said 'may have been started,' did you not?"

"I did."

"Arson! There is no crime more craven!" exclaimed the mayor.

"Tenebro, I need you to delay your departure down river."

"Sure, for how long, Sir James?"

"Put the crew to work helping clean up the boatyard and building a large shelter there; one we can close up later as a warehouse. Where is Virgil?"

"He just came in an hour ago with a full load. We are transferring the wool sacks now."

"I need him to stay in the City, as well."

"I'll let him know."

"Other than an anchor watch, please have both crews at the priory, just after evening prayer. They will get supper there and they should bring their bows. Slip them in gradually and use the friar's boat, too."

"We won't attract any undue attention. May I ask what we're about?"

"I'm not sure yet. Arrange an archery competition. *Marie's* against *Christine's* and both against Whitefriars. Figure out something for prizes. Keep them at it until everyone is sharp. That is all for the moment."

St. Leonard's Hospital has over two hundred beds to care for the injured and the infirm. It is the only hospital in Yorke and may be the largest in England. Through it the Church feeds the poor, the prisoners, and has a nursery for ill and orphaned children.

Injured townspeople slowly begin to make their way over the Ouse to Lendal Street and the gate to St. Leonard's. A vaulted passageway leads to the undercroft of the chapel, which is the main infirmary. Katherine Blackwell gently flushes grime from a deep gash in a man's upper arm where he had been hit by a timber from a collapsing building. "I do not believe your arm is broken. The swelling and bruising will get better, but if the pain persists, then I may have been mistaken and you need to return." As she was putting stitches in his arm, she said, "Do you understand?"

"Aye, Doctor, I'll be alright, thank yee."

"If it is broken and you continue to use it, then it will heal badly and never be right. Be sure to return if it still hurts after a few days." She did not think that he would.

Sister Coletta gently wound a bandage over the stitches. "I know his wife, Doctor, I'll tell her; Eustace is too stubborn for his good," she said, looking him straight in the eye.

"I am under siege; can a man find no peace?"

The hospital is similar to a monastery. Thirteen brothers live by the rule under the authority of a prior and there are eight sisters. In addition, there are choristers and servants. Doctors and surgeons in the city, such as Katherine, sometimes help out. The regular staff of over seventy see to the burned, injured, and homeless from the fire. St. Leonard's humanitarian mission is well endowed with enormous gifts and property to fund its task, but it is also required to turn no one away. Resources are stretched this day.

Katherine is exhausted when she leaves Saint Leonard's, but at least she had been able to have a hearty supper before she departs.

"You think this was Hubert the stone carter's doing?"

"If the fire was deliberately set, which seems unthinkable, and the boatyard was the target, then that is a possibility that is hard to ignore Sir William, but I have nothing other than unfounded suspicions to go on."

"Maybe more than that, James," the Sheriff replies angrily. "Hubert threatened the money lender yesterday, just as you warned me he might. Your barge was ordered by the archbishop to replace him and his wagons. To put him out of business – that's his reason for the crime!"

"Unless we can find witnesses, that is still a dangerous accusation."

"For you, James, but not for me. I am the sheriff here! I intend to haul him in and ask him his whereabouts last night and if anyone can vouch for him. At least four people died in that fire."

James' scarred shoulder began to tingle where the skin had been burned years ago. "Burning is a bad way to die. You might want to pick up some of his men and see if they crack. That fire surely spread beyond their intentions, and they may be remorseful or frightened. They'll be heading out the Micklegate Bar for Tatecastre before noon."

There is an unruly crowd filling the street at the Micklegate Bar when Sheriff William and his party ride over. Hubert is standing up in his wagon brandishing a long iron bar and yelling back at the mob surrounding his teams. His men try to regain control of the draft horses, but the crowd has a hold of the bridles.

It seems that the townspeople suspect Hubert, thinks the Sheriff, but do they actually know something or have rumors just gotten out of control? "Make way, there! Make way for the sheriff!" his men slowly push through the crowd on their horses asserting his authority. The people are still shouting and throwing stones until the sheriff is next to Hubert. It is clear that the mob is well aware people died in the fire and that Hubert's shouted threats at Benjamin the money lender are also known. They seem to know that Swain was building a barge that would put Hubert out of business and have come to the same conclusion that both he and Sir James had. It takes a while to get the wagon teams turned around and headed back into the city, over the Ouse Bridge and into the castle courtyard.

Master Swain sits on the blackened barge talking to James. His face glistens with a thick layer of pig fat, and it obviously hurt a great deal.

"So, what you are telling me is that these timbers are only charred on the surface and that the barge survived?"

"The blackened outside protects the thick timber from burning. We can clean it up and the hull will be fine. We've lost the sweeps, the rigging, and the materials we need to finish her, though."

"Buy what you need and hire some of these people that lost their homes to get the yard cleared up. I'll send some men over to put up some shelters for them. We can add walls later and use them to store supplies for the boatyard."

James walks over to Prior William where he and the Whitefriars are providing meals. "thanks for jumping in Prior William. If the boatyard was intentionally burned, then this is all my fault."

"Because the archbishop asked you to build a barge? Nonsense. Whoever struck the flame is responsible and no one else. And no need to thank us – this is God's work."

James has rarely seen Prior William happier. "Nonetheless, I feel partly responsible."

The priory has plenty of food and a bakery. They are able to get more from The Swan. Their boat on the Foss makes meal transport to the boatyard from both priory and The Swan simple as the yard is just a bit downstream from where the Foss joins the Ouse.

Sheriff Sir William pays a visit to James' townhouse. "I'm releasing Hubert and his men tomorrow; I've no witnesses and they all swear to each other's whereabouts that night."

"You believe them?"

"Hell no! I don't believe them. My gut tells me Hubert set the fire. I know it, but I cannot prove it."

"The people of the city seem to agree with you. I wonder if Hubert will keep trying to bring stone here?"

"He would be wise to clear the city gate and never look back. I'm releasing them about mid-morning; just thought you might want to know." It would be most unlike Sir William to be asking him to take the law into his own hands.

Did he feel his hands were tied? How else to explain the sheriff's words? Merely a courtesy or a suggestion?

Paul Fitz-William sat his horse calmly on the road from Yorke to Tatecastre. Will sat his horse beside him. It is less than ten miles from Yorke to the quarry and Geoffrey chose a spot just after a wooded curve about six miles from Yorke. There is only one road. There were no witnesses to swear to Hubert's starting the fire. His men swore they had all been asleep in the cathedral yard when the alarm was sounded.

No one tried to enforce the curfew during the fire emergency. It would have been impossible in the chaos. Everyone was streaming into the streets in the night and the bridge gates were open. People were moving across the bridge to fight the fire after the bells started ringing. Except Hubert and one of his men had been seen crossing the Ouse Bridge going in the other direction by Oliver, James' fishmonger, who has his shop on the bridge. He noticed just because they were going in the wrong direction and he was absolutely certain. Hubert was quite recognizable as he had driven his heavy wagons with many loads of stone across the bridge past his shop. For James, there was no doubt he had not been asleep in the cathedral yard.

A whistle from the forest signals that the heavy wagons and their teams are in sight. But it is unnecessary as Paul can hear them coming. The wagons are empty and headed towards the quarry at a good pace.

"While I appreciate your morality in not compelling a confession, I must also confess to my frustration."

"I share it James!" a visibly agitated sheriff replied. "Don't think me squeamish; we did apply some pressure I assure you."

"Well, I am told they rolled out of the city today with the scorn of the populace fully expressed."

"That stone carter left with a smirk on his face that I will not soon forget. I hope a well-aimed chamber pot found him with its contents. My appetite is not what it should be as a result; which is a shame as this meal is most elegant."

"Perhaps some more wine, then, Sir William?" the ever-present Malcolm offers. They dine upstairs in James' townhouse.

"If no one has come forward as a witness and they all swear to each other's innocence, what is next? We have four deaths and homes and properties burned to the ground. It seems that justice has not been served. I do pray that he takes his business elsewhere. I do not want more of an arsonist's kind of trouble."

"Agreed, but I will not punish Hubert based on suspicions and give in to public demand for a hanging, no matter how much I want to."

"I have another matter for your attention, Sir William. My boatyard is unpaid for three vessels built last year. I have had the Court of Chancery issue writs of capias et extendi facias to you for imprisonment of the boat owners."

"Did you speak to them first?"

"I had Swain tell them I would take legal action if they did not pay him what they owe."

The sheriff took the documents from James. "This seems in order. They operate on the River Ouse and come to Yorke?"

"The first two come in about once a month. The third is a fishing boat that only gets as far upriver as Selby."

"They can pay the balance, or you get their boats until they do. Is this why Swain was in arrears with Benjamin the lender?"

"It is. The ten pounds would have kept him current on the loan and if you can collect it on his behalf, then I can get out of owning a boatyard."

"I'll send out a bailiff."

The first wagon team rounds the bend and comes to a halt thirty feet short of Paul who makes no effort to get out of the road. There are two wagons each pulled by six large draft horses; the carter's men are in the wagons. The men in back stand up to see what has blocked their progress. "Well, if it is not a struttin' peacock without enough sense to get out of the road," Hubert laughs scornfully from the driver's seat. "Get out of my way or I'll run you down and be glad to do it."

"Innocent people were burned to death in that fire. I call that murder."

"Are you the sheriff now? He had no proof, and neither do you. Seems to me Swain was careless."

"It would be best if you all dismounted from my wagon teams and walked away peacefully."

"Your wagons! I've a mind to crack your stupid skull open."

"Yes, my wagons, I am taking them as compensation for damages."

"Ha!" Hubert cracks his whip to move his team forward.

Paul draws his sword and points it at the head of the nearest horse. As in his past experience, the big horse shies and refuses to impale itself on the sword. Sometimes horses are smarter than people. Will raises his halberd. They do not move from the road.

Hubert reins in again in a fury. The front of his team is stopped just a few feet from where the horsemen stood. "Get after them!" His men leap out of the wagons with the heavy iron lever bars used for moving the massive stone blocks. Another man stands in the leading wagon with a crossbow and begins to level it at Paul. Hubert rears back with his whip.

Paul brings his sword down and ducks behind the big draft horse. At the signal arrows fly from the woods; a score of men emerges and charge across the short gap to the wagons. Two arrows pierce the man with the crossbow under his arm and in the thigh. Three strike Hubert in the hip and side. The biggest man, with a lever bar, leading the way towards Paul is dropped where he stood. Another falls to his knees grabbing his belly where one of the two arrows buries itself. The rest start to run away in all directions. Paul slashes one across the neck. Will stands in the saddle, swinging his halberd with both hands as he rides down two more. The last three are cornered by the charging Virgil and his crew of big oarsmen against the front wagon; fear momentarily paralyzes them. They think to drop their weapons a bit too late.

Hubert cries out in pain and fury. Even with the arrows sunk deep he lashes out with the whip, missing into the air next to Virgil. Tenebroides is up over the side of the wagon in an instant. He plunges his long knife deep in below the breastbone and upward to the hilt. Blood fills Hubert's mouth and runs down his chin. Tenebroides smiles and softly snarls, "Your troubles are over now, and we will have no more trouble with you." Hubert's eyes roll back in their sockets.

Without a word the bodies are tumbled into wool sacks and loaded into the empty wagons. The entire encounter has taken only a moment. The *Christine's* crew and the men from Yorke depart back towards the river south of the city. Paul says, "Let's get going. It is a long way to Richmond. I will see you all again. Virgil, you will need to hurry to get back into Yorke before the curfew."

"We moored *Marie* north of the city," Virgil replies; which meant they would not need to pass through a city gate before curfew. "Not much of a fight," as he disappointingly slides his halberd into the wagon.

"Good thinking." With that Paul and his men get the big wagons moving.

In the late afternoon, the road to Richmond skirts a deep ravine. They take a break to rest the horses and throw the bodies off the wagons and into the dense brush below. Paul Fitz-William takes a look through the items on the wagons. There is plenty to make a decent supper here without the provisions they brought with them. There is a lot of money in the lockbox under the driver's seat. Either Hubert was not planning on a return to Yorke or this is where he always kept his funds. Sir James could use the money to repair the boatyard or add it to the Companie profits.

"Coletta, thank you for meeting me."

The older woman smiles, tiredly. "Do I get some fresh fish for my trouble?"

James nods, they are meeting on the Ouse Bridge at Oliver's shop, both pretending to be waiting to be served and standing next to one another. "Any kind you want. Tell me about a surgeon named Katherine Blackwell."

Chapter 6

Fistula in Ano

JULY 1372

Yorke is an independent city. Once it had been governed by the lord sheriff, based at Yorke Castle, who is responsible to the king for all of Yorkshire. The citizens bought the right to rule themselves from King John, over a century ago, for £200 and some horses when he was desperate for funds. Now the citizens collect and pay their own taxes to the crown; that 'farm' is £160 each year. The city is run by the elected Lord Mayor, currently John de Gisburn, and the city council.

Today is Thursday – market day. Yorke Market is the largest outside London and the city swells with shoppers and sellers from the surrounding countryside and towns plus merchants from the entire region and even overseas. It is difficult to be certain, but Yorke probably has a population of between thirteen and fourteen thousand souls; on market days it is surely twenty-five thousand!

The market drives the economy of the city and the city leaders zealously regulate trade to generate revenues from city gate and river tolls. The four corners of the main market square have posts and chains to assure the collection of fees from those coming to the market.

After raising the 'farm' some of the toll money is used to maintain the bridges, roads, and riverside piers; more is used to keep the rivers Foss and Ouse clear of obstructions. It is important that food and raw materials are in adequate supply to the city. All of it comes in from the countryside in wagons or from river barges. Any unauthorized fishing nets blocking the river are removed and the owners fined. Food provisioning is one of the largest occupations in the city followed by the cloth and wool trades. Leatherworkers and metalworkers come next.

Master Tenebroides and the crew of the *Christine* have been up before dawn. At least monthly, when they are docked in the city, they try to get two market stands for which they pay stallage to the city bailiff. This is in addition to getting all of Sir James' merchandise to his partners with shops and stalls of their own. Oliver the fishmonger has fresh fish in the summer at his shop on the bridge; Owen the butcher has pork cuts and mutton; his son the poulter, at the next stall over has hens and eggs. In July Tenebroides has no grain or dried beans to sell and there will not be any until after the harvest next month. Finer cloth is sold by Janice the weaver, but canvas, sack cloth, and lower grade cloth, which is all most can afford are sold in the monthly stall. So, are beeswax candles that fetch almost seven pence a pound, and honey is brought down river by Virgil. Cutlery items: knives, shears, scythes, sickles, iron tipped spades, and axes are bought in Sheffield by Sir James' wool buyers and brought by Thomas down the River Trent to him at Barmby. The cutlery is the best that can be had at any price. Judd the tanner sells his cured skins to artisans in the leather industry to make gloves, clothing, scabbards, purses and more.

Wine is imported by the tun at Kingston, the mead that Virgil brings down from Richmond, and the ale that Bertrand will buy in Tatecastre is sold wholesale in the market to taverns by the Whitefriars at their booth. No city fees are charged to the Church. Brother Hugh sees that the proceeds make it to the Companie coffers. Mason and carpenter tools for the massive cathedral building project are sold outside the market to the construction foremen and Master Tenebroides takes full advantage.

The bell tower of Saint Peter's rings Prime: the market is open. Nothing can be sold before the bell. Sir James makes his rounds each week to see that his booths have goods and are selling. The shopkeepers act as though they fully own their business and careful to treat James like any other customer. Any problems are addressed later or on the sly. It is always a busy day and James has a great deal of merchandise and money moving. John de Thornton is one exception; he has a wonderful selection of spices but does not know that James is one of his suppliers. Spices are strictly a wholesale shadow business for James in Yorke. It would be very difficult to compare any spice sales to import duties paid in Kingston, or in this case – usually not paid. He checks in on Tenebroides' monthly booth before heading to the Ouse Bridge to see Oliver the fishmonger. "Tenebro, we are not the only ones with cutlery today."

"And don't I know it. Bargaining is tough. Something of interest to you, Sir James – there are men wearing the livery of Lord Yarburgh in the market. Brother Hugh insists that you be careful." Tenebro slips him a long dagger.

"Hmm," James strokes his chin beard thoughtfully. "Odd, he does not make a habit of visiting Yorke." As a knight he is allowed to wear his sword, but he does not make a habit of it. He sidles past Malcolm to alert him to the news and have him pass the word. "I'm headed to look in on Oliver."

The Ouse Bridge is packed with people. There are over thirty shops plus tenements, the City Council chambers, and even a chapel crowded on the bridge.

"Well met, my good cousin James. A moment of your time?" A flabby, round-faced man in fine attire blocks his path.

"My Lord Yarburgh, I'm afraid that I've much to do before the gates are closed; another time perhaps?"

"I said I wanted to talk to you..." Yarburgh growls and shoves his forearm into James' chest to push him into a side alley. His dirk is now at James' belly. James instinctively seizes the wrist and twists it behind the younger man's back spinning his face into the side of the building. "You bloody knave, Allan." James pounds his knee into his thigh – twice. Allan gasps and sinks to the ground. His cousin's coddled existence gets under James' skin; Allan has always brought out the worst in him: probably envy.

Two men hurry out of the back of the alley towards James wielding short wooden clubs, but Will, Malcolm, and Paul Fitz-Williams have now rounded the building into the alley, too. This brings Allan's men to a stop, but one raises his baton. Will deflects it and smashes his fist into the man's mouth. Paul slips out a war hammer and the second man starts to run.

Paul starts after him. "Let him go and put that thing out of sight," James orders. Then, pointing at the man with the bloody mouth, he says, "The barge is close; get these two there and then across to the sheriff at the castle." He brutally twists Allan's dirk out of his hand and yanks his cousin up off his knees and shoves him to Will. Then he heads back across the Ouse Bridge to see Sir William de Acton, High Sheriff of Yorkshire. The pain in his lower back is suddenly excruciating. Fortunately, the castle is less than a five-minute walk away. Downriver, in the angle formed by the joining of the Foss to the River Ouse.

Sir William is only recently appointed by King Edward. Fortunately, he is well acquainted with James, and his connections to Prince Edward and the Duke of Lancaster. Royal correspondence to Sir James passed through the sheriff recently. Lord Yarburgh has no holdings in Yorkshire and little influence here. The sheriff readily agrees to James' request to lock him up and issues a warrant for men wearing his livery.

The next morning, James returns to the castle escorted by his squires, Malcolm and Will. He is elegantly attired and wearing his jeweled sword. Lord Yarburgh is brought up to the sheriff's hall by two men-at-arms.

"Attacking citizens will not be tolerated, Lord Yarburgh, no matter who you are," Sir William asserts. "Why are you in Yorke and what is your business here?"

"I assure you that my mercenary cousin attacked me, unprovoked!"

"Really? Then this is not your dagger? And the witnesses that saw you strike Sir James on the street are mistaken?"

"His men are liars, not witnesses."

"Sir James has a fine reputation here and with me. There are several other witnesses, which happens when you attack someone in broad daylight." The color is rising in the sheriff's cheeks. "Take him back to his cell."

"Quite sorry to trouble you for such a short interview, James, but it seemed best to let your cousin sit in his cell a bit longer to see if that improves his understanding of the seriousness with which I hold his actions here in Yorke."

"Family conflicts are often the bitterest ones. I do appreciate your confidence in me, Sir William. Did you really find someone that saw the fight?"

"Actually, yes! Mayor John de Gisburn was here earlier demanding jurisdiction. I persuaded him that the city wants no part of a dispute between you and Lord Yarburgh."

"I hope he agreed."

"Citizens reported the fight and apparently some of Yarburgh's men got a bit rough in a tavern last night. He has them and will deal with them. I think he wanted to insure you were going to be favorably represented."

"In that case I appreciate the mayor's concern."

"I heard that it wasn't much of a fight!"

"I had warning and took precautions. Else it might have been different. My cousin and I have had our differences, but if anyone would be aggrieved it is me. Makes no sense."

"The mayor said that Yarburgh has serious debts in Lincolnshire. His men spoke of it."

"I did not know that." But it may be why I saw him there with that horse-turd Latimer, James thinks. His rich brother-in-law getting him out of trouble again. What pound of flesh did Latimer extract as his quid pro quo? Am I feeling sorry for cousin Allan? First time ever.

"Another matter," Sir William confides, "there is ill news from across the channel. The king's fleet has been utterly defeated at La Rochelle. The Castilians have taken the war chest. Now there is fear of invasion."

"Then the Crown will be raising a new fleet and a new army. It will mean more taxes, and La Rochelle likely to fall before anything can be done. I've been caught in all that before and certainly intend to stay well clear this time."

"I understand that." The sheriff nods in agreement. "Would not we all. I pray it blows over."

"Lord, hear our prayers. When did this happen?"

"Late June. The king's envoy is here now seeking funds and men-at-arms, just as you said."

James enters an apothecary shop near Saint Leonard's hospital tucked in on this side of Saint Mary's Abbey. An elderly woman is being instructed in the application of a poultice for her husband and he waits for her to leave.

"May I help you?"

"I do hope so; you are Mistress Blackwell?" He had expected an older woman.

"I am Katherine Blackwell."

She was tall and slender. "The same that studied with John Arderne in London?"

"My father worked with the surgeon when he was in Nottinghamshire; I assisted him after my father died. He taught me surgery. Why do you ask?"

He pulls a letter out of his purse and hands it to her. "I am James. I watched Arderne perform a surgery on a comrade of mine some years ago in Brittany; I believe I have the same problem – 'fistula in ano.' John states that you may be able to help me."

"There are several highly regarded surgeons in the city." Katherine sits down on her stool and reads the letter. "John says here that you assisted in the surgery, Sir James."

"He is being generous; I handed him things while he worked." She has passed his first test: she reads Latin. She also picked up his rank from the correspondence, which he brought for fear she would refuse him. She grasps things quickly – he does not want a fool cutting on him.

"Arderne is kind to recommend me, but he has not examined you. You do not appear to be in much pain. Have you had a drainage of pus?"

"I have begun to find that being in the saddle is more than I can bear. I did have pus, but I have not had it in a while. I hoped my problem had solved itself."

She looked the tall, broad-shouldered knight directly. "I will need to examine you."

"Of course; perhaps your husband should assist?"

"In the interest of propriety, Sir James? I appreciate your concern, but I have seen plenty of bare bottoms." With that she latched the shop door and turned a closed sign in the window. "It will only take a moment to evaluate your diagnosis. Please step back here into the light and remove your doublet."

James did as he was directed, setting his doublet neatly upon the counter, then pulling up his shirt, unlacing his hose and leaning over the counter. His back to the light revealed a large, angry lump below the base of his spine and between his buttocks.

She pressed her fingers against the inflamed lump. It was not an uncommon problem. Knights that spent too much time in a wet saddle could develop the affliction. "You have an abscess and I am certain that is causing you great pain. I am somewhat surprised it has not burst. It is possible there is also the fistula; when it was unable to drain the abscess formed."

She moved back around to the other side of the counter to face him. His pulled-up shirt had revealed a host of scars. "I will need to drain the abscess and then look for the fistula. If, indeed, it is the fistula, and it does need to be cut out, that will be very painful. I have not performed this particular surgery in a number of years." With the light on her face she did not appear so severe as she had at first. Her hair was actually a chestnut brown, not black, with a touch of grey; she did not dye it.

"You are willing to perform the surgery, then?" He said as he tucked in his shirt.

"I am. I do occasionally perform surgery in the mid-mornings at Saint Leonard's. I have someone who can assist me there. Tomorrow would be best; I do not want it to burst."

"Tomorrow will serve. I would prefer a well-lit room at the Whitefriars' Priory than the chaos of Saint Leonard's. I will provide my own very capable assistants." He was tall and well-built with piercing blue eyes. A man used to being in control of the situation and obviously not pleased to put his life in another's hands.

"You are concerned about my discretion?"

"Your discretion I take for granted. That of others, I do not. I'll send a man to carry your things."

Katherine watches him as he strides down the street. Two men ease in quickly behind him as he walks away. Then Sir James stops to speak to one of the men and points to her shop. She concludes that will be the man she will see in the morning.

She had not thought about John Arderne in years. He made quite a name for himself as a famed surgeon and charges hefty fees to the wealthy for his services. He must be sixty or seventy years of age now. How different things would be if she had accepted his offer and become his mistress after her father died. Instead she moved away, unwilling to sleep with a man so much older in exchange for the comfort his wealth could buy. Pride, maybe. What was a fine education worth if you lived in near poverty? He had always been kind and generous to her. He taught her so much. Would she make the same decision again? Katherine wasn't so sure.

Bertrand followed in the *Christine's* wake down the Ouse as far as Cawood. This heavy new barge will be a tough pull up the River Wharfe past where it is tidal; two mules are aboard for that purpose. For now, they tie up here where the Wharfe meets the Ouse to await the turn of the tide. This is Bertrand's first trip as master of his own barge after a few years working with Virgil. The crew is half from the other barges and half men that came up from Lincoln. Everyone aboard is a Companie man.

Master Tenebroides went with him to Tatecastre last week to meet the master at the quarry. He assured them he would have the limestone blocks on the dock below the ford. The crew had practiced loading and unloading a heavy stone block using the boom crane aboard under the eye of Sir James until he was satisfied. It will be easier without him watching; he made the new men nervous.

Transporting the stone alone will not be profitable. To that end he is also supposed to pick up ten kegs of ale from the brew houses. Justin, Sir James' wool buyer south of here, is attempting to secure next spring's shearings from the flocks in the area. The wool would make it all worthwhile, but that is a competitive business. In addition to the other wool merchants in Yorke, Flemish and even Italian buyers will be making offers.

"You will address me as 'my Lord,' you insolent bastard."

"Oh, Cousin Allan, I am an orphan now but never a bastard. The last man to pull a dagger on me has no more problems in this life. I am thinking that tossing you into the river will at least give you a peaceful slide into hell. I really do not think the sheriff will mind, your jailers tell me they find you irritating."

"I need funds and I know you've got them."

"So, what has it been – four years? And as I recall you had nothing but contempt for me, then. I'm a worn-out old soldier, and I've nothing for you.

You got the manors and the land, not me, as you well know." Lord Yarburgh is his father's older brother's son; the family lands are his as they were his father's.

"Nothing? Maybe you think I believe that. I know damn well you plundered half the continent with Sir John."

"I barely got back to England with my own skin, which is better than Sir John managed."

"I'll tell the Duke of Lancaster where you are, and he'll enlist you to his new campaign across the channel. I know he is desperate for experienced men."

"John of Gaunt knows exactly where I am. And so does Prince Edward. He doesn't need you to tell him how to conduct his campaign. You are a greater fool if you think that will curry any favors from him. I have stood shoulder-to-shoulder covered in blood next to him…that is a bond you know nothing about." James' voice is now low and menacing. "Prince Edward knows his loyal subjects!"

Near tears, Yarburgh pleads, "This time when I cannot pay the king's demands he will take everything from me. I know you have reason to despise me, but you surely won't let this happen to Marjorie's children!"

"Go beg from your vicious brother-in-law for all I care. You deserve each other."

"He will not loan me anything more!"

"Sir William, you mentioned that you need to raise three hundred men for Lancaster?"

The High Sheriff smiled. "I take it you have an offer."

"I do not believe my cousin can pay the fine to free himself and his men."

"No, I do not think he can. What mischief are you considering?"

"I'll pay Yarburgh's fines, and you commit him and his men to your levy."

"I accept your generous offer," he said, laughing. "Gets him well out of your way for a while and maybe permanently."

"Well, hopefully not as bad as that. The French mostly seem to avoid a full 'all or nothing' battle when they know they can just wait our campaigns out."

"I have more information from the battle at La Rochelle. The king's envoy is still here and insists on speaking with you."

"Sir James?" A man that can only be Sir David strode into the hall. Sir William and James both immediately stand. "Sir William, I did not mean to intrude."

"No intrusion, Sir David. I was just mentioning you. We were discussing domestic and foreign difficulties. I will make my departure."

"Greetings from His Highness, the Duke of Cornwall," he says quietly as they sit. "You have heard about La Rochelle?"

Duke of Cornwall was one of Prince Edward's many titles. "I just recently heard that the fleet was completely lost. Is it that bad?"

"Worse than you can imagine. Pembroke and four hundred knights captured. They attacked with fire; thousands burned alive."

A ship is wood and tar with rope rigging and sails – all of it highly flammable unless it is wet. Fire has always been a great fear of sailors. Once burning it is nearly impossible to douse. If you are on a ship, there is no place to go other than jump overboard. The few that do know how to swim would still drown weighed down in fighting armor. "Burning is a horrific way to die. The Earl and four hundred knights captured. So, it is truly a great disaster! I have heard about Greek fire, although I have no understanding of it."

"I do not believe it was the legendary 'Greek fire' but was thrown oil, which was then lit with flaming arrows."

"Indeed!" James wondered just how oil would be thrown from one ship at another without endangering the throwers as much, or more, than those being attacked.

"Another source says they used fireships."

"That seems more likely to me. Wait for an advantageous wind and tide and launch your fireships into the packed fleet at anchor. And the treasury taken, as well?"

Sir David nods his head sadly. "Twelve thousand pounds sterling!" Then, handing James a packet, he says, "I am instructed to give this to you in person. Our prince has spoken with his brother to remind him that your campaigning days are over and wishes to bring another matter to your attention. You remember Sir Gerald de Rabuk?"

"Good morning, Doctor, I am Brother Hugh!"

A large, cheerful man in the white cassock of a Carmelite friar stands at the door to Katherine's shop. Well, Sir James did say she would be going to the Whitefriar's Priory this morning, so why not a Whitefriar to escort her there? "I am Katherine Blackwell. I am a surgeon not a doctor."

"May I carry your bag?" Hugh said as he takes it from her.

As they head past the market square, Katherine notices the man she saw yesterday with Sir James slip out from a shop to follow them. She resents Brother Hugh presuming to carry her bag a bit but, then again, it is heavy. Yet he swings it like it is nothing at all.

"I am told you do work at Saint Leonard's Doctor; you perform surgery?"

"Some surgery; people who cannot pay do not seem to be as concerned with the gender of the surgeon."

"You are doing the Lord's work!"

"Yes, I do feel that is so. It does cover the rent on my shop, but it does not buy much bread."

"No, but the Lord provides for his servants."

My dress is of common cloth and nearly threadbare, she thinks. My last decent meal was served from the same pot that Saint Leonard's uses to feed the starving. The gate to the Whitefriars opens as they approach and then closes quickly behind them.

Brother Hugh guides her across the courtyard. "This is Prior William's study, and this is Will, one of Sir James' squires."

"Good morning, Doctor; please excuse me while I let Sir James know that you are here."

Will left, and when she turned, Brother Hugh is holding a blindfold. "I am sorry about this, but it is just for a short moment."

"I do not like this at all."

"Oh, I assure you are completely safe," he says as he gently but firmly ties it around her head. "You can't see, can you?" he teased playfully. "I am just going to turn you a bit to the right and out the door and then to the left and then the left again, and spin you around, and in through this door, and just along here a bit, and here we are!"

Brother Hugh removes the blindfold and she is in a dim stairwell. "Just head on up and Will is at the top of the stairs with your bag."

At the top of the stairs is a curtain that is being held back for her. "You made it!" Will says, smiling. "And now this way."

Sir James is standing in a loose robe with his back to a magnificent oriel window. In front of him is a table. She can see the rising towers of Saint Peter's over the roofs of the houses across the street.

"The light is excellent here as you promised." The table has sponges, a bowl of hot water, and soft towels.

"This is Malcolm, he will be assisting you."

Malcolm's shirt is rolled up past his elbows and his hands and fingernails are spotless. He wears a white apron like a butcher.

"You have assisted in surgery before?" Katherine begins to lay out her scalpels and surgical implements.

Malcom nods. "I have Doctor."

Katherine moves around the table to where Sir James stood. "I have some pain medicines."

"I do not want them."

"It will be very painful."

"Of that I have no doubt."

Malcolm takes Sir James' robe and slides around to the side of the table out of her light. James leans over the table onto his elbows and spreads his legs.

She notices that his back had been viciously lashed with a whip many years ago. She kneels with a damp towel and wipes the area clean, although clearly that had already been attended to. "Towel." Then, with her scalpel she makes a small slit in the bulge on the inside of his butt cheek. Thick puss spews from the incision. She gently presses the rest of the fluid out into the towel.

"Are you doing alright so far?"

"Yes, not much pain as yet."

"Remain still." Katherine, then, slices the skin across what had been the bulge and uses the sponges to squeeze vinegar into the wound and rinse it out thoroughly. Malcolm holds a towel to catch the drips. "You were correct; you have a fistula." The accuracy of his self-diagnosis surprises her. "It does not seem to be very far below the skin." A fistula is a tubular passage between an infected gland and the skin that weeps fluid. She gently inserts a flexible probe made from the spine of a goose feather into the passage. "This may be painful." She cuts a slit along the surface and down to the probe along its entire length; then peels off the sides of the tube with her scalpel.

"Yes, it is!" James gasps. It stings like fire.

The wound bleeds profusely. She rinses it out, and the gland cavity with a golden colored tea made of calendula petals. This will help stop the bleeding, act as an antiseptic and promote healing. The fistula needs to heal from the inside out. She pats it dry as Malcolm hands her a clean towel.

"Press the edges together while I suture it closed." Seven, small stitches later, the inch-and-a-half wound of the abscess is closed with the hollow quill of a feather to allow drainage. "The hope is that the fistula will now heal itself closed, but this does not always occur. I do not think you will be able to admire my sutures, Sir James."

"No, they are in a spot where very few will evaluate your skill. I'd laugh, but it stings too much just now."

Katherine soaks a dressing in calendula ointment, places it against the wound and then winds a bandage through his legs and over his hip to hold it in place. She hands the jar to Malcolm. "You will need to refresh his dressing twice each day and replace it after any bowel movements. Loose clothing, do nothing stressful, no riding for a while. Make sure he behaves Malcolm."

"We'll all gang up against him if he acts up, Doctor."

"Enjoy it while you can," James growls through the pain. In a much kinder tone, he says, "A humiliating location for an affliction. Thank you very much, Doctor."

The whole blindfold routine is done again and then Brother Hugh escorts her home.

"Here is your payment Doctor," Hugh said, handing her a sheepskin pouch of coins.

"Thank you, Brother Hugh; you are aware of why I came to your priory?"

"I appreciate your coming very much, indeed, and should you ever need help, we are at your service. Please do call on us if you are in difficulty."

That was hardly an answer. Katherine sits down in her shop and opens the pouch. What a strange morning. It is mostly smaller coins, but there are plenty of shillings and…several pound coins. It appears to be about six pounds, all told. An amount the most esteemed surgeon in Yorke would charge for such an operation. It was more than she had made the entire previous year. Obviously, Sir James had not used her as his surgeon to save money, but was it so important that no one knew about his condition?

In the early morning hours, James slips down the back staircase to Prior William's study and across the compound. Carefully he is helped into the white robe of a Carmelite friar that is held open for him. Then the five of them make their way out the quay to the priory's boat. The brothers hold the boat steady and gingerly help James down into it. They unmoor and pull easy on the oars across the King's Fishpond, 'the stew,' until the Foss joins the Ouse below the castle. Here James is lifted up into Master Tenebroides big barge.

"All safe and sound, Hugh. These are for you," Tenebro said, passing down sacks of barley, beans, and two of mixed grains used to make maslin bread.

"And these are for Sir James," Brother Hugh replies, passing up two large wardrobe trunks.

"My God, how long does he expect to be away? This one feels like a shipment of lead!" Tenebro knew it wasn't as that cargo was already aboard.

Several hours later, squires Malcolm and Will together with Geoffrey and Paul Fitz-William ride out of the courtyard of Sir James' Yorke townhouse, onto High Ousegate Street, and head towards the Layerthorpe Gate and bridge to leave the city. Paul rides James' courser, and wears his riding cloak and feathered hat. They are fully armed and wear hauberks of chainmail under their tunics.

The countryside glides by peacefully as the barge rides the outgoing tide and current of the River Ouse south. The farther they get away from Yorke the better the river smells. Odd that he had assumed the river caused the stench of the city, when obviously, it is the city that contaminates the river. James is as comfortable as he can be reclining on pillows upon the raised stern castle of the barge; no wonder Cleopatra travelled this way! The difficulty is that even though the barge is presently moving along at a good pace, the river makes so many serpentine turns that the distance to Barmby is many times as long as a ride down the old Roman road. Not to mention that when the tidal bore heads upriver Tenebroides must tie-up or anchor. The trade-off, of course, is that it would take a pack train of over a hundred mules to move this cargo.

"That is Biscupthorpe, Sir James."

"Where the archbishop has a manor house?"

"A better view of that in just a moment; it is right on the river. Chapel, too."

The river is becoming considerably wider now and Master Tenebroides calls out the manors and villages as they glide by. Next is Acastre, a village held by the Fairfax family. Then the River Wharfe flows into the Ouse just north of Cawood – where Bertrand takes his barge for the archbishop's stone in Tate-castre. Cawood village is owned by the Archbishop of Yorke and over the years successive archbishops have built an opulent palace there.

Several more farms and villages pass until they reach the larger town of Selby on the west bank of the river. James had passed through many times before, on the road, of course, and knew it well. The stone tower of Selby Abbey Church is easily visible from the river as are the towers of the entry façade and its lengthy lead roof. "They should be a customer for salt and salted fish Tenebro."

"Too close to the fishing villages and Kingston. Hanse salt from southern France is easy for them to get. The farther upriver we take salted fish the better the price."

"That makes sense, every barge or ship coming upriver to Yorke passes right by here."

"We'll need to anchor now. The tide has turned." Tenebroides shouts to the crew of the *Christine* to pull in the sweeps and throw out the anchor. A moment later, a small wave lifts the barge and she tugs on the anchor dragging it until it bites. "That is the tidal bore. Not too bad here, but it can be deadly in the Humbre, if you are unwary." Then the cook gets a brazier going to prepare a meal. Master Tenebroides has anchored about forty feet from the bank on the Selby side of the river at the southern end of the town.

"I like to stay out of mid-river. Less tidal pull and out of the way of craft heading up with the tide."

"Low chance of trouble this close to the town, too."

"We will be back under way before dark. I've yet to have trouble from the shore in daylight."

Four hours later, the tide ebbs against the natural flow of the river. The river has swollen to double its previous width, so they are now over a hundred feet from the bank.

"Out sweeps." And then to James, he says, "We will row over the anchor, so we can pull it up more easily."

James nods, a crew member is easily turning the windlass at the bow as the barge moves down towards the anchor. "Up and down," is the shout from forward.

"Avast rowing."

"She's up."

"Give way all. Soon the outgoing tide will really get us moving again."

It is late afternoon when they pull up at Barmby-on-the-marsh and tie up at the dock. Malcolm is waiting for them and reaches over to steady James as he transfers his weight from the barge to the planks. "They were waiting for us," he says quietly.

"Were any of you hurt?"

"Paul's shoulder was grazed by an arrow; nothing serious, didn't penetrate the mail."

"A warning or a poorly sprung ambush?"

"My guess is they expected us to turn north and were set up in that direction. When we turned south, they attempted it any way."

James agrees. "Interesting, I told a very few individuals that I was heading north for Richmond this morning. If your theory is correct, one of them either purposely tipped them off or accidentally spoke to the wrong person."

"Well, you were right that we might be attacked, sir."

"They should not have shot their bows; now we are on to their intentions. They lacked the patience to wait for another chance – also interesting."

"Any ideas? Your cousin?"

"Oh, I have ideas. Lord Yarburgh has other concerns at the moment. Geoff did not attempt to loose an arrow?"

"No, we were clear, and I had no notion of how many they were."

"You did right, Malcolm."

The arrival of the mounted party had given Sigismund a few hours to prepare for James' visit and he put it to good use. The guest cottage was transformed from 'adequate for barge crew stop-overs' to 'suitable for their lord and his retinue;' a convalescing lord at that. A hog had been slaughtered and his wife, Isabelle, was supervising the preparation of a dozen dishes.

"Welcome, my Lord!"

"Thank you, Sig. My apologies for the lack of notice."

"Do you need to rest?"

"It feels good to walk for now; it has been a very relaxing trip. No one made me pull on an oar."

"Ha!" he laughed. "You are lucky; Master Tenebroides can be a merciless taskmaster. How long do you plan to stay?" It was a natural enough question for the lord's steward at an infrequently visited manor.

"The barge continues on to Kingston in the morning. I will join them again here for the trip back upriver to Yorke." James has been strolling towards the salterns during this conversation. Men are filling buckets in the pond, carrying them to a lead trough, and emptying them there. "Even in July we have to heat the brine?"

"We do, but not for very long."

Barmby is a farm and the usual location for transferring goods from Thomas' barge, which normally went from here to as far south as Gainsburgh, to Tenebroides' barge, but it is primarily James' salt production operation. When the tide comes in the low-lying marsh floods naturally with the salt-water. This was controlled by the creation of rectangular ponds, called salterns, and water channels to allow only some of them to flood. Those that were not allowed to flood on a particular tide continue to evaporate in the summer sun, reducing the water volume and concentrating the brine.

In warmer climes the salterns become concentrated enough for the salt crystals to form through the heat of the sun alone, and they can be raked out into piles. In Britain, since Roman times, the brine has to be heated in lead troughs to achieve the required concentration. It must be watched carefully, if too much water evaporates the lead pan will melt. The trick is to get the brine just to the crystallization point and then pull away the burning peat and let the pan start to cool. When they were first learning they would place an egg in the brine – when it floated it was ready. Now they just stick a finger in the trough and taste it. If the spring was a wet one the salt making season would get a late start. A rainy fall and it ended early.

The first saltern here may have been Roman. James recognized its remnants from his time campaigning in Brittany where there were huge piles of salt next to the ponds. They dug it back out and added a several more over the last few years. You needed to wait for the river to be at its highest point, the saltiest, to open the sluices and flood the pond.

"There is lead being offloaded from the barge for two more pans. How is Nicholas working out?"

"Now there's a good lad for you; always busy making them barrels. I was hoping for more lead; we ruined a pan last week."

"I am dealing with some demands on our lead supply. Hopefully that situation will get better. I want plenty of salt and barrels ready for the herring by winter. At least a hundred bushels and two hundred barrels for salt fish. That's besides the bushels we produce to sell as salt and use ourselves." Salt is one commodity that he both uses and could sell many times the current production. All butchered meat needed to be dried, smoked, or salted or it would spoil unless it was the middle of winter. No big piles accumulated here.

"Understood, my Lord. Nicholas makes a barrel each day and he now has an apprentice. I will need more lead pans and more laborers. We will also need to dig out another salt pond."

James grimaced. "I'll work on that. Not so easy." Maybe Coletta can find someone suitable in Yorke, he thinks.

"Isabelle has been busy preparing a feast for you!"

"I hope she has not gone to too much trouble, especially with my dropping in on you like this. I have spent much of my life wondering if I would have anything to eat for supper at all. I am not picky."

"I tried to tell her that some simple fare would be perfectly suitable, but she would have none of it. So, I made what you might call a strategic retreat!" Sigismund had been on campaign with James and also knew days without food. Villagers and farmers on the march fled at word of their approach or had already been picked clean by other soldiers.

"Discretion is often the better point of valor, Sig."

Fortunately, the meal is an occasion for everyone in the village; even the salt workers join them when they would normally have worked until dark. July is a challenging time of the year as the winter grain harvest would have been all used up and the spring planting would not yet be ready for harvest. Isabelle knew how to take advantage of what the salt marsh and this location on the river could offer, so nothing was lacking.

The green porry was not only leeks and chards but included watercress and smoked pike. Prawns were served over roasted aubergine with garlic and cheese. Fresh trout was pan fried. Mussels were cooked in ale with orache. The main dish was the roasted pork; it was served with a sauce of fresh raspberries. James is lavish with his praise for Isabelle and all those that had labored so hard.

After spending the morning with Sigismund to see the crops, check the salt grass harvest that had been brought in last month, admire the new fishpond, and meet Nicholas at his cooperage, James sits down to explain the primary reason for his visit. "Sig, these sacks contain a soft pinkish mineral," James says, pulling out a fistful. "Now there is good stuff in here and waste material. We need to separate the two."

Sig nods without understanding. "Just tell me what you need me to do."

"What I believe is that the good stuff will form white crystals if dissolved in a concentrated solution."

"Like a brine will form salt crystals."

James nods. "I want to dissolve this pink material in fresh water. My premise is that the waste material will settle to the bottom and the good stuff will stay dissolved in the water, but it could be the other way around. Then we skim off that water and heat it up in one of your lead pans until the crystals form."

"Will they form while the pan is hot? Salt crystals form as the pan cools or you ruin your pan."

"I do not know, but we will find out. Let's start by mimicking what you know of salt crystallization."

"We rinse our salt crystals with fresh water several times before they are pure. Do we do that with these crystals?"

"I do not know that, either!"

"Are you going to tell me what the crystals are?"

"They are used to dye wool in brighter colors. You know, salt is a valuable commodity; we get just about one shilling two pence a bushel in Yorke. I will just say one bushel of these crystals is worth over fifty bushels of salt."

"Whew, that's a lot," Sig suddenly gets more interested.

"Well, this pink stuff was not easy to get, and we've got about two hundred pounds here. I do not think we will end with even half a bushel of the crystals when we are done. Assuming we can get them at all."

"Worth the try, though; what happens if we can't get the crystals to form, my Lord?"

"I'll see if I can get more of the pink mineral and we will try to figure out another method."

There is a fair wind from the northwest as the *Christine* passes the confluence with the Trent and the river is called the Humbre. "Lower the dagger board, all hands loose sails," Tenebro shouts from his position at the stern manning the steering oar. The two large triangular sails quickly fill into a hard curve. The effect is immediate as the barge heels over in the wind and picks up speed. "If this wind holds for the next hour we will be in Kingston before the tide turns."

Kingston-upon-Hull is the major English port north of London. Today there are seven ships anchored in the estuary flying Dutch and Flemish flags, as well as that of Hanover and Norway. There is not a ship flying the Hanse banner. The Hanse, or Hanseatic League, is a powerful merchant trading guild that started in the German states and now has a presence from deep in the Baltic, Scandinavia to Spain. They are his usual customers for wool, dyestuffs, and skins, which he trades for spices, wine, and sometimes salt. The salt in the early spring and late fall when the weather is too cold and wet for Sigismund to produce any at Barmby. The Hanse still get it from southern France and Spain.

If a Hanse ship had been here, the king's customs agent could come aboard for a ship-to-ship transfer and collect the duties. Now his cargo will need to be brought ashore to the Hanse warehouse. "Take in sail and then pull up the leeboard." The leeboards swivel down from *Christine's* sides to reduce her downwind slippage through the water and hold her course under sail as she does not have much of a keel. With the leeboards raised Tenebroides can bring her right to the wharf and tie up.

Unloading went quickly and each trip to the warehouse brought a purchase back to the *Christine* – wine, oil, and a modest quantity of spices. The huge tuns of wine contain 252 gallons and literally weigh a tonne. The tuns are rolled aboard and lowered into the hold using tackle from the masts. They await the next incoming tide for the return trip up the Humbre to the River Ouse.

Late the following morning, the barge ties up at the fishing village of Blaketofte. Four of the families here fish in boats that are partly owned by the Companie including Cnut and his wife Freydis. Five salted herring sell for one pence in Yorke once the weather turns cold. Tenebroides and Thomas bring them barrels and salt. Cleaned fish are layered with salt in the barrel. Water comes out of the fish to make brine, which prevent the fish from spoiling. It can last for years if done properly. Each barrel holds about a thousand herring. After paying for the fish, salt, and barrel the profit is about six shillings a barrel. Sir James is pushing for two hundred barrels this year – just over sixty pounds sterling!

Sir James' villagers at Barmby produce the salt through owed labor, rent for their land, in lieu of working his fields. Oliver the fishmonger can sell every barrel and, of course, Oliver is a Companie man.

In the morning, twelve full barrels of salted herring are loaded aboard the barge. "Freydis how are you for barrels and salt?" Cnut had left several hours earlier in his fishing boat.

"We should have enough until you or Thomas bring some more unless we have a big run." Sometimes the herring are so plentiful you can fill the boat with every cast of the net. Freydis pats a barrel she has been leaning on. "One more for you, Master Tenebroides."

He nods and counts out payment for the herring and the additional barrel. "No trouble?"

"No trouble."

Master Tenebroides rolls the last barrel himself to the *Christine*. Spices do not weigh nearly as much as a full barrel of fish. He paid for the barrel yesterday in Kingston with Master Schiffer's agent; today he just paid the 'transport fee.'

Thomas had been to Barmby while they had sailed to Kingston. He left some cargo for them: picks and shovels in addition to the usual cutlery items and iron billets from Sheffield. There are also four hogs, crates of chickens, four sheep, and three ram lambs. The tide is favorable and Tenebroides is anxious to take advantage of it, but Sir James is still deep in conversation with Justin the wool buyer, and as James is to be his passenger heading back to Yorke he has to wait.

Justin knows wool. Wool varies in quality and therefore value. Most of the wool in Yorkshire is in the middle of the price range, but some flocks do command a premium. Justin is one of those people whose warmth and open countenance make him instantly likable. Blonde and blue eyed he clearly descended from Norse settlers. He is good at gaining the trust of tithe-men, manor holders and their reeves to buy their wool. James has Justin visit these customers several times a year to establish a relationship that a foreign wool buyer cannot.

"If we can transport the wool from the villages to the river landing, then I believe I can secure the spring shearings around Tatecastre. The current buyers expect them to get the wool to Cawood themselves and wait; they complained bitterly about that."

"That seems like something we can manage. Good work Justin." We already have a pair of mules on the barge to help get us upriver and go to the brew houses, James thinks, if we can put a wagon on the barge, as well, then surely we can pick up the wool. Giving herders a reason to sell to us that doesn't require raising the price is the kind of advantage he is looking for. "Have you heard anything new on the Flemish wool buyer?"

"He is still around. I think he is having trouble figuring out how to collect the sacks to a shipping point. Everyone is sheering at the same time and you've got to be everywhere!"

James has received a letter from sources in London that suggests his old enemy Lord Latimer may be helping the Flemish community there become major buyers of English wool in England. A fee paid directly to the king's accounts, managed by his chamberlain – the same Lord Latimer, will allow them to ship the wool directly to their own ports and by-pass customs.

Tenebroides misses his tide and must wait another eight hours before the next incoming tide overcomes the flow of the Ouse and he can move upriver. Sir James has a much lighter trunk heading back and is in a very good mood.

Chapter 7

La Petur

August 1372

Virgil's timing could not have been worse from his crew's point of view. They had arrived after a long pull upriver at the dairy yesterday only to be sent into the fields today. The previous week had been dry and sunny, but how long would it last? Joel had put everyone: the weavers, brewers, and dyers into James' fields with the villagers. When the demesne fields had been harvested the peasants could attend to their own.

The eight oarsmen spread out along one side of a golden field of winter wheat in the cool of the morning. *It will be hot ere long.* They grab the long stalks in their oar calloused hands, well below the ears of grain, cut it with a sickle, and then gather the next fistful. Two villagers gather the cut stalks into bundles behind the reapers. Virgil had acquiesced to ten days of harvest provided the weather held. They should be able to bring in forty acres in that time. Virgil did not really report to Joel in the pecking order of the command structure – he reported to Tenebroides, but they did live in Richmond all winter. It was important to keep the peace. "Only those that wish to eat need help with the harvest," Joel had argued. It was an argument too similar to the Companie way as expressed by Sir James to be debated: 'Your share of the spoils depends on your contribution to the task.' He and Joel spent the day cutting rye with long-handled scythes. Once you got the technique down it was not too bad. Matilda the brewer and her brother Gus gathered the cut rye behind them.

Once the winter crops of rye and wheat had been harvested, the spring grains – barley and oats came next. Again, if the weather cooperated, all crops in by the end of the month. At the end of each day a white habited friar from the Carmelite Priory in Yorke supervised the Church tithe – one sheaf in every ten – collected from the field and into their wagon. By law the tithe is taken not only from the lord's demesne but also the peasants' fields.

The villagers and members of the dairy community in Richmond barely control their resentment as the Church takes its legal share. How the priory in Yorke secured jurisdiction over the local parish for the fields was surely orchestrated by Sir James. Virgil had to laugh because he knew that not only was the "Companie" priory getting the tithe, but Sir James would collect part of it back as a fee for shipping it down the River Swale in *Marie*, and that would be in addition to his charge for having the villagers thresh it! Virgil would be sure to have the river tolls waved; the Church was exempt!

The harvest must be threshed with a flail to separate the individual grains from the ear. A flail is a wooden pole with a second rod attached by a leather thong to beat the sheaves. After threshing, the grain is winnowed to remove chaff and straw by tossing it in the air and letting the breeze blow the lighter chaff away and leaving just the grain kernels.

The dry spell has left the ship La Petur stuck in the River Ouse just below Yorke. She is out of Bristol, a port on the English west coast where the river Avon meets the Severn, and her captain had taken advantage of a rainy day and a high tide to get as close to the city as he could to shorten the lightering distance to unload his cargo. When the tide went out the ship rested on the bottom. Perhaps if they had unloaded more cargo they would have re-floated on the next tide as expected, but they didn't. Each new high tide was lower than the last one as the August heat set in. La Petur had not floated for three weeks now.

Bertrand slowly rode the last of the rising tide past La Petur with a barge load of stone for the cathedral to the city docks. "How much water do we have under us?" A sudden panic struck him; he did not want to be stuck, as well.

Christopher pushed a pole down along the hull walking sternward as it went down and the barge continued moving upstream. "About another five feet," he estimated looking at the wet length of his pole against the depth of the hull. "That one has a deep hull. She hasn't budged since our last trip."

"And she is unladen." An officer aboard the ship's stern castle gazed down at them as they went by. Bertrand waved with a sympathetic shrug.

"Brother Hugh, what brings you to my shop? Is Sir James doing alright?" Katherine's first thought is for her recent patient.

"He is as far as I am aware. I am to get a salve for a rash that Prior William is suffering."

"There are apothecaries closer to your priory; on this side of the river."

"I am not permitted to visit Master Anketin's shop if that is who you mean."

"Really? Why is that?"

"His hands are dirty. He does not wash up after working in his herb garden."

"So, fastidious are you, then?" Then she thought about Sir James and how impeccably clean Malcolm's hands and fingernails had been when he assisted her; no, he would not approve of dirty hands compounding medicines. But then Sir James should hardly determine which apothecary is patronized by the White-friars. "Rashes may be caused by different things. What does this rash look like?"

"Doctor, I was just told it is itchy, red and ugly."

"I suggest applying apple vinegar. If that does not help, then I really ought to examine him."

"Just pour it on the rash?"

"Gently dab it with wad of soaked wool. Let me mix up a poultice to help with the itching."

Katherine mixed some dry clay and honey into a paste and put it in an earthenware jar. "Just one penny if you'll bring my jar back."

"May I help you?" A man she has not met previously fingers her broadcloth.

"This is Flemish cloth?"

"It is made by Flemish weavers," Janice replies.

"Please produce your customs documents with their cocket seal."

"I am not an importer, and who are you to make such demands?"

"My name is Edmund and I am a customs agent. Where do you get your cloth?"

"She gets it from me." James enters the shop with his squires having heard the man was in the city and outside the weaver's shop. "Listening to unsubstantiated accusations can create undesirable difficulties. You should be more careful."

"As yet I have made no accusation d'Arzhon, but I am obliged to investigate complaints! Lord Latimer suspected you might be in the middle of this," he sneers.

"You are a long way from Kingston to demand a cocket seal."

"Tariffs are due on imported cloth. I am authorized to demand evidence of payment!" he said stubbornly.

"Any and all payments due the customs house have been paid; you need to validate your assumptions."

"Then prove it with your documents."

"Attempting to intimidate a legitimate competitor by legal means requires more that jealous suspicions. You have my word as a knight that no laws have been broken here nor duties evaded."

"The word of Sir James d'Arzhon is of no account to Lord Latimer."

James put his face inches from the shorter man's nose. "You would do well to mind how you address your betters. Time for you to leave if you wish to do so unharmed."

"This is not the end of this!" but Edmund was clearly shaken as he left. He knew his words had gone too far.

"All payments due have been paid. Be sure to tell Lord Latimer I said so," James iterated after him. "And be sure to tell your complainer that making false accusations can have consequences!"

"Continue keeping an eye on him, and now make sure he knows it." Will nods and trails behind him all the way to his lodging in the castle. "Janice, they should leave you alone now. They will channel their efforts on me."

"Are you in danger?"

James laughed. "Not at all! There is nothing illegal going on here. This is exactly where I wish Latimer to occupy his mind." However, a letter to Prince Edward appraising him of the situation will be a good insurance in the event Latimer gets too aggressive; he intends to see to that this evening.

"Master Tenebroides?"

The *Christine* is tied up at the City Docks in Yorke. The crew had unloaded a cargo of grains from the fields at Barmby and those shipped there by Thomas down the Trent from Gainsburgh. Tomorrow they will load one last consignment of Quixley's wool for Kingston. "Aye," Tenebro stands up from his deck chair and gazes upon a tall, hawkish man standing on the dock legs akimbo and hands on his hips.

"I am Master Cornelius of La Petur. May I come aboard?"

He waves him aboard and heads down the short staircase from the stern deck to meet him at the top of the gangplank. "To what do I owe the honor of this visit Master Cornelius?"

"A member of my crew was at The Swan last evening. He overheard you saying that you could get my ship off the river bottom."

He had been discussing the plight of La Petur with Bertrand. "I said that I observed a method using barges in the Netherlands that I thought should work. I have not attempted such a thing myself."

"A barge such as yours?"

"This one and Master Bertrand's barge working together; one on each side. Bertrand's barge is the heavy one there that transports stone for the cathedral construction," he points upriver near the Ouse Bridge.

"I have seen it. I am told that I might not re-float until late September unless we get a lot of rain, and that would be unusual before then."

"Sounds right."

"I am losing money right now. Will you share this method with me?"

"A barge is secured along each side of the vessel to be raised. This is done at low water and the barges are laden to the gunwales, so that they sit deep, as low against your sides as possible. Then the barges are unloaded. As they rise, they raise the vessel between them."

Cornelius rubs his palms hard together in thought. "And the tide comes in to help, as well."

"Counting on that. The biggest issues are securing the barges tight against your hull, so they cannot just come up without you, and breaking any suction holding you to the bottom."

"We would need additional barges to offload yours. You know this Bertrand?"

"I do. We have the same owner, and I may be able to use a third barge, as well."

"A day to load. A day to secure the barges. A day to unload and wait for the tide."

"Then float you downstream a mile or more to deeper water and untie. And return to Yorke with the barges to recover your cargo and stores and bring them back downstream to you and reload them."

"Five or six days, then…provided it works."

The sheriff has sent for James. One of the delinquent boat owners has asked to speak to him from his cell in Yorke Castle. "I do not have the money to pay you."

"Then your barge is really now my barge."

"You would take away my livelihood?"

"You order a boat you cannot afford and expect to use it as though you own it while the boat builder goes bankrupt, Master Gervase? Forgive my lack of sympathy."

"If you take my barge, Sir James," he said sullenly, "I won't be able to earn enough to get it back, even if I am released. What good does that do you?"

"None. At the moment, I have no need for your barge. I will try to find a buyer."

"If you let me have my barge back, then I can pay you something each month from what I earn until I have satisfied the balance!"

"Normally I would be agreeable to such an arrangement, but that is what you told Master Swain and you paid him nothing these last six months."

"Aargh! Tough times I was having. I'm good for it! I have an agreement to ship wool to Kingston now."

"Sure you do, and now you'll make your payments," James scoffs with disbelief.

"At least fifty sacks to ship for a Flemish woolman!"

"Now, that is interesting. I think your boat will sit in my boatyard."

Much of the grain falls to ground during harvest and Joel invites the poorest peasants and widows in Richmond to glean the field. This is a common tradition. The poor can gather quite a lot of grain, but they must be diligent, or the birds will beat them to it. The demesne harvest collected in Richmond,

Joel goes with Alfred, the Whitefriar, and his wagons up along the Swale to Sir James' villages of Ghyll, Kelde, and Waite in the hills to the west to collect the tithe and James' portion of their harvest.

Virgil strides across the River Swale bridge above the castle and into the city of Richmond. The road wraps around castle hill to get to market square and Matilda's brewery. He hears a muffled welp of pain and picks up his pace. Her brother, Gus, is protecting his face from two young men that appear to be roughing him up. "Gus! Are you alright?" he shouts and breaks into a run.

Gus' assailants are in a corner formed by a rock outcropping. They are taken aback by Virgil's unexpected arrival and alarmed by his size and menacing appearance. "We didn't mean no harm, just having a bit of play with him."

"Gus, go on and take your sack home." His sack of partially spilled rye sits on the ground next to him. When he bends down to pick up the sack Virgil sees his bloody nose. His anger rising. "Go on, I'll be along shortly."

The first baskets of grain from the threshing floor are loaded by the crew aboard *Marie*. Fine cloth, skins, candles, livestock, and parchment make a good load. The parchment is a new item that he suggested to Joel last winter. Cloth is a better cargo than wool because it takes less space and sells for far more. Same is true with parchment being better than sheepskins, although not nearly to the same degree. Skins for transport have been de-fleshed and most of the hair has been removed, but they have not been tanned. To prevent them from spoiling they are packed in a barrel of light salt brine – a heavy item to ship. Virgil had learned the art of making parchment during his unhappy, though brief, time in an abbey and taught it to Joel's son, Stephen.

They have plenty of sheepskins for Judd the fellmonger to tan in Yorke. About half are then traded in Kingston to the Hanse. More are brought to the city on live animals and removed by Owen the butcher or at The Swan; in any case, Judd has all he can tan and as the flocks grow there will be more and more. Transforming a sheepskin into parchment is a simple process; it just takes time and patience. The first step is to select the best hides. No thin spots, holes, or scars. If the animal had a healed wound it is still a flaw in the skin that will ruin the sheet. Stephen's advantage for making the best parchment is that he has plenty of skins to choose from. The skins are soaked in a barrel of lime solution to loosen the hair. After a week, it scrapes off easily. Then the skin is stretched on a frame and the flesh side is scraped clean – this takes some effort. When it is fully dry, he has parchment. The wet skin sells for just 3 pence; but the parchment will sell for 8 and packs as a nice dry roll with many sheets.

Marie is coaxed off the pebble beach, the oarsmen jump aboard, and they head downstream. Before long they are out of the boat and hauling her across a shallow. There may be quite a bit of this until they pass the ford at Catrice. It's the heavy lead ingots causing her to sit so low in the water. The smelter is producing more than ever.

Sir James has three more small villages along the Swale. It is the same there; every village and manor in England is bringing in the harvest. They will pick up more grain, honey, mead, and fresh fish. The fish are netted from the fishpond after they arrive and are quickly cleaned and tossed into barrels with cold spring water. Fresh fish sell for a premium. If the remainder of the trip to Yorke takes too long the fish will spoil; Oliver's customers will complain, and he will have to lower his price.

Securing the royal charter for a fish weir was essential when Sir James was first granted these plague devastated villages. It almost guarantees the peasants will have something to eat and something to sell. Each of the weirs is set in the side beck above the village, well before it joins the River Swale. Weirs that pose a threat to navigation are not allowed and Virgil has used the wapentake courts to have several unchartered weirs removed from the river. Weirs are v-shaped post and woven branch fences that channel the fish into a fish trap. The trap is made of a small woven cone set inside a larger cone – the fish can enter but have a hard time getting out. The live fish are removed and tossed into the fishpond to hold until they are needed. The trap is pulled out periodically, so the beck is not over-fished.

There are many lean days of the year, at least one or two every week, when eating meat is prohibited by the Church. So, there is always a demand for fish at the market and the religious houses in Yorke.

Farther south up the River Trent, Thomas and the crew of the *Suzanne* are pressed into service, harvesting the flax stalks at the farm in Moretun. "Cut them off right at the ground!" Francis the Reeve insists once again as the crew swing the scythes too high. The longer the fibers, the better. This is from the seed that his lord sent him for the spring planting, a man he had only met once, and he did not want the crop mishandled. The blue flowered stalks rise just about to the reapers' waists. They would beat the tops later for seed and then soak the stalks until the outer skin rotted leaving the fiber and the pith.

Tenebroides, Bertrand, and Master Cornelius sit opposite Sir James in his study and describe what they propose to do. "What is the risk of damage to our boats, Tenebro?"

"Minimal, if any, I should think. Stress on the hulls will occur when the barges try to rise and La Petur holds them down if she is stuck to the bottom. This riverbed is firm, and I do not think that will happen."

"Could water come over the sides and sink them?"

"I don't see how. We would cut ourselves loose if the water got close."

"Four days is a lot of time, and that does not include our coming back up-stream to get your cargo and stores, everything you've off-loaded, and bring them back down river to you."

"I would obviously pay, even if the attempt does not work, Sir James."

"Why stone to lower the barges? Won't the barges come up with the tide, even if they are empty?"

Bertrand speaks up. "We have easy access to the stone, and it is compact and, of course, heavy."

"We won't get enough lift from the tide alone. It doesn't raise the river that much here in Yorke," adds Tenebroides more to the point of James' question.

"Stone takes a long time to load and unload; it needs to be transported from the cathedral yard. The Catherine is not built for it. Why not timber? We load it at the boatyard and unload it into the river – it will float."

"Keep it tethered and pull it back to the boatyard, which is right nearby, fast and easy!" enthuses Tenebroides. Laughing, he says, "We can use your new barge."

"Very amusing but, yes, we can. Using timber, we should be able to do it in two days. Tenebro, you and Master Cornelius agree to a failure price and a success price. If we have to cut loose due to stress or danger of sinking – you still pay the failure price and the decision to cut loose is Master Tenebroides' alone. I will speak to Simon Quixley about a delay loading his wool. I'll just tell Archbishop John that La Petur will be an obstruction danger to shipping his stone in another fortnight if nothing is done."

"You are actually in the right on that, Sir James," Cornelius said quietly. "The lord mayor proposes to fine me a shilling a day if the river channel constricts further. As an obstruction to river trade."

James' eyes twinkle and he gives a slight smile. "We are agreed, then."

This time it is Prior William himself that makes his way across the Ouse Bridge to Katherine's apothecary.

Katherine pauses from the mixture she is compounding. "Prior William, is your skin rash doing better?"

"Perhaps a little better; it is not itching so much and no longer spreading. I am afraid it is something serious."

"Well, perhaps you would be willing to let me take a look at it, then. Come over here into the light."

"It is across my back."

"Prior, you will have to remove your habit if I am to examine your back." William self-consciously slips his arms out and lets the robe down to his waist.

Katherine looks at the swollen red welts across his back. "Hmm."

"Is it…?"

"Is it what?"

"Leprosy!" he shudders, his voice breaking. "Punishment for my sins!"

"No, it is not leprosy; I am quite certain of that."

"Aaaargh, thanks be to God." He gasps.

"I would say it is Saucefleme. Interestingly some do say it is caused by one's sins, but some say that about every affliction."

"Can it be cured?"

"It can be quite painful and may last a while. You need to keep it clean with the apple vinegar and after a bit pat it thoroughly dry. Wear a light dressing and avoid chafing. Be sure to regularly clean your habit and all of your garments that come in contact with the rash."

Prior William nods as she repeats the five things he must do. "Do you need more of the poultice to keep you from scratching it?"

"Yes!" he said, producing the empty jar.

"I want to see you or hear from you in two weeks about how you are doing."

The weaver's guild has a grand social event this evening. Janice and her apprentices, plus their families, are attending. The guild master presides over the affair and it is a big to-do. It seems that everyone involved in the cloth trade is present including a fair representation of dyers, tailors, and fullers. With such a crowd it is easy for Janice to avoid any scene with the master – although it is clear that some are anticipating such an encounter. Whether that anticipation is one of dread or glee depends upon where the individual's loyalties lie. Weavers trying to gain entry to the guild wisely pay homage to the master and steer clear of Janice. On the other hand, the tailors seem quite interested in pleading for particular colors and patterns that will delight their wealthier customers.

Tenebroides slips over the wall and into the dark courtyard behind the guild master's home and shop. It is quiet and empty. The workshop is on the second floor towards the south-facing courtyard. It is likely there to get enough light to work. The street front store is on the first floor and the family lives above; a typical arrangement. The ground floor windows are shut tight. Those on the second story are open wide to encourage any breeze in the August heat. He is strong and wiry. A windowsill, then an angled bracing timber, a handhold from a hole in the daub, and he soundlessly pulls himself up, over and into the upper story. Much easier than scaling the walls of a castle.

Two looms sit quietly in the dim light. One has a dark pattern nearing completion and the other is in the process of being set-up for a new bolt of cloth. Shears sit on a worktable nearby; they easily clip the taut warp threads that have been so carefully threaded through the heddle to set up the loom. It takes little effort to pry off the treadles, rollers, and intricate heddle. Yarn makes an excellent fire-starter in the empty fireplace. It catches Tenebroides' spark immediately and blows into a flame. The dry splinters of the heddle kindle nicely and successively larger wooden parts of the loom build a hot fire. The largest elements will not fit nor break easily. Tenebroides stays near the open windows. It is too warm near the fire as it hungrily consumes the dry wood. In its light he admires the plaid on the other loom – nice work. After a while, he banks the glowing embers to the rear of the hearth to prevent any danger of a spark catching the house afire.

"You were in there a long while. Did ya destroy both loo looms? No tra-tra-trouble?"

"No trouble at all. Just one loom. Did you hear anything?"

"As-sa-sa-silent, as always. Shudda done 'em both to bits."

"No need to completely ruin him. If I wrecked them both, then he would have nothing left to loose. Now he will worry that if he makes more trouble, he could lose the other one."

"Da-da-da do you expect him to ga-get the message?"

"We shall see, Judd, we shall just have to wait and see."

"Would be a shame ta-ta-haft to come back."

"As our captain might say, some are slow learners."

"He doesn't like slow learners, Master Tenebroides."

"No need for him to know anything about all this Judd."

Judd smiles his nearly toothless smile and put his finger to his lips. "If he is questioned, then he don't know nothin'."

This was not the best time of year for the barges to have an extended stay in Yorke. At least it is not the middle of the wool season, but it is the harvest season and there is plenty of cargo to be shipped. Master Swain had moved timber and uncut logs to the river edge in preparation. One by one they are rolled into the river, floated to the anchored barges, and then lifted aboard. The stone barge uses its crane and Tenebroides uses the long yard arms of his masts to lift the logs clear of the bulwark and then swing them aboard. The largest logs weigh several tonnes apiece and placing them to keep the barge on an even keel is a delicate operation. The *Christine* was not built for timber hauling. If a log came loose at the wrong moment, it could crash right through her hull.

The stone barge, it had never even been given another name, was less temperamental. Her heavy construction made her less apt to list as the logs are added first to one side and then to the other. She would never be a pretty boat – missing chunks of wood from hauling stone and the original scars from the fire had seen to that. She was like Bertrand, her master, sturdy and dependable. It took all morning to load and by noon they sit low in the water. There is now just three feet of water under the stone barge and five under *Christine*.

Tenebroides waits for the ebb to maneuver to Le Petur pulling hard on the oars to move the sluggish barges just upstream of her. Then they use the river current and tow cables aboard Master Cornelius' ship to slowly ease along-side. They could no longer use the oars on the side against her. Cables could not go under Le Petur because she was firmly on the riverbed, but they could be brought under the sweep of her bow and her stern counter. Many lengths of cable are pulled tight to form a sling. They will stretch some before they begin to lift. If they stretch too much, then she will not come up off the bottom.

"Let's start to unload – slowly and together!" Tenebro has a fear that Bertrand would just start rolling logs off into the river while he was still half loaded. The squared timbers are on top and off-loaded straight to poor Gervase's barge for return to the boatyard. The big logs are lowered into the river and tethered together, so they do not float away downstream.

"The strain is on! I can hear it." Indeed, the ropes utter low-pitched creaking noises, and so does *Christine*.

"Let's take a break, then, for a moment and talk this through, Cornelius. Bert, join us aboard Le Petur," Tenebroides hollers.

"We still have your anchor down but no guarantee it will still be holding when you come loose."

Cornelius says, worried, "Or, that we can raise it to free ourselves."

"We can ease upstream when the tide is at its peak and ride it out…"

"If we can go upstream enough to get directly above the anchor, there is no reason we should not be able to get it up. We can cut the cable if we must, but then I lose my anchor."

"My fear is that we come free from the bottom and drift before we are under control. Bert, we need to be ready to throw out our anchors if we still have logs aboard and come free."

"Will do. Let's get some more over the side now; it is two hours until high water."

"Agreed, I don't want to sit here another twelve hours. Have your outboard sweeps ready after a couple more logs. This could get interesting."

Bertrand nods and gestures to the spectators on both banks. "You're going to give the commands from here when we start crabbing down the river?"

"Right." They would be three vessels wide on the river. Starboard oars on the stone barge would not be able to see the larboard oars on *Christine* because Le Petur is in between and higher than either barge. Tenebroides will have to coordinate from Le Petur's high poop deck. The big ship's rudder might be a help if the sling cables are not in the way. Otherwise they would have to steer entirely with the banks of oars.

"All assuming she comes free."

"Oh, she will; I can feel her!" Cornelius enthuses.

"So, Sir James is all of this effort going work?" James has arranged for a dinner to be served atop Clifford's Tower because it has an excellent view of the proceeding. The Lord Mayor, John de Gisburn, and the new High Sheriff, Sir William de Acton, attend with their wives. Archbishop John was invited but is out of the city at the moment.

"The explanation seemed promising, but I am out of my element here. It could be a huge disaster. In any case – not to be missed! Some more Gascon wine?"

"Disaster? What might go wrong?" Elizabeth de Gisburn's eyes gleam at the prospect.

"Hopefully, nothing! However, the near barge, the *Christine*, is not built for this kind of thing. There is a remote possibility she could shatter."

"How awful! She is so pretty; named for one of your conquests, Sir James?" teases Lady de Acton.

"My youngest sister – died twenty years ago."

"It is nice that you remembered her, then."

"You are being paid for this?"

"Oh, yes, John; even if we are unsuccessful."

"May I inquire about your fee?"

"It is five pounds for making the effort – already paid. Ten if we get her off the bottom, and an additional ten to get her downriver to Selby and then ferry all of her stores and cargo back down to her. They were removed to lighten her as much as possible."

"Surely if you get her off the bottom, the job is done."

"As I understand it, if we were to untie from her, she would sink right back to the bottom. The barges will be keeping her up until they reach a deeper section of the Ouse. Master Tenebroides is also quite concerned about navigating the three tied together down the river – very wide and hard to maneuver. There are shallows and the river will want to push them against the outside bank where it curves."

"Are you a betting man, Sir James?"

"My Lord Mayor, in a sense I already am!"

At the moment a large log went into the river everything moves. "We're afloat!" hollers Cornelius.

In hindsight it made sense. The weight of the log was still born by the stone barge, even though it had been lifted off the hull by the crane. It was when the log was in the river that the burden was off the barge. Everything moved upriver and then grounded again, but they were free.

"I told you the river bottom was firm!"

"Oh, sure, you told us alright!" the crew laughs. If Le Petur had been stuck in mud she would have popped up when the suction was overcome; instead, they just started moving with the tide.

"Throw the anchors out. No, downriver!" Tenebroides did not want them floating upstream until the few remaining logs were off-loaded. The tension is off Le Petur's anchor upstream and it is pulled up and brought aboard. The waterline of the two barges had been lowered about four feet with the overload of logs and timber. Now, empty, they sat about a foot-and-a-half deeper than normal – that was the portion of Le Petur's weight they were bearing.

"Sweeps out! Starboard oars!" He would work them to the middle of the river as the tide turns and the current begins to overcome it. They are moving downstream. "Anchors up!" There is scattered cheering from the riverbanks. If any vessels were in their way, then they had better get out of it because this three-hulled ship was taking her share right out of the middle. In another thousand feet the river turns hard right, so he began moving towards the inside of the curve; the river will throw them back to mid-stream as they come around the bend. "Larboard oars!"

Chapter 8

Desecration

October 1372

Katherine arrives nearly breathless at the Whitefriars' Priory having been bustled quickly through the city by Brother Hugh. His normal nonchalance was replaced with a sense of urgency and he had moved through the tight streets aggressively. He had not said why she was needed. When she arrives, Sir James cut off his conversation, crosses the room, and guides her by the elbow to an alcove in the refectory.

"Doctor, thank you for coming so quickly. Across the room you will see Prior William speaking with a girl and her brother. They have both been beaten rather badly."

She could not see the girl's face at the moment, but the boy was slowly spooning food to his mouth in what seemed to be a trance-like state. The side of his face was bruised, and his hair appeared matted with blood. He looked to be about fifteen.

"The girl's name is Mary. I suppose she is about thirteen years of age. She has certainly been beaten and molested – perhaps worse. Malcolm has a room for you in the infirmary with hot water, sponges, towels and so forth. I want you to take her there, do what you can for her and then get her to go to sleep. I have sent for a sleeping gown; it should be here shortly. The boy is Daniel. He has been unwilling to leave her side, so you will have to gain their confidence."

So, cool and calm when children have been hurt Sir James, she thought to herself. Then she took a deep breath and crossed the room to where they were sitting. A wiry man with a closely trimmed red beard stepped in as she arrived.

"Daniel, Mary, this is Doctor Katherine," he said gently and then stepped back away.

The poor girl's dress was muddy and torn; her face bruised. She had clearly been crying. "Mary, my name is Kate. I am here to help you. Would you please come with me?"

Paul Fitz-William and Geoffrey hustle across the Ouse Bridge towards Micklegate Bar. Master Tenebroides had found the boy and girl several miles from Yorke on the west bank of the river. If the man they sought was headed to the city, then he would enter at this gate and they would see him if they were in time. Tenebroides said he was a monk in a black cape that ran when his barge came around the bend. That should at least help narrow the possibilities among all the people streaming through the gate.

They did not have long to wait. A Blackfriar strode through the gate and headed towards the Dominican Friary. Paul strolls up to the gatehouse. "Who is that friar, John? He looks like a comrade from my last campaign in Brittany."

"I doubt that Brother Thom has ever been out of Yorkshire," the guard replied.

"How so?"

"He has been with the Dominicans since he was just a boy."

"I could have sworn…maybe he has a twin brother. Thanks."

Brother Hugh brings Daniel to the other bed in the room and pulls back the blanket for him. Mary is sleeping now. The lad was cleaned up and in a man's shirt that came down to his knees. Hugh picks up Katherine's bag and motions her out. "Doctor, this is Brother Alfred; he will keep watch over them." A gaunt brother with a pock-marked face sits on a stool, just outside the open door.

"Who attended to the boy? He did good work."

"I believe it was Malcolm. From necessity we are rather good at battle wounds."

"Really?"

"Most of us campaigned together across the channel."

They walked silently through the now empty refectory, into the court-yard and towards the gate. "I appreciate your concern, but I am capable of walking home."

"That I have no doubt of," Hugh replies, but he kept walking alongside her.

"You have nothing more to attend to, such as finding the bastard that did this?"

"Vengeance is our Lord's and surely it will be taken in His time."

"You are all so damn smug, you men, a young girl has been hurt and life just goes on. 'Ah, well, these things happen, don't ya know.' And Sir James: 'see what you can do for her doctor.' He certainly would not want to get a speck on his doublet; all aloof and serene. No one will do anything!"

"Oh, I would not say that," he replies with a wry smile.

Katherine stops and faces him, fire in her eyes. "Whoever did this will do it again!"

"That is what the captain said, but perhaps not."

"Do you know who did it?"

"I do not."

"I see. Vengeance is the Lord's and you will leave it to him. I suppose you will pray about it."

"I certainly shall pray about it, but the Lord has disciples of many kinds."

"What does that mean?"

"The Lord used Saint George to slay the dragon did he not?"

They walked the remainder of the way back to her shop without speaking. "You said that you do not know who did this."

Hugh nods.

"Someone else does?"

"I think maybe so. This is for your help today."

"I do not require payment for what I've done."

"Everyone has to eat; I was told to pay you."

"I will not take it."

"Please do. Sir James has been cross since the children were found. You don't want to get me in trouble, do you?"

"He did not seem to be very upset to me." Then Katherine thought about the way Hugh had thrust through the people in the streets when he escorted her to the priory. He was actually a tremendously big man. Maybe Sir James was cross.

"And no other friars came in? Black robed or brown?"

"Not for the next two hours, Captain."

This might not be as difficult as James had feared. There were not that many Dominicans in Yorke, although this could be a visitor from another house. "Keep a watch on their gate. Paul, make a note of all comings and goings; if 'Thom' leaves their gate – follow him but take no action. We have to be certain."

"No, no, she is still here."

Katherine had decided to check back the next day on her patient unbidden but had been asked to wait in Prior William's study. Before too long, Sir James, not the prior, strode in.

"I would like to see how she is doing if that is alright."

"I am glad you came. You told Brother Hugh she was not raped. You are certain?"

"He did not need to know."

"Ah, well, that is upsetting. When you see her, if possible…I am hoping for anything she might remember about her attacker; anything that might help identify him."

"She may still be too traumatized to talk about it."

"I will let you be the judge of that, but time is of the essence if we wish to snare the perpetrator. She is in the cloister. Hugh will take you there."

"I really do not need Hugh to escort me everywhere, Sir James."

"Hugh needs to be kept busy."

Sure enough, Hugh was waiting outside the prior's study to walk her over to the cloister. 'Hugh needs to be kept busy' he had said. What on earth does that mean? Mary was sitting next to another young girl.

"Mary, do you remember the doctor?"

"Doctor Kate," she replied.

"Quite right. Maude, would you please come with me, so the doctor can talk to Mary?"

Mary is wearing a beautiful silver-grey gown made from high quality broadcloth; far better than she could afford for herself since the death of her father. "You are still badly bruised, but the swelling has gone down. How are you feeling?"

"Better I suppose, it is peaceful here. I hope I never have to leave."

"I don't think the priory ordains women, so that could be a problem," she said gently. "Do you feel safe among all these men?"

"Perhaps I should be afraid, but I am not. I do not know why."

"Not all of the men I see here have taken a vow of celibacy."

"That doesn't mean anything. Are you afraid here Doctor Kate?"

"No, not afraid but a bit cautious."

"Why?"

"I do not know why, either. Not everything here is as it should be. What did you mean when you said that about the vow of celibacy?"

"Nothing."

"Was one of the brothers here the one that hurt you Mary?"

"No, not one of these brothers."

"But a friar or a monk?"

Mary was silent but tears started down her checks.

"It does sometimes help to talk to someone. Did you know the man?"

Mary shakes her head no.

"So, how is our girl coping, Doctor?"

"She is having a tough go of it. Mary feels safe here and doesn't want to ever leave. I assume that would be a problem."

"Oh, eventually Prior William will start in on me about that. For now, the sentiment amongst the brothers is much in sympathy towards the youngsters."

"It was a monk, or a friar named Thomas."

"She knew him?"

"No, he said his name, though. She can't get it out of her head."

James sat quietly in deep thought.

"She bit his hand; that is why he hit her so hard. Deep enough to draw blood."

"That could be useful; which hand?"

Katherine thought for a moment. "It must have been his right hand because he hit her with his left on the right side of her face. She bit the side away from the thumb."

"High chance he is left-handed, then."

"Do you know who this 'Thomas' is?"

James did not reply but stroked his beard in thought.

"Are you going to report this to the sheriff?"

"Sir William de Acton is a good man. We had a conversation. I would rather not say more."

"You mean I shouldn't worry my little feminine brain about it?"

"No, I do not mean that at all. Some conversations end up going in directions best left unspoken." She clearly did not understand the point he was trying to make." Hmm, why don't you have this conversation and take both parts?"

"What do you mean?"

"I'll start you out: 'James, you reported to the sheriff. What did he say?'"

"How am I supposed to know what he said?"

"Just think it through and give it a try."

Katherine thought for a moment. "Alright, I'll try: 'this will be the word of two young people versus the word of a monk and difficult to prove.' Oh, me, this would not even go to the sheriff's court – it would go to an ecclesiastic court!"

James put his finger over his lips. "Hmm" was all he said.

"So, you're going to take matters... Oh, alright, I see what you mean about some conversations."

"Something bothers me, Katherine. Why would he let her know his name?"

"I think he was talking to her while he molested her. A 'come-to-daddy' sick fetish."

"Strange."

"She has on a beautiful dress."

"She is well-born. The lad is not her brother but a servant."

"And the broach is her family crest?"

"No, that is something we use around here to say she is one of ours; an homage to an old friend. I'll get Hugh to escort you home."

"To keep him busy."

"Exactly."

"Brother Hugh, tell me about the broach Mary is wearing."

"How do you mean Doctor?"

"Please call me Kate. Sir James said it was a homage to an old friend."

"Sir John Chandos."

"A friend of yours, too?"

"He was a good man to follow into battle. I did not know him personally."

"Sir James did?"

"He was his squire for many years."

"Sir James said the broach marks her as one of yours. Does he mean the priory or his retinue?"

"I guess both. Sir James is a generous benefactor to us."

"Is Sir James your Saint George?"

"He is a very good friend to me, but hardly a saint. Why do you say that?"

"You said the Lord has many different servants."

"Ah, yes, I do remember that conversation. Not a saint but perhaps a dragon slayer just the same."

"My Lord Sheriff."

"Sir James, what brings you back so soon? Nothing to do with your cousin, I trust."

"Our river barge interrupted an attack on a young orphan girl and her servant a few miles south of the city. As they came around the bend the crew shouted when they saw what was happening. The attacker fled and was long gone by the time they were able to throw out an anchor and get ashore."

"Did they raise the hue and cry?"

"No, it is an empty stretch of the river."

"And where are the victims now?"

"They are at the Whitefriars' Priory. Cleaned up and being taken care of; I had a female doctor attend to the girl. Beaten and raped."

"Perhaps your men stopped murder, as well. Did they get a good look at the attacker?"

"He appeared to be in the garb of a Dominican."

"A Blackfriar!"

"I sent some men to watch the Micklegate Bar to see if anyone matching that description entered the city. A friar named Thomas came through at about the right time, and the girl said her attacker talked to himself using the name Thomas."

"I will arrest him, but it becomes a matter for the ecclesiastical courts. The testimony of a little orphan girl is unlikely to carry much weight."

"There is another problem. The man's hood fell off as he ran away and showed him to have a full head of black hair."

"And Friar Thomas?"

"Light brown and tonsured."

"You want me to visit the Dominican Friary?"

"Their prior, a social call. William, I want you to act more like a leader in the religious community of Yorke."

"Bullshit James, what are you up to?"

"Now, William, so suspicious!" Laughing, he says, "In this case, quite justifiably. It is possible that a brother of that house attacked Mary and Daniel."

"I did hear something to that effect, but why do you think that?"

"The attacker was wearing a black cape over a white tunic like a Dominican."

"The Blackfriars have well over fifty brothers. I really do not see what I would be able to do. I mean I cannot just walk in there and accuse them."

"I did not realize they were that numerous. He could be from another house or even an Augustinian. Absolutely no accusations. As I said, a social call one prior to another. You are relatively new at this William. You have twelve brothers here, they have over fifty, go to learn. I know you are having trouble finding your way. Seek advice. Make their prior a mentor; build a relationship."

Prior William put his head in his hands. "Is it that obvious?"

"Many leaders of religious houses are appointed by the king and have no more prior experience than you do. Actually, that's funny – no more 'prior' experience! You wanted this life and you are sincere about it. I am not faulting you. Hell, I helped make it happen. The biggest difference is those men took over leadership of houses with established structures and lieutenants to help them. This house was nearly wiped out by the plague and you've had to start from scratch. Confide in their Prior and ask for help – in all sincerity."

"Alright, that is actually a good idea for the health of our house. That may help me. You actually want me to be disingenuous in building a relationship, though, and find the attacker; that bothers me. It is dishonest."

"Don't get all wound up. You may be clearing an innocent man of suspicion. A man being set up falsely for some reason I do not understand. Or you are helping to remove a vicious rapist from their midst."

"I can see what you mean. A man like that can eat a place up. I still do not see how I can find anything out. Their Prior is not going to just tell me who their rapist brother is."

"Do not mention the attack at all! Just have the conversation looking for guidance. Sense the feeling of the place. Is something wrong in the interactions between the brothers? I don't know if you will be able to discover anything at all. The man we are looking for may have an injured right hand. Take Hugh along to converse with anyone he can while you are in with the prior."

"Hugh is a keen observationist, isn't he?"

"Yes, he is. Now if you can, ask how they support themselves: benefactors, manors, villages they own. Do brothers ever leave the friary, and if so, where are they going and who goes?"

"James, they are a preaching order; Dominicans are supposed to leave the friary all the time."

"Sir William, I have found out a few things that may be of interest. Your insight would be most appreciated."

The sheriff motioned for his bailiff to leave the room. "And I learned something this morning that may weave into the situation, as well, James."

"First the orphan girl is the Lady Mary and I believe she has the dower rights to Appleton Rabuk manor."

"Sir James, her guardian, a Roger Elford, sent me a letter today stating that she has gone missing a week. So, it is the same girl."

"Seems Elford intends to betroth Lady Mary to his son and gain control of the manor for good. Sir William, can you find out about Roger Elford discreetly?"

"I already know a bit. He is Ales Perrers' man. His letter made that clear to assure my cooperation I suppose. Do you think Elford is responsible for the attack?"

"The king's mistress; that complicates things. She is not one to wield her influence with subtlety. The Lady Mary did not know her assailant, but it could still be them, just using the friar as a scapegoat because he happened to be there preaching. I just don't see the reason for attacking the girl if you've already got control of the manor as guardian. It is still most likely to me that Mary that just happened to be in the wrong place and the attacker took her for a nobody. I think it best to keep Mary's whereabouts unknown until we know more."

"Be careful James, the stakes just got higher for both of us. I was told in confidence that Perrers now owns dozens of manors and villages. She is using the courts and stealing them as greedily as she takes jewels from the king."

"My Lord Sheriff, I'm about to increase the stakes again. Friar Thomas is the Dominicans' choice to be their next prior. A choice supported by Archbishop John but opposed in London."

"By whom?"

"Seems that Lancaster and Latimer have a candidate of their own."

"A relative of theirs I am sure! You are well-known to John of Gaunt I know."

"Yes, I am still on reasonably good terms with Lancaster – we fought together. I fought with Latimer too, but we are less than friendly. I have always been more Prince Edward's man."

"I witnessed a bit of that. You think they are trying to ruin Friar Thomas' reputation? That is the reason for this whole thing?"

"Maybe to get the Archbishop to withdraw his support. This is an important Dominican house with a significant annual income from rents and tithes. Whatever else is true of the king's mistress, Latimer, and Lancaster they desire riches above all else. The reputation of some friar and the life of a girl do not signify. Would you be willing to visit Appleton Rabuk and see if anything raises your suspicions?"

"I think I will do just that. To look into the missing girl, of course. I am more our prince's man, too, and the Perrers woman goes too damn far for my taste!"

"On that we are heartily, but silently, agreed. By the way, you are looking for a man whose right hand has been bit deep enough to draw blood."

"It is time for me to have a talk with Friar Thomas. Would you like to join me for that?"

"Yes, I would. May I suggest that the knowledge that you are talking with him slips outs, even have him brought here publicly, although not the reason for bringing him in."

"Right, if Thomas is not under suspicion, they may do something else to incriminate him, and harm some other innocent. If you are correct that the rapist is not clergy, and we apprehend him, then it is back in my courtroom, not the Church's."

"If he is the Lord Chamberlain or the Duke of Lancaster's man, I do not envy your position."

"Not convicting is a perversion of the king's justice. Convicting would submit me to the fury of one of the most powerful men in the realm."

"Pray for the health of the prince."

Katherine rises as James enters his sitting room. A most persistent woman. "I see you have located my abode."

"I wished to check on my patient."

Which one? He thought. "I am doing very well, thank you; although I have not taken a full day's ride since the surgery."

"Do you know who attacked Mary?"

"We thought we did. Things have turned out to be more complicated than they first appeared."

"I do not understand."

"It is possible that this was not about Mary at all. It may have been about ruining a man's reputation."

"She was still the one that was raped!" Katherine fumed.

"And that is why the culprit will be tracked to the ends of the earth if need be! But it also may mean that a Benedictine monk named Thomas did not commit this heinous atrocity."

"So, Brother Thomas was framed."

"It appears that way, and now finding the real rapist is more difficult."

"Who would want to ruin his reputation?"

"Perhaps someone that does not want him to become the abbot here. He is the brothers' candidate for the vacancy."

"Then that is who we are looking for!"

"That is my current line of thinking. Them or their liegeman."

"Both them and their man."

"That may be difficult," James replies as he appraises Katherine anew.

"Why address the symptoms if you can effect a cure? Someone else has put forward a different candidate?"

"The Duke of Lancaster has recommended someone. Others have also suggested names."

"And how do you know this?"

"I asked someone that would know," James said coyly.

"So, it could be one of Lancaster's men that raped Mary."

"John of Gaunt has his faults, and they are many, but this is not something he would do. I just can't imagine that."

"One of his men could have done it, then, without his knowledge," insisted Katherine.

"Lancaster is powerful and arrogant. He will believe that his father will appoint his choice."

"No need to stoop to rape, then."

"No need to discredit some insignificant monk."

"Who makes the decision?"

James replies thoughtfully, "I believe the king will endorse the archbishop's choice."

"Has someone been here promoting their candidate?"

Of course! "Now, that is something I should be able to discover."

Malcolm slips in with two goblets of wine and silently retreats from the room.

"My Lord Sheriff, you sent for me?" Friar Thomas has just been openly escorted by the bailiff and his party to Yorke Castle.

"I did. You were south of the city on the fifteenth of this month?"

"Two days back? Am I under arrest, my Lord?"

"When did you leave the city, where did you go, and when did you return?"

"I left on the thirteenth for Selby Abbey and returned late afternoon on the fifteenth."

"Please tell me the purpose of your journey to Selby."

"I was on friary business I assure you."

"Of that I have no doubt. I understand that the Dominicans are without an abbot at present and that you have been forwarded as the friary's choice, was that the business you were about?"

"My Lord Sheriff, surely this is not a matter for your concern?"

"It may be very much my concern. There has been some violence that may be related to the vacancy. Please answer my questions."

"Violence? I was speaking to Abbot John at Selby Abbey about our vacancy here. The archbishop suggested that I secure additional advocates for my candidacy."

"And was John de Shirburn supportive?"

"Apparently I was not the only one seeking his endorsement. He would not commit."

"Friar Thomas," Sir James had been lounging on the window seat, "was another supplicant present at Selby Abbey during your stay?"

"No, not personally. He had an advocate there on his behalf."

"Can you tell us who that individual was?"

"No, I did not ask."

James raises an eyebrow. "But he was still at the abbey while you were there?"

"He was."

Master Tenebroides eases *Christine* up against the wharf below Selby Abbey. "Tie up!" Selby is a number of miles south of where they had rescued Mary and Daniel, but it is the nearest village of consequence, of course, dominated by the abbey. The idea is to spread out into the village and the abbey and see if there are any, or had been any recently, guests staying here. Sir James had said to be very obvious about their presence. Try to give every man in Selby a hard look-over. 'Whack the hive and see what flies out.' That was good as his crew was not a subtle bunch. The man may well be in Yorke, of course, and they had all been actively on the hunt, but Yorke is a large city and filled with walled religious houses, shops, and residences. If he is in Yorke, he will be hard to find.

So, they split up into pairs, leaving one pair at the boat as they have cargo aboard, and head into Selby. Tenebro's own assignment is the abbey cellarer to see if he can turn him into a customer. No better customer than one he went right past on the river every trip upstream and down. While he speaks with the cellarer, his son Peter will see if anyone had been staying at the abbey guest house.

"Brother Cellarer, I am Tenebroides the bargeman."

"I am Brother Reginald; how may I be of service?"

"I pass by the abbey on my trips between Kingston and Yorke and have often thought you may desire cargo I carry or could get for you."

"I have seen you on the river many times bargeman; what goods do you carry that would interest me?"

"Certainly, you have sources of fish from the river. And wine, salt, and spices in Kingston as good as mine or better. You have manors for grains and poultry. Let me show you a few things that may be of interest. I can get blankets and coarser material, too, but take a look at this best quality cloth woven in Richmond that I can offer at better prices than imported cloth in Kingston."

"This is a high-quality cloth."

"The weavers are Flemish immigrants using looms made in Flanders. I also sell these cutlery items – scissors, kitchen knives, axes from Sheffield if that is of interest. Do you make your own parchment here? If not, we make a fine parchment in Richmond – here is a sample. Also, honey and beeswax candles…"

"We may be able to do some business after all Master Tenebroides. Would you be able to transport goods I have ordered in Kingston to me? I sometimes have difficulties with that."

"I carry cargo for folks all the time. Usually wool to Kingston and salted herring to Yorke."

"If you go all the way to Richmond and Sheffield you don't come by as often as I need."

"I do not go that far myself. I have a partner that runs the Swale from Yorke to Richmond and another that runs the Trent. I go from Yorke to Kingston at least monthly."

"Can you offer me the same price I would pay in Yorke?"

"Yes, the same prices I sell for in Yorke at the market or better as I will not be paying fees to the city. I will write out your order and our agreed price for what you want, so there is no disagreement on delivery."

"If you can give me an hour, I would like to place an order."

"Excellent, by the way, there is a foreign wool buyer that has been out trying to contact me in the area. Have you had anyone come through recently?"

"There have been a number of guests lately; you might check with Prior Francois."

Paul Fitz-William and Geoffrey the longbowman settle in a copse of trees along the road west of Selby Abbey. If Master Tenebroides and his crew's presence in Selby made anyone nervous enough to make a hasty departure, there were high odds he will take this road. The barge crew had seen him, and he knew it. That they had not seen him well enough to identify him – well, he did not know that. Squire Malcolm stands in the road pretending to tend to his courser's wrapped ankle.

Chapter 9

Misericorde

NOVEMBER 1372

This is the last trip of the season. There is no ice on the Swale as yet, but it will not be long now. Virgil and his crew row the boat up past the new dock and nose into the pebble beach below the dairy. "Let's get the load up the hill and then we will haul the boat out."

The barrels of salted herring are rolled up the slope, the baskets of salt carried up by the handles, shovels, picks, axes, and other tools passed up man to man until they are all stacked at the top of the hill. The valuable crates of shears, knives and canvas packages of spices are handed to Joel to take straight up to the house. Oars, anchor, mast, spar, and sail are pulled out or unrigged as required and toted up. A pulley is rigged to the big oak and long logs arranged every six feet or so in front of the barge. Then everyone: oarsmen, weavers, dyers, Nicholas the cooper, the miller, and even the carpenter takes a hold of the cable and pulls down the hill through the block to haul the boat up. Once up on the first roller log, she moves more easily. It is just a matter of overcoming the weight to get her up the incline. Soon *Marie* is resting in the grassy meadow to sleep until March. Virgil does a quick visual inspection of the lower hull to check on some of the worse scrapes from hauling over the shallows earlier in the year. He will do a more detailed check later.

Joel and his family live in the house at the dairy and Virgil still has a bedroom there. Joel was a hungry orphan caught stealing bread and sentenced to lose a hand. Sir James was 'helping' Virgil out of the same cell and Joel tagged along; he has been along ever since. His wife, Leia, serves as the cook for everyone when they are at the dairy. She runs the household and Joel runs the business as James' steward. They have two young daughters and a son. The boy is twelve.

Joel could not read, write, or do figures at first. Perhaps it was the survival instincts of an orphan, he has always been quick-witted, that led him to understand that the reason James usually had something to eat or was the one telling everyone else what to do, was in part because he could read and write. He was forever at James' elbow and as French is the usual language of commerce and of the nobility he now reads and writes in French. Virgil has brought a letter from Sir James that is longer than usual.

Joel looks up after reading the letter. "You know what this is all about, Virg?"

"I know that I am supposed to take the crew up to see Clyde and that bunch and build a big shed and barn before it gets too cold. I brought up the cooper for a few months and I'm told you've got seasoned oak for barrel staves."

"I am supposed to visit Clyde with you and bring half a dozen lead salt pans. Nicholas is to build large tubs and barrels. He knows what he is to do?"

"He met privately with Sir James in Yorke; he may know more about what is afoot than either of us."

Many miles south, outside Selby, a lone horseman heads out of town. Malcom bends down to pick up his horse's leg and inspects the dressing as the man arrives. Geoffrey nocks an arrow onto his bowstring.

"Selby Abbey is just ahead, is it not?" Malcolm asks.

"Aye, less than a mile," the horseman replies reining in his mount.

"We can limp the rest of the way, then," Malcolm replies, caressing his horse's neck. "A bit late in the day to be starting out for Leeds."

"This road does go there, but I am not for Leeds. I was delayed in my departure."

"You look familiar to me."

"Have you fought across the channel?" the horseman asks.

"Aye Auray and Nájera and more, I am currently trying to avoid going back!"

"By the Virgin Mary, anyone that made it back from Nájera should not push their luck further."

"That is my feeling. My name is William, and I will not delay you further," Malcolm replies. Then, noticing the decoration on the saddle cloth, he says, "This is Lord Latimer's livery, is it not?"

"Simon," he said, "I am in the service of Lord Latimer."

Malcolm grabs his wrist with both hands and throws his own weight down to twist him out of the saddle and onto the ground. Simon hits hard on his rump and starts to roll to his feet in the same motion, but Malcolm locks the wrist under his armpit in an arm bar and slams his knee onto his chest to pin him to the ground.

"Bastard!" Simon grunts out and reaches for his dagger, but Malcolm's is already at his throat.

"Shut your fat mouth." Geoffrey and Paul Fitz-William now join-in to gag him and bind his ankles and wrists. He struggles until Geoffrey cuffs him across the cheek. He pulls off Simon's woolen cap to reveal a thick mane of black hair.

A wool sack is pulled over his head and bound below his feet. None too gently the bag, with Simon, is thrown over his own saddle and tied in place. "You saw his bandaged hand?"

Malcom nods and remounts his miraculously cured courser to head on into Selby to tell Master Tenebroides and the barge crew what has taken place. Geoffrey and Paul lead the third horse with its load south of the abbey and to the river. When the sack squirms or makes a noise, it gets a good whack. An hour later, the wool sack is aboard the *Christine* and headed south on the River Ouse. Simon's horse is relieved of a black cape and white robe, his purse, and some correspondence; the horse is left on the road to Leeds.

"Did you learn anything in Appleton Rabuk?" James has stopped by the castle to make a call on Sir William, the sheriff.

"Only that they are truly anxious to have the Lady Mary back, even if for the wrong reasons. I have also looked into the 'court ruling' that placed Roger Elford there as guardian. I believe it to be a sham as there is no record in the wapentake court of Barkston Ash and the bailiff there has no knowledge of it."

"The ruling was in the wapentake as opposed to a London Court?" James raises an eyebrow.

"The jurisdiction is Barkston Ash and that is what Elford declared to me. He has some armed men there to enforce his rights as acting lord of the manor. The peasants are sullen, to say the least, and that has gotten worse, I'm told, since the Lady Mary's disappearance. They seem to believe Elford is behind that, or at least that he and his wife made her miserable enough to flee."

"Are you able to intervene?"

"I would hesitate but the Lady Mary's father, Sir Gerald Rabuk, died in service with the prince at Nájera. I believe he will not be pleased to see this perfidy at her expense, and I have asked him to step in."

"Your request will join mine, then. Does Elford know I have the Lady Mary?"

"Certainly not, I did not write that to Prince Edward. Did you?"

"I did," James spreads his hands open. "It would not serve for him to find out later and that I failed to mention it. He does not like being manipulated."

"No! I am sure of that."

"He believes his father is surrounded by thieves. They abuse the king's authority to gather riches to themselves. I do not want to ever give him any reason to think the same of me."

Joel brought the carpenter along with Virgil and the crew of the *Marie* in three mule drawn wagons north to Yarm and then east into the North Yorkshire Moors. Two of the wagons are heavily built and good for weighty loads having been once used in the transport of building stone. Under the canvas covers are three large oaken tubs, lead salt pans, assorted tools, and provisions.

There are four stacked stone cottages built together into a hillside. The cottages provide some shelter from the frigid wind blowing in off the sea to the women at a cooking fire. The smoke swirls until it rises above the eaves to be snatched away by the wind. The smudge of soot is on the women's aprons and on a small child playing nearby.

"Clyde, Sir James has entrusted me with a letter for you."

"You will need to read it for me Master Joel."

"I can read it, but I certainly hope that it makes some sense to you as it makes none to me." He begins reading: "Now, this is the odd part: 'Completely dissolve the soft pink material in the tubs using clean warm water. The impurities will settle to the bottom of the tub. Ladle the water into a lead pan and heat until the water is reduced to one fourth the original amount. Remove the heat and let cool. Crystals will form. Mind the lead pan the entire time it is on the fire. If too much liquid is lost the batch is ruined and the lead pan may also be lost.' Does that make any sense to you?"

"Aye, please read it through again for me, though."

Trees are felled and dragged to the building site opposite the cottages using the mules that pulled the wagons from Richmond. The logs are squared by David, the master carpenter, making shallow cuts with the saw and then taking off the material in between with an adze.

Virgil supervises the digging of holes for the vertical posts and then the manhandling of the beams set across the top; each post sits in a pocket notch cut into the beam. Auger holes are bored through the beams and wood pins driven in to secure them. A diagonal timber is fit into each resulting square formed by posts and beam to make the structure rigid. Simple roof trusses are built: horizontal beams spanning the structure from wall to wall with a post on top in the center, the so-called 'king post' to support the ridge beam. Finally roof rafters are laid from the ridge to the side walls with a diagonal added on each side from where the king post met the beam to the rafter.

A grid of wood battens is attached atop the rafters. Reeds harvested from the nearest wet areas are bundled to create the thatched roof. This is done by tying a row of reed bundles to the battens along the bottom edge of the roof followed by a row on top, which overlap the first layer by two-thirds and continuing up row-by-row until the roof is complete.

To form the walls sticks are woven between the posts in a mesh – the 'wattle.' A sticky mixture of clay, straw, and the lime and hair residue from cleaning sheepskins, the 'daub,' is applied until a thick and solid wall completes the barn. A large shelter is built next. James' instructions call for just poles and a roof, but the wind is too aggressive. A wall is built on the long side towards the prevailing wind from the sea, and halfway across each of the short sides. Window gaps in the walls can be closed with large shutters.

Upstairs in the private dining room back in Yorke, at The Swan, Paul says, "Sometimes Sir James, I think you know more than you let on."

"Oh? Explain yourself."

"A man named Simon hot-footed it out of Selby on the road to Leeds; with a thick head of black hair, a bandage on his right hand, and this black cape and white cassock in his saddle-bag. And, he is Latimer's man. Exactly as you said."

"Tenebroides has him now?"

"Headed down the Ouse, Sir James."

"Geoffrey, your ale mug is empty," James pours him full. "The cook has done wonderful magic with the smoked salmon in this pastry; won't you have another portion? Malcolm, surely you have also worked up an appetite."

Malcolm helps himself to another helping and sits back comfortably in his chair. It has been a while since Sir James has been in such a good mood. The grant from the Prince of Wales sparing them another campaign across the channel, and success capturing the Lady Mary's rapist are at least two worries off his mind. His Lord is going to enjoy the moment for a change instead of configuring plans to meet unexpected setbacks that usually never happen.

"You've all done well. You were unobserved?" A good theory based on some information from his Prince and the known facts had paid off; if his men assume he knew more than he did…Well, James was fine with that.

"I am as certain as I can be of that," Paul Fitz-William assures him. "These items were also in his saddle-bags."

"Good. Now put the matter out of your minds entirely; it never happened." James pulls a cord behind the drapery, which rings a bell in the kitchen. Soon a man of the inn arrives upstairs with a timid girl, scrubbed spotless with a white apron, to clear empty dishes and set out a tray of sweets. He deftly refills their mugs despite missing a thumb on his left hand.

It is past curfew when the gathering concludes. The city gates are closed for the night and the watch keeps the streets clear of potential troublemakers. A lantern with blue glass is hung in the high gable window of the inn and, before too long, the boat from the priory arrives on the Foss. "We were just coming out of our prayers at Matins when we heard you hung the lantern. Is everything alright?"

"Aye Brother Hugh, you may rest easy on that score. All is well, indeed."

The King's Fishpond is warmer than the night November air and their arrival at the priory pier is shrouded in fog. James and Malcolm slip quietly through Prior Williams study and up the back staircase into the townhouse. Will stumbles awake and lights more candles in Sir James' bed chamber.

James opens Simon's purse and envelope of letters onto a side table. "It is late, my Lord," Will said gently.

"I will not be much longer. You may both turn in." Tomorrow would be an interesting day. A bolt of cloth will be offered for sale at the market at twenty-nine pence an ell. It is from the batch of wool dyed using all the alum from Clyde's chance discovery and his experiments in Barmby. If it all sells at full price it is worth close to six pounds.

Katherine carefully shops the Yorke market for just the right material to have a new dress made. She notices a commotion at the next stall over a length of an expensive bright aqua cloth, which quickly sells out. When the shoppers disperse, she is drawn to see what else they might have.

"Doctor Kate!"

"Maude?" It is the young girl that had been sitting with the Lady Mary in the cloister of the priory. She is wearing the same enameled broach, a white shield with a red triangle pointing down, that Mary had been wearing. "Were you wearing that same beautiful pin when I saw you at the priory?"

Her eyes sparkle. "I wear it always, of course. Are you shopping for material?"

"I was considering have a new dress made but am having trouble making up my mind."

"Doctor Katherine, my daughter told me about you, my name is Janice, and this is my stall. I also have a shop just down the street."

"Your aqua material created quite a stir this morning. Of course, that would not be something for me." Sumptuary laws prevent commoners from dressing in more expensive colors, imported material, or furs.

"This dark green is first quality as is this midnight blue."

Katherine notes that Janice is also wearing the shield broach as she inspects the green and the blue. "It is very nice, but this is imported, is it not?"

"No, it is perfectly alright for you to wear. It was woven in England."

"Expensive, though?"

"Which one are you considering?"

"How much is the midnight blue?"

"The best tailor in Yorke is Valentine; I'll get the material to him and let him know you will be stopping by for measurements. You know his shop?"

"He makes dresses for the wealthy; I just don't think..."

"Doctor, you will not have to pay for this dress; that I can assure you."

"Now, Janice, I cannot accept..."

"Please, go see Valentine to be measured. You don't want to get me in trouble, do you?" She winks.

Trouble? Trouble with Sir James? "No, I do not want to get any one in trouble." Janice the weaver hardly appears to feel threatened by the possibility. Just some confidential amusement she must share with Brother Hugh and Sir James.

"You will be so beautiful!" Lithe little Maude spins and dances in happiness at the thought.

Across the river, James pays a visit to the fellmonger. "Sir James, to waa-waa-what do I owe this visit?" he says, rising to his feet.

"I want to get some papers to a Blackfriar named Thomas."

Judd scratches his chin and thinks for a bit. Sir James could obviously simply hand them to the man himself. Confused, he stuttered as understanding dawned on him, "Straight into his ha ha-hands alone without any way of na-na-knowing whence they came?"

James nods.

Judd stretches out his bum leg before it becomes stiff. "Does this Ta-Ta-Thomas ever leave the Benedictines' gate?"

"Yes, usually after the midday prayer and returns before vespers. Geoffrey can point him out to you."

The fellmonger glances across the street and sees Geoffrey lingering outside the public house. "Leave it to me, then." The sealed canvas folio remains on the bench with a few pence when James casually strolls back towards the Ouse River Bridge. At the end of the street Malcolm, Will, and Paul Fitz-William join him.

The cellarer at Selby Abbey has wine and spices in Kingston with no way to get them to the abbey available at the moment. Master Tenebroides is all too willing to be hired for that transport as he is headed there anyway. As long as the weather held, he will continue sailing the Humbre to buy tuns of wine and spices from the Hanse representative to sell in Yorke, as well as baskets of sea coal and fish from local boats including those of Companie men. He has aboard some grain, cured sheepskin, beeswax, and high-grade iron ingots to trade to the Hanse, to offset some of the cost.

Sir James wants him to negotiate a purchase of kermes grain in Kingston if the Hanse will sell it to him. If not, he has to sail two to three days to Bruges or Antwerp in the spring and try to make the purchase there. That means putting out into the North Sea; although the coast would be nearly always in sight, it was still a bit chancy in the *Christine* if the weather got rough.

Most cloth dyes are plant based, reasonably priced, and have alternatives. There are numerous ways to get browns, yellows, blues, and greens. There are also expensive dyestuffs. Tyrian purple dye comes from Mediterranean Sea snails; it literally sells for its weight in silver, which makes purple the color of royalty as whom else could afford it? Kermes is a bright red dye that comes from the dried eggs of beetles infesting Kermes Oak trees; the dried eggs look like grain.

Kermes is very expensive but produces the most premium woolen cloth, which is referred to as 'scarlets' even when the final cloth color is not red. The 'grain' comes from southern France, Spain, or deeper into the Mediterranean just like many of the spices he buys. The Hanse can get it, but will they sell and at what price? The cost of the kermes grain can be one fourth the final sell value of the cloth or more, but that selling price, 90p per ell, is over three times the price of first quality broadcloth. That is why Sir James wants it. To be in the premium end of the wool cloth market.

Before the *Christine* arrives in Kingston there is another matter requiring attention. The scattered fishing boats out in the Humbre estuary this morning are at a distance when Simon is brought out into the dim, morning light. He is still bound hands and feet. The wool sack is pulled down to his waist to reveal that the side of his head is bruised, swollen, and ugly where they had repeatedly thumped him to keep him quiet. His head is pulled up with a yank on his thick mat of black hair.

"Tenebroides!" I should have known it was you. "You stinkin' bastard; I won't tell you nothing," Simon spews out.

"I'm not asking you anything," Tenebroides smiles and sets his long, narrow misericorde dagger on the step next to him.

Panicking, he says, "We weren't trying to kill d'Arzhon! Just give him a warning."

"Oh?" Was Simon responsible for the ambush outside Yorke? Tenebro wonders to himself and grabs the man's wrist. He unbinds Simon's hands and then rips the bandages from his right hand. Tenebroides meets the man's incensed stare with a hard stare of his own. The half circle bite mark is plain to see.

"What a coincidence, the man I've been looking for was bitten on his right hand by a young girl. I see your tastes have not changed."

"That's what this is about? That spoiled little bitch! Don't think I won't see you all hanged for this! No court will convict me of any crime and believe me when I tell you I know people at the king's court." Tenebroides violently rebinds Simon's wrists.

The crew begins slipping smaller ballast stones with him into the wool sack. Simon desperately tries to push the stones away. "You are nothing but a pack of stupid jackals. You won't get away with this! I can pay you enough to see reason. Lord Latimer will hunt you down; you'll never escape him. You'll all die over a worthless scrap of a girl."

"We may hang but you won't see it." With that Tenebroides places the dagger point against the base of Simon's left eye and punches the hilt with his palm through the eye-socket and deep into the brain. A vicious twist of the knife and blood runs out over the haft and Tenebroides' hand.

"Sew him up."

Chapter 10

Desperate

There are often children begging outside the arched brick Blackfriars' gate. The gatekeeper shoos them away as Brother Thomas returns; it is almost time for vespers.

A determined young urchin eludes his reach and careens into Thomas almost knocking him into the gatekeeper. "Your purse Thomas," he hisses and slaps a leather purse hard into his mid-section before scrambling away.

"Oomph!" Thomas gasps, grabs his belly and the purse involuntarily. It is too late to reach out for the boy disappearing fast around the corner. "Impudent boy!"

"Did he rob you Brother?"

"No, no he did not. The opposite it would appear," shaking his head in bewilderment.

Inside the walled compound of the Benedictines, Thomas sits down at the abbot's desk and looks over the black satchel that is not his but clearly meant for him. He had been unable to collect himself properly for prayer at vespers wondering at the incident outside the gate. Perhaps now he will be able to make some sense of it. He turns it over, but it is not monogrammed or distinctive in any way. There is nothing left to do but open it and see what it contains.

Thomas begins to read a message to a man named Simon. The message directed him to incriminate or otherwise discredit Friar Thomas of the Benedictine house at Yorke. A notation in the margin indicates the sender is the king's chamberlain, William Latimer. Simon was to assure that Thomas would no longer be eligible to become abbot of the Benedictines. Thomas sat in stunned befuddlement. Where did this message come from and who penned the margin notation? Should it be believed? If so, did the king himself oppose him or just his chamberlain? Who is this man Simon and where is he now? Was that the man who visited the abbot of Selby? Is this somehow connected to his interview with the sheriff and the violence he mentioned? And...what was he to do now?

"What was the expression you used: 'are you saying I don't need to worry my pretty little head about that?'"

"I should not have said that, James, I apologize."

"Well, what I am saying now, Kate, is that if you were worried about it you no longer need be."

Katherine swirls her wine glass and stares briefly through it into the candles. She had never drunk from a goblet made of glass; surely The Swan did not serve all customers like this. "And if I remember rightly, it would be best not to continue this topic of conversation any longer. So, I will just say that I am relieved and try not to think about anything that might imply." And she did not want to think about it too much. Certainly, she was angry at the man that raped the Lady Mary and wanted justice, but having a romantic relationship with a man that had a hand in that 'justice' without the king's authority was unsettling to ponder, to say the least.

James smiles slightly over his claret. "That might be best."

Changing the subject, she says, "Thank you for this new dress, but you should not have had another made for me. One was quite enough." This dress had also been made by Valentine and was made of a fine silver-grey cloth, just like the one she admired that the Lady Mary had been wearing.

"Hugh said you liked the material. Please consider it not as a gift but payment for a surgery well done. I no longer experience any pain and it shows no sign of re-occurrence." For a single woman to accept a gift from a man could legally be interpreted as agreement to marriage.

"I will have to be careful what I say!" One thing is apparent to her, when she wears this dress, or the dark blue one that James had also given to her, people in the city step aside, nod politely or touch their hats in respect when she walked past. They never did that before. "I noticed that it arrived with this little shield shaped broach pinned on. Does that mean you think I am part of your Companie now?"

"Valentine did a lovely job; it suits you perfectly. I am in the cloth trade, you know, so surely I can give a dress now and then." Valentine had her measurements and this dress was quite form-fitting above the full skirt when the laces across the back were pulled snug. "The broach just helps our people know to look out for your welfare when they see it." He grins. "Unless of course, you fought with Sir John across the channel in which case..." James waves his hand at Paul Fitz-William who has just peered around the corner. Paul nods and returns with an attractive young woman. It is past mid-day and The Swan is settling down after the busy dinner hour. Will slips in to tend the fireplace behind them here in the small upstairs dining room. They look out over the River Foss through south facing windows.

"Kate, you know Paul, and this is Diane," he said, rising to pull back a chair for her to be seated. "I for one have worked up an appetite today."

Malcom brings more glasses and pours warm mulled wine. Then he returns with a platter of smoked pike, capers and spermyse – a creamy cheese flavored with herbs. He slices the smoked fish and places it on thin toasted bread with some of the spermyse and capers for each diner.

"I usually have ale with this pike, but I hope the wine will serve." James says as he offers the platter to each diner in turn. Then he helps himself to the smoked pike. "Delicious!"

"It is a lovely starter; I am afraid I've become tired of salted herring this winter," Katherine pouted.

"Ha! Do not disparage salted herring too strongly at this table," Paul teases. "Sir James makes a handsome profit on barrels of it this time of year."

"Are you in the fishmonger trade, as well, James?"

"We do all right with the salt fish and it gives us a good cargo coming back up the river. Wear your new broach and visit Oliver the fishmonger on the Ouse Bridge, if you can stand anymore salted herring. He could even have some fresh trout packed in snow and ice – never salted! You just may get favorable treatment for your pence."

"Another of your Companie, I presume."

Diane adds, "Perhaps the cook here at The Swan has a sauce that will make it more bearable. I will see if I can persuade him to share some preparations."

"He certainly has a lovely parsley sauce," said James. "I am partial to his flaky pastry pie full of carrots, leeks, and pease with the herring, but I am also looking for other options than salted fish today. Fortunately, Paul had a successful afternoon at the hunt yesterday, so we will not be going hungry."

"Paul brought the cook some beautiful pheasants to roast for our meal today!"

"Diane do not give me too much of the praise; Geoffrey and Hugh were the marksmen of our hunting party. I just managed the hounds."

"Brother Hugh?"

"He needs to be kept busy, Kate." James eyes twinkle with mischief.

"So, I have been told. I just did not realize he was an archer." Katherine always thought of archers as being long-limbed and lean.

"A very skilled one if I am any judge," adds Paul.

As if on cue, Malcolm brings out the roast pheasants and the cook follows with a tureen of turnips with pease and bacon. "Michael stuffs the pheasant with butter and wraps it in bacon." The cook nods in solemn agreement to James' commentary as Malcolm deftly carves the birds without disturbing any of the splayed feathers decorating the platter.

"Smells divine Michael," Diane coos warmly.

"Perfection," said James, having a bite. Michael beams with happiness at the compliments and retreats with visible relief to his kitchen.

"I have never had pheasant this succulent; it is wonderful." Kate contemplates the little gathering: Malcolm serves, which is certainly a squire's duty, Will tends the fire, which may normally be the establishment's responsibility, but if privacy has been requested, then certainly the guest's own man could be doing that. A wealthy and frequent guest could bring game to be prepared and the cook could be nervous about pleasing that guest. Nonetheless, Katherine senses that Sir James presides over the meal and inn with more than a guest's level of comfort.

"William, your priory has four villages and five houses with shop-fronts here in Yorke to support twelve friars plus yourself. That is more than sufficient, far more than sufficient I assure you."

"It is the Lord's work that is my concern James. I did not become a prior to manage farms and rents," he replies with indignation.

"They come together, and you cannot escape that fact. The villages belong to your order and you are the head of the order. You are the villagers' lord. If you are unwilling or unable to be a manager, then get Hugh or Alfred or one of the others to act as steward."

"You seem to have a gift for making money and directing people. I am just not..."

"Not what?"

"I was going to say greedy but that is not really fair. Tenacious might be a better word." Prior William stammered, "Not that it isn't necessary. I do not mean to sound judgmental."

"Fair enough, let me put it differently – the people in your villages are your people. You are responsible for their well-being. If they are suffering, then it is your problem. You can call it being a lord or you can call it the Lord's work, but abdication is unacceptable."

"It is not my fault if they are going hungry!"

"Maybe not but it is still your responsibility. You avoided the word 'greedy' but let us use it for a moment. If I am greedy, which makes me more money: a large village full of healthy peasants or one that is struggling and starving?"

"Well, obviously, the healthy village."

"In the long run looking tenaciously after the well-being of my people enables me to make more money. The two are one and the same."

"I am not starving them."

"You are ignoring them. Not a sin of malice but of incompetence."

"Each village has a reeve; isn't this their responsibility?"

"Yes, but the reeve is your representative. If he is unfair or incompetent it falls back to you."

"They were elected by the villagers before I even got here. I don't even know them!"

"You should; they are less than seven miles away. Let's start by speaking with the four men that have come to the priory with grievances. It was a long walk in winter to come here and they have a right to petition their lord."

"So, if I understand right, the problem started two years ago when your seed rotted after it had been sown and you had no more seed to re-sow?" James sat down with Prior William and the unhappy villagers to guide the conversation.

The men nod nervously. "It wasn't that we sowed too early – the weather just turned bad again late that year! Rain, rain, and more rain." The men have dark sunken eyes and threadbare clothes.

"I am not blaming you. That happens some years."

"What do we do, Sir James?" asked Prior William, clearly out of his element.

"You must support the villages with food until harvest starting right now. Secondly you must provide enough seed this spring to get a proper crop in the ground."

"Will you help?"

"Yes, I will. We need to get a wagon load headed to each village in the morning."

Back in the Prior's study, he says, "I am going with the wagons, and you are coming along, too, William."

"I thought you might say that," William said glumly. "You want me to meet the reeves."

"Yes, and get their measure. They should have told you they needed seed two years ago."

"They sent a message; I told them to make do as best they could. This is my fault."

"Shit, William!" James says, exasperated. "Well, the important thing is that you now are accepting responsibility for your flock. You cannot change what is in the past, accept it, learn, and move forward. The reeves should still have come here in person long ago to plead their case."

"These people have been starving."

"Yes, and it will cost your treasury dearly and your conscience more so."

"I should resign."

"Don't be such a coward, William. Step up and meet your responsibility to these people and make things right. I have made many such mistakes and I continue to! Look at me." William was staring at the floor. "There are many, many villages suffering the same neglect all over England from negligent or over demanding landowners. You are not alone. Just resolve to be better and not let it happen again. If you do that, then they will be most fortunate in the future."

"Oh, and what mistakes have you made?"

"Well, for one, I was rewarded with rights to all of these manors only to find that my grant was having the most plague decimated villages dumped on me. That cost me more than they were worth when parliament granted the king the fifteenth!"

"What did you do?"

"I got a little 'tenacious' to use your word before I went bankrupt!"

"You did not cause people to starve."

"That I did across the channel fighting for the Crown – my incompetence, as well as that of my superiors. Not only the French, but our people starved, including myself, at times. I got damn good at securing provisions."

"I well know you did. I was a beneficiary of that. This is not a war here."

"Are you sure? I certainly feel like we are in a fight of a sort. Listen, the English serf is hardy and resilient. Lord knows they have had to be. You are fortunate in that your villages are so close. Many lords have property scattered all over England and also some across the channel. Now how many people are in each village?"

"I don't know."

"You should. Ask the ones that are here for a head count and get the bakehouse busy. The cooks need to prepare a mutton stew. Speak to your cellarer and have him get sacks of grain, beans, and turnips ready for transport. I will get the wagon teams here from The Swan and get some salted herring from Oliver. Don't let Mark be miserly; these peasants cannot have helped but notice how full the friars' table was at dinner today while their families have nothing."

Prior William nodded, feeling guilty at the obvious unfairness of the peasants' predicament. "We will fast here upon our return to atone for our gluttony."

Whatever makes you feel better, thought James.

If Oliver was concerned about half a barrel of herring being diverted into baskets and cutting profits, he was wise enough to keep those concerns to himself. As long as Sir James did not complain when his payment was due about a shortage! In truth, if anyone was scrupulous about accounts it was Sir James; he would already have calculated the shortfall. Paul Fitz-William escorted the wagon to the bridge and Brother Hugh was driving it. It appeared to be a full expedition in the making.

The wagons are not heavy, but the teams are doubled; four mules are less likely to have much difficulty pulling each wagon on the frozen road. Paul rode ahead with four men from The Swan. Geoffrey and two others kept pace out on the left. Ben did the same on the right. Alfred and three brothers brought up the rear, and in the middle, James, his squires, and Prior William rode with the wagons. No one smirked at Sir James' elaborate precautions. Was Sir James acting the soldier again or merely taking prudent precautions when taking two wagon loads of food through country with people concerned whether they will make through the winter? Whether he knew they were riding into potential danger or just thought they were getting too pampered of late did not really matter. When he gets like this it is best to do as you are told. The four villagers ride in the wagons.

They departed the Layerthorpe Gate and stayed at The Swan last night. They cross the Foss Bridge before daybreak, which is before the city gate would have been opened. They should easily reach the villages by mid-day and return to The Swan before nightfall. Ahead, some down trees block the road and put James on alert. "Spread out and create a perimeter. Will, get some men with axes up there." James himself rides forward to where the trees had broken off at the ground. "This just looks like winter storm damage. I see no sign of a deliberate effort to block the road." Malcolm nods his head in agreement. "They about have the road clear now." Will had merely used the horses to drag most of the branches clear of the road. Very little chopping had been necessary.

The foodstuffs are distributed in both the villages of Supton and Elfwynton by early afternoon. Fields, a small wood, and the frozen Derwent River is all that separates them. Many of the villagers seem dazed and moving without purpose as they are roused from their wood and thatched homes. Space is cleared in the tithe barn to get a fire going and heat the mutton stew. James makes certain that every home is searched, so he can be sure every single villager gets a bowl of hot stew and a thick slice of bread with a slather of butter.

Many of the huts did not have a fire going. The people were just snuggled in with each other for mutual warmth. They stood shivering in torn blanket remnants that did not hide how thin they were. James has some of his party remain for a few days to cut wood, get fires going, and insure they get something to eat each day. It is worse than he imagined. The villages will need to be checked on every few days for the next month or they may all die in their sleep.

James is not impressed with the reeves who seem more concerned that some villagers had gone to Prior William in disregard of their authority than the plight of the village. One of the men that went to the priory, Miles, is appointed reeve of both villages by the prior at James' suggestion. He seems the natural leader. It will be interesting to see if the villagers confirm that choice at the next election.

There is no threat of robbery now that the wagons are empty for the return trip, and it is unlikely that someone with a grievance will even know that Sir James had left the city, but James keeps men out on the flanks from habit and his natural sense of caution. When they get to the site of the trees that had blocked the road, they hew them into manageable lengths and fill the wagons. The Swan can always use firewood. They have the wagons back to the stables just after dark and enter the city, well before curfew.

A message is waiting for James from the Archbishop and the Lord Mayor to attend them at his earliest convenience; that meant immediately.

It is late and Archbishop John resides closer, so he went there. To his surprise John de Gisburn is still there. "My apologies for the late hour of my calling, my Lords. I have just returned to the city and received your summons."

"Sir James! I was afraid you would not be back until late tomorrow. Have you rescued the priory's villages from starvation?"

"Your Grace is well-informed." Too well, thought James. "Yes, for the moment; they have clearly suffered a great deal. I expect that Prior William will need to make several more trips until the harvest comes in." He wonders if Prior William spoke to the archbishop, or if it was someone else.

"Stepping into that situation was well done. Are you aware of the situation across the channel?"

"I understand that things went poorly in the summer."

"Poorly! A disaster in every respect! We spent two days of the parliament listening to all that went wrong and the reasons for it." The Archbishop of Yorke holds a seat in Parliament.

"Did you find them valid, your Grace?"

"Of course, the king always wants more money. More money than the treasury can possibly support and as we lose control of the Aquitaine, Poitou, and Saintonge we lose those revenues, too. In fact, at this point, they are costing us money to defend."

"I know Lancaster is planning on raising a new army for a campaign in Brittany and I am also aware that the subsidy on wool cargoes has been continued."

"Yes, you would be aware of that. All imports and exports, not just wool, will have customs duties continued and increased to pay for armed convoys in the Bay of Biscay and in the North Sea. That is the other cause of our troubles – no royal fleet. Parliament has authorized the king to build fifteen large war galleys to be funded by the port cities including Yorke."

James just nods thoughtfully. That explained why the Lord Mayor is here: they want money.

"Are you still owner of that boatyard, Sir James? I know you were hoping to divest yourself of it," the mayor has finally spoken up.

"Yes, it is still mine from a financial position. I am no shipbuilder myself, of course."

"No, of course not, but could your yard build a sixty-five-foot war galley?"

"Yes, Master Swain built the *Christine* for me in that yard before I owned it. She is fifty foot and patterned after the great Venetian trading galleys that I saw in Bruges. Much smaller, of course."

"What would such a war galley cost the city to build?"

"I guess I would need to know more of the details and get with Master Swain. Have they provided specific plans?"

"Forty-four oars, equipment for forty archers, two masts with fighting platforms, top castles, and as I said, sixty-five foot in length. That is all."

"These are usually of lighter construction than cargo ships for speed and maneuverability. That needs to be carefully balanced with seaworthiness. I have served on them only briefly."

"That makes you the expert in the room!" laughs the Archbishop leaning back in his chair.

The mayor perks up. "Were you actually in a fight?"

"Just once, we sheared off the oars of a French galley with our bow as we came along side. We boarded them and then the ships moved suddenly apart. That left me and not too many others stranded and outnumbered on the wrong galley!"

"What did you do?"

"Fought like a madman to clear her stern castle and try to hold it against the rest of the ship. Fortunately, the two ships ground back together again fairly quickly, and archers were pouring arrows into her waist from our ship the whole time. I did determine that I would learn to swim after that."

"Exeter is trying to raise two hundred pounds to build their galley."

"Master Swain and I will figure out how to build and not exceed that. I should not say this without speaking to Swain but, offhand, that seems more than ample."

"Less would be better."

"Did you learn how to swim?" teases the Archbishop.

"I certainly did! Although you would also need to get out of most of your armor soon after hitting the water to have any chance. That might prove extremely difficult."

The archbishop ponders that for a moment, thinking about all the little straps and buckles securing armor. "Yes, I suppose you would."

Kate wears the dark blue dress. It is market day, Thursday, and she had agreed to meet James on the Ouse Bridge outside the shop of Oliver the fishmonger. She wears the Chandos broach on her heavy hooded woolen cloak because he would surely notice its absence. The cloak is new and had been purchased from the fee she received for James' surgery. Even her hands are covered in woolen mittens, so he might never find her in this crowd.

"Good morning, Kate!"

"You managed to find me in spite of being all covered up in this cold," she laughs. "I see that Will, Malcolm, and Paul will be keeping us properly chaperoned."

"I tried to convince them that you meant me no harm," He says, smiling mischievously.

"Clearly, they can sense danger," she responds. "Friar Hugh is not here to stand up for me, then? Oh, what do you know…he is just across the way, pretending to be interested in goose feathers at the butcher's."

"You can probably get good measure at that butcher. Owen is his name."

"A Companie man?"

"And Hugh actually is trying to corner the market on goose feathers at Owen's son's stall – the poulter."

"For the prior's mattress I suppose or maybe yours."

"Those would be the little breast feathers. He is supposed to be buying tail and wing feathers." He guided her across the bridge towards the market square.

"For writing quills or just being kept busy?"

"They are for arrow fletching; supporting the king's war effort."

"I never know whether to believe you or not."

"I know an excellent stall for garden shears; the finest Sheffield cutlery."

"Some vendor you might know James?"

"I think you met Master Tenebroides at the priory, so yes."

"One hundred forty pounds, John."

"Well, that beats Exeter's contract by a great deal." The mayor delightedly rubs his hands together. "Still an expensive undertaking, mind you."

"Indeed, that includes the ship with two masts, rigging, anchor with cable, fittings, and sails; the oars, ballast stones, bows for forty archers and over 1,900 arrows – which are two sheaves apiece. What it does not include is stores or embellishments such as carving and gold leaf decoration. We'll paint it one color – green. If you want a different color, then we need to adjust for any cost difference."

"I like green just fine. If the City Council wants decoration, they can raise additional funds for that. We will need to increase river tolls and market fees as it is."

"I expect my barges will be free of those when they are bringing materials to the boatyard. In fact, I insist upon it."

"That is fair enough; we should not increase your cost to build our own ship. We will write that into our agreement. So, you know the Council is aware you were coming back with a proposal and have asked some of the other yards for bids. Does that change yours?"

"It does not. Blind bids?"

"I will not reveal yours until the others are received. The galley must be launched and fit out by the end of August."

"When are their bids due? The sooner I know whether or not I am the builder the better; that is a tight schedule."

"End of this week."

"Please, do not share my price, then, with anyone, including the archbishop or members of the council. I also ask that their proposals fully list what is included, so we are quoting the same thing."

"Not too trusting, are you?"

"I feel quite certain that with a contract involving this much money, if you share my price, at least one of the other yards will know it by evening."

"I cannot fully dispute that, although I would like to."

"Also, please protect yourself against any low bids that allow for cost overruns later."

"I would tell you that we know how to manage our expenditures, except you will then remind me that the Ouse Bridge construction eventually cost double what we were quoted!"

"Big projects are hard to estimate. The problem is that once you have paid an enormous sum, but the project remains unfinished, you are somewhat trapped."

"I can tell you that Archbishop John has agreed that he and the Lord Abbot will contribute one-third the cost and he favors you as the builder."

James laughs. "Perhaps he feels responsible for my owning the boatyard!" Doubtless the two churchmen travelled back from London together, both having seats in parliament, and determined their share. "Does Kingston need to build a galley?"

"No, not this time anyway. Possibly judged to be too small a town to bear the cost."

"They have in the past. Maybe they need to have a share in the cost of ours, then."

"I doubt that they will make that offer, but they could be required to... Interesting, Sir James, interesting."

"Sell enough shares and Yorke could make money on this ship!" James winks.

"Master Swain our proposal won the contract. Total is now 150 pounds, which includes ten pounds for embellishments. Not only were we preferred by some stakeholders, but we also quoted the lowest cost."

"Then no one can have any complaint of favoritism, Sir James."

"Oh, there will be griping from the other yards – this is a huge contract. We need to build a fine galley and not have any cost overruns."

"Remind me to have you review the next major agreement that the city enters into Sir James."

"Oh, has something gone amiss?"

John de Gisburn laughs. "Quite the contrary, Kingston is now contributing fifteen percent of our war galley costs! Archbishop John agreed that they should help the effort and so did his Majesty." The mayor slapped the table, stood up and twirled about. "That is not all; Scarborough has been told to contribute fifteen percent, as well! The smaller ports cannot be expected to finance a ship on their own, but they can contribute to the one being built in here. They are in Yorkshire, too."

"So, the City of Yorke's share is now...fifty-five pounds?"

"Actually, sixty-five; the Church has insisted they are a third of the balance after Kingston and Scarborough's shares are deducted. They are paying thirty-three pounds and I have that here for you."

"Bless you! That will help a great deal as we are getting ready to make our first purchases."

"Prevents you from using your own money or promising to pay later."

"That and money up front usually gets a better cost."

"Timber from Supton and Elfwynton villages can be rafted down the Derwent to Barmby. We will build a saw pit there and cut it into planking. That will give the villagers something to do this winter that will make them a bit of money." Prior William nods as James is talking to him at that moment. "Tenebro, you will have Justin get us the saws they will need from Sheffield and obviously bring the cut boards upriver to the boatyard."

"Bertrand, Master Swain gets his framing timber near Tatecastre, so transporting that is your job and he needs that as soon as the river is navigable."

"A priority over stone for the cathedral?"

"They can't lay stone until it warms up and they already have enough on hand for when the weather breaks. Get two loads of timber first and then we will just have to watch the quantities on hand at both the cathedral and the boatyard."

"If snow stays on the ground, we can move it here by sledge now, Sir James."

"Bert, I like the way you think. Use the mule teams at The Swan. Master Swain you will need to go on the first trip to arrange the purchase and pick out your timber."

"Aye, the sooner the better – keel first."

"Janice you are in charge of getting the sailcloth woven. We will sew the panels together later to make the sails, so the exact shape is not important yet. Just produce the canvas bolts."

"Tenebro, these are sample deck spikes, and these are planking nails. We need hundreds of the one and thousands of the other. Every smith we've got from Richmond to Gainsburgh needs to get started. Justin needs to get more iron billets to keep them supplied and, of course, you need to get them here when they have been completed." He paused. "You also know how to make rope. See if the farm in Morton did well with the flax seed I sent. I thought it would be for fishing nets, but they should already have the fibers spun into cord over the winter, which is the starting point for either. If they have enough, set up a ropewalk and make or buy whatever machinery you need. Teach Francis to make rope or have Walter make it in Gainsburgh. If we don't have our own flax crop you will need to find a source quickly."

"What am I leaving out?"

"Long bows and arrows."

"Thank you, Master Swain. Nathan is our bowyer in Barmby, so he will need to make fifty bows."

"I'll let him know. We can get yew in Tatecastre, Bert. I'll have Thomas get flax cord to him for the strings." Tenebroides looked back at James. "Arrows?"

"We will need ash for the shafts. Bodkin points as soldiers aboard ships wear armor. Goose feathers for the fletching. Barge crews will make arrows; assign every boat a quantity – we need at least 1,900 in total."

"There are.. thirty-two oarsmen on our four boats. Most were long bowmen and are well-skilled at making and repairing arrows. That is about fifty arrows each."

"Master Tenebroides, we here at the priory were once busy with the bow – put us down for four hundred arrows. If you will get us the iron billets, we will set up a forge here and form blanks for all the points."

"Thank you, Prior William."

"Tenebro you will need to ride south as soon as you are able. The rest of us will meet back here in two weeks. I know it is winter, but what we do now before spring plowing is essential to our success.

Swain rubbed his hands together. "Sir James, your barges will bring in my timber, your weavers will make the canvas, your smith will make the fittings, your bowyer will make the bows…I think we're going to make a fair profit!"

"That is certainly my intention."

Chapter 11

Unrest

The nights are still cold, but winter has finally passed. May is a hard month, even though it is Spring and warmer, because the fields have nothing yet that is ready for harvest. In April, the drier fields have the soil broken up by yoked plough teams for the planting of barley and oats. Now the beans and pease are dibbled seed by seed into the newly turned rows. Haymaking is done by cutting the plants down with the scythe and spreading the stalks out to dry for a few days before gathering them into the barns. If they are not dry, they will rot, and there will be nothing to feed the animals over the winter.

Prior William and some of his brethren have headed east to Supton and Elfwynton with the promised seed grain, four bushels to the acre for the barley, and additional foodstuffs. The villages will need to be supported to some degree until August when that harvest comes in. The crop that was supposed to be planted last autumn of winter wheat and rye will be a sparse one.

There are more peasants in the City of Yorke seeking work and something to eat than usual. Whatever food they managed to stockpile for the winter has run out. Saint Leonard's has a que outside its gate each day of people desperate for a meal. Each day the line seems a bit longer than the day before. Their hungry eyes tug at Katherine's heart, and she wonders if this winter was harder than usual or if it is something else is going on. When she asked James, he just shook his head and shrugged. He did say that if the people were begging in the city, then they are not getting the spring crop sown, and potentially that will only make things worse.

James meets Coletta on the Ouse Bridge at Oliver's. She has a shawl over her head and stands on one side of a corner post and James is on the other. Quietly, he says, "I saw some men lined up this morning that look able."

"Some are. Looking for laborers?" Her eyes focus on the fresh trout in front of her.

"Men of the soil and shepherds to send north. Sig can use a few more, as well."

"That should not be difficult. How many?"

"Six or eight. Another two or three for salt pans in Barmby."

Coletta nods. "Send them to the priory and have them ask for Brother Hugh?"

"Yes."

"If they have families?"

"That is good, if all are healthy. The area is remote." He gets Oliver's attention. "Four of the trout, please." He points on the sly with two fingers to the fish and then to Coletta. He slips Oliver a few extra pence as he receives his trout. Oliver passes the pence to Coletta when she gets hers.

The woodlands and valleys have turned green again, the weather warmer, and the sheep shearing has begun. Wool from James' flocks begins to pile into the barns. From Gainsburgh to Barmby, from Barmby all the way up the Ouse-Swale valley to Richmond, out into Swaledale, to the edge of the North Sea, and on to Yarm over ten thousand sheep are being sheared in the Companie's flocks. His buyers pay hard coin on the spot to secure additional wool that manors and villages committed to sell them along those same river courses and on to Sheffield, Tatecastre, and into the hills farther from the rivers. Wool belonging to Quixley, Graa, and other leading merchants in Yorke is also brought into the barns by their men and carefully labeled for shipment.

Catherine swirls her glass of warm hard cider and considers the last time she had been at this table and smiles.

"I believe I know what you are thinking from that smirk on your face Kate!" James laughs.

"Well, at least I arrived by way of your front door this time, and without a blindfold. It is a lovely dining room." The table that had formerly served for surgery is covered with an expensive cloth. A vase of spring flowers serves as the centerpiece. The voices of Prior William and the young Lady Mary can be heard as they came in from the next room. They had all entered the town-house together to preserve customary proprieties.

"This is a celebration dinner for you, Lady Mary. Roger Elford and his men have been sent back to London by the authority of Prince Edward and the wapentake court. Our sheriff saw them on their way. You are now free to return to Appleton Rabuk as lady of your manor."

The following week, James slips silently through the woods to the east of Po-peltone village where he spent the night as a guest of Abbot William. The Abbey of Saint Mary's owns this village just north of Yorke on the River Ouse. The sun is beginning to rise but has not yet lit up the valley to his left; it is still blocked by the ridge and the trees. He is downwind of the valley, and as yet cannot discern any potential prey through the mists and half-light. Geof-frey is ahead and Paul Fitz-William and Friar Hugh trail behind.

Geoffrey puts up his hand and they all stop, but James still cannot see any-thing in the shrouded valley. Geoffrey then motions to get down and he nocks an arrow. They all do the same.

A herd of deer slowly materialize in the valley just fifty yards away. James pulls his bow to a full draw; the arrow fletching just grazing his cheekbone. When Geoffrey clicks his tongue, James releases as do the other three. The stag raises his magnificent head as two arrows hit him hard behind his shoulder. The remainder of the herd runs to cover, and the men sprint after the three wounded deer. The doe goes down before she can reach the far side of the val-ley and they run past and leave her for Hugh. She was his kill.

The big buck staggered into a thicket just ahead and dropped. James pauses for a breath and grins at Paul as they pull out their long knives. James is exhilarated and relieved; Hugh and Geoffrey are much better archers – he did not want to be embarrassed missing his mark in front of them.

Geoffrey drags his smaller buck back to where Paul ended the stag's suffering. He deftly begins the process of gutting the animal, so that it does not spoil before it can be butchered.

A hunting horn is heard in the next valley. "Sound our horn."

Paul nods and blows a blast. "The abbot's party has been successful too."

It takes another blast to guide the villagers to their location. Once there they quickly dress the kills and tie them over horses for the trip back. A groom dismounts from James' fine coarser and holds the stirrup for him to swing into the saddle. "The Lord Abbot is waiting for you at the bottom of the valley, Sir James."

"Three! Same as us – a good hunt," Abbot William greets him with enthusiasm.

"Your villagers must be respecting the forest laws."

"I have no tolerance for poachers!"

"The deer certainly are plentiful."

"Then we must have another hunt!"

"If that is an invitation, then I graciously accept!" responds James. On the ride back to Yorke it is agreed that one deer will go to each of their own kitchens, another to the Whitefriars, and the three remaining to Saint Leonard's to feed the poor, at James' suggestion, but well received by the abbot. James is hopeful that this will be the start of an excellent relationship with Saint Mary's. The abbey commands extraordinary wealth and influence in Yorkshire and the kingdom. They own many villages, forests, thousands upon thousands of sheep, and parish churches. They also spend incredible amounts of money. The abbot enjoys the very best of food, wine, and the finest clothing and vestments in his manors and palace-like homes. Surely the abbey can be a customer for imported cloth, wine, and spices. Of course, the abbey also charges a toll on the River Ouse; James would like to continue to find ways out of that.

Work in the boatyard now gets going in earnest. The frames of the galley that had been shaped in the open sheds for the last month are pulled out and placed in sequence on the keel. At James' insistence work had been pieced out to other yards to try and stay ahead of schedule and salve any hard feelings. It appeared to him that various council members had shared the Exeter cost estimate, just as it had been shared with him, and then the other yards used it to guide their proposals. When he came in so far under it raised suspicions in them, but fortunately not in the city leaders as they knew his bid came in first and before he knew that others had been asked to submit.

At first Swain had been resistant, but as the frames rose on the keel with their bracing, he grudgingly admitted that they were in a good place on the build. James' view is that there will be a complication at some point that will cause a delay, so be prepared to absorb it. The widest section of the hull is at the theoretical waterline, but it is very difficult to know exactly where she will sit when fully loaded. At the widest point, a 'king plank' is run along each of the frames from bow to stern. This keeps the frames aligned and is the first step to planking the hull. Now they work from the king plank down to the keel and up to the top of the deck rails to form the sides of the ship.

The sawpit at Barmby was created in the peat bog. The advantages were that it was easy digging, and they dig peat and dry it to heat the salt pans anyway. The downside was that it becomes a wet hole in spite of the shed roof as water oozes from the bog to the open hole. Eventually a wooden deck was built on the floor of the pit. Men trade off sawing the planks as it is tiring work. The saw is six-feet long and one man stands above the log and the other below – in the pit. Naturally, the saw dust is always coming down on the man below, so the sawing is done at an angle to try and keep him clear of most of it. The intent is to cut all the planks the same thickness from end-to-end, as well as to each other, so it is skilled work. If there is enough light to see, then a team is working in the sawpit.

On the North Sea coast, Clyde sees the heavy wagon coming across the moors and wipes his brow. He has a batch going right now, so he works almost exclusively nursing the lead pans of alum liquor over the coals. James' directions for producing the alum crystals seems to be working, but you have to mind the pan, or it will burn up. It seems to go from just right to too dry very quickly.

The liquor appears to be the right concentration, so he rakes the coals out from under the pan to let it cool.

"Welcome, Joel." The steward came to pick up the alum in person. "I see you've brought me some people?"

"They need work on fair terms, and you need workers. Be good to them Clyde."

"I will, I will! Any experience with shepherding?"

"Two say they have been shepherds and the others are farmers."

Clyde rubs his hands together in anticipation. "Did you bring me a new lead pan?"

"I did. Is everything going well here?"

"It is, indeed. Let us sit down; I imagine you are hungry."

"I've brought bread, cheese, and ale with me," Joel said as he got down from the wagon. "In addition to your usual food supplies. I've also brought seed for pease and beans; you're supposed to start farming this spring. That's what the new men are about. They can dig shale on two days as James is not expecting you to farm demesne land for him."

"So, their owed labor is on our confidential business. Hard to disagree with farming. We are becoming a larger community here now and need to become more self-reliant. I did understand that message! Their women and children can help gather sea coal on the beach." Sea coal is created by erosion of the land and sea floor. When rain and surf churn the sea floor, or bring down the cliffs into the sea, any chunks from an exposed seam of coal float until washed up on the beach. A steady easterly wind and a low tide is the best time to gather the coal. On many days, the coal can be gathered by the ton. Craning it up the cliff by means of an extended beam, tackle, and mule is the limiting factor. The coal is polished shiny by the sea and burns cleanly with little ash.

"Good, I am glad as I did not want to have an argument. Initially you can use the days they owe to build their own cottages."

"Ah, well, Sir James doesn't mince words with me; never has. We aren't just outcasts tending sheep anymore. I think we're going to become a village over time!" Indeed, it appeared that was exactly James' intention. Finding and digging out the alum rich shale was now the full-time work of four men. A wagon team and three additional men hauled it to piles where it was burned with brushwood and sea coal to get it started. Once the coal that is contained in the shale is burning, the mound is sealed with clay and left for as long as possible; preferably a year or more. Currently six mounds of different ages smolder between the circle of dwellings and the cliffs. Every two months they are supposed to add an additional pile. Then there are still the sheep for the men to mind.

As others came up and help the driver unload the wagon, Clyde and Joel sit down and break bread. No one interrupts, Companie rules – business first; pleasantries later. Do not disturb the 'officers' until their discussion is complete. "Do you have another good quantity of crystals for me?" The word 'alum' is not to be spoken.

"Five bushels."

"We're supposed to use barrels to transport it now. I've brought some kegs that Nicholas made down in Barmby. I brought kegs of piss too; what is that for?"

"Seems to help separate out the good stuff. I don't know why, but it is working, so we do it."

"Dyers use piss, too. Wool?"

"About five hundred shearings so far; still a way to go."

"Not quite to the halfway point, then. How much have you been able to increase the size of your flocks, Clyde?"

"We have about ten score more to shear this year than last." New lambs typically needed a year before their first shearing, "and we have three times that many just born." Clyde quietly said, "That wool buyer you told me about rode through here."

"You sure it is the same one?"

"Arrogant Fleming told me if I didn't sell him my wool, I would regret it."

"Sounds the like same man, Clyde."

"I don't like being threatened."

"No one does."

"He won't do it again."

"Oh?" replies Joel. "He had two men with him."

"I believe he did."

Thomas began to pace across the orchard in Gainsburgh. He needs eighty yards in a straight line for the rope walk, so he continues past the last apple tree and along the manor wall to drive his stake. At one end he places a 'traveler trolley' and the other the 'gear box.' Francis, the reeve from Morton Farm, stands by with enormous spools of flax yarn that had been spun over the winter. Harold, the steward, has three lads to run the thread back and forth down the rope walk.

The lines start at the gear box where there are three hooks. Two threads go from each hook all the way to the single hook at the other end on the traveler for a total of six lines. Now the large wheel on the gear box is revolved. The teeth on the wheel engage with three smaller cage gears, so that each revolution of the wheel spins the small gears many times. The small gears, then, spin the hooks and twist their pair of threads together. Now where there had been six small threads there are three.

At this point the work moves to the traveler with a crank and a single hook at the other end of the rope walk. An acorn shaped wooden 'topper' is wedged between the three lines tight to the hook. Now as the crank spins the hook the three lines begin to twist into one rope and the topper is slowly pulled back. This keeps the twist tight. The wheeled traveler begins to move because as the rope forms it becomes somewhat shorter.

The traveler is returned to its original position and six new lines run back-and-forth to the hooks. This time Thomas stands back as Walter and the boys make the rope. "Widdershins not sunwise" he calls out as they began to spin the wheel in the wrong direction.

As each rope came off the rope walk Thomas sits down to teach Francis the art of splicing ropes together. Finally, the frustrated reeve is elbowed out by his wife. A long splice is being used here to reduce the thickening of the rope at the joint. This involves untwisting the three strands on both rope ends and then winding one of the strands from each rope in replacement of an opposite one on the rope it is being joined to. Each of the six ends are then woven back into the rope in three separate locations, so that in no place is the rope more than four strands in thickness. If a short splice had been used the resulting rope would have a thick spot that might hang up in pulleys. To make heavier cable the new ropes are wound together in the same fashion on the rope walk as the twine had been.

"Sir James, the *Marie* has arrived."

"A full load of wool, Paul?"

"Wool, lead, and first quality cloth. Virgil came by to make sure you knew. He seemed to think it was important."

"Janice has it now?"

"She has two bolts. Two more are on your table upstairs. Why the royal parade?"

"Each bolt is worth almost six pounds." James replies as he bounds up the stairs.

"Six pounds!" Paul gasps. "What does a bolt of good English cloth sell for?"

"Second quality sells for less than two pounds." James holds the bolt up in the light and runs his fingers over it. "This color is exceptional. This is what we need to do more – weave the finest cloth and sell it here; not export it as wool. Parliament has agreed to continue the subsidy to the Crown on wool this year. We will pay forty-three shillings four pence on every sack we export through Kingston again."

"I thought we had to pay the fifteenth?"

"We pay that, as well! Plus, tunnage on wine and six pence on every pound we import or export. Between the cost of this war, the thieving of Latimer and maintaining the king's greedy mistress there is sure to be a rebellion. When this cloth goes on sale Thursday, I want Janice to have some help."

"Protection?"

James looks at Paul intently. "If it is selling, then I want the money secured. There is also the likelihood that it will attract more attention from the weavers' guild."

"Trouble?"

"Unlikely I hope, but possible. Certainly, some people could be upset."

"We had some first quality broadcloth before in the bright blue."

"Just half a bolt; it sold fast and was gone, but I assure you it was noticed."

"I thought I would deliver this parcel to you in person in hopes you might part with any information I should know." Communication from Prince Edward to Sir James typically passed through the sheriff, and though it remained unopened, it provoked his curiosity. James maintained frequent correspondence with the crown prince. The fact that the prince wrote back raised his status with the highest nobility and officials in Yorke. Prince Edward valued independent sources of information throughout the realm and in his present poor state of health delighted in memories of past triumphs.

"My prayer is that my prince is sharing news of his improved health, Sir William."

The sheriff smiles, saying, "I share your prayer."

"Please make yourself comfortable while I see what he has to say." Malcolm brings two glasses of wine and then retreats to an adjoining room.

"This has been dictated; it is not in his hand."

"Is that unusual, Sir James?"

"Somewhat, it may be because his health has worsened. He writes that the Castilians have marched into Portugal and taken Lisbon. Don Fernando has proven to be inept."

"What does that mean for us?"

"Lancaster is supposed to cross the channel with an army to retake the Crown's possessions in France and Brittany with John de Montfort. It is suspected that his real intention is to march on Castile and make good on his claim to the crown. Without the support of Portugal that is no longer realistic. It also means that Castile is now free to send its fleet to support the French against us."

"The prince suspects Lancaster of using the army for his own purposes?"

"He does not say that nor would he. I am reading into things. Lancaster had to surrender the Honor of Richmond to Montfort last year because of his claim to the throne of Castile. To me that means he intends to pursue that claim. How else would he do that?"

"So, your overlord in Richmond has changed to the Duke of Brittany. Is that bad for you?"

"Hard to say; if Montfort loses Brittany, then I may have an overlord in residence, which would be new for me. I think it more likely he will spend his time near London."

"You think we could lose Brittany!"

"I have believed that for some time now."

"How well do you get along with Montfort?"

"Thankfully, quite well; better than with Lancaster!" James saw no reason to relate his new overlord's demands for money to help fund this new campaign.

What will Lancaster do now?"

James shrugs. "He is not one to give up easily, but obviously neither is Henry of Trastámara – the King of Castile. One thing I am sure of, and that is that I have no intention of being persuaded to join Gaunt in a march across the whole of France to win him the crown of Castile!" He read further, "There is more, William de Montagu, the Earl of Salisbury, has assembled a fleet and an army. He is sailing for Saint-Malo in Brittany. Salisbury is a capable soldier – hopefully, he will reverse our fortunes."

"I came by for another reason, as well; a less pleasant one, I am afraid." The sheriff is a bit uncomfortable. "An accusation has been made that your stone barge is bringing other cargo into the city without paying tolls. Is that true?"

"Interesting; who is behind the accusation?"

"You are not answering my question, Sir James."

"The stone barge also brings other cargo – all of which is exempt from the river tolls. Most of it is for the war galley we are commissioned to build for the city."

"Such as?"

"Pine tar, timber, nails, wool for the sail canvas…I have an exemption for that from both the city and Saint Mary's."

"Nothing else?"

"We bring in ale from Tatecastre for the Whitefriars. They sell it in the market; also exempt. If anything else is aboard, it is not my cargo, and that would surprise me."

"I have been asked to board your barge and inspect the cargo."

"I appreciate the warning. You know I could easily contact Bertrand before his next arrival and remove any non-exempt cargo."

"Maybe not; my men should be boarding now just north of Cawood."

"And who made the accusation?"

"For now, I need to protect my informant. I hope you understand."

"Well, my Lord Sheriff, I am beginning to."

"I have a job to do. Don't make this personal."

Prince Edward's letter had some additional information that James had not shared with the sheriff. It was his father's mistress, Ales Perrers, that had manipulated the courts to take control of Lady Mary's manor. He thought it possible that her life had been in peril to end her dower rights. This would clear the way for Perrers to take the manor in her own name. Needless to say, she had not been happy with the prince's interference or with our sheriff's role in bringing the matter to his attention. By this time, it was known that the Lady Mary was under the protection of James. He is suspected of being involved to Perrers' disadvantage.

A man named Richard Lyons has left for Yorke to make her displeasure known. Ales Perrers will use Lyons to make it clear that she could use her influence with the king to have Sir William's property holdings revoked. His term as sheriff lasted one year and was almost over; to lose his manors would destroy his income. The prince thought Lyons would threaten the sheriff to get to James; perhaps that is what is happening now.

"Sir William, our informants were correct!" his bailiff proudly reports. "I have the barge tied up below the castle on the Foss; they are not just carrying stone."

"What else did you find aboard?"

"Barrels of pine tar, timber, kegs of ale, and wool!"

"Nothing else?"

"Surely that is enough!"

"The lord mayor has confirmed that d'Arzhon has an exemption from city and abbey tolls for all war galley construction materials."

"What about the wool and the ale?"

"Supposedly to weave the canvas for the sails. The ale is a consignment for the Whitefriars, Prior William confirms that, too, and, of course, they are exempt. If he is bringing in additional wool or ale; that will be difficult to prove. We would have to inspect every shipment and compare the totals."

The bailiff is crestfallen.

"How did the crew react when you boarded? Did you have any impression that they had been tipped off?"

"No, they were quite surprised, offended, and asserted their innocence certainly; a bit angry, too. If you want me to board them again, then I should bring more men."

"Better release the barge. I do not want to be blamed for a delay on the galley construction or on a late stone shipment to the archbishop's cathedral."

"Calm yourself down, Bertrand, the more merchandise we transport the more agitated competitors will become."

"Sir James, I had nothing on board that was subject to the river tolls!"

"I know it and that is most fortunate. Think about some other barge master paying all of these tolls, and then watching you pay nothing. He naturally will think he is being treated unfairly. So, he complains. I am surprised it took so long."

"You knew this would happen?"

"No, but I am hardly shocked. I thought because we were bringing in materials for the cathedral and building the war galley that those relationships would prevent this sort of thing. I am hoping that since everything was in order on this occasion, the sheriff will hesitate to board us again. For now, make sure none of your crew are bringing personal cargo aboard. Justin did a good job of securing the wool from flocks around Tatecastre, so you will have more to transport. Can that be transferred to Tenebroides on the river? No point paying a toll to bring it into Yorke only to ship it to Kingston." James did not however believe this was the result of a complaint from some lowly barge master.

"I may need to take it downriver to Barmby. It will add two days' time to my return trip."

"It will be a total of about 3,200 clips – just under fourteen wool sacks." A wool sack is the standardized customs quantity. Each sack weighs 364 pounds and typically required the 'clips' of 240 sheep.

"I can move that in one trip if it is all ready for me," Bertrand asserts.

"Quixley won't like it; he would prefer it all be sold in the Merchants Hall. I'll have to speak with him."

"Will, Master Tenebroides left Yorke three days ago. Ride for Barmby and get there before he passes back through on his way north. Tell him that Bertrand was boarded and searched by the sheriff just above Cawood."

James then looked at Paul. "I would like to know everyone that our sheriff is seeing over the next few days."

"That seems only fair. There has been a rotation watching your house this last week."

"Do they follow me when I go out?"

"I did not think so until yesterday, but one follows you and one stays across the street."

"Hmm maybe looking to break in while we are gone. Where do they go when they are relieved?"

"I don't know."

"You should Paul, find out."

"Perhaps we need to have a conversation with one of them in a secluded place."

James nods in agreement. "Tomorrow would be a good time to ride for Hambleton Hills to take possession of our wool purchases there. I will have Malcolm make the necessary arrangements."

Janice the weaver had spoken to the finest tailors in the city and shown them a bolt of the brightly colored aqua cloth. She told them she would have just two bolts for sale at the Thursday market and they quickly called on their most exclusive clients. As a result, all the cloth was sold within moments after the opening bell.

"Will you be getting any more?"

Janice is apologetic. "I do hope so, my Lady; shall I send you a message if I have some?"

"Yes, please, Valentine told me I should get here early but I had no idea it would be gone at the bell!"

"Lady Gisburn, I do not believe it will go so quickly next time, but I do have a shop where I can hold it for you."

Eleven pounds sixteen shillings is quickly removed from the stall by Judd the fellmonger and dropped off surreptitiously to Friar Hugh at the priory's booth where they are selling ale and wine casks to the tavern keepers of the city. From there Will and Malcolm, James' squires, pick up the money and take it to the townhouse. Only the most prominent in the city would see that much money in a full year's time.

"Sir James, the man that followed you through the market today ended up at Saint Mary's and visited a guest there named Richard Lyons. He has been at the abbey for a week. I am trying to find out who Lyons is. He paid a visit to the sheriff this morning."

"Interesting Paul, I already know a bit about Lyons."

"Oh, someone of concern?"

"A very wealthy London vintner, he is involved with Latimer in managing the Crown's finances and customs revenues to his own benefit. So, yes, someone to be concerned about."

"Do we still go to Hambleton Hills?"

"Oh, yes."

The next shale mound had burned for a full year and collapsed in upon itself. This occurs because the burning consumes about half the mass inside of the pile and the outer crust eventually caves in. Clyde and his crew shovel off the crust to expose the pile to the weather and search to see where the grey mass has turned to the desired material. He finds a large pocket and pushes his hands into the good stuff. "This will do nicely. Good work; go ahead and wet it down." That meant to douse the pile with water and urine from the barrels.

He then returns to the previous pile that has been left to weather. Here the task is to shovel the soft pink mineral into carts and take it to the first of the large open vats that had been made by Nicholas the cooper when he had been at Richmond. Buckets of fresh water are then added to the vat and the whole stirred into thin slurry. After a few days, the liquid is transferred to the next vat and the sediment that remains is re-stirred with more fresh water. Then that liquid is also transferred to the next vat, and the remaining sediment cleaned out and hauled away. After the third settling vat the liquid is taken by Clyde to his lead pans and concentrated over the sea coal fire.

When the pan cools the crystals form, but these crystals are not yet pure enough. They are re-dissolved in boiling water and allowed to cool in a barrel. After a week, the hoops are knocked off the barrel revealing a block of pure alum crystals and a small layer of yellow waste on the bottom. They are still a long way shy of the goal of a barrel each week. The crystals are now always referred to as 'antisepsis salts' to cloak the production and are supposedly sold to the wealthy in London. These medicinal 'salts' are used as a valuable skin treatment paste for acne, dark spots, body odor, and foot fungus. As an oral rinse it is claimed to cure mouth sores, bad breath, and whiten teeth. Taken in small doses it is a cure for diarrhea. Clyde is shocked to find that it seems to work for these purposes. The women in the small community beg small quantities to use as beauty treatments, which makes the story highly plausible! Eventually the alum is just called 'natron salt.'

James rides out of the townhouse's courtyard at the break of dawn with Malcolm and Will towards the city gate. Extra men have been pulled in the night before to guard the house in addition to the usual household servants against a possible burglary attempt. At The Swan, they pick up more men and wagon teams for the trip towards Hambleton Hills. Paul Fitz-William had left The Swan several hours earlier with Geoffrey.

"Do you think we are being followed?"

"We will know soon enough. I keep wondering if their intention is to get into the house."

"That would be a mistake today."

"Yes, it would." Hambleton Hills is about equal distance from Yorke and Richmond but to the east of the River Swale. They will be going about ten miles today, which is only halfway to Hambleton, but it is where they have purchased the wool from three flocks of sheep. James is hoping to buy the rights to a village in this area as it is halfway to the North Yorkshire Moors seacoast where Clyde and his companions are, a good area for sheep, and they make pottery here. Pottery would be an additional market item and any village with a craft that kept the people employed over the winter seems like a good prospect.

Just after noon they reach the first village and are able to secure half the clips and get them loaded. They should return in another two weeks to get the rest. James pays the reeve 180 shillings on the spot. No promises of payment later or buying on credit. The reeve and other leading villagers seem more than pleased and anxious for their return. Malcolm and Will cook a dinner for everyone and James attempts to get to know and befriend as many village leaders as he can. As they depart, he seems confident he has secured agreement to purchase their wool again next year.

They get started back a bit later than they hoped, but the journey back is generally downhill, and they make good time. About halfway back they encounter a scruffy pock-faced man that has been badly beaten and robbed struggling to limp back towards Yorke. His legs have been whacked and his shoes stolen. Initially he is very afraid when he sees them, but Malcolm gently cleans up his head wound and bandages him. James carefully inspects his wounded leg. "This is badly bruised, and I am sure it is painful, but I do not believe it is broken."

They help him up into the wagon and pack the wool sacks around him to make him comfortable. "How long ago was it when you were attacked?" James asks.

"Ah'm not sure, but it was certainly several hours past. I've been robbed of my purse."

"Do you want to try and eat something? I've got a bit of pork pie and a flagon of ale if you're up to it."

"I'd be grateful, sir."

"Try to rest and we'll get you to Yorke to see the sheriff."

James laughs. "Oh, yes, we picked him up on the way back. Can he identify you?"

"No. We tied a sack over his head. I assume he will live?"

"He should be fine in a month Paul. What did he have on him, anything?"

"Here is his purse and his knife. It amounts to a little over eight shillings."

"Doesn't that seem like a lot to you?"

Paul nods. "It did to Geoffrey. He would know better what should be in a commoner's purse. No one attempted to break in while we were gone."

"That's almost a shame. It would have been helpful to catch them breaking the law."

"A man calling himself 'Jack Straw' and a peasant mob have taken over Saint Mary's Abbey!" Janice's daughter, Maude, brings the news to the Carmelite Priory and is quickly shown into Prior William.

It is not long before Sir James appears in the study. Maude again recites her message: "A man calling himself 'Jack Straw' and a peasant mob have taken over Saint Mary's Abbey. They have broken into the cellars and beaten Archdeacon Jacob."

As James asks further questions to no avail it becomes clear that little Maude is only passing on what her mother had her memorize. "I wonder where my Lord Abbot William is right now."

"I thought I heard he is hunting again at Popeltone," Prior William volunteers.

"I am certain that our new sheriff, Sir John, knows already but I will seek him out."

"Be careful!"

"I will not be alone. I suggest securing the priory in case they come here next looking for food."

"That I doubt. Did you not hear that Archdeacon Jacob had three men branded last week for deserting an abbey manor?"

"No, I did not hear." James sighs. "No good can come of such an act and now he is in the hands of unsympathetic judges."

Chapter 12

A Bad Bargain

JUNE 1374

Sir John Bygod is the new sheriff of Yorkshire and James finds him in the courtyard of Yorke Castle assembling his men. "You have heard, then, about the uprising?" James says, dismounting. "We have not had an opportunity to become acquainted, I am James."

"Sir James d'Arzhon?" He looks over the twelve men that have entered with Sir James. All are clearly experienced men-at-arms. His few men lack the professional edge of the newcomers. "My predecessor had to send most of his men to the Duke of Lancaster."

"Not an auspicious beginning, Sir John. Perhaps you will allow me to support you?"

"Certainly! All I know is that a peasant rabble have taken over Saint Mary's Abbey and blockaded the gates."

"I am told they have Archdeacon Jacob and beaten him."

"A serious offense with serious consequences. How many of them are there?"

"I do not know their numbers. I am told that Jacob branded several laborers for abandoning abbey manors last month, Sir John. Their leader calls himself 'Jack Straw.'"

"A 'nom de guerre' I imagine. I will not tolerate a peasant mob taking justice into their own hands."

"Certainly not, how do you wish to proceed?"

"We can attack from the city side and gain entry to the abbey compound."

"Easily done but slaughtering them in the abbey until they retreat to the sanctuary of the church is awkward, at best. Might I suggest we discover their numbers and quality of arms to be certain we don't put ourselves in difficulty? A few well-sited bowmen high in the abbey could pose a significant challenge."

"I see your point; we are but thirty and they may have a hundred. What do you suggest?"

"Let's find out what they want. I believe that once their initial passion passes, they will become worried about what they have done. I mean what can they possibly hope to achieve besides being hanged?"

"It would not serve for me, as sheriff, to appear to negotiate with them."

"No, that might embolden them, and my Lord Abbot should not put himself at risk either. Perhaps this 'Jack Straw' would talk to me? Meanwhile we can block the main abbey gate to the west and gather more men."

"I have sent word to the abbot at Popeltone to bring men. The mayor is also attempting to round some up, but it seems that the townsfolk are in sympathy with the miscreants – unbelievable!"

"Dislike of wealthy nobles and the Church has become a popular sentiment. We may need to watch our backs."

James took off his sword, helmet, and gauntlets to slowly approach the north abbey gate. Saint Mary's is perhaps the wealthiest and most powerful Benedictine Abbey in England. The abbot, *the Lord Abbot*, has a seat in the House of Lords. Their walled, over twelve-acre compound, is sited on the east bank of the Ouse along the outside of the city walls and runs from the river up to Bootham. There is movement in the gatehouse… "Halt! You—halt there."

James stops. "I am here to talk to your spokesman."

"Wait, wait there."

Finally, the small wicket door opened in the gate and he is waved closer. "Identify yourself?"

"I am, Sir James. I represent the sheriff and mayor of Yorke."

"What do you want?"

"First to understand what you seek, and then to see if we can resolve any difficulties peaceably."

"You are unarmed?"

"I am unarmed."

James emerges through the gate into the courtyard next to the abbey church and cloister. There are about twenty men there armed with a variety of weapons ranging from swords to clubs and spears. One man does have a bow. None of the men give the appearance of having been soldiers, just field laborers, but it is hard to be sure. They are a mixed bunch. To James they appear to range from wronged peasants to thieves and troublemakers seeking spoils.

"Here is one of our oppressors sent to keep us starving while they live in luxury." The men nod and growl. "What do you have to say for yourself, Sir James? Do you enslave people on your lands, forcing them to work for your enrichment while they starve?"

"May I call you Jack? Surely you have a plan; something you wish to achieve by being here?"

"We have demands!"

"That seems a good place to start, then."

James departs the abbey and meets the others nearby in the council chambers on the Ouse Bridge. "They demand higher wages and the right to refuse work; particularly to refuse working on Church land without any wages. Also, they seek the restoration of common pastureland, and free pannage rights. They had plenty more to say but that is the crux of it."

"Essentially they want a reversal of the Crown statutes of 1361 and of common law!"

"Yes, in part, my Lord Abbot."

"And what of Archdeacon Jacob?" the abbot is in a fury.

"And how many men do they have?" Sheriff Bygod wants to know.

"We did not speak about the archdeacon. As for men, I saw perhaps thirty, variously armed, some with bows, but I did not get to see very much of the buildings or grounds. They are holding some other people there; your guests that were staying at the abbey."

The sheriff asserts, "We do not have the authority to reverse common law nor laws enacted by parliament."

"Not everything here is the law. Some of what they seek could be said to enforce the law."

The abbot becomes wild-eyed. "You think we should give in!"

"I think we should get them back in the fields before we miss the spring planting. If their rights have been abused, then as their lords we have an obligation to protect them. The statutes are a result of labor shortages caused by the plague. We should be able to find a way to give them enough time to work their own fields, so they don't starve. We don't need more of them abandoning the land to line up for meals at Saint Leonard's. That only makes the situation worse for everyone."

"Sounds reasonable to me."

"My Lord Mayor, you are not a landowner." Sheriff Bygod holds several manors.

"The right to refuse work at low wages affects us here in the city, too."

The abbot, reminding them that he is a member of the House of Lords, states firmly, "Fixed wages are enforced by the Statutes of 1361."

"Nobody follows them, though; you have to pay what someone else is willing to pay or no one will work for you," the mayor says matter-of-factly.

"I have three manors," Sheriff Bygod notes. "Common pastureland is, indeed, part of the old rights. I know some lords have taken it away to put more ground to the plow. Some do charge a pannage fee but letting their pigs forage for forest mast without a fee violates no law. However, the land is the lords and how he chooses to make use of it is certainly his prerogative alone."

"Well said, Sir John. If the Church gets the tithe what law forces the people to also work Church land without pay?" poses James.

"How are we supposed to get our work done, then?"

"My Lord Abbot, your manors and villages have typical demesne labor obligations to work them just like the rest of us. How much of an issue is this?"

"I don't agree to bargaining with a violent mob. We have courts if they have complaints."

"True. That is how they should have proceeded: taken their complaints to the courts. Instead the pot boiled over when your archdeacon put a branding iron to some people's foreheads. Allowed by law but not very Christian or very smart."

"They are the ones that broke the law, Sir James; not Jacob!" The abbot is back on a tear.

"But it is landowners that have forced their workers beyond the law. Let us reaffirm the law for Yorkshire with a bit of clarification. We can affirm the legal requirement of the tithe and prohibit additional forced labor to the Church. We can insist that traditional common grazing lands be restored to that purpose and that pannage rights be without charge. We can affirm that serfs owe three days labor each week to demesne lands and no more."

The sheriff nods. "If we are affirming the law and that landowners and workers must follow it... What is to be objected to?"

"We have not addressed the right to refuse work, Sir John."

"No, Mayor, but we have said that a man cannot be forced to work beyond the requirements of the law. I can present that as addressing their real concern."

"What about Archdeacon Jacob and damages to the abbey?"

"We will need to assess exactly what damage has been done to both. The sooner we get them back to the fields and out of your abbey the less damage will be done. Some of them appear to me to be knaves out to loot the abbey's riches and larders."

"We must punish the ringleaders," says the abbot.

"Your desire for vengeance is understandable but will not help us resolve our dilemma."

"Are we to just forgive their damages and let the leaders go?"

James shakes his head. "Preventing them from stealing abbey treasures must certainly be done. They would never be able to pay for any damage, no matter what judgment is made against them. Pretending otherwise is folly. These people have no money."

"That is sadly true. The best I can hope for is to have them out of my abbey as soon as possible without hauling off Church property."

"Our sheriff can state that he will pursue the ringleaders once they have been identified – particularly if Jacob has been seriously harmed. As we do not know their leaders or the real identity of 'Jack Straw' that allows you considerable wiggle room. I'll have another meeting with 'Jack Straw' and then draw up our reaffirmation for everyone's agreement. If they agree, then we can affix the seals of the city, the sheriff, the abbey, and after I speak to Archbishop John with you, my Lord Abbot, he can add his seal."

James reads the proposed proclamation to 'Jack Straw' and the men with him. "No one in Yorke can refute a statute of the Crown. I can't, the sheriff can't, and the mayor can't. Demanding something that is beyond anyone's authority is pointless. This reaffirmation restores your rights under the law. Virtually all of your demands are due to landowner abuses of laborers' rights."

"You write it out and get the seals on it. Then we will have it verified."

"I understand; I'll do it as quickly as I can." They must have someone who can read Latin that they trust. "In the meantime: don't further injure the archdeacon or damage the abbey and figure out how you all get out of here safely and unrecognized. If anyone loots the treasures of the Church, you will all be hunted down. You must understand that. There were now several hundred men-at-arms surrounding the abbey." Those inside are much more sober now and rightly concerned for their lives.

"We want safe passage."

"I will get them to agree to that, but once you are out of the abbey, I am not sure everyone will honor that promise. You have much sympathy among the citizens of Yorke – consider that when you make your plan."

"It is a bad situation, and this will only temporarily quell the tensions, but it will get them back where they belong and out of the abbey." The Archbishop of Yorke shook his head. "I will affix my seal and enforce what is agreed on Church lands, as I am able."

"This sort of a bargain will come to no good!" Abbot John snarls. "They must be punished, or they will be emboldened to make further demands."

Calmly, the Archbishop offers, "Possibly, or trust their betters to redress wrongs through the courts after being fairly treated. James, you must make clear that the authorities will not forgive further such actions."

"I will tell them that they are likely to find forced employment in the Duke of Lancaster's army across the channel if it happens again."

"You may not be far wrong in such a threat. Montfort has been forced out of Brittany. The treacherous Bretons have deserted him and welcomed the Duke of Bourbon and the Viscount of Rohan with open arms to save their own skins."

The mayor gave James a smile. "It would appear that the rebels left in the night through the city and then likely the Monkgate Bar. My men watched the main abbey entrance to the west and Bootham Bar."

"The sheriff is pursuing them?"

"He is James, but he was caught flat-footed and they are several hours ahead."

"I thought we were to pull back to allow safe passage. I certainly did."

The mayor laughs. "He complained that you pulled out after the agreement was presented. That left him too thin to cover the entire abbey perimeter."

"Nonetheless, they must have had cooperation from the night watch and the sentries at the gate."

"I would not know anything about that," said the mayor with a conspiratorial grin. "The sheriff and the abbot were certain they would take the shortest path out of the city. They stationed their men well back to tempt them."

"I would never suggest you might have any knowledge."

"The archdeacon, Jacob, was branded on the forehead. Some of the people trapped in the abbey joined the pursuit this morning. They mean to catch them in spite of the promises made."

"If a fine point is put on it, they were given free passage out of the city. With their head start the deal was kept, even if some do not plan to honor it. If they keep moving and scatter into the woods, then they will get away as long as they did not try to carry off anything."

"Paul, since we have an armed company already assembled please escort the Lady Mary back to Appleton Rabuk."

"How many men do you want me to take, Sir James?"

"Just a dozen mounted; make certain that she is well received there. Stay a few nights to make sure. If any bad actors are still hanging about that will give those loyal to her a chance to confide in you. I may need a bit of a presence here when Lyons and the sheriff return from the hunt. Whether they return empty handed or not, things may get a bit ugly."

"Would you rather we stayed here, then? We can always take her back later."

"No, you will not be far and still together. I will send for you if you are needed. Take Brother Hugh with you. There is no good reason for Richard Lyons to stop at Appleton on his return to London, but if he does, you stay there until he has gone."

"You're expecting trouble for the Lady Mary, aren't you?"

"I just know that these are people that do not give up easily."

"If Lyons shows do you want me to make him feel unwelcome?"

"I want you to make him feel watched and nervous for his safety without any specific reason to do so. I've a letter to Prince Edward for you to post in Selby." Forcing laborers to work for low wages when there was a labor shortage since the plagues is not realistic. The recent unrest in Yorke is not at all the first in England and James is certain it will not be the last. If nothing is done to alleviate the peasants' plight it can only get worse. He wants to make the prince aware of his fears. And, he no longer trusts this sheriff to post his letter.

Katherine looks up from her mortar and pestle to the customer that just entered the apothecary shop. "May I help you?"

"Ah, Miss Katherine Blackwell, haven't I seen you in the company of Sir James d'Arzhon?"

"I don't believe I know you; may I assist you with some ailment?"

"So, how do you feel about the man that promised safe conduct to the poor peasants trapped in Saint Mary's Abbey only to betray them?"

"I really do not know what you are talking about, but I do think it is time for you to leave my shop."

"Some might say a villainous man to keep company with." The man with the London accent stepped very close to her. "You should be more careful."

At that moment, Geoffrey steps hurriedly into the apothecary with two other men. "Doctor Katherine, would you look at this rash on my arm... Oh, I did not realize you were with another customer; my pardon, sir."

"I was just leaving. Do think upon what I have said."

"Is everything alright here?"

"Yes, of course, have you been watching my shop Geoffrey?"

"No, I've been watching the man that just left."

"Is he dangerous?"

"Sir James wants him watched while he is in Yorke. I assume he has a good reason."

"Geoffrey, did Sir James go meet with the men that took over Saint Mary's Abbey?"

"Yes, he did; several times."

Malcolm and Will shadow Sir James from a bit farther behind than usual as they head across the Ouse Bridge to the west side of Yorke. Just close enough to react quickly if something happens on the crowded bridge. He is in a surly mood and best left to his own thoughts. Eleven bodies now hang rotting from hooks over the city gates, and James had stared daggers at the new sheriff as he rode back into the city with his prisoners. The population of the city is restless and seething. They head out of the city through the Micklegate Bar and down to the boatyard to check on progress.

In the boatyard the galley is now fully planked on both the sides of the hull and the deck laid. Bertrand had brought pine tar from Tatecastre, which is being used to seal the seams and make her watertight when tamped in with bits of untwisted rope fiber. Master Swain stops his work and goes to walk by James as he looks around. Malcolm puts his finger to his lips and Swain takes the hint and only answers when spoken to.

"Sweeps?"

"They are ready." The long galley oars had been contracted to another yard to both keep the work moving and spread the wealth.

"Masts?"

"We will step them by the end of the week. Most of the cordage is here as is the sailcloth."

James stops to look carefully at the stern. The ship has a stern rudder instead of the usual side steering oar. This is becoming more common on larger vessels but is new to James. With the steering tiller amidships, the helmsmen will not be as exposed to the weather or enemy arrows. The lines of the vessel are sleek and clean as he sights down the sides of the hull. She should be a fast ship. "At some point we will need to add ballast stones."

"We'll put in some before she slides down the slipway. Then after we see where she sits in the water we will add more."

"I am thinking we should load on stores and a crew of 120 men to understand where the waterline truly lies. Then see if we can find the ideal amount of ballast for speed and stability."

"If we get it close the captain will adjust that as he wishes."

"Provided that he knows his business Master Swain; provided that he knows his business."

"We are being followed."

James does not turn to look back. "I know it. He is one of Lyons' men; the little furtive fellow pretending such interest in Clifford's Tower across the Ouse. Time for this to stop. Is he alone?"

"There is another one back in front of the public house. Judd is back of him."

"As we head back into Yorke, they should switch places if they are working together." They pass each man in succession as they walk towards the wall and ditch of the City. When they pass Judd, James touches his throat with one finger.

James picks up his pace along the city wall before turning into the barbican's dark passage of Micklegate Bar. They are briefly illuminated and then back into the cool darkness of the gate itself. To their left horse drawn wagons lumber through the main street portion of the gate. He ignores the bodies of the recent captures mounted on pikes high overhead. Without looking back they continue along High Street towards the Ouse Bridge.

Malcolm and Will still follow. Close behind trails the man that had been in front of the pub, he is followed by Judd, and finally by Lyons' man that watched them in the boatyard. A heavy wagon drawn by six horses is moving through the barbican as Judd, in the darkness of the gate tunnel, slips behind the huge pier between the side pedestrian passage and the street. As the little man hurries past Judd smashes the pommel of his blade against the back of his head with one hand while yanking him by the collar and thrusting him down into the street in front of the on-coming horses. The driver in the darkness of the barbican sees nothing in the street ahead.

The big horses clop over the man and through the gate pulling the wagon after them. The driver feels the bump under his wheels but cannot see anything as he twists to look back around the side of the loaded wagon into the dark. Then he returns his attention to directing his team down the crowded street.

"I want all of our own wool north of Yorke to go to Richmond to be woven into cloth. The wool from Tatecastre we will weave in Yorke, as well as that from Supton and Elfwynton. Everything else goes straight to the Kingston Customs House for export. There is no point in paying river tolls in Yorke if we don't have to."

"We are buying and producing much more wool this year than you think, Sir James. We have more wool north of Yorke than we can possibly weave in Richmond."

"That is a good problem. How many sacks do you expect north of Yorke?"

"Over thirty sacks and we should use about ten in Richmond."

"So, I missed the mark badly. That is quite an increase, so well done to you. We need more weavers."

Master Tenebroides continues, "I expect another twenty-five sacks from around Yorke plus another six from Tatecastre. Our weavers will use four here."

"How much of that can be moved down the River Derwent to Barmby and then to Kingston?"

"All of it can come down the Derwent rather than through Yorke; if we have a boat to run that river."

"Why don't you pay a visit to Master Gervase; he is no longer being held in Clifford's Tower, but we still have his barge. See if he is willing to work for you. Then tell me your plan for shipping our wool sacks."

The hospitium of Saint Mary's is near the river within the twelve-acre walled abbey compound. Pilgrims and other well-born guests may enjoy the hospitality of the abbey here during their stay. Richard Lyons has left his room to pay a call on the sheriff to see the body of a man trampled by a wagon. Lyon's groom has been called to the stables to attend to one of their horses. While they are absent several of their leather-bound travel trunks go missing.

The hue and cry are raised in the abbey and the gates are locked down, so all workmen and merchants can be thoroughly searched. The quarters of all guests and even the barns, granaries, mill, bakehouse, fish house, brewery, the chapter house, refectory, and in short everywhere is searched to no avail. It is concluded that the trunks must have been spirited out of the compound before the gates were sealed. Several wagons that already left are pursued and searched.

Eventually the emptied trunks and their shredded contents are found at the base of the river wall. They are in the waste of the privy house and covered in excrement. If the tide had come in it would have all been washed down the river. In any case, Richard Lyons is livid; his expensive wardrobe is ruined. Clearly robbery was not the motive.

Both Lyons and the sheriff suspect that the furious Sir James d'Arzhon is behind both crimes. As he has been watched it is clear he was not personally involved, but it is well-known that he has numerous henchmen. Naturally, Sir James vehemently resents the accusations and responds with several insults of his own. There are many in Yorke that are bitter about the heads on the pikes; it could easily have been someone besides Sir James. Lyons wisely determines that he has neglected his responsibilities in London long enough and departs the City of Yorke.

"So, Virgil will bring just over twenty wool sacks in through Yorke. Four of those we will hold for Janice and our weavers here. We can sell the rest at the Merchant Hall or take them on to Kingston. Then we will bring about fifty sacks directly to Barmby and then on to Kingston ourselves."

"Did you speak with Master Gervase, Tenebro?"

"He had some rather strong words about you; so, no, he does not want to work for us. If we can still use his barge, then I can put a crew in it."

"It is legally our barge. Who would you put at the steering oar?"

"Ben."

"Can that be a regular route or are you thinking we would only run it during the wool season?"

"We can bring timber down like we did for the galley construction. Most of the other items we pull from the villages are best brought overland here for sale in Yorke. It is faster. Particularly the fish – which Oliver sells fresh the same day. So, I would say we only run the Derwent when we have a reason."

James presses the tips of his fingers together. "I will see if a craftsman can be found to build weaving looms to match those we purchased from Flanders. I want to be in the cloth business more than the wool business with this oppressive tariff."

"Perhaps Swain knows a woodworker that does finer work and is not employed for the archbishop in the cathedral."

James nods. "Good idea; I'll ask him. Will you find out about the kermes grain on this trip to Kingston?"

"They should have some for me. I want to take as much cloth as possible to trade for it and offset the purchase price."

"Six full bolts of our best cloth are about what you will need to trade for enough kermes to dye eight bolts of scarlets. That's about 224 pounds of kermes grain. So, don't be shocked at the price Tenebro."

"I warned them that everyone may not hold to the bargain, Kate."

"They believed you and now eleven of them rot at the city gates!"

That is the least of it, thought James as many more were killed when the sheriff, Lyons, and Abbot William caught up with them. "If the fools had kept moving and scattered into the woods and fields instead of staying on the road it is likely they would still be alive. Several were caught with abbey treasures. That was stupid and greedy."

"So, now it is their fault they were murdered!"

"In a way yes! They let their emotions drive their actions and did not think through the consequences."

"They trusted you!"

"I cannot control the sheriff or my Lord Abbot, or the thieves among the men that took over the abbey, for that matter. I can only expect that they will honor their word on both sides!"

James resolves to counter the rumor that he tricked the laborers into leaving the abbey under a false safe conduct agreement. When you add up the population of the priory, The Swan, the boatyard, and all the tradesmen and women…plus, their families – almost three hundred people in Yorke have an entwined relationship with James. He has them point to those that actually pursued the peasants versus the man that pulled his men from surrounding the abbey. It does not take long to re-direct the anger of the citizens to what James feels is a more accurate target. They all watched the sheriff and Lyons bring the prisoners into the city.

Chapter 13

Warp & Weft

JULY 1373

The completed hull of the war galley slides down the shipway at high tide with a great deal of pride and celebration. She is christened *le Mare Majstro* by the new Lord Mayor, Roger de Moreton, and blessed by Archbishop John de Thoresby. She has just enough ballast to keep her upright when she floats in the River Ouse. Sir James pointedly ignores the new sheriff and the abbot of Saint Mary's is busy elsewhere.

The high sheriff of Yorkshire changes every year at the end of June as appointed by the king. Typically, they are Yorkshire knights with several manors. The mayor also changes each year; each February third, Saint Blaise's Day, a leading citizen is elected from the city council. Therefore, James knew de Moreton, not particularly well, but he had not known Sir John Bygod at all. If you built a good relationship with the sheriff it did not last particularly long, but if you had a bad one at least it only lasted a year. James needed to wait this one out.

"Well, Brother Hugh, I did not expect to see you in my apothecary again."

Hugh smiles broadly. "I hope I am still welcome here."

"Of course you are. Here for an ailment," Katherine questions, "or is this a social call?"

"Just social; thought I would see how you are doing."

"So, you heard that I am no longer seeing Sir James."

"I did. He can be difficult, at times. Is it fair to say that you had not met Richard Lyons before he came into your shop last month?"

"Is that the man that Geoffrey and two of his men interrupted here?"

"It is."

"Never saw him before or since. Did James send you?"

"He does not know I am here. Lyons has returned to London. He was guest of the abbey when the peasants took it over and forced him to stay there as their prisoner during the conflict. Then he joined the sheriff and abbot in the pursuit of them when they fled. So, if he accused Sir James of double-crossing the protesters, then he was misrepresenting himself and the facts."

"He told me that James promised the people safe passage out of Yorke. He also knew I was seeing James."

"His men have been following Sir James since they got into town, so they would have seen you. So, we started following them. That is why Geoffrey got here so fast."

"Why would he have James followed?"

"That is a question for him. I do know that Lyons is thick with Sir William Latimer, the king's chamberlain. Latimer and Sir James are not on the best of terms. In any case, Richard Lyons had no purpose in visiting you other than to stir up trouble and get under Sir James' skin."

"Doesn't sound like a good enemy to have."

"It is an old acrimony. No, Sir James believes both men use their positions primarily to enrich themselves at the Crown's expense. Apparently, they are very good at it because they have become extremely wealthy."

"I am sure that is not uncommon."

"Probably not, I think their greed goes well beyond the usual. In any case, Sir James did not care for Latimer when they fought in France together, so there is something deeper. I just want you to know that Sir James feels he was played for a fool by the sheriff and the Lord Abbot when they told him they would abide by the grant of safe passage. Sir James pulled all of his men out of the encirclement of the abbey. I can also tell you that he and our new sheriff had some very strong words for each other."

"I'm afraid I had some very strong words for James, as well."

"I am not suggesting that Sir James is an easy man or that you should be seeing him again. I am just saying that if the reason you stopped seeing him is

because you think he betrayed the peasant mob that took over the abbey…
Well, that is not what happened."

"I actually know very little about him after all this time. He is very obscure
about his…um, activities."

"Maybe you should ask him, then."

"Sometimes he says I don't want to know. Do you trust him Hugh?"

"With my life."

"Coletta, I am looking for quick minds and nimble fingers," James declares.

"Women, too?"

"Provided they seem to be of good character."

"The war has caused many women to be without means. Is it alright if
they have young ones?"

"Yes, I find that the need to provide for children creates good workers."

"Just no bug dumb oafs, eh? May I ask what they will be doing for you, Sir James?"

"Hopefully, weavers."

"They'll have trouble getting in the guild."

"I know, but they can work in other places or work for a master. They
need to understand that if I decide to keep them on, then I may locate them
elsewhere than Yorke."

"Shall I send them to the priory?"

"Yes, to Hugh. Have them tell the gatekeeper you sent them."

"Sir James, this is Elias." Swain nudges the man forward towards the corner
table at The Swan. "He was let go by the master joiner at the cathedral and
sought work at my, err your, boatyard."

"I still think of it as your boatyard so you certainly can, too. Elias why
were you let go?"

He let out a deep sigh. "I should have just stayed quiet and done as I
was told."

"Why didn't you?"

"There is a right way to do things and when you cut corners it only creates bigger problems later."

"Have you ever made fine furniture?"

"I was working on the choir stalls and cathedral furniture. That is quite fine work I'm telling you...Sir James."

"Indeed, it is. Do you have a family?"

"A wife and two small ones. She is upset with me right now."

"How well I understand that. Do you have your own tools and shop?"

"I still have some tools. I had to sell some to buy food and pay the landlord. I worked in the cathedral sheds."

"He could work in a shed at the boatyard," Swain chimes in.

"Men that work for me give me their very best efforts, Elias. I expect them to tell me when something is not right, but I also expect them to do as I say."

"I take much pride in my work, Sir James."

"Here is six pence – two days wages. Master Swain, please take Elias to meet Janice the weaver now. "You know where her shop is?

"I do."

"Elias meet Janice, and then go take care of your family needs. Tomorrow morning, first thing, show back up at her shop."

"Yes, sir, thank you, sir."

"Don't sell any more tools."

"I won't, sir."

"Some fresh trout arrived this morning, Katherine! Caught on the Derwent and sure to be good." The fishmonger pulled the canvas tarp back from the tub. "Still swimming in cool water!"

"How much for one, Oliver?"

"For you, one ha'penny."

"I thought it might be more today."

"Never know when I will be wanting a good doctor. Um, in case you wish to avoid somebody, he might be coming through the archway..."

"Please, put one in my basket Oliver; too late now to make a graceful escape."

"Good morning, Kate, I hope Oliver has something to your liking."

"Good morning, James; of course, he does. You well know that he has the very best. Brother Hugh believes I have judged you harshly."

"I thought I was keeping him too busy to get into trouble."

"He told me the Lady Mary was happily received back at Appleton Rabuk."

"That seems to have worked out well; at least for now."

Katherine slipped her arm in his. "I thought you told me that I didn't need to worry any longer."

"There are some that tried to challenge her dower rights to the manor. That has been dealt with for now, but these are powerful people that do not give up easily. I will need to keep a guardian's eye over her."

"Not to mention that she had a horrendous experience."

"That was why I sent Hugh along – to make certain she would be safe there."

"Will she be?"

"I think so. Fortunately, her manor is not far from the river and we are going by often."

"James, if we are going to continue seeing each other I believe I should know more about you."

"I'm just a simple guy with a few barges trying to sell a little broadcloth," his eyes twinkle as he laughs. "Surely that's enough."

"Not hardly." She shakes her head, but she is smiling.

"Why don't I pick you up tomorrow for dinner, and we can talk with a bit of privacy."

Janice strolls through the dyers' workshops, inspecting the various color wools and cloths drying in the sun. Ben, one of the Companie men that had been in the sheriff's custody in Lincoln, is with her. "What are you looking for?"

"Consistent color, vibrancy of the color, and in the case of the woven cloth if it is distressed or deformed after the dying."

"There are not many brighter colors here," Ben smirks and whispers "no alum." All the colors are drab greens, browns, and russets. One dyer named Adam has some brighter colors.

"I was able to get a bit of alum again," he said. "This cloth is already sold, but you seem to have your own sources Janice."

"Well, the dyer does; I am buying the wool already dyed."

The long diagonal spars are hoisted up the masts as the galley nears completion. Next comes the heavy standing rigging that supports the masts: fore stays and back stays. With the masts secure the fighting platforms are erected. From these high perches, archers will be able to rain projectiles down into enemy ships. Fore and aft platforms are built above the main deck. The sides of these are 'crenelated' just like the top of a castle wall, so that an archer can be protected behind the high part and shoot out of the lower.

Then the running rigging, moving lines that control the spars and the sails, is run through the pulley blocks, and belayed to the rails. The heavy iron anchor is attached to three hundred feet of hawser that has been coiled in the cable tier and then raised up to the cathead projecting out from the bow. The ship has a windlass to raise the anchor from the seabed. Rowing benches are built, and the long sweeps brought aboard along with tubs of arrows and the bows as specified in the contract. Stores such as fresh water and food are not part of the contract, but James had Master Swain load the ship to simulate the weight, so to better gauge the waterline. More ballast stones are added until the ship sits in the water just where Swain wants her to be. Finally, the sails are bent onto the spars and attached to the rigging.

"Leave the *Christine* at Barmby and then you and your crew make your way back to Yorke and stay aboard the galley. I do not want an army of two score men on the march for two days from Kingston back here after delivery." The crews of the *Christine*, *Marie*, and the stone barge are to be combined to sail her to Kingston for delivery. Even then half the oars will not be manned, but it is enough to control her with the outgoing tide and keep her in mid-river.

"It might not be a bad show of force after recent events."

"I'll have wagons from The Swan meet you in Kingston with provisions for your return. The last thing I want right now is for our sheriff to think he can solve his recruitment needs for Lancaster with our men. He will believe he has solved two problems!"

"I may be able to sell you some alum if you are looking for more," Ben has returned to the dyers' lane and speaks on the sly to Adam the dyer who Janice thought was one of the best.

"Really? How much would it cost?"

"I need to get four pounds for a bushel with an additional condition."

"That's a steep price. What is the additional condition?"

"You only dye for Janice."

"If I buy your alum, then surely what I do with it is my business."

"Sorry we could not come to an understanding." Ben walks on with the hope that Adam will re-consider and chase him down. He doesn't.

Paul Fitz-William and Diane, the manager of The Swan, join James as they meet Kate at her apothecary shop near Saint Leonard's. Kate is wearing the dove grey dress with the narrow waist, long tight sleeves, and full skirt. She notes that Geoffrey and some other men she recognizes trail a way back in the crowd behind them. Even though the street is crowded, people step aside to let them pass; touching their caps or bowing their heads.

After a cool glass of wine and a dish of pickled herring in a small room at The Swan, Paul and Dianne excuse themselves, which leaves them alone. "You never married?"

"No, I suppose I got myself caught between my social status when my father was living and the reality of my circumstances after he died. The men that expressed interest seemed beneath me or lost interest when I had no dowry. Then somewhere along the way men stopped being interested. You?"

"No, the girl I loved married another and I left for the wars." James is thoughtful. "I guess marriage wasn't much on my mind after that. Campaigning across the continent, always fighting, is not really compatible with being married. I had no inheritance to pass on."

"Campaigning with Sir John Chandos." She touched the broach on her dress.

"Eventually as his squire and then as one of his mercenary captains after I was knighted. Sir John never married, and I suppose I modeled myself on his example."

"Were you with him when he died?"

"I was already back in England. The war in Spain was bad enough to call it quits. If Sir John were still alive the situation across the channel would have never become such a mess." The knock at the door is Malcolm. He brings in a lamb pastry, refills their glasses, and leaves as quietly as he entered.

"And you brought back your men with you?"

"The ones that survived the diseases and had no place else to go when they got back to England. More have come since. Some I served with, and some that heard I could find them work and a place to stay."

"Like the priory."

"Turned out that way. Strange how things happen sometimes."

"Do you own The Swan?"

"That's perceptive of you. I own most of it. Diane has a small share and so does the chef, Michael. Michael is a Companie man and was always a wonderful cook for Sir John. What prevents most from getting established is the initial cost of building an inn, or a boat, or buying a weaving loom for instance. I try to find the right work for our people, or find the right people and set them up in a business I need or want to be in. They get a share and manage it for me. In this case Diane's family owned the little inn that stood here. When she got it, she was heavily in debt."

"Is that the same with Oliver and Janice?"

"Yes, Oliver is a Companie man. Janice has an ability I needed. The cost of the shop and guild fee to get started was an insurmountable barrier."

"So, you pay that and then they work for you."

"And for themselves. Quite a few could buy me out if they wanted to. Some really didn't need my help in the first place."

"Why don't they?"

"I think they still like being connected to the Companie. There is a security there. Sometimes competition, local nobility, or representatives of the Crown can get a little rough. Being alone can be difficult, but when they learn you are not alone, they find someone easier to push on."

"You push back?"

"It usually does not come to that. When you show back up at the tavern where you got hassled with twenty friends the problem usually goes away. Our men also value the comradery. I see that when they come into Yorke, or when I'm down in Barmby or Gainsburgh. In truth I selfishly feel important still being their captain."

"You like the status."

"I do and I did not want to give that up. I guess I feared being a nobody again when I returned to England."

"You could have stayed over there."

"Eventually it became obvious that could only end one way; just like it did for Sir John." They sit quietly for a while.

After a bit, Katherine raises an eyebrow and asks, "You came back from the wars with enough money to do these things?"

"I did."

"Honestly gained?"

"Most was fairly gained as gifts from the Crown or from the ransoms of French nobles. Some was plunder of French towns and great residences. Even that was as I was directed, not with any consideration of humanity, though. Certainly, I caused a greed deal of misery. War is like that, but no one in England is ever going to make an accusation against me for any of those things."

"Are ransoms a great deal of money?"

"The ransom for King Jean of France was 750,000 pounds."

Katherine gasps. "Did you have a high noble?"

"For a moment I did! I was obligated to turn him over to Sir John. He did pay me two thousand pounds for him. Even a knight can fetch several hundred pounds. Abbots and bishops can be very profitable. We did rather well."

"Abbots and bishops!"

"If they put on armor and march into battle, they will suffer the consequences of defeat just like any other noble."

"Was Prior William with you when you were marching through France?"

"He was and gradually became very troubled by it. That is why he decided to become a man of the cloth."

"Are you troubled by it?"

"Not in the same way. He has his own ghosts. My nightmares seem to be about being in battle with my helmet twisted sideways, so I can't see, and getting knocked down with my face in the mud and people trampling over me and pinning my arms, so I can't move or breathe."

"That doesn't sound pleasant. Did that ever happen to you?"

"Not to me. I witnessed it once and it seems to have festered in my brain."

"How long were you in the wars?"

"Just over sixteen years."

"So, now you have a few barges on the river and try to sell a little broadcloth," she said, smiling.

"I was given some nearly deserted villages and I had some men that really were ill suited to work the soil. So, we started out by raising sheep and moving other people's wool to market with the barges. Things just went from there – trying to find goods that we could transport or sell up and down the rivers."

"Such as the salted herring."

"Some of the men grew up as fishermen but they needed a boat and nets. So, we found a boat to buy, had a few more built, and then started taking their catch to market. We started buying salt and barrels, but we could not always get them. So, we started making our own. There are probably twenty-five men working on salt, barrels, and fish now, and that does not include the barge crews that transport it, or even Oliver. If you consider their families – close to a hundred people are supported by our salted herring sales. None of it planned out by me. One thing just led to another. I never imagined I would be involved in fish mongering!"

"But you do make a nice profit."

"I don't really make much on fish. That is partly because we eat much of it ourselves. Sheep is where the money lies: wool, broadcloth, skins, and meat. Like this marvelous lamb pastry. Oh, and cheese. Ewe's milk makes wonderful cheese and that has turned out to be very profitable."

"So, you compete with Quixley, Graa, and Selby?"

"I am a much smaller player. Over six thousand sacks of wool paid customs duties in Kingston last year; I did less than fifty of them. We'll do more this year."

"How many sacks do our leading Yorke merchants export?

"Well, we transported over three hundred for Simon Quixley alone last year and we are not his only shipper."

"What are you going to do with those empty villages?"

"They have actually grown quite a bit. I have not given up on them."

"Did people from your villages take over Saint Mary's Abbey?"

"I doubt that."

"Why?"

"First, the villages are not that close to Yorke, except the priory villages. Second, I think my stewards would have sent word, and lastly, I honestly believe the people feel that they are fairly treated."

"Really?"

"Otherwise they would leave. Several of my villages have grown because the serfs left their original homes."

"Isn't that against the law?"

"It is. I do nothing to encourage them to come, but we try to give them a reason to stay."

"Are you in charge of the priory or is Prior William?"

"Ouch! I said that is a bit strange. Obviously, Prior William is in charge of the brothers day-to-day and of ensuring that they keep to the rule. I seem to have ended up playing the role of steward there, or maybe chamberlain is more accurate as they do have a brother steward."

"So, you manage their finances."

"Yes, but not the daily transactional ones. I have to admit that if I told the brothers to stand up, they would, and if William told them to sit back down, they would likely stay standing."

"So, Prior William does what you tell him to do?"

"Well, I try not to do that and certainly only in private. He does seek my counsel. Are there other things about me that concern you?"

"Why do you have guards everywhere you go? Are you in danger?"

"I...well, I take care of the men I fought with and they think they need to take care of me. I am allied to some powerful people such as the Prince of Wales and that puts me at odds with some other powerful people. Every so often, someone tries to remove a pawn from the chessboard, so we take precautions."

Janice is having the strangest of days. First a young woman, Juliana, arrived with her son and a note from Sir James to 'see if she has an aptitude for weaving' and that Elias the joiner would be returning that morning. She was to put them both to work at the weaving loom. So, she had spent the morning showing them how to use the looms while her daughter Maude watched the little boy.

"I am a joiner not a weaver."

"Elias, I am certain Sir James knows that."

"Then why are you showing me how to weave?"

"I believe he must have a reason." To her surprise both of them were doing a decent job after a short while, but slow! She and her journeyman weaver shake their heads in bewilderment. They would not be able to complete an ell all day. However, the woodworker was meticulous, and she could find no fault with his result. That was unusual.

At mid-morning, a dyer she recognizes enters her shop. "May I help you?"

"I am Manser – a dyer."

"I noticed you yesterday. You do nice work."

"Thank you; another dyer said the man you were with offered to sell him alum."

"I believe they were unable to strike a bargain."

"True. He complained bitterly about the terms. I am willing to be more open-minded."

"I believe that man is still in Yorke; do you want to meet with him?"

"I do."

"Do you know The Swan?"

A sheriff's bailiff stops by the townhouse in Yorke to deliver a parcel from the Prince of Wales that arrived at the castle. Malcolm pointedly confirms that it has not been tampered with, signs the receipt, and then shuts the door without giving a gratuity.

James waves Malcolm to a chair as he slits open the parcel and unfolds the letter. "Our prince is still unwell in body and spirit. Lancaster has finally crossed with his army to Calais and Montfort has joined him. An easy crossing, but that is a long march to Brittany!"

"At least he is out of England and we will not have to worry about being coerced into being a part of his army." Malcolm had no desire to cross back over the channel, either.

"I hope he takes Paris, ends the conflict, and these wool subsidies. I am not sure how long we can continue to afford this war." James returns to the letter. "The prince is troubled by my predictions of more peasant unrest in the future and asks my council on how it might be averted. That will require some thought." Elias the joiner has just been announced.

"I do not understand why you have hired me if the only work you have is weaving cloth."

"Tell me about weaving."

"Well, I don't know what to say. You press the foot pedal down to raise half the warp threads and slide the shuttle through and then you let the pedal up and push the shuttle back through it the other direction."

"Is that all there is to it?"

"No. No, you have to slide a stick between the threads every few passes and pull on it to tighten the weft threads up."

James nods. "The beater."

"Yes, the beater, and when it is time to start a new bolt of cloth it is a difficult job to get everything set back up again."

"How so?"

"Every thread must start from the front roller and go through the…the heddle, that's it, and then onto the back roller. Everything must be very orderly, no tangles, no crossovers and kept evenly taut. Each warp thread is the full length of the final bolt of cloth – some twenty-four yards! There are dozens of them, and it can quickly become a hopeless mess. It took all day for two of us and we did not complete the task!"

"I want you to make a loom just like the two Janice has in her shop."

Elias thinks for a moment. "I can do that. The heddle is a fussy bit of work, similar to a confessional screen in a way, with the vertical slots and thread holes."

Manser, the dyer, is directed to a small room at The Swan when he arrives at the appointed time in the middle of the afternoon. The dinner crowd is gone now, but it is Sir James that rises to greet him.

"Have a seat, Manser, and a tankard," James invites. "You know the terms?"

"Four pounds for a bushel and Janice buys everything I dye using the alum."

James nods.

"I have only twelve shillings; can I pay you the balance after I sell my cloth?"

"I can sell you just the twelve shillings worth if you wish."

"I am good for the balance and I will certainly have it after I use the alum."

"You do nice work Manser. Perhaps we can work something out."

"Such as?"

"What if I provide you cloth, dyestuffs, the alum and you do all of your dyeing for me. I'll pay you a fair wage based on how much cloth you complete."

"So, I work for you? I am a Freeman of the City, a master dyer, and a member of the guild, you know!"

"Otherwise, I would not be trying to strike a bargain with you. I'll pay you twelve p a bolt for cloth. If you can dye six bolts a week and I think you can…that's seventy-two pence a week without the expense of buying cloth, or dyes."

Manser sat back and drank from the tankard shaking his head.

"What do you make now, five p a day? Thirty a week?"

"Close to that after I pay my helpers. Can you assure me I will have at least six bolts of cloth to dye each week?"

"Or the equivalent in skeins of spun wool. Yes. Think of it, you won't have to negotiate for wool or cloth to dye, you won't have to find a buyer for your goods, and you'll be dyeing some of the finest cloth in the city."

"Even less what I pay my journeymen and the apprentice I think I can earn another twenty pence a week."

"Think how much that is in a year. Four pounds more a year than you make now?"

The dyer is still hesitant.

"What if we make a three-month agreement and then talk again; you can back out if you do not want to continue, and so can I."

Master Swain now joins Sir James upstairs at The Swan as his dinner guest. It is just the two of them in the small, private dining room. "I did not know this room was here."

"It was an awkward corner when we added on. I have found it useful. We have received most of the payment for the galley. I have your remaining wages, and a share of the profit. She is a beautiful ship and you have every reason to be proud of her."

"I am quite pleased. Using the other yards to help with part of the work turned out well. Your web of suppliers for cordage, iron fittings, sails, and sawn planking, not to mention all the longbows and arrows – that made all the difference!"

"You've got a decision to make. James sets a coin purse on the table. There is enough here to buy me out of your boatyard, and you can resume the payments to Benjamin, you can keep it all and continue to work for me in my boatyard, or you can pay me half of what you owe me and we become even partners. It is up to you."

Swain sat for a moment and considers while helping himself to another portion of the chicken pastry. "I'm thinking partners. You have been a reasonable and fair man this whole time. I would never have gotten the galley contract to build – you got that work with your connections. If I want to buy you out in a few years is that still an option?"

"I don't see why not. If Elias does well making the weaving looms that may lead to different kinds of work. If we don't have any boats to build, we need to be open to that. If we want to keep your workmen with us, then we need to keep the yard busy."

First thing in the morning, Ben leads a mule cart into Manser's dye-yard. Together they unload twelve bolts of cloth woven by the Flemish dyers in Richmond and cleaned in the fulling mill; then come the bushels of powdered dyes, and finally a half bushel of alum. "I was told to ask for three emerald green, three forest green, three bright blue, and three yellow; and that it should be two weeks work."

Manser looks over the cloth and nods appreciatively. "This is very nice broadcloth. Was it made here?"

"In Richmond by Flemish weavers," Ben recites.

Then his eyes take in the alum and thinks: I have never seen this much alum in my life! "We'll get right to work."

"If there are any difficulties be sure to let Janice know right away."

Chapter 14

Prison

Normally James merely shares what he sees taking place in Yorkshire with Prince Edward in his correspondence. He always chooses not to complain about things like the expensive wool subsidies he is paying on exports to the Crown because that income obviously went to king to fight the war and the prince would hardly be sympathetic. It did not matter whether Prince Edward actually wanted his thoughts on the hardships of the serfs, he had asked for it, and James felt obligated to respond. Trying to explain the plight of people struggling to survive to a man who had never had a moment of want in his life or any desire that had not been immediately attended to is a challenge. James had some difficult times in his life, particularly campaigning across the channel, when meals could be hard to come by, but he, too, had been born to a noble family with the many advantages that entailed.

He started by bluntly stating exactly that challenge. Edward had certainly seen peasant hovels and their poverty while on campaign. He ruled a large number of possessions including the Aquitaine and all of the people living there. The prince had a reputation for getting every penny out of his holdings. Whether he had ever taken a moment to consider the lives of those people was another question. James now asked him to do so. The real issues were around excessive labor demands and constraints on pasture and forest usage. A man's family could be starving near woods full of game or a river full of fish and not be permitted to catch any of it. Lords had not responded to the reduced population from the plague with accommodation. Instead, they had passed laws fixing wages at pre-plague levels and making it a crime to refuse work. Eventually the situation must erupt in a tide that cannot be resisted and will cause great damage. The strength of the realm depends on the strength of the nobility; the strength of the nobility depends on the strength of the people.

On a more personal topic, a noble is expected to ask his overlord for permission to marry. James owes fealty to several overlords because like many others his manors and villages are spread over a broad area. Many are to the north but Montfort, Duke of Brittany, and more importantly for James also Earl of Richmond, is in France, so he asks Prince Edward for permission to marry Katherine. There is no law against his marrying a commoner, but it is not encouraged.

Customs officials of the Crown have now boarded the *Christine* for the second consecutive month in Kingston. "What do they expect to find, Father?"

Tenebroides grimaces at his son. "They are counting wool sacks, skins, and grain before we unload, and wine barrels that we load for the return trip, Peter. I imagine they are comparing that to what we are paying at the customs house to insure that are getting all that they are due." Tenebroides is annoyed by their suspicions.

"Will we be in any trouble?"

"I don't see how. All of this wool belongs to Quixley, although they may not have known that prior to reviewing the manifest. We paid on the skins and the wines. The Hanse paid on the dyestuffs and the officials are already well aware of that. The sea coal we are bringing aboard is not imported from overseas, so we do not need to pay on that. What troubles me is that they are not searching anyone else."

Tenebroides decides to ship any spices waiting in Barmby up the Derwent to Elfwynton in Ben's barge in case he is searched again on the Ouse. From there it will go by wagon to The Swan and the Whitefriars can pick it up in their boat and slip it into the city. The two barrels of kermes for dye will go that way, too.

The priory owns five attached properties near Market Square on St. Andrew-gate. They had been bequeathed them many years ago. Each has a small shop on the ground floor and living space on the floor above. It has taken a number of years for James to finally get the full use of all of them. Prior William was unwilling to evict anyone, and James was not fully prepared to utilize them all yet, so it just took patience.

Janice has been in the first shop and residence above for several years. Last year a smith was established in the yard behind the last shop. This was done in James' usual fashion: Coletta found a capable young man needing work and James made him an apprentice smith in Barmby; he took to the work and was eventually judged capable of running his own forge. Then James spent the five pounds on hammers, anvil, bicorns, and bellows, had the forge built, and shipped in the iron billets from Sheffield to get him started here in Yorke. The boatyard and customers with their horses and wagons at The Swan keep him busy. The walls behind the shops that separated the lots into individual yards are removed to make one large courtyard. The wall material is reused to build a stone warehouse across the back of the space after Katherine declines to move her apothecary and herb garden there.

Now a bakery, pie shop, and an ale house are established in the other shops to take advantage of the opportunity presented by all the workmen swarming over the cathedral construction. The second floor is opened up into a weavers' workshop and a common space. The third floor is expanded with dormers and windows in the gables to become the sleeping quarters. It is into the second-floor workshop that Elias assembles and finishes two new looms. Another young woman is working there now. She was also sent by Coletta.

Sheriff Bygod's bailiff and men board the *Christine* for inspection as it docks in Yorke. Master Tenebroides has to tell his men several times to stand aside as the barge is searched. Crates of tools are dumped out as are the baskets of sea coal and salt into the hold and onto the decks. The baskets of eggs and the chicken cages are tumbled. Then they dump over the six barrels of salted herring and smash in the tuns of wine. Only the sheep and the hogs are left untouched. The crew spends the next few hours putting fish back into barrels and shoveling up the sea coal. Tenebroides files a complaint with the City Council and goes to meet Sir James with the news.

"If you stop coming upriver to Yorke until spring, and only work the lower river from Selby to Barmby to Kingston...what is the cost?"

"Everything we've worked for, Sir James!" Tenebroides exasperates.

"The wool we planned for export this year is already gone. We can sell salted herring to the Hanse in Kingston."

"It will not bring as much and we will have to pay export tax," he complains. "But yes, we can sell any surplus harvest to the Hanse if you want to and get a reasonably good price. This is Quixley's last shipment of wool for the year," he begins ticking items off his fingers. "I can send enough grain up the Derwent to supply The Swan and the bakery. Sea coal and iron billets for the smith can go that way, too."

"Cloth can go down the Derwent and the Hanse will buy that."

"Provided the sheriff does not board Ben's barge."

"True; so, the biggest losses will be to Oliver and Owen the butcher."

"All of our sales at the market too. We won't have dyestuffs to sell to the Hanse."

"I will not have a surplus to sell if the dying here continues to go well. Tenebro, anyone that attempts to board the barge on the Derwent should be assumed to be thieves and Ben needs to be prepared to act accordingly. Do you understand me?"

"I do!" he replies with enthusiasm. "There are two barrels in the hall behind the Prior's study. The top is wheat, but the bottom is Kermes."

"You sent that up the Derwent?"

"I did."

"We paid the import duty?" James asks.

"The Hanse did, and I have their certification."

"Why the wheat, then?"

"I thought it best to disguise it because of the value."

"When Ben goes up the Derwent with spices or kermes, I want outriders on the shore."

"On both banks?"

"Just this side. Six Companie men should suffice. If someone attempts to ambush that barge…"

Roger de Morton has finally located James at The Swan. "There you are!"

Rising, he says, "My Lord Mayor, please join me and tell me what brings you here." Diane hurries over with a loaf of fresh bread and another tankard of ale. "Sorry, no wine today."

"Yes, I heard. A fishmonger, butcher, and poulter have given notice that they will not be paying the stallage for next month and the foreseeable future. Apparently, they said that their supplier is no longer going to be coming to Yorke. That's your barge isn't it?"

"It is."

"So, they just stop doing business here?"

"If they have nothing to sell…"

"But you can bring more!"

"As you know, Mayor, that has become a problem. I am attempting to find other markets where things are…less troublesome shall we say. Surely I do not bring enough food into the city to be noticed when I stop."

"I think that the absence of Oliver and Owen will be noticed, and I am always concerned about victualers in my city." The mayor is exasperated.

"There are other fishmongers and butchers. Your problem is not with me. If the sheriff compensates me for the damages and agrees to stay off my barges, then we can talk again. I've already told Archbishop John that if the sheriff boards my other barges and destroys merchandise, then he will need to find another way to transport his stone and a supplier for lead."

"You have every right to be angry, but let's see if we can work things out. I've already protested to the sheriff and I'll bet the archbishop will, too…"

"I have spent a lot of effort in Yorke, and it would be a tremendous setback if I need to start over elsewhere, but I will do it."

The sheriff and his men arrest James outside the market. There is no warning or opportunity to resist; not that resistance to the king's appointed sheriff is a viable option. He is accused of not paying the wool subsidy on his exports and confined to Yorke Castle in a tower on the east curtain wall. These are fairly comfortable quarters as befits his rank and he is permitted to walk in the bailey twice each day. Bygod is cautious about pushing a knight of the realm and a man well-known to be loyal to Prince Edward too far.

There are three small windows in his room looking out onto the River Foss. He is allowed visitors and may either purchase food from the garrison or have it brought to him. Obviously, he chooses to have it brought in twice each day. The meals are inspected, and a guard is always in the room when guests are there. The exception is the servant he is allowed and this alternates between Malcolm and Will.

"The guard made a hell of a mess of Sir James' pie. Stirring it around making certain nothing was in there."

"Likely just spite, Malcolm." Tenebroides shakes his head. He is uncomfortable sitting in James' study. Not only does he not like being cooped up indoors but he does not like serving as the Companie captain, even if Sir James remains in daily contact.

"James wants Oliver and Owen to set up their shops in Richmond. He thinks the fish weir in Brecken and our villages on the upper Swale can keep them supplied."

Tenebroides nods. "Alright, I'll tell them. Virgil can take them along this trip. We will stop taking sheep, hogs, and chickens to Yorke and keep them up north. Anything else?"

"He wants Joel to make the village of Wilsham disappear. We're supposed to help."

"As in kill everybody and burn it to the ground?"

"No!" Malcolm laughs. "As in relocate everyone and everything of value without a trace."

"Where is Wilsham?"

"A little more than halfway from here to Bollebi."

"Up in the North Yorkshire moors?"

Malcolm says quietly, "The village belongs to our good sheriff."

"Interesting, I am starting to get the idea. Bygod is to understand that he is not invulnerable. He is to know in his gut that we are behind his loss without having a shred of evidence to support the notion."

"That's the sense of it, and it will give him other things to worry about besides what might be in our barges. Sir James has too much time to think while he is sitting confined in the castle. He gets more restless, and surly every day."

"Where are we to put these villagers?"

"Should be about sixteen families. Joel knows the place – tried to buy their wool in the spring. Move some to Bollebi, some to Brecken, and some to Richmond."

"And what if these peasants don't want to go?"

"Sir James does not think that will be a problem. Some of their men took part in the protest and never made it home. Their widows are still there for now. I don't think they want to stay; they just don't have an alternative."

"What about the reeve?"

"He seems to spend most of his time here in Yorke."

"What if someone talks?" Tenebroides worries. "Someone always does."

"They risk branding and a forced return to Wilsham. Once they are with Clyde up in Bollebi who are they going to tell?"

"I'll ride to Richmond and speak to Joel. Tell no one else about this Malcolm. No one."

"Paul is in charge while you are gone?"

"I'll let him know. I think I will take Brother Hugh with me."

"Sir James wants Hugh to check in on the Lady Mary in Appleton Rabuk."

"Prior William and Geoffrey can do that. I'll tell them."

"Sir James said to tell Hugh that the attack on Mary was no accident."

"In that case I will send Paul Fitz-William along, as well!"

"What exactly are you being accused of?"

"I am charged with not paying the wool subsidy to the customs house in Kingston."

Katherine rearranges the skirt of her emerald green dress. It is difficult to have a candid conversation with James' jailer standing nearby; she wants to frame her questions carefully. "Are you concerned?"

"Any time you are accused by officers of the Crown and taken to court it is a concern. I am not concerned about these charges, though. I have paid the wool tax on every sack exported and I have the documents to prove it."

"Then why are you being charged?" She is careful to act indignant and not worried. Hugh had told her to act aloof and ignore the sheriff and his men as if they were not even there. 'Surely you have known women like that?' he had asked. She had known many. Aristocratic women in London of noble birth could make you feel small and insignificant when they choose to. Hugh had said that was exactly the sort of woman she needed to be if she visited James. In this expensive dress and jewelry, the act came off more easily than she had imagined.

"There are several possibilities. It could just be a simple error: the customs officers are counting wool that we are shipping but do not own."

"For Simon Quixley."

"Quixley and Graa; Tenebroides shipped over five hundred sacks of theirs to Kingston. Once in Kingston it is up to them to pay the subsidy on their wool, and I am certain that they paid. They have both been here to see me and to see the sheriff."

"Then the charges should be dropped!"

"I think when the evidence that I paid over two hundred pounds to the customs house this year is shown to the grand jury, and Quixley and Graa attest that the rest of the wool is theirs it will seriously injure our sheriff's reputation." James said this clearly enough for the guard to hear well. "When the mayor, archbishop, and several leading citizens are telling you they intend to attest to a man's reputation in court it may be time to listen."

"Yet you are still here."

"It may be that certain other factors are at play."

"Such as?"

"The customs agents may be being pressured by Richard Lyons because of my wool purchases this year. His mother is Flemish, and he represents the Fleming merchant interests in London. We bought wool that they expected to buy again this year out from under them. Some of the Flemish wool buyers were angry enough to make some threats to both my buyers and the sellers. Lyons, and Latimer, for that matter, represents the king's monetary interests in customs collections. Using their position to intimidate through the Royal Courts is certainly a real possibility."

"Base vindictiveness, then."

"It depends upon how suspicious you want to be. Sitting confined here seems to make me very suspicious. This could also have to do with our recent disagreement over the peasants' take-over of the abbey. Or my role in thwarting Ales Perrers' attempt to own Appleton Rabuk."

"Now you are…" She wanted to say, 'frightening me,' but instead, she said, "…infuriating me! This is just another way to try and remove a 'pawn' from the chessboard, then! What can you do?"

"The Royal Court of the Exchequer's judges of the King's Bench come twice a year to settle cases in Yorke. If the charges are not dropped, I sit here until then. Normally that would be another three months. I understand that they have been told to be here within the month," he lifts a letter off the side table in evidence. The messenger had been instructed to give the letter directly to Sir James and not to the sheriff; although certainly the sheriff did know that it had been delivered. "His Royal Highness, Prince Edward, also sends you his personal greetings, Kate."

"Oh, what nonsense!"

"Second paragraph."

"The Prince of Wales has given you permission to marry me."

The sheriff's men search Virgil's barge but do not do significant damage, other than from a little clumsiness spilling grain as they dig through the bushels. Perhaps the complaints of the mayor have not fallen on deaf ears or, more likely, Master Tenebroides' suit for damages has gotten Bygod's attention. It really makes no sense as the *Marie* is still free from river tolls because of the lead she brings for the cathedral. While some in the City Council resented the exception, nothing had been done to cancel it. It seems that if the council intends to get in another legal squabble with the archbishop it needs to be over a far bigger issue. If they owe no fees, they can hardly be trying to avoid paying them. They did not find any alum aboard.

If the search had not taken place as they tied up at the city wharf but, instead, along some remote stretch of the Ouse...Virgil would not have been so restrained. Instead, he just seethed.

Joel and Brother Hugh drive the wagon east from Richmond into the North Yorkshire moors. He brought inexpensive cloth and some tools along for his stop in Wilsham. It is unlikely they have any money to purchase his goods, but they might have something to barter; they should be bringing in the harvest now. In any case, it gives him a reason to visit and see what is going on in the village. The reeve should be present during the harvest to oversee his lord's demesne lands and the tithe. If he is going to evacuate this village it will have to be after the harvest and when the reeve returns to Yorke, provided he does, but he and Hugh may be able to learn a great deal. If they sell nothing it is no loss, Clyde will be able to use it all in Bollebi. Which is their eventual destination.

It turned out that the reeve's son assumed his father's duties for the harvest. It was also obvious that he is not well-liked. Wilsham has seventeen cottages, which include the reeve's and the three recent widows from the uprising in Yorke. They are still working on bringing in the harvest from the lord's fields, and as they are shorthanded it is taking a long time. Only when that is completed will they be able to bring in their own. They work sullenly and look at the sky hoping they will be able to get it all done before it rains. If they are going to get the villagers to desert Wilsham, then the reeve and his family need to be considered.

Lord William Latimer and a modest entourage canter through the gate of Yorke Castle. "My Lord, we only received word of your coming early this morning!" Sheriff John Bygod stammers as he holds the lord chamberlain's bridle for him to dismount.

"You have suitable quarters for me here in the castle? I understand that Saint Mary's Abbey is not secure from criminal mischief. I do hope that you are more efficient in these matters than your predecessor."

"We do, indeed, my Lord." Sir John had cleared out his own sumptuous suite for Lord William's use just moments before his arrival.

"I will take some refreshment and then pay a visit to the prisoner."

"This is a rather comfortable accommodation. Too comfortable, I should say; that will have to change. See to it, Sir John." Lord Latimer ignores Sir James for the moment and began to peruse the correspondence on the side table. "You are checking all of this? You must not make it too easy for the prisoner to continue to conduct his criminal business."

"I do, indeed, check everything coming in or going out of this room."

"Hmm, it appears that Prince Edward is aware that you are inconvenienced. You continue your attempts to make a fool of a very sick man. How pathetic."

"He is not nearly as easy to play for a fool as some might think," Sir James responds.

"Ah, yes, always so clever, but nearly as clever as you think you are. There are no customs receipts for any alum imports sold to you through the Hanse at Kingston or Boston or Yarmouth or any other English port. You will be forced to prove your compliance with the king's laws, or you will sit here until hell freezes."

"I have been respectful of letters from the crown prince, my Lord! They are delivered from the courier directly to his hand by order of the prince."

"He plays to your fears, Sir John."

"You should know that d'Arzhon's men watch and report everyone that enters the castle. They know that you are here. In fact, the Lord Archbishop is paying a visit to Sir James, even as we speak. No doubt alerted to your presence here and insuring his welfare."

"A meddlesome old man. Move d'Arzhon to a cell without any windows. Stop coddling him as though he is of man of importance. A fortunate looting of treasure on campaign does not make him a worthy noble. He and his base-born criminals are undeserving and never should have been allowed to return with it. You are too lenient; far too lenient. Time to squeeze him."

The night is cool, and the Foss is warm, creating a thick mist as Brother Hugh and the Whitefriars row from the Ouse back up towards the quay of the Carmelite Priory. Tenebroides slips over the side of the boat without a splash and swims noiselessly to the bank at the base of the castle wall. There is a moon, but this side of the castle is in darkness as he climbs up the steep bank to the base of the tower's batter. The batter provides a wide foundation for the tower and makes the task of siege engines or miners more difficult trying to bring the tower down. It is a steep incline, but the mortar joints are worn and provide easy handholds. He sits at the top of the batter with his back to the corner where the tower meets the curtain wall, takes a rest, and listens for anyone sounding an alarm.

It has been many years since he climbed his way into a castle at night. The garrison is fairly small, perhaps a score, and most of them should be asleep. Those awake are tasked with guarding the scores of prisoners and the gatehouse. The tower is nearly vertical as he begins the climb. It has not been well-maintained; too expensive to repoint the joints between the stones. He finds toe holds in the corner on both the wall and the tower easily. Tenebroides is a wiry and tough little man used to the outdoors and the rigor of life on the river. He keeps his hips tight to the wall and stone by stone works his way to the top. A thin line uncoils from the bank below tied to his belt as he ascends. At the top there is no sentry on this section of the wall. There may be one atop the tower, but he does not hear a sound. Always easier to slip into a castle when they are not expecting it. He has climbed into some during a siege, but that requires a diversion such as an attack on the opposite wall to occupy the defenders and create noise and confusion. Slowly he hauls up the thin line, hand over hand, until he feels the heavier line attached to the end of it. He hooks it unobtrusively to an arrow slit in the battlement.

He understands Latimer is staying in the sheriff's usual quarters. Thinking about Sir James in a situation where he is at the mercy of his enemy is causing a physical pain in the pit of Tenebroides' stomach. If anything happens to him while imprisoned, he will do what he has wanted to do for years and no one will talk him out of it. Once inside the castle, Tenebroides walks boldly across the bailey towards the range of buildings built against the curtain wall. The door is closed but not secured. He heads up the staircase at the end of the great hall. A hound raises his head and then goes back to sleep. The door to the sheriff's suite is closed. He knocks softly and then turns the handle. Locked. He knocks more loudly and hears feet shuffling towards the door over the snoring.

The door is unlocked and opened. "What is it now?"

Tenebro's knife slashes the sleepy man's jugular vein as his gloved other hand smothers his cries. The gurgling soon ceases in the man's throat. Another man slumbers on his side facing the wall. He never even struggles.

"It would appear you have traitors right under your nose! You are an incompetent fool!" An understandably furious Lord Chamberlain rages at the sheriff the next morning. "Two men in my antechamber, right outside my very door, murdered in the night. It is only by the grace of God that I was not murdered, as well. What are you doing to find the murderer?"

"The gates all remain locked. We are searching the grounds and questioning everyone here."

"I certainly expect you will have the bastard before long!"

"There are courts here and administration of fines and revenue collections. Many people come and go each day. The entire grounds are not thoroughly searched before we lock-up for the night. It could be anyone, although as yet we have not found someone that should not have been here overnight," responds Sir John.

Latimer screams, "You know full well that schemer d'Arzhon is behind this!"

"Entirely possible, but he was securely locked in a windowless cell with a guard outside and spoke to no one."

"He has stinking criminals in his employ. You are afraid of him!"

"I am certainly not afraid of him. Unless I can find the man that actually committed the murders and then get a confession out of him, I will have a tough time proving Sir James' guilt.

"He gave the orders. Hang him!"

"His servant was dismissed upon your arrival. After that he saw no one."

"You are just a damn coward," Latimer snarls. "It is obvious to me that one of your men has been treacherous. Find the one in the pay of d'Arzhon!"

"Perhaps one of your men decided to settle an old score last night!" The sheriff responds angrily to the accusation, "They were heard gambling and arguing. Who else would they have unlocked the door for?"

"Bah! Find someone and make them confess. If you can't find someone, I will!"

Each of the guests at the castle have been questioned. All of the sheriff's men-at-arms present last night are berated endlessly to no avail, particularly those on duty. Sir John and Lord Latimer are now out of patience with each other. In any case, Latimer has no intention of being murdered in his sleep.

"When I come back, I will bring my own guards and d'Arzhon had better be ready to tell me everything I want to know!" Latimer is nearly screaming. "Or you will both be sorry!"

An uneasy sheriff considers the murders in the castle. He hires more men to the garrison despite the expense. While he believes it most likely that somehow d'Arzhon is responsible, there are other possibilities. Lord Latimer is reviled by many. If it was d'Arzhon, then is the message: you are not safe in Yorke Castle if something should happen to him? Most of the prison cells are grimy, foul holes. He returns Sir James to his previous quarters after the lord chamberlain's hasty departure as the lord archbishop promised he would be back today. The prisoner gives no indication he is aware of what took place in the night. James blinks his eyes in sleepless confusion as he is escorted out of the dark cell.

The sheriff is an unhappy man. His efforts to do his duty as ordered by the king's chamberlain have left him at odds with the mayor, the archbishop and the leading citizens and merchants of Yorke. Not to mention Sir James and his men. Men that are willing to resort to violence when they think it is necessary.

"And sometime in the future, you are not going to regret having made a poor match with a commoner?" It has been a few weeks and Katherine is still considering James' offer.

"I simply wrote him that you were a most uncommon woman and I always look forward to your company. Kate, I am nearing forty years old now and I have no desire to be matched with some child because she brings a large dowry. The king is not going to raise me to the peerage, no matter whom I marry; nor am I seeking it."

"Yet you spend a great deal of effort to make money, increasing your lands, and influence. The right marriage could help all of that."

"I can do that without the marriage. Such a match can also bring difficulty and attention that I wish to avoid. Do you not wish to marry me?"

"James, you know I do love you. I have just been on my own for quite some time now – without a man telling me what I can and cannot do. You will want me to live in your house."

"Certainly."

"And give up my apothecary and garden."

"I have never thought you would be willing to do that. You will not need the income if you choose not to."

"My work at Saint Leonard's?"

"If you wish to then, of course, you may. That is important work. There are quite a number that may need your expertise in certain manors, villages, barges, and a priory for instance that I am apt to think should come first."

"Your manors and villages."

"Yes."

"We have never really talked about all your holdings. Just barges, wool, and cloth. May I ask how many people you are talking about?"

"I don't know how far from Yorke is sensible unless I am going too, but here alone we have almost five hundred souls when Elfwynton and Supton are included."

"I had no idea. How can that be?"

"The two villages I just mentioned, the priory, The Swan, the boatyard, two barges, shopkeepers, and workshops and, of course, their families. Even just at the house: Malcolm, Will, Paul, Geoffrey, grooms, cooks, maids—all their families live here, me...soon you and your maid?"

"You have also mentioned holdings in Richmond, Barmby, and elsewhere. How many in all?"

"With Yorke, well over a thousand; we keep growing and they have ailments and injuries that go wanting for expert care."

"I am going to need a bigger herb garden."

"I'll find gardeners to help you. Do you want your own lawyer to write up the contract before we post the banns?"

"I will write it out myself and make you sign it." She laughs. "If you get dragged off to prison again and again before we have children, I will need some security! Assuming you get out of here at all!"

"Children?"

"Clyde arrived today."

"Problems Malcolm?" The weeks confined in Yorke Castle have James agitated.

"He came through Settrington recently." Sheriff Sir John Bygod's primary holding is the manor of Settrington. The estate is not too far from Scarborough and Clyde's little hamlet of Bollebi; it is on the way south to Yorke. "We still want our sheriff to have a run of 'bad luck'?"

"This does not sound good. What did he do?"

"Nothing yet. He says that the manor house is sited below the mill pond, and that the levee is not as well-maintained as it might be."

"Let's keep personal residences out of this. There needs to be some limits of propriety."

"I'll tell him. He just wanted me to ask you about it."

After eight weeks confined under arrest in Yorke Castle, the judges of the King's Bench arrive. James is released before a grand jury is even convened to weigh the evidence. Sir John Bygod, the sheriff, had to be satisfied at having put him in prison for a time. James already had the rumor spread in the city that this was the sheriff's petty retaliation for his trying to resolve the uprising peaceably. The citizens of Yorke are ready to believe the story, which actually may be completely true, after the executions and news that Lyons and the sheriff killed many other peasants that they caught became broadly known. This release before trial seemed to substantiate that the charges were spurious.

The leading merchants in the city are quite agitated with the sheriff's actions of imprisoning Sir James and the destruction of merchandise on his barge. They all use the river to ship goods and are subject to the tariffs on imports and exports in Kingston. A threat to one is a threat to all.

"Manser has been questioned by the city bailiff on his alum supply," Janice confides to James.

"Alum is a common item for dyers. Expensive and sometimes hard to get to be sure, but not something out of the ordinary."

Janice had slipped out the back of her shop and then to The Swan to meet with Sir James as she had arranged. "We offered to sell the alum to another dyer first, but he would not agree to our terms. He has complained."

"On what grounds?"

"That the alum was not sold at the market as is required by the city but was an arranged sale. Manser told them he did not buy the alum, nor does he own it or the broadcloth. He is being paid wages to dye the cloth. They asked who pays him and he did tell them he brings the finished product to me and receives his pay."

"The city only requires that *victualers* must sell at the market. Has the bailiff come by your shop?"

"He came by with that dyer today, but they only looked at what I have to sell. They did not ask me any questions. The other man is named Adam; he is dean of the dyers' guild. I am recognized now as one of the best clothiers in the city. No one else sells the fine colors or quality of broadcloth that I do."

"That is exactly what we sought to achieve. I will have a discussion with our lord mayor. Surely we can bring raw materials into the city for our own use without also offering them for sale at the market."

"I thought you wanted your involvement to be somewhat unknown."

"It may be time to show myself as a larger factor in the commerce of the city."

Clyde and his party come down from the north and help get Wilsham's flock of sheep moving along. They have just over twenty miles to go and he wants this particular flock on the far side of Bollebi, so that anyone trying to find them will have to go past several flocks first. That should obscure any trail. Four families come with the sheep and help to herd them along. Their harvest and worldly goods are packed in two wagons, which Clyde sent along the old road out of Wilsham east and then north. Brother Hugh went with the wagons and the women. "Clyde, these people are trusting us only because they do not believe they can survive where they are now. They are leaving everything they know. They are our people now."

The plan is to keep them hidden for a year and a day. A year and a day and they are freemen. The reeve's son had gone to Yorke after the harvest. May God keep him there through the winter. Clyde looks skyward and crosses himself, then shakes his head; it is a long time since he had prayed. Joel and his men have taken the other twelve families west towards the River Swale.

Prior William slips up the back staircase into the townhouse to see James. "How is the Lady Mary managing, William?"

"She was glad to see us. They had some unwanted guests, so I was glad Paul brought so many men over my objection."

"The guests thought it best to end their stay?"

"Indeed, they did. I was not part of that conversation and I did not ask for details. The manor steward was visibly relieved when they departed."

"No notion of whose men?"

"Paul may have an idea. He did not hesitate to let them know they were not welcome!"

"The Companie has taken a very protective stance over our young Lady Mary. Another item my old friend – Katherine and I are hoping you will witness our wedding. Just vows at the door of the priory church…nothing elaborate."

"My congratulations! I will be delighted, of course. I am sure she is getting another new dress out of this."

"She is writing up a contract in case I am thrown into the Tower of London for life."

"I correctly judged her as a perceptive woman, then. If Prince Edward dies your enemies may have a free hand."

"You still know nothing about women, so it is good that you have taken a vow of celibacy. Everyone has constraints on their actions, but things could get rougher. He did give us his blessing."

"The prince?"

"Yes, it seemed best to ask. He also wrote that Salisbury has returned to England after relieving the siege of Brest; du Guesclin withdrew his forces at least for now. That is some good news from Brittany for a change. Lancaster and Montfort continue their march across France, so perhaps the tide has turned."

"Any other news?"

"Your villages had a decent harvest from the spring planting."

"They will survive the winter, then, but I meant from London," for most Englishmen, including Prior William, any news from London is of interest.

"No rye or wheat, of course. I've sent seed to them, so they can get a winter planting in now. At your expense, of course. There has been little news from Lancaster."

"I understand. Thank you, James, I realize that you are turning the situation to your advantage, but they benefit, too."

"Certainly, I've got them busy in many ways now. The priory also benefits."

James and Katherine go together to post the marriage banns outside the door to the city council chambers on the Ouse Bridge. This public proclamation provides the opportunity for anyone to raise a legal or religious objection. As James had spent much of his adult life across the channel it was unlikely anyone would claim that he was not free to marry. The couple certainly are not related.

"You asked to speak with me, Sir James?"

"I did Roger and it is good that Thomas is here." Thomas Graa is a leading citizen of Yorke, as well as a wealthy wool merchant.

"If this is about our sheriff, both the mayor here and I have made our complaints known to him."

"I appreciate that. This is another matter. I am paying wages to a dyer to do work for me; he is a member of their guild. Another dyer has made complaint that the dyestuffs I am providing him are not available for sale at the market."

"I am familiar with this matter," Mayor Roger speaks up. "I did not realize that you were involved in any of this. The dyer says he has alum, which is not easily available, to dye superior colors."

"He does. I provide the alum and the cloth for him to dye. I pay him a wage to do so. I also want to point out that it is just victualers that are required to sell only in the market."

"He is not buying the alum, then? You are?"

"I acquire the alum elsewhere and bring it here to Yorke for my own use."

"Our bailiff says that it is Janice-the-Clothier that is paying him and sells the cloth he dyes."

"She works for me."

This statement is met with stunned silence. "If another dyer was buying alum in Kingston and bringing it here for his own use surely that would not be an issue," Graa asserts. He and James have known each other for some time.

"My dyer is not the only one in the city using alum. It is just difficult to get, at times, and always expensive. We offered this Adam a deal to dye for us first and he turned us down."

"Materials can be purchased elsewhere and used here, of course. Now I can see why the dyer is upset – he is at a disadvantage…but you offered him the deal first? Interesting."

"My wife says that Janice has the finest broadcloth in the city, or I guess you do. I was also surprised by the amount of wool you moved of your own through Kingston. Now that your books were shamefully forced open for us by the sheriff's allegations; I have learned a bit!"

"Not an amount of wool that even approaches yours, Thomas," James replies.

"No, but you have created quite a business network with your barges, the fishmonger and butcher, and now we know more about the extent of your cloth endeavors. I am impressed!"

The mayor nods. "Your wool, your weavers, and your dyers."

"And his alum! If the other dyer wants some, he needs to find his own source; his competitor cannot be forced to share his. The competitor being you James," Thomas Graa is warming to the fight.

"What are you asking me to do?"

"Mayor, I want to know that neither the guild nor your bailiff is going to seize cloth or alum or anything else that belongs to me claiming a city ordinance has been violated."

"As you say the ordinance is for victualers, so no law has been broken. I will make certain our bailiff understands this. The guild has its own rules, but they cannot violate the law."

"My dear James, my wife wants to have a small party, just the women, for your intended. Is that alright with you?"

"I think she would like that Thomas. Thank you. You may want to offer Maud some thoughts on whom she should invite."

"As in whom she should not invite! Ha! I will make sure that Lady Settrington is omitted. I imagine your Katherine is still cross with her husband, our sheriff."

James strolls over to the clothier shop. "Janice I have been assured that Manser will not be bothered by the bailiff and you will not be, either."

"Well, that is good news. I was afraid you would respond by selling all of our cloth to the Hanse in Kingston and I would be out of business here."

"Don't think I didn't consider it. The cloth fair at Saint Bartholomew in London is another option."

"But we won't need to do either now, right?" Janice puts on a pout.

"Not at the moment, but it is good to prepare options. You are pleased with Manser's work?"

"Very; I think he is excellent."

"He is satisfied with our arrangement?"

"Oh, yes! Our alum and handling of all the buying and selling responsibilities have let him concentrate on what he does best – dyeing. He struts around like the pre-eminent dyer in the city now."

"Good, I want to meet with you and Manser at my townhouse this evening. Will that be convenient?"

"I am sure it will be."

Chapter 15

Atonement

EARLY OCTOBER 1373

Malcolm lights the candles in the drawing room, and Will stokes the fire. The room is still partially illuminated by the setting sun, but in a moment, that will be gone. "Sir James, Janice is here with Manser the dyer."

"Please, show them up."

"Won't you have a seat?" The table is set with smoked fish, bread, butter, and cheese. Malcolm brings tankards of ale for each of them.

"Thank you for joining me this evening; I apologize for the short notice." James spread some of the soft cheese on a slice of bread and takes a bite. "Please, help yourselves."

"Manser, you are content with our arrangement and wish to continue it?"

"I certainly am more than content! I was dying poorer cloth much of the time and using inferior mordants before. Janice...err, I mean you? Provide me with fine broadcloth, pure dyes and, of course, the alum."

"What do you need to produce the finest cloth in the City?"

"I believe that I already am doing just that!"

"Have you ever produced scarlets?"

"That requires a prohibitively expensive dyestuff. I have seen some of that cloth being worn by nobility, but not sold here. So, no, Sir James, I have never produced scarlets."

"If I was able to supply you with kermes grains, then would you be able to produce them?"

"As I said, the kermes is prohibitively expensive and must be imported from the Mediterranean. A much higher quantity is required of the grains to dye a bolt of cloth than other dyestuffs."

"I was told twenty-eight pounds of the kermes for each bolt. You do seem to have some knowledge of this dye."

"If you could actually get some, which I doubt – no offense, my Lord, I would be able to make the finest wool cloth you have ever seen."

"I will be the judge of that. Malcolm has weighed out twenty-eight pounds for you to take back to your workshop. I would like to see your result in one week. Manser, we have aroused a good bit of envy with other members of your guild so, for the moment, please keep the kermes grains away from prying eyes."

The dyer just sat quietly for a minute. Then staring at James as if to assess him. "I may need to put up some sort of a fence, then."

"That may induce even more curiosity! Perhaps you can make it clear that the fence is a response to other dyers' complaints about your supply of dyestuffs."

"I could say I am concerned about someone stealing my alum."

"People may find that prudent after the complaints. At some point you may need to expand your dye yard and make it more secure."

"If I am dyeing scarlets, then I certainly will need a better way to lock-up."

The village of Brecken sits well back from the River Ouse because of the broad flood plain. There are but eighteen cottages if the vacant ones are not counted. Joel has had a crew in to repair those six over the last month. This consisted primarily of replacing bad timbers, re-daubing the walls, rebuilding the chimney and fireplace in one instance, and re-thatching all of the roofs. The road from the east was washed out years earlier, so now only a footpath and single log bridge cross the beck. In short, the village is isolated; you need to be going there to end up there.

Joel leads six families from Wilsham through the fens and across the Beck. Each family has a mule to carry their belongings besides what was loaded on the wagons. Upon arrival each family is shown to a cottage and waiting there are the items entrusted to those wagons. "Virgil just finished unloading a few hours ago," the reeve offers.

"I did not know if the *Marie* would get here before we did. Make them welcome, Samuel. I want them given ground and to be part of the winter sowing, even if part of it comes from the demesne land. I need them to have put their own work into this place and have a reason to stay through to the harvest."

"We will be able to get more cultivated in the spring than before to make up for it, Master Joel."

"That is exactly what needs to happen. Let them know they are free to gather firewood and hunt small game."

"I'll make certain they get some fish from our weir, too."

"Check in on them often in case someone has second thoughts and runs. That would cause us a great deal of trouble. You will have to hunt them down."

"I understand," Samuel replies solemnly.

Joel visits each family before he departs for Richmond. They seem pleased with their cottages and reassured to see again the chickens, pigs, and household goods they put on the wagons. That had certainly taken some trust when the wagons departed to meet with Virgil's barge on the river. They should be pleased, he thinks, these homes are better than the shoddy hovels they left behind. The remaining five families, including the three young widows, are on the barge and headed north to Richmond. Other than the reeve's own home the entire village of Wilsham has been vacated. Every person, sheep, sack of grain, chicken, tool, bed, stool, and bit of cookware is gone.

Virgil and Clyde had wanted to empty the reeve's home too, but Joel had stood firm. People's homes are off limits according to Sir James. He hopes Clyde does not return to Wilsham and finish things up the way he wanted.

The widows had been the most adamant about taking Joel up on his offer to find them all a new home. Not only were they understandably upset about losing their husbands, and fully aware their lord as sheriff had a role in that, but in the very desperate situation of having no land now or even a firm right to the roof over their head. The reeve's son had made it clear that he expected certain favors in return for letting them stay and having enough for their young children to eat. It was when Virgil learned about that that he was ready to remove any evidence the reeve's home had ever existed.

"Keep Elias here in Yorke making more looms. Send an apprentice to Richmond with the two, new looms."

"I know just the apprentice to send, Sir James. He will do a good job assembling the looms."

"Master Swain, you know that I have been under some duress from officials of the Crown."

"Well, the sheriff locked you up for two months if that is what you mean!"

"I believe he is but a pawn in all of this, but a damned willing one. It is the inspection of my barges and damages to merchandise that I am speaking about."

"What do you have in mind?"

"I need to be able to go around Yorke and Kingston if necessary. I want you to build a ship that can transport our goods to Antwerp, or the Merchants of the Staple at Calais."

"Knowing you as I do, I expect you have thought about this vessel's design?"

"I have. Here is a drawing. It is a preliminary drawing only. You are the expert here, but this should be a fast, seaworthy ship not a fat, slow cogge. I expect to ship smaller, high value cargoes and prefer to make more quick trips with less merchandise."

Swain looks it over. "This hull is eighty-one feet long at the waterline and has an eighteen-foot beam. That's a...a..."

"Four and a half to one ratio."

"But this is not a galley."

"No, oars are only for maneuvering in harbor or perhaps on the Humbre or Thames. Two, big, lateen sails on two masts. If she is chased, then she can sail closer to the wind and get away. I just do not see her becoming becalmed on the North Sea very often."

"You are funding all of the wages and materials?"

"I am. She will need a smaller barge to lighter cargo ashore and head up small rivers such as the Tees."

"Very nice. When do you want her completed?"

"In eight to ten months if possible. If you need to hire workers let me know if you want help finding them."

"We will have a new sheriff by then. Perhaps your problems will stop?"

"I do not think this sheriff is the root of the problem."

"We currently have a fishing boat being built and a coastal trader being refurbished. I should have both of those done by the time the timber arrives to frame your ship."

"You might confide to a few people, in the strictest confidence, that this is part of my plans to move my business out of Yorke because of the way I have been treated."

"That will cause a stir."

"Exactly so."

"I can call on Master Tenebroides to help pull in all the necessary building materials?"

"He is working on that now. The framing timbers for the hull I am leaving to you."

"No one is disputing your duty to enforce the law, nor your right to inspect a vessel's cargo. What is in dispute here, my Lord Sheriff, is whether the Crown is liable for damage done in that inspection."

The second judge from the King's Bench now queries, "You have stated that the customs officers in Kingston suspected this vessel." He shuffles the papers. "The *Christine* of transporting cargo without paying duties and they inspected it there. Did you discover any such cargo during your inspection?"

"Not on this occurrence."

"Ah! Then you have discovered cargo on this vessel in the past for which proper duty was not paid?"

"Not as yet."

"Meaning you have never found such cargo. On this list the only item aboard subject to tariff is the wine. Three tuns are listed here and here is the receipt for six shillings paid. Am I missing something here, Sir John?"

The sheriff shook his head 'no.' "Is this not a matter for the 'Staple Court' rather than the Exchequer?" he challenges.

"We have been directed by His Majesty Prince Edward to hear this case in particular while we are here. Indeed, we were directed to change our circuit plans to hear all Crown cases in Yorke immediately!" the judge says pointedly. Sheriff Bygod shuffles his feet uneasily.

The second magistrate spoke, "Now, we have a claim here for twenty-four pounds six shillings fourteen pence in damaged merchandise. This appears to claim reimbursement for the wine tariff and labor to salvage some portion of the cargo. Master Tenebroides, is the salvaged cargo included in this claim?"

"Not what we could save, my Lord, but I do have a list of what was salvaged. It greatly exceeds the labor cost of saving it."

"What was salvaged?"

"The unbroken eggs, three barrels of salted herring, twenty bushels of sea coal, five bushels of salt, and all of the tools and cutlery." Tenebroides ticked the items off on his fingers.

"All three tuns of wine were lost and that appears to be majority of this claim. None of the wine could be saved?"

"No, the tuns were smashed in."

"My Lord Sheriff, do you contest this assertion?"

"We were told contraband might be hidden in barrels."

"It makes no sense to pay the import duty on an expensive item such as wine and then ruin it by opening the barrel and putting something else in. What did you suspect them of putting into a wine tun that would have a higher tariff charge than the wine? I can think of very few things!"

"I do not believe the bailiff thought that through in regards to the wine tuns. He was searching for alum. No duty was paid on alum in Kingston."

"Yet no alum was found aboard in Kingston or here?"

"No, but we know Sir James is bringing alum into the city."

"Master Tenebroides?"

"I am not transporting alum, which is why none was found."

"They must be bringing it in a different way," the sheriff asserts.

"Sir James?" asks the judge.

"I am bringing alum into the City. I have never denied that. I do swear that to my knowledge no import duties are being avoided on any alum that I am bringing into Yorke. This is a deliberate pattern of harassment and intimidation; not enforcement of customs collections."

"So, you are paying import duties on your alum?"

"I am not importing the alum. I have no reason to believe that my supplier is not paying any duties that are due."

The sheriff speaks up, "Who is your supplier of alum, then?"

"I do not feel obliged to reveal my sources for the benefit of my competitors. I have stated that to my knowledge all duties due the Crown are being paid."

"You know your supplier is paying the duty?"

"Alum is difficult to buy. My purchases began prior to parliament's authorization of the poundage on imports. Since then, I have not presumed to ask my supplier if he is a smuggler. I have every reason to believe that all duties due the Crown are being paid on alum that I bring into the City of Yorke."

"Sir James, without asking you to give away information that you consider to be proprietary, about how much does alum cost?" The judge continues, "I mean, just what are we talking about here?"

"My Lord, I believe that the Hanse, for example, pays about fifty-six pounds for a tonne of alum. Of course, I am not buying alum in those quantities."

Bygod points his finger at James. "So, the Hanse is your supplier and there should be a record of their tariff payment in Kingston."

James says, smiling, "I certainly did not say that."

"So, assuming the Hanse or whoever your supplier might be is not exempt from the duties, at six p to the pound the duty owed...one pound, eight shillings for every tonne of alum imported. My Lord Sheriff, you have just destroyed over twenty-four pounds worth of merchandise searching for less than two pounds in lost revenues! May I respectfully suggest that you be more careful in the future?"

After a brief discussion between the two judges of the Exchequer Court, he says, "Damages are awarded for the full amount claimed and are to be received by the clerk of the court before the end of the session. Next case."

The marriage ceremony is to be just James and Katherine at the priory church door, with Prior William as witness. James comes down the hidden staircase to William's study where Kate has changed into a form fitting sapphire dress with a wide neckline baring both shoulders and full sleeves. Blue is the traditional color for a bride's gown.

"Spectacular!"

"Me or the dress?"

"Both, but especially you," he said, kissing her on the neck. "Mmm."

She twirled to show the white inserts in the folds of the full skirt. "Do you approve?"

"It appears you inspire not only me but Valentine, as well!"

"There are quite a number of individuals anxious to make sure you are pleased besides myself."

"I will be sure to tell them how beautiful you look today. Ready?"

As they step out to cross the small courtyard it becomes apparent that the ceremony is not going to be quite as private an affair as they had agreed. "Your doing?"

"Mine? No, perhaps the breach in security is your prior?"

"He has had a tendency to change my plans in the past, but I thought I had cured him of that... My Lord Mayor, so glad you could come!"

They face each other and James presents Katherine with a gold ring saying, "Katherine, I take thee to wed."

She accepts the ring and puts it on her finger saying, "James, I take thee to wed."

"A toast and light refreshment in the refectory, then?" suggests Prior William.

As the couple step inside they are greeted by the applause of almost a hundred people. Not only are all the friars and James' key partners in Yorke there, but so are a number of leading citizens and their wives. "Light refreshment?" James smiles seeing Diane, Michael, and several others from The Swan arranging an enormous feast on several banquet tables.

"I thought you said just an exchange of vows outside the church with Prior William as witness?" Kate laughs with her eyes sparkling.

"I suspect a conspiracy against me!"

"Let me be the first to confirm it and you should know that there are many enthusiastic conspirators!"

"We need to be sure to greet all of them and thank them for coming, then!"

"My congratulations Lady Katherine."

"Thank you, your Grace," she replies with a curtsey to the archbishop. "The title may require getting used to."

"You look every bit the part."

Kate gently glides just the very tips of her fingers across the scars on James' shoulder. "Burns are very painful."

"I'll be the first to agree with that."

"In fact," she says as she touches various scars as though counting them up, "you've had a rather hard life."

"Not at all; just a few very bad days."

"You'll have to tell me about them sometime."

"Most of them I would prefer not to think about too much again. If I start shouting in the middle of the night, try not to be frightened!"

"Does that happen often?"

"You may need to ask Malcolm as he comes in and wakes me. I usually have no memory of it in the morning."

"That may be my responsibility now. I don't believe I want him pulling back the bed curtains in the night."

James runs his hand over her thigh. "I see your point. I'll let you work that out with him. Perhaps now my dreams will be filled with more delightful thoughts."

"I've given her more keel than you had on your original plans. She'll draw more water but sail closer to the wind." Swain pokes the keel beneath the first timber ribs being erected on the shipway with the toe of his boot.

James looks at the framing. "How much more?" It was hard to compare to other ships because you rarely had a chance to see the bottom of their hulls.

"I think she'll draw nine feet."

"Good idea Swain. No need to fuss with elaborate cabin cabinetry; this is a commerce trader not a show piece. In some ways the less attention she attracts the better."

"Understood, Master Tenebroides is to be the captain?"

"I need him to manage the barge network, so I am looking for both a captain and crew. I do have a number of my own men in mind for the crew, but more are needed. If you know someone, send them my way. Tenebro will put the word out in Kingston, but I am worried about that. I do not want someone that is available because the owner dismissed him or because he wrecked his ship on a reef."

"You may be looking for an experienced first mate, then, that is ready to become a captain."

"They have stopped searching Virgil's barge."

"That is because they are trying to find the alum; we know that for certain now, and everyone knows that alum is imported from Africa or the Mediterranean." James leans back on the window seat cushion in the stern cabin of the *Christine*.

"So, the sheriff believes I am bringing the alum up the Ouse from Kingston." Tenebroides raises an eyebrow. "Meaning, I am the one liable to be searched again."

"Or getting it here from Kingston some other way; just not down the Ouse and Swale from Richmond. Tenebro, if they were not sure before, then they are now. First because they have searched the *Marie* on at least three occasions and found nothing, and second because I suggested that the Hanse controls the supply of alum at the trial. No doubt they have since confirmed that. As I am not paying an import poundage on alum in Kingston, they have come to the conclusion that it is not being paid at all. I've confused that issue by leading them to believe I am buying from an intermediary. Now they want to find out whom."

"The sheriff's bailiff has been watching Manser's yard and sending someone to follow every cart that goes in or out."

"Exactly my point. So, he knows by now that the alum comes to Manser from Janice's shop. Now he wants to know how it gets there. I have admitted that I bring alum into the city, so there is no point to seizing it at Manser's or Janice's. He will be trying to catch us bringing it into the city without paying the fee at the gate or taking possession of the alum from our supplier."

"What's the point, then? We don't bring it through a gate or buy it at all."

"He doesn't know that. I am trying to think about it from his point-of-view. If it does not arrive on Virgil's barge and it did not come in on your *Christine*, then he has to conclude we are bringing it in through a city gate or smuggling it into the city some other way."

"When we bring wagon loads into the city, we pay a flat rate on the load, no matter what is on the wagon. We don't have to bother saying what we've got, so we could have anything."

"I'll need to remember that." James smiles. "Then I think he wants to know where we get the alum."

"Why?"

It depends whether he is acting on the orders of the sheriff or someone else,"

"Like Latimer."

"Like Latimer or even the dyers' guild here in the city. They may be trying to identify our supplier to get the alum for themselves by outbidding me or threatening them. Or, maybe they are just trying to ensure that the import duty is being paid. If he is acting on his own, then he may be trying to steal the alum and resell it."

"Alright," Tenebroides replies. "How do we find out which?"

"Have Thomas come all the way up the Ouse and meet Bertrand's stone barge at Cawood. He can transfer tools, cutlery, and baskets of sea coal – we still need all of that here. Cover up the baskets of coal, so that anything could be in those baskets. Let's see if our bailiff boards the stone barge again."

"That is simple enough. Eventually he will discover that we are bringing goods up the Derwent."

"If he has followed our wagons back to The Swan and on to Elfwynton, then he already knows. I would expect him to search the tithe barn there."

"He won't find anything, Sir James."

"Not alum no, but make sure he doesn't find anything else. When we bring a wagon through the gates from Elfwynton be sure to take it to Janice's shop. Keep him chasing possibilities other than Virgil's barge."

"We stop there anyway to bring in ingots and sea coal for the smith."

"Just pull all the way into the courtyard, so he can't see what is being unloaded, and bring something to Janice every time that looks like it could be alum."

"The kermes will serve that purpose."

"Oh, shit. We are hiding coal behind diamonds."

"Sister Coletta! What brings you by my apothecary? Are you unwell?

"I am quite well, Lady Katherine. I have been asked to find someone to help you in your garden, so I thought I would stop by and see just what that entails."

"You've been asked?"

Coletta moves the bib of her smock to the side to show Lady Katherine the broach she is wearing.

"I had no idea. Have you always worn it and I've just never noticed?"

"You are very focused on your work at Saint Leonard's, but I am also wearing my smock when I assist you."

"So, you are an associate of the Companie, then."

"My husband fought with Sir John. He died in Spain."

"I am so sorry to hear that. May I ask just what it is you do for my husband?"

"Mostly I find people. Right now, I am trying to find a good person to work in an herb garden instead of desperately begging for a meal at Saint Leonard's."

"How do you know if they are a 'good' person and not a thief or a rapist?"

"Sir James seems to think I am very good at just that."

"I don't suppose he asked you to find him a wife?"

"No!" She laughs out loud. "But he did ask me specifically about your skills and habits as a surgeon. Apparently, he already had a recommendation and was double checking. Actually, knowing your husband, much longer than you have, he may have been triple checking."

"Will he double check your recommendation for a gardener?"

"Oh, yes, of that you can be sure. You have met Brother Hugh?"

"Interesting."

"Sir James, I thought lead was a nuisance cargo: heavy and low value."

"It is Virgil, but it seems to be in demand and bring some other benefits."

"May I ask?"

"Obviously, you know that we currently enjoy a river toll exemption on your total cargo because of the lead you bring for the cathedral roof... I believe I can extend that indefinitely if we become the only source of lead coming into Yorke, or at least control the vast majority of it."

"So, if I make an arrangement with all the smelters, I can find in Swaledale, and I really do not know how many there are, can't someone else still bring lead here from someplace else?"

"They can but I don't think they can match our price once they have shipped it. I'm willing to break even on the lead to bring all of our wool, cloth, and victuals in without the tolls. Plus, there seems to be a shortage of lead available and we may have room to increase our price."

"What if our guy is the only smelter up there?"

"Some other barges are bringing lead down the Ouse to Yorke. I think there are other smelters and I seem to remember Paul saying so. If not, see if our smelter is getting all the lead ore or even set someone else up as a smelter. My guess is that some of the free miners are digging too far away from Paul the smelter's location."

"And if you can't keep the exemption on tolls?" Virgil seems unsure about all this.

"We can use some ourselves for salt pans and alum pans – even our own roofs. The rest we can stockpile in Richmond until the price goes up or someone is ready to make a deal. I am betting that eventually someone will."

"It should not be too difficult to find out who is getting lead west of Richmond and shipping it down the Swale. There are other ways of putting an end to competition."

"Let's try to dry up their source of supply first Virgil. An ingot here or there is not a concern."

"I would still rather carry pigs that squeal than pigs of lead."

Paul sticks his head around the corner into James' study. "I just found out that our bothersome bailiff has been dismissed."

"Either that means the sheriff never told him to damage our merchandise, or he has been guilty of upsetting Sir John in some other way. He can't board our barges then, but our sheriff could still send another bailiff."

"Costing him over twenty-four pounds is certainly something to be upset about. The odd thing is that he is still watching Manser's yard and Janice's shop."

"Time we watched him, then. I want to know whom he talks with, where he lives, and everybody that might be working with him. He may be up to some mischief of his own or be serving a new master."

"I thought you might say that." Paul Fitz-William smiles. "We've been following him around since you said he might search the tithe barn in Elfwynton. He hasn't gone that far yet, but he did follow our wagon there. Should he have a bad day?"

"First I want to know if someone is paying him. If they are, I want to know whom."

"He met with a man this morning, near Lady Katherine's apothecary shop. Geoffrey followed the man back to the castle and will find out who he is. Judd is keeping an eye on her shop right now. I've sent a few Companie men over there from The Swan to relieve him. Have you considered closing her shop?"

"No. That is not an option. I doubt any of our men have knowledge of medicinal plants?"

"I can ask around. Sir James, I've been thinking about the Lady Mary's manor."

"Appleton Rabek."

"She needs a way to get some income, and I was thinking."

James leans back in his chair; this is not typical of Paul. "Did you have something in mind?"

"They need a flock of sheep. That's how we make our money – right?"

"That may be something we can help with. Have you discussed this with Mary or her reeve?"

"They seemed open to the idea but unsure about the cost of buying the flock. Each ewe costs about seventeen pence."

James nods. "At the Yorke market." Paul was doing some checking; now that is interesting! "If they committed to selling their wool to us, then we could do a bit better."

"This is a spectacular scarlet!" James is visibly enthused.

Manser nods. "I used the best bolt of broadcloth I had."

"From Richmond, Janice?"

"Yes, from your Flemish weavers there. Would you consider having one of them come here to manage our weavers?"

"I have been thinking about that both for here in Yorke and in Barmby. It is not as easy as you might think. They have a little community up there and I do not want to upset things. So, is this bolt of cloth worth the princely price of eighteen pounds?"

Janice thinks, after a period of silence. "I will show it to Valentine. If he tells his wealthiest customers about it, then we have something."

"That gives me an idea. Take it to Valentine in secret to make a dress for Katherine. If he asks, you don't know if you can get any more. Have him put white in the pleats of the skirt like he did on the dress she wore on our wedding day."

"He will tell everyone!"

"Those he doesn't tell will know when she walks with me through the market on a Thursday morning."

"Nicely done Manser. Malcolm has another bag of the kermes grains for you. I want a bolt for trade in Kingston. Think about how you might increase the amount of cloth your shop is dying for me. I want to export, as well as sell in London, besides here in Yorke."

"I believe some of the dyers in the city may be open to doing piece work for me."

"Start them out on some second-quality broadcloth before you start providing them with alum. If you and Janice are satisfied, then please show their results to me. Just because they are members of the guild doesn't mean I am willing to provide them with cloth and dyestuffs. We intend to be the clothier with the best cloth in Yorke and perhaps all of England. Just to increase the stakes, Janice, you might want to warn Valentine that I intend to be at Katherine's first fitting on this new dress."

Chapter 16

Too Close to Home

OCTOBER 1373

"Well, do you wish to buy her? The City paid you a 150 pounds to build her, as you well know, James, and you can buy the galley back for half that—just seventy-five!"

"I don't think so."

Thomas de Howme, the recently elected Mayor, acts surprised. "Surely, she is well-built, and I am told you have laid down the keel for a new ship in your yard. Buy this one and you can save time and money."

Now that the emergency need for ships has passed, the Crown sent the galleys back to the cities that built them to save the expense of maintaining them. "That galley is exceedingly well- built, but she needs too many oarsmen and lacks enough cargo space for my purposes. Not a profitable equation. We designed her to fight not to be a merchant trader. In hindsight perhaps I should have considered what would happen when the Crown no longer wanted her, but I did not."

"When the Crown needs ships again they will demand her back and pay good money to the owner."

"They will promise it and maybe even pay it, but the ship still needs to have a useful purpose in the meantime to make financial sense. The ship I have laid down is quite a bit bigger and designed to be a sailing vessel."

"The city will have to put her up for auction, then," the mayor's hope for a quick sale is not turning out the way he planned.

"If the bidding stays low enough, I may buy her for the timber and fittings."

"I hope another buyer steps forward, then. I would dearly love to recoup more of the money the city spent to build her." The mayor leaned back in his chair. "On another matter, I've been asked to speak to you about your barge, *Christine*. You are still not shipping goods upriver to our city."

"Perhaps in July we will try again."

"July! Ah, when we have a new sheriff. Sir John has assured me that he will not be damaging goods again in any barge inspections. After the financial compensation the court made him pay, I certainly believe him. Surely you can resume shipping earlier?"

"I may start taking consigned wool out earlier for Graa and Quixley – say April. My wool and sheepskins can wait."

"But not bringing goods into the city all winter?"

"I am still bringing some shipments in on the barges that also bring construction materials for the cathedral. Archbishop John has told me the sheriff will not board them."

"You threatened to stop bringing in the lead and the stone; I am told my Lord Archbishop had strong words for the sheriff. Don't think I don't realize that was at your instigation! The City Council is very concerned. I know you seem to believe that you are but a small portion of food and goods coming into the city, and have said that no one will even notice, but I assure you that people have noticed!"

"How many times would you allow over twenty-four pounds worth of merchandise to be destroyed? Yes, I was awarded the money paid but I do not want to go to court every time some oaf boards me. Shipping has plenty of risks already without an overzealous sheriff, and no, I do not trust him."

"I agree that is an awful lot of money to lose until a court decides in your favor – if it does. What if the city insures your cargo against any damage caused by the sheriff? I realize it is a usual offer, but as Sir John has guaranteed me, he will not damage anything the city really is not taking on any risk."

"You are a persuasive man Thomas. I will have Master Tenebroides make a trip up the river provided the weather holds. If he is inspected in a manner that damages merchandise in any way…no more shipments until the next sheriff takes office."

"Kate, we have an appointment with Valentine this morning."

"We do? You have a surprise for me!"

"You are to be part of my devious scheme to make every woman in the city jealous of you."

"Why I thought they were already."

"Indeed, some of them are not yet fully aware of just how jealous they should be."

Malcolm and Will wait outside of Valentine's shop as James held the door and they go in. Janice and Manser rise from their seats and bow slightly as Katherine enters. Valentine hurries out from behind the counter. "Lady Katherine, welcome."

"Katherine, you know Janice. May I introduce Manser who, as you will soon see, is perhaps the finest dyer in the city."

"A pleasure my Lady and thank you for your gracious compliment, Sir James."

"Lady Katherine, won't you please come this way? Anne will assist you."

"Have either of you seen the dress?"

"Not yet, but I inspected the cloth we brought, of course, and I saw a sketch last week." Janice adds, "I am as anxious as I can be."

Manser stood up again as he said, "Here she comes now!"

Katherine's smile lights up the room in the most brilliant scarlet dress any of them have ever seen. Valentine fusses about her as she twirls first one way, and then the other. To James the fit seems perfect, but the tailor makes small chalk marks and pinches at the material here and there.

"Well?"

"I am still catching my breath – you are stunning." The white inserts in the pleats of the full skirt make a dramatic contrast. "Katherine, are you pleased?"

"It is beautiful, and now I see why all of you are here. I won't be easy to miss when I wear it. Is that part of your plan, James; you are shamelessly using me to sell broadcloth?"

"Very expensive broadcloth; I hope the perquisites to your assignment offset any possible resentment?"

"Oh, I don't know," she said, smiling slyly. "How often do I get a new dress?"

"I guess that is something we will need to negotiate over dinner. Valentine, it is beautiful. If there was any doubt that you are the finest dressmaker in the city, then there will be no longer. Will it be ready for market this Thursday?"

"Certainly, Sir James, it will be my pleasure; just a few, minor adjustments. Thank you for bringing your patronage to me. It is a pleasure to work with such fine material for a beautiful Lady."

"Tanned sheepskins, yarn spun over the winter, and six bolts of good broadcloth."

"That is not a very good barge load Paul." James is re-routing shipments from the Ouse to the Derwent to avoid the sheriff and the river tolls charged in Yorke. The priory's village of Elfwynton, just a few miles east of the city, lies on the Derwent, which joins the Ouse at Barmby. "And our ex-bailiff, Gilbert you said is his name, saw the barge being loaded."

"Oh, yes, first he watched it being unloaded into the wagons and then re-loaded to go back down the Derwent."

"Then he will not attempt to board going back down the river – he can't have any interest in skins and yarn; maybe the cloth if he recognizes it for what it is worth, but it was all wrapped up. What would he have seen being loaded into the wagons?"

"Seven barrels of wine; we transferred the wine from two of the tuns bought in Kingston into them. There is no way to handle the full tuns on the small barge. Paul reads down the manifest. "We also had two barrels of kermes, twelve baskets of sea coal, a barrel of spices, and six bolts of coarse cloth for wool sacks. The down-river cargo was in baskets, sacks, and the cloth is as you said in a canvas wrapper."

"So, what he sees is eight barrels and twelve baskets, which could contain anything, but he may believe had alum, and the cloth. All of which is now here in the city?"

"All of which is at The Swan. We'll bring one wagon into the city when the gates open in the morning."

"And at the city gate, we simply pay a flat fee on the wagon load. They don't ask what is on it?"

"No, Sir James, not typically."

"If he stayed to watch the barge being reloaded, then Gilbert does not know the wagons are at The Swan."

"Oh, yes, he does!" Paul quickly interjects, "He had two other men with him that followed the wagons there."

"Any one you recognize?"

"I'll make inquiries."

"He cannot legally board one of our vessels now. He could be playing informant for the sheriff and they could board, or he is planning a robbery. Work it backwards Paul. If you planned to rob us, how would you do it? Then we will try to set him up."

"I did an inspection of the galley as you asked, Sir James."

"And your assessment, Master Swain?"

"The timber is in good shape and we can re-use a great deal of it. The planking alone will save us a lot of time. The masts can be salvaged but one of the spars needs to be replaced. All of the cordage and sails are a bit worn. The anchor hawser can be re-used. There are enough good oars for our new ship."

"How much is she worth to us?"

"Twenty-five to thirty pounds as salvage?"

"You'll do the bidding but keep an eye on me. If someone is trying to run up the bids, then we are out."

"She is a beautiful vessel and close to my heart. Have you considered re-fitting her to be your merchant vessel?"

"I don't think she has enough cargo capacity."

"Well, I was thinking we could add another deck. You know, maybe just five foot of hold space between decks."

"Too top heavy."

"Not if we remove those heavy fighting platforms up high on the masts and take down the castles at the bow and stern."

"Interesting, you've been thinking about this."

"I can add a bit to the keel if we pull her all the way out of the water and increase the size of the spars, so she carries more sail."

"If you add to the keel can we get her out of Yorke?"

"We can leave her near empty and float down to Barmby for the final fitting out. I would still say she could come here, except in the late summer."

"Draw up your plan and estimate the cost. I like this idea. All of the cordage and sailcloth we are producing for the new ship can be used to refit this one. All we lose is the keel and framing timbers that you have completed."

"All timber that can find a new purpose," Swain points out.

"Bid for salvage value only. Your limit is twenty pounds unless I give you a signal to go higher."

James waited until the sun was high enough in the sky to bathe most of the market square in sunlight and warm enough for Katherine to wear her scarlet dress without a cloak covering it. Then, with Katherine on his arm, he set off to make his rounds of the vendors. Amongst the dull brown, olive, and russet clothing, the brilliant red stands out like a cardinal in winter.

"First my wife's favorite fishmonger disappears from the Ouse Bridge, and now she is desperate for a new dress! I lay both charges at your feet, James."

"Guilty on both counts, Thomas; I beg your forgiveness. It does appear that the Lord Mayor and I have come to an agreement that will bring Oliver back to Yorke. Perhaps that will assuage her. If it is a scarlet dress that you need to keep peace with Maud at home, then may I suggest she see Janice at her shop? I have heard whisperings that she has more from this bolt."

"If broadcloth this fine is now available here in the city, then I may not have to take her to London."

"Katherine, may I introduce Thomas Graa?"

"Lady d'Arzhon, we met at your recent wedding."

"Of course we did, and your lovely wife was so kind to invite me to your home."

"Is it accurate to conclude that Valentine made this dress too? Your doting husband has started to put the pressure on."

"He did! Maud is a beautiful woman and deserving of the finest that the city's leading wool merchant can provide."

"Your husband seems determined to give me a run for that title."

"James says that you and Simon are the kings, and he is but a pawn in the wool trade."

"Surely you have learned that he plays chess many moves ahead."

"I think I have been distracted by a few vendors a bit too long if you two are comparing notes," James winks at Thomas Graa.

"Another willing conspirator to help me James; I need my allies." Kate smiled coyly.

Graa laughs easily. "You appear to have met your match, my friend. But you will begin shipping back into Yorke?"

"Provided the sheriff keeps his dogs on a leash – yes."

"I am starting with the assumption that Gilbert does not have a boat." Paul Fitz-William pauses to assure James understands the significance of his point. "That means he can't attack the *Christine* on the Ouse as it is too wide and deep. I believe his best chance is to attack Ben's barge on the Derwent at the ford below Elfwynton."

"Is that what you would do?"

"I would not want to tangle with Ben's crew hand-to-hand, so I would use arrows from cover on the bank in an ambush."

"Confirm that he does not have access to a barge. Then tell me how we prevent him from killing Ben and his crew. They will be helpless against archers up on the bank in the open barge."

"Gilbert will need to keep watch at Barmby to know when we are headed upriver, then will need to send word back to his men in time for them to get to the ambush site. That barge moves surprisingly fast when it rides the tidal bore. He won't have much time."

"We can either load the barge in secret, so he doesn't know until they put out, or let him see us load the night before and be ready for him. Don't underestimate him. He could put a snag in the river to stop the barge or some other trick that has not occurred to us."

"I've spoken to Ben about not letting market day, nor the *Christine's* arrival in Barmby make his trips too predictable. If Gilbert knows in advance when the barge is going, he can pick any place on the river."

"Make sure he knows we are watching him. Crowd him a little. Maybe we can get him to think the better of whatever he may have planned."

The man would not even look Katherine in the eye when she spoke to him. Instead, he kept his head directed at the ground in a subservient manner that she found most irksome. What had Coletta been thinking when she chose him? "Miles, please look at me when I am speaking to you. This is Horehound. It spreads aggressively, so you have to watch it. This is Flax and it keeps coming up, but we don't need it anymore. Go ahead and weed it out."

"Lady Katherine, what is the Flax used for and why don't we need it?"

At least he is trying to learn. "Flax seeds are used to help with bowel movements and a single seed placed in the eye will help remove a speck of dirt there. We do not need it because Master Tenebroides brings me Flax seed from the farm at Moretun and I can use the space in the garden for other things now."

"The busy little man with the red beard."

"That's him," she answered.

"And this?"

"Turnips."

"What do they cure?"

"Hunger. This is mugwart for treating the feet and some feminine needs. I want to harvest the seed from these dried flower heads. Wait a moment, and I will get the jar."

"Inside on the shelf? I'll fetch it." A moment later, he is back with the correct jar.

"You can read."

"Yes, my Lady. I was in a monastery."

"But not any longer."

"No, I met a woman, fell in love, and got married."

"I have heard they have a problem with that."

"Yes, they did. I was declared apostate and had to flee."

"You could not go back to your family?"

"Uh, no, that is why I ended up at the monastery in the first place."

"That explains why you ended up in line at Saint Leonard's."

"I did not tell this to the big Whitefriar."

"Brother Hugh. What happened to your wife?"

"She is here with me in Yorke. You won't tell him, will you?"

"Hugh is not going to report you to the sheriff. Coletta knows you can read, and I assume write?"

"She saw me writing a message for someone to earn a penny. Maybe that is why she picked me out for you?"

The auction begins with the mayor speaking to the considerable expenditure, and therefore value, of the war galley. Then her captain, Robert Carter, spoke of le Mare Majstro's speed and seaworthiness. There are not many bidders present, much to the mayor's chagrin. The galley's very virtues for war made her useless as a river barge or a trading vessel – just as James had said: too much crew to man the oars and not enough cargo space. The other potential bidders are the shipyards south of the city and they, too, were interested in her scrap value. Swain buys her for twenty-one pounds seven shillings after getting the nod to bid higher.

Immediately the fighting platforms are removed from the masts and the castle decks pulled off fore and aft. This reduces both the weight of the ship and lowers the center of gravity. Whether the ship is to be scrapped or rebuilt according to Swain's plan they have to come off any way. Then the heavy anchor hawser is attached to the foremast and run to a large capstan anchored at the top of the yard's main slipway. Six mules are harnessed to turn the arms of the capstan and slowly pull the galley up out of the water. As she came, pairs of log rollers are laid on each side of the ship to keep her upright and move her into the boatyard. Even so, when the galley is halfway into the yard the capstan will no longer turn.

First the rest of the ballast stones are hauled up out of the hold and dropped over the side. On the pitched deck that is more than just a little awkward. Then additional teams of mules and heavy draft horses are yoked to cables on either side of the ship. The reduced weight and the additional pulling power finally inches her out of the river and completely into the yard. Immediately bracing is angled to both sides of the hull every eight feet and timber wedges driven under the keel to keep her from rolling back into the water.

"That was a task well done, Master Swain!"

"I thank yee, Captain. Touch and go for a bit there."

"It's a bloody shame she's to be broken up as salvage. A sweeter ship does not sail the channel."

"Where do you go now, Captain Carter?"

"I'll take what's left of my crew and try to get a ship in Kingston. December is not a good time to be finding a ship. If there is nothing, then I'll try in Boston, then Yarmouth..."

"You should have a talk with my partner, Sir James. He may be looking for a good captain."

"For what ship?"

"Well, you should speak with him about that. You can ask for him at The Swan out the Monk Bar, or I do expect him to come by here sometime tomorrow to look over le Mare Majstro."

"Our 'friend' the ex-bailiff seems to have gotten skittish. No sign of anyone watching in Barmby. No sign of anyone riding north after the tide turned and no one laying in ambush. Ben brought his barge up the Derwent yesterday without any trouble."

James is pensive. "Good news, Paul. Hopefully, he has decided the risk is too high. The difficulty is that someone could waylay the barge at any time. In some ways it would have been best for them to attempt it when we are expecting them. Now we need to vigilant all of the time."

"I rode along the bank the whole way. I see your point – we just can't have a squad of outriders every trip."

"Interesting. It might be good to do it occasionally, though. Keep them nervous."

"Master Tenebroides has put a boarding axe at every rower's station on the *Christine*."

"His oarsmen are higher out of the water and have added a gunwale to protect them. We should add at least a foot and a half to the sides of Ben's barge. Then the men can get behind something if arrows start flying their way."

"They will be a much smaller target behind the higher bulwark. We've got planks in Barmby. All right if I ask Swain to send a man down to supervise the work?"

"I'll stop by the boatyard myself. I believe Elias has two looms ready to set up in Barmby. He can go and do both jobs. I want to build a work room there for weavers and a bigger warehouse. Janice's journeyman will come down with us to lead that shop."

"You're going to Barmby, Sir James?"

"Yes, also Lady Katherine. Please make preparations for the trip with Malcolm."

"What did you do before you became captain of *le Mare Majstro*, Captain Carter?"

"I served as mate aboard *La Petit Mighell*, Sir James."

"Trading cogge?"

"Aye, eighty-tonne small cogge. Mostly between London, Portsmouth, Bruges, Calais, and Antwerp."

"You are able to navigate out of sight of land?"

"Well enough to cross the channel or the North Sea. I have never gone south of Biscay nor into the Baltic. I cannot say that I would be comfortable for a long time, say more than a day, without sighting land."

"An honest answer. I have known many a captain to become anxious in bad weather or fret getting caught at sea after dark. Did you have responsibility for buying, selling, paying tariffs?"

"No, the owner had a man aboard to manage all of the cargo."

"Master Swain is making some changes to the galley to make her a trader. Mostly wool from Kingston to Calais; tuns of wine on the return. London for the cloth fair. As far north as Stockton-upon-Tees. Interested?"

"It will be hard to make money with such a large crew."

"She will have larger masts and sails and fewer oars; crew of about twenty. Swain has removed the fighting platforms from up on the masts and the castles – fore and aft. They stay off. We estimate her capacity to be about twenty-eight tonnes. No more than one week to Calais or Antwerp and back."

"She'll be a fast sailer. I've still got some crew here with me. May I hire them on?"

"I'll want about half the crew to be my men. The rest can be yours. I may be able to employ the rest of your men on river barges if you vouch for them and they can handle an oar."

Swain walked James through his suggested changes to the galley. "I think the ship we started to build would have had a cargo capacity of fifty to sixty tonnes. This ship, after the changes, will be closer to thirty." Building Swain's additional deck really only required adding to the hull side amidships and then decking it to make the existing quarterdeck connect to the fo'c'sle.

"If we are shipping wool, then we will fill the hold before we get to thirty tonnes. One hundred sacks are about eighteen tonnes and I doubt we can cram a hundred sacks into her. Ten tuns of wine – yes, but I want you to figure just how many wool sacks she will hold before I agree to this."

"How many does she need to hold?"

"At least seventy-two."

"I think we can get there. She's no hundred-tonne cogge and never will be, but you never asked for one."

"Just a fast run to Bruges or Calais from Yarmouth or Colchester – three days there and back. We're not going to Genoa. She still needs to be able to outrun a Castilian galley."

"If there is any wind and she has a lead, they will never catch her before their rowers are exhausted. The captain just needs to take her to her best point of sailing and make his escape."

"Now that I see her with the castles removed, I think we can add back a new higher quarter deck. Ponder that through and then let me know what you think."

"I was planning to suggest just that. I'll want to keep it small."

"Hugh, my new gardener, is hiding from a monastery; he is apostate."

"That was my assumption. Coletta thinks his wife will make a good maid for you Lady Katherine. Have you seen her?"

"Not yet. What do you think?"

"She is not from a peasant family; that I am sure. We have her selling meat pies from a basket up by the cathedral. She is pretty and the workmen are attracted to her." Hugh smiles, "She sells a lot of pies."

"I was considering letting Miles live above the apothecary. I have not been up there in weeks."

"If you think he will be a good gardener we can get your possessions moved."

"Doesn't my maid need to live at the townhouse?"

"At least one of them should."

"I can't imagine I will need more than one."

"You'll want more when the baby comes."

"Hugh!"

The bailiff's cudgel pounds on the door of James' townhouse before first bell. "Open in the king's name!"

Will quickly sends Geoffrey down the hidden staircase to the Abbey. The bell in the courtyard starts ringing to wake up the entire household.

When the door is unlocked, they shoulder in shouting "In the king's name!"

"Stop that damned bell!" Sir John Bygod hollers, and two men lumber out to do his bidding only to retreat quickly back to the house in the face of all the people coming from the kitchens and stables armed with whatever is at hand to deal with robbers. Sir James and Lady Katherine are not in residence, but the staff is well-drilled and soon the sheriff's party is badly outnumbered inside the house. "Get back! In the king's name, get back!"

People begin running from James' cluster of shops on nearby St. Andrew-gate: weaver, bakery, smith, pie shop, and tavern. Will keeps letting them inside until every sheriff's man has three or four of James' around them, crowding them, as they try to continue their search. "Get back! This is the business of the Crown." The house continues to fill with men impeding the sheriff's progress. They come in all directions: the stables, the front door, even from the second floor.

"What exactly are you looking for, Sir John?" Will asks innocently.

"I'll know when I find it."

"Do you wish to steal Lady Katherine's jewelry? Sir James' purse?"

"You watch your foul tongue."

"Seems to be a good question, my Lord Sheriff," the Archbishop of Yorke enters the room with Prior William right behind. "What are you hoping to find after forcing entry into Sir James' home? While he is away, I might add."

"You are interfering in the king's business, and I will not stand for it." Then, abashedly, he says, "My Lord Archbishop."

"Not interfering at all; merely making certain that it is King's business that you are about." A crowd is gathering outside started by Whitefriars, joined by men from The Swan, and now the commotion has attracted a considerable crowd.

A sheriff's man tumbles down the stairs after some aggressive pushing and shoving. Some of the women of the house begin verbally abusing the bailiff as he goes through Lady Katherine's wardrobe and then get very much in his face. Finally, the sheriff and his men back out of the house only to be confronted by the crowd in the street. Stones and horse droppings begin to fly from the back of the mob until the sheriff's party turns the corner.

Will stands at the bottom of the staircase. "Geoffrey, take three others and ride for Barmby to tell Sir James what has happened. Put everything in order and let me know if anything is damaged or missing. Elizabeth, please offer his Grace and our Prior some refreshment."

"Will, what would the sheriff have been seeking?" Prior William asks innocently.

"I have been asking myself the same question Prior William. We do not store alum here if that is what he wanted, but even if we did Sir James has not denied buying alum."

The archbishop rearranges his fine robes. "Ah, thank you, my dear. I am glad Sir James has resumed shipping wine up the Ouse. Yet you were clearly prepared for the sheriff's intrusion."

"Prepared for thieves, your Grace. Sir James thinks that when he is away with a large escort people may think the house is vulnerable. I do not believe he expected the sheriff to force entry. I am indebted to you for coming."

"Prior William came and got me, so thank him. I am glad I did. Things may have gotten out of hand. I imagine there are things here that Sir James does not want the sheriff to find?"

"I'm sure he does not want anyone to find the money kept here. As a merchant and shipper there is naturally some on hand. He keeps financial ledgers and that sort of bookkeeping here, and if they were taken, I am certain he would be quite inconvenienced. If there is something warranting the sheriff's intrusion here, I am unaware of it."

"If James has something illegal to hide, he probably keeps it in your Abbey, Prior William!"

"He might, but he would not tell me about it. He does not involve me in his business dealings. Thanks be to God."

"Do you think we are going to have a confrontation between Sir James and our sheriff?"

"I will be surprised if we do not, your Grace! James may have intended to wait out his term in office for another six months, but this may well change that."

"That would not be good for Yorke or the realm. I may compel them to sit down at the same table and discuss their issues in my presence."

"We have a little problem, Judd."

The big fellmonger nodded, stuttering, "I sa-sa-saw him, Hugh."

"He is not from here; been staying at the castle. Name of Edmond."

"The one I saw speakin' with our interfering ba-ba-bailiff."

"Ex-bailiff; haven't seen him around lately."

"No. Th-Th-This Edmond was with the sheriff this morning. I don't like pee people that don't belong there poking around Sir James' house."

"None of us do. We are concerned."

"Enough said, Hugh. Enough said. He sees a particular woman at nigh night sometimes."

"Always risky to pay for certain companionship."

Edmond is frustrated by the confrontation at d'Arzhon's townhouse and loudly rages at the sheriff over what he saw as cowardice in the face of it. He storms out of the castle gate and into the city in a huff. By early evening, he heads down the narrow streets in the dark shadows cast by the overhanging stories above. Dogs bark and this part of the city reeks of urine and refuse in the street. He swats at the flies. There is no response when he raps on the door, but it is open, and he goes up the staircase. The door at the top is slightly ajar. "Missy?" he says as he slips in.

She is not there, but he feels the presence of someone behind him in the room. Edmund grabs for his dagger and steps forward quickly to give himself space – too late. The steel head of the hammer strikes him on the temple as he starts to turn. He staggers and crashes to the wall and then the floor. Blood begins flowing profusely. Judd pulls a long narrow spike from his apron and inserts it deep into Edmond's ear. A single rap with the hammer drives it home.

"The prostitute claims to know nothing, of course."

"My Lord, she was here at the castle with your reeve's son last night."

"Leon's son, my reeve at Wilsham?"

"The same, Sir John."

"They were waiting for him, then. He went to her often?"

"Often enough, I guess," the bailiff replies. "I believe Sir James is still in Barmby, but he could have been told about our entry in his house and sent back orders. Plenty of time for that."

"A spike left in his ear. Have we seen that before?"

"Not in my time as a bailiff. I would remember that."

"Why not just smash him in the head again? We are supposed to remember this killing. I don't suppose this is a spike from Master Swain's boatyard?"

The bailiff handed it to the sheriff. "Just a typical building spike. Any smith could have made it. Edmund's purse was missing."

"Simple robbery? I think not."

"One of Richard Lyons' men was run over by a wagon team in June under the Micklegate Bar."

"Oh? That was not mentioned to me when I became sheriff."

"It was after the peasants took over Saint Mary's. He was with the sheriff's party that hunted them down."

"Which irritated d'Arzhon."

"Yes, d'Arzhon and most of the citizens of Yorke but I am told he was following Sir James when he left the house. Then Lyon's wardrobe was found in the abbey's latrine."

Sheriff Bygod's fingers drummed on the table. "Do you know if one of Sir James' men rode back from Barmby before Edmond was killed?"

"No, we all came back here. No one has been watching the house today."

"Ask at the gates. No one saw anything on the street where the woman lives?"

"If they did, they're not saying, but it was after dusk – past curfew. Even if someone did see somebody, they would probably not be able to identify him."

"So, the idiot goes to visit a prostitute past curfew and gets himself murdered; after we force ourselves into Sir James' home at his instigation!" The sheriff shakes his head.

"Sir James doesn't know that."

"He may suspect it."

The bailiff suggests, "If he knew, he would not have left the city."

"If he knows that Edmond is Latimer's man, then he may well blame Latimer. No love lost there."

"Sir John, I must admit I think the man was an ass. I will not miss him."

"He wore my patience thin today, as well."

"Do the rest of us need to watch our backs? I mean are we going to be murdered for…"

"Assuming Sir James is behind the murder, then I imagine he believes the message has been sent. He will not be so bold as that! All the same, it might be best if you not visit whores after dark."

"That is not one of my vices, Sir John."

"I feel I am being used in a personal feud. As a result, the archbishop, the mayor and, most dangerously it would seem, d'Arzhon himself are arrayed against me."

"What do we do now?"

"The archbishop has invited me to meet with him. We shall see. Time for my reeve in Wilsham and his son to depart Yorke and head home."

Chapter 17

Tempest

NOVEMBER 1373

"Thank you for coming to see me, my Lord Sheriff."

As if I had much choice in the matter, thinks Sir John Bygod. "How may I be of service, your Grace?" he replies as he kneels to kiss the ring of the Lord Archbishop.

"I do not want matters to get further out of hand between you and d'Arzhon. It seems to me that things may be about to escalate in ways that do none of us much honor."

"I half expected him to be here."

"He sent his apologies to me. He says he needs to 'calm stormy seas' at this moment, whatever that means. I am told he has had numerous visitors the last few days."

"Numerous, indeed. We lost tally when it became too dangerous to watch his house."

"How so?"

"When a dozen men surround my bailiff and carelessly bump into him in the street…"

"Your bailiff was watching Sir James' house?"

"I had men watching his house, the Whitefriars, his shops on Saint Andrewgate, at The Swan, and his three barges that have all shown up on the docks, which is unusual in November. His men are staying in all those places. Mine have all been intimidated off their posts and none too gently in some cases. He may be a dangerous man to cross. Lord Latimer believes him to be a criminal."

"It appears you have whacked a hornets' nest."

"I estimate there are over a hundred of those angry 'hornets' in the city, your Grace. Some of these men look fairly brutal."

"You do understand that d'Arzhon finds work for veterans of the Crown's war in France, don't you? Many of whom served with him. Two things do seem clear to me: first, Sir James' reach is bigger than I knew, and second, when you forced entry into his house the alarm bell began to ring literally, as well as figuratively. What made you do that?"

"I was told that valuable commodities for which proper duties had not been paid were hidden there."

"By whom?"

"The king's chamberlain sent his man here."

The archbishop nods. "Sir William Latimer's man?"

"Yes, we found him murdered in the home of a prostitute last week."

"So, the man comes here and directs you to search d'Arzhon's house and then ends up dead. I do not know if Sir James is a criminal. All my dealings with him have been lawful. Scrupulously so. If anything, I have graver doubts about dealing with Lord Latimer. That is a man I do not trust. I will speak to d'Arzhon soon. It does seem that in each instance where there has been trouble the situation was instigated by someone else. You may wish to consider that. In the meanwhile, please do not do anything further to acerbate the situation."

Prior William leads Tenebroides, Sigismund, Joel, and finally Sir James into the priory church. Everyone turns as they enter and conversation ceases. The nave is full of men and a few women. Twelve Carmelite friars in their white robes and three novices stand in the chancel. Prior William begins with a prayer praising God, asking his forgiveness for our many sins, and for his blessing upon the gathering. It is not a large church, but it had been built when the priory had been much larger. Everyone stands and the church is full.

"It is early for our yearly meeting." James walks to the front of the assembly. "And many more of us are here than usual." It is an understatement. "So, let me start out by welcoming everyone to Yorke and thanking Prior William for offering us the use of the priory church. We do not have another place out of the weather to meet large enough in the wintertime. Just so you know, we will not be distributing shares here in the church..." Some laughter greets the comment as Prior William would surely be indignant at money being passed out in the sanctuary. "There are some new faces with us. Some are old friends in arms that have recently made their way back across the channel or have been here a while but sought us out in the last year. Others have joined us as a part of ventures we have entered. Master Swain, would you please stand? Master Swain owns a boatyard with us here in Yorke. His yard built the war galley for the city and we made good money on that contract. We recently bought the galley back and Swain is modifying it, so that we can trade along the coast, as well as to Calais and Bruges." Heads turn to get a good look and think about the ramifications of what Sir James has just said.

"Janice, please stand. Janice is responsible for our shops here in Yorke. She has been with us for some time weaving and selling cloth here, but now also manages the money side of the bakery, pie shop, smithy and tavern that are clustered together near the market." Janice sits back down next to Coletta. There are only three women in the church; the third being Diane from The Swan.

"More on our trading ventures in a moment. Obviously, you are all here because of concern over recent events: my two-month stay as a guest in the castle..." There is some laughter and some growls. "And the attempted search of the townhouse a week ago." Louder growling follows that remark. "There have been some other incidents, too – repeated searching of our barges for instance. I was not here, Lady Katherine and I were in Barmby, but Will, Prior William, and many others that are here acted promptly and effectively to get the sheriff and his party out of the house." Some cheering and enthusiastic exclamations of 'Well done!' are offered in response. "Well done, indeed."

"Nothing was taken from the house. They did not have enough time to make any sort of a thorough search. Many of you have been by the house and will confirm that everything is in good order. I believe that justifiable concerns grew in the re-telling, but I assure you that everything is very much under control."

"What if they come back with more men?" is shouted from the back.

"Then they, too, will be shown out the door in an even more aggressive manner, and…our actions in response will also be stronger."

"Has anything been done to prevent such a violation in the future?" Prior William asks, and the sentiment is echoed throughout the church.

"You all know that I prefer to play those cards in the shadows. We have successfully used the courts to redress damages with a little help from Prince Edward, the archbishop has intervened on our behalf, and I assure you that we have taken other actions that I will not further explain."

"Perhaps this sheriff needs to be taught with whom he is dealing!" This was followed by "Hear! Hear!"

"That education is very much in progress. That all of you arrived here in November turns out to be very much a part of that education. It is important not to over-react. My belief is that the sheriff is being manipulated by some powerful individuals in London. He does need to understand that is a risky game he is playing, but he leaves office in six months. Then Yorkshire has a new sheriff. My intention is to help the people in London…um, change their behavior. Otherwise it never stops."

"Who are the people in London?"

"They are people that have gotten very close to our king and are using that authority to fill their own purses. They have made many powerful enemies, so we are not alone in this. I understand that there is a feeling, that with all of us here, that we should do something. Please be patient. I assure you that I know where to find you if such actions are necessary." James waits. "May I move on to discuss our ventures?"

"Our Companie made over 1,700 pounds sterling in profit this past year. That is after all wages were paid for those of you that receive wages and all duties on imports and exports were paid. That works out to three pounds, ten shillings each to all single shareholders. Multiple shareholders can work out your payment. Last year we paid out two pounds per share, so that is a good increase. There is no poundage on imports and exports this year, so unless parliament acts to reinstate those duties, we stand to keep over two hundred pounds for ourselves that we lost last year."

"Cloth sales are, by far, our biggest source of profits followed by wool exports, cheese and then mutton. From the shepherds, to those involved in producing dyes and dyeing, wool shearers and spinners, weavers, fullers, skinners, butchers, fellmongers, and our barge crews...anyone touching sheep or wool, which is almost everyone, is contributing to our main source of profit. For me, the big surprise is the amount we are making on cheese. Up until recently, we were consuming most of the cheese we made from sheep's milk ourselves, but now we have grown our flocks to the point that we are producing a very marketable surplus. We do make good money selling surplus grain, tanned skins, and salted herring. Also, on imports such as wine and spice. I like to eat and drink, and so do all of you; those of you that produce things that we don't sell but keep to support ourselves are essential, too."

"If you feel guilty about not taking up your sword or bow and joining Lancaster's campaign across the Channel, then realize that we paid over 360 pounds to the Crown in duties and wool subsidy last year to support the war. We, you, are doing your part."

"I can't say as I was feeling guilty, my Lord!"

After much laughter, he says, "Well, you shouldn't, Walter! Shares will be paid out in the priory refectory. You may take any or all of it or add it to your account. Those not present will have it added to their account but may withdraw it at any time. Malcolm and Joel will have the ledgers. Virgil and Brother Hugh will have the coin. While you wait there is wine, ale, and plenty of food. I will be pleased to speak with any and all of you. It is really great to see us all together again, no matter what the circumstances!"

Swain recognizes Ruddy from the crew of the barge *Marie*. "What do you do with your share?"

"I'll take ten shillings to buy something special here in Yorke for my wife and our girls. The rest I add to my account."

"How do you know there really is an account with real money when you want it?"

"I counted my purse yesterday. It's all there and now it will have another three pounds."

"So, your money actually sits in your purse."

"In my purse, in the *Marie's* lockbox, in the strong room. I can take money out if I want to. Oh, I've been down the chimney," Ruddy laughs.

"Just like that."

"I have to make an entry on my ledger page with Malcolm and Virgil to sign. The ledger amount has to match the actual amount in my purse."

"How much is in your purse?"

"Enough."

"Each year you add a few pounds and you have enough?"

"It goes on top of what I brought back from France."

"You trust Sir James not to take it. Why?"

"There are a number of reasons. Where else would I keep it for one?"

"Point taken; what else?"

"Well, if he took all of our spoils, he would have a lot of men after him. Now wouldn't he?"

"There is that. So, everyone in this room has spoils."

"Not everyone. The fellas that showed up this last year, for example, probably came because they have nothing and need work. If you got back the first time with Sir James, you had a little; if you came back with him after Auray, then you got a lot; after Nájera, then a bit more. If you weren't in Sir John's Companie or with Sir James, then you may well not have come back with anything. He made sure we got back with what was ours...course, we made sure he got back with what was his."

"You get just one share?"

"Unless you have a lot of responsibility, such as a steward, you just get one share. Almost everybody gets one share."

"I get two shares and I just joined. That doesn't seem fair to you does it?"

"You are responsible for the boatyard and everyone that works there. The war galley was a big project. I pull on an oar, move cargo, and do as I am told. That is just the way I want it to be. Look at Master Tenebroides – all full of worries and nervous energy. He earns his twelve shares. No, thanks."

"Twelve shares...that's almost forty pounds! How many shares does Sir James take?"

"He gets a third."

"Just one third of a share?"

"No, one third of everything before any shares are paid."

"So, he took over five hundred pounds and you get three pounds."

"Right."

"You accept that?"

"It is same rule for spoils as we had in France, except we don't have to give a third to the king...unless you count the duties we had to pay. I guess that was damn near a third."

"That sounds unfair."

Laughing, "that is how the world works! I came from almost nothing and now I have a family and I bought a home in Richmond. It's a good life. Why do I have it? Because I fought with Sir James and was able to return alive with my share of the spoils. He got me back alive... Don't you understand that?"

"Seems to me that I saw lots of old campaigners limping about and begging for food in London when I was there."

"I am not limping, and I am no beggar. That is my point. And another thing, even if I was an invalid, Sir James would have made sure I got back with my share. And have a roof over my head, and food to eat, and work to do to earn my living!"

Swain sniggers, "bah, I don't see any invalids here. Well, a few."

"Next time you are at The Swan or the bakery look a bit more closely. There are lots of things a man with one arm or a bum leg can do as well as you or me. Pulling an oar ain't one of them, though, and heading down from Richmond to Yorke in November wouldn't be a smart decision, either. We stick together here just like we did over there."

"I am told your army has dispersed, James. I take it you were able to calm things down."

"Hardly an army, but yes for now, your Grace."

"Impressive to gather that many men with snow on the ground, but you need to be able to control them!"

"They did not assemble in response to an order from me. I do not like to work that way." Attracting attention to the number of men he could call on was the last thing James wanted. "I would say...they gathered in response to a perceived threat. Everything is under control. Your Grace, please understand they are all free men and not my bondmen. Our bond is based on mutual benefits not compulsion. When there is a concern, they do expect it to be attended to."

"Like Latimer's man?"

"I heard about that. I do not know anything, and I certainly had nothing to do with it. He also had some violent words with our sheriff that day; so, there are other possibilities."

"You and Sir William Latimer are not on the best of terms, that much is clear."

"That goes back a long way. I do not know if this current conflict is personal, aggressively farming the customs or an attempt to enter the wool trade. To this point I have been very restrained in response to repeated provocation. Everyone is not in agreement with that restraint. They made that clear. I pray that Sir John Bygod's other many responsibilities as sheriff take all of his attention for the rest of his office. Destruction of our property, forcing entry into my home, putting me into custody without reason, and threatening my wife are not things I am able to further tolerate."

"This has gone too far. I have encouraged him to do just that. Latimer may well keep his own greedy interests foremost, but he is still the king's chamberlain."

"I am most mindful of that your Grace."

"I believe Sir John realizes he has been unwittingly involved in a most dangerous situation. Your gathering of former comrades-in-arms has certainly made him nervous. I imagine you will deny any knowledge of the murders in the castle when Lord Latimer was here in person."

"I assure you I was locked in a dark cell when that happened. Obviously, I was made aware of what took place by the sheriff. He did make some accusations. None of my men were in the castle that night. Lord Latimer has made many enemies. I have no desire to keep fighting with Sir John, but the man continues to antagonize me without reason! If he is nervous, and that serves to back him off, then that is a good outcome. If he musters a substantial force to assert his authority, well...that is something I certainly hope to avoid at all costs."

"What do you mean no one is there?"

"The entire village was empty, my Lord Sheriff."

"Disease? Murder?"

"There were no bodies and all of their possessions are gone. I would say they have been gone for a while." Sir John Bygod's reeve for Wilsham is bewildered and nervous before his lord.

"A Scottish raiding party? Surely, we would have heard. Was there a trail to follow?"

"There was snow on the ground; if there was a trail it is not there now."

"So, you are telling me that I have lost an entire village! One entrusted to your authority I might add. That is entirely unacceptable! You will get back there and find those villeins. I have some matters to attend to here, but then I will join you and we will find them."

"Lady Mary, what brings you to Yorke in the cold of winter?"

"Oh, Doctor Kate, things are not good," she sighs despondently.

"This does not sound like a matter for me here at the apothecary."

"No, I have been called to court for debts."

Katherine looks at the drooped shoulders of the little girl, what is she thirteen or fourteen years old? "Surely you have a steward or reeve to represent you in court?"

"Yes, the steward is here. We used all our money to pay the fifteenth two years ago and have nothing to pay them for last year."

"I fell behind with the city bailiff myself until I was paid to perform surgery on Sir James. Why don't I close the shop and the two of us go see my husband?"

"I don't want to bother him with more of my troubles. He has done so much already."

Katherine shoos Mary before her as she heads out the door, "Miles, I am headed out for a bit; I should be back before too long."

"Lady Katherine this is Richard, my steward. Should he come with us?"

"Most certainly."

"Lady Kate I have the sense that some men are watching us."

Katherine turns and points to two men that are following them. "Those men?"

"Yes!"

"They are keeping an eye on me. My husband is afraid I will run off with a wealthy Flemish wool buyer." She winks at Mary. "You aren't Flemish, are you, Richard?"

"Oh, no, my Lady."

"Well, Richard, you are the steward, how did it come to pass that the manor entrusted to your care has no money to pay the taxes?"

"Sir James, we had money. It was gone when I became steward again."

"After Roger Elford was forced to depart."

"Yes."

"That should not come as a surprise. Did you report the loss to the sheriff?

"No, I guess we were glad to see them gone and hesitant to make an accusation that would be hard to prove."

"Forgive me Kate, but would you and Richard please step out? And ask Malcolm to join us." Katherine smiles and holds the door for the steward.

"Mary, your father, Sir Gerald Rabuk, died in service with our prince after Nájera. Disease preyed on our encampment and those of us that returned consider ourselves fortunate. Did you know that your father served with Sir John Chandos?"

"I do not recall hearing that name. Is it important?"

"I see you are wearing your broach. That is Sir John's shield; it is how we remember him. The greatest knight in the realm after Prince Edward, oh and of course the king. Ah, Malcolm, Lady Mary would like to make a withdrawal from her account."

"Of course, I will bring her ledger. How much would you like to withdrawal?"

"Fifteen pounds should be enough Mary?"

"Sir James, I do not have an account."

"I brought back your father's share from Spain. I was waiting until you became a bit older to have this discussion, but now seems to be a good time."

After some time has passed Malcolm returns, "Thank you, Malcolm." James came over and sits next to Mary. "You see what this says?"

Her eyes widen, and she bobs her head, but nothing comes out.

"Malcolm has written fifteen pounds withdrawn, and dated it today, January 25, 1374. This pouch has fifteen pounds. Please count it."

"Fifteen."

"Now I will sign the ledger next to Malcolm's signature and you will also sign it."

"Good. Take the eight pounds seven shillings that you owe and pay it to the clerk of the court today. You will not need to go to any trial in the morning."

Mary begins sobbing and James hugs her tight. "Tomorrow we could talk about Appleton Rabuk's finances if you would like. There is no fifteenth approved by Parliament for this year, so at least you will not have to worry about any taxes for a while. If something happens and you need help, then you know where to come. Otherwise it is always best to keep financial matters a closely guarded secret."

"Paul Fitz-William thinks we should have a flock of sheep; do you agree?"

"You can sell the wool for income. Slaughter some for meat and skins. And you get milk; some of which you can use to make cheese."

"Paul said you might be willing to help us get a flock if we commit to sell you our wool."

"James, she looked like she has been crying."

"A release of tension, I imagine. A fourteen-year-old girl can only hold it together for so long."

"You loaned her the money to pay the taxes?"

"Mm...not a loan. I had some money here that belongs to her. I was waiting to give it to her when she was older."

"Really?" She clearly does not believe him. "I don't believe you are telling me everything."

"I'm not, but what I did tell you is absolutely true. Her father, Sir Gerald, was a member of Sir John's Companie."

"And the Companie takes care of its own."

"Yes, we do, but the money I gave her did rightfully belong to her father, was entrusted to me, and is now rightfully hers."

Sir James' townhouse has twenty-seven feet of street frontage. On the left side as you face the house, through a stone arch is an alley leading to the courtyard behind it. The street is almost right up against the stone front of the house. The door is up three steps and recessed back from the main façade. The second-floor main living area, overhangs the first, is timber framed, and extends over the alley arch right up against the adjacent house next door.

Purchase offers have been made, but not yet accepted, to the owners of the houses on both sides. Mid-winter is not a time when people want to move away from their warm hearth. In the meantime, a wrought iron gate is hung on hinge pins inserted behind the alley archway, and quarters for eight Companie men are established on the ground floor. Behind a thicker new front door an entry hall is created ending in a second door. Any visitor can now be allowed in out of the weather without having access beyond unless so invited.

Paul Fitz-William has the unenviable task of sitting through all cases before the wapentake court of Barkston Ash. "As you surmised, Sir James, a man did inquire why the court was not hearing Appleton Rabuk's tax debt case."

"Ah, a local man?"

"No, I followed him back to his lodgings at the Black Bear. He got his horse and left the city."

"Did he give a name or place of residence to the inn?"

"William Elys of Yarmouth is what he told them."

"The Elys are a prominent family in Yarmouth. William is a customs agent and therefore connected to Lyons and Latimer. That fits my suspicions. I will make some inquiries."

"Sir James, I also bear some bad news. Archbishop John died last week at Cawood."

"That is, indeed, sad news. He was a good and prayerful man." Not to mention that he was a helpful ally, thought James. "Find out about funeral arrangements, please."

Chapter 18

War at Sea

"Sir James, we find ourselves in the awkward position of requiring you to sell back to us the galley that we so recently sold to you."

James is surprised that the two, prominent men have braved the cold day to come to his townhouse; he would have expected them to send for him to attend them in the cathedral complex. "Not much has been done to her since the purchase my Lord Mayor, it has been too cold, and so your request is easily done." James sips his glass of warmed wine while Malcolm adds a log to the fire. "May I ask why you need her back?"

"We have received word that the Castilians will be sending a fleet into the channel as early as March first," replies the archbishop who stood in his fur collared robe with his back to the fire. "The Crown is assembling a fleet to defend the coast." Alexander Neville is the newly elected Archbishop of Yorke. His election has yet to be confirmed by the pope, but he has been approved by the king and is in the city. He is a younger brother of the steward of the royal household – John Neville; a man closely aligned with William Latimer. The Nevilles are a powerful family in northern England and are in many prominent positions. His attainment may become a difficult situation for James and his Companie.

James nods. "And the city is ordered to send the galley back again."

"We are hoping you will be willing to sell her back for the same salvage price."

"The ship needs new sails, cordage, a main yard, some oars, and to have the fighting platforms re-assembled."

"We can manage to be certain that your boatyard gets that work. Even if we still owned it, we would be obligated to have all of that done. We also need to re-equip the ship with bows and arrows. James, would you make a complete list and tell us the cost?"

"Certainly, Thomas, but may I suggest an alternative? The city does not need to own the ship; just to provide a ship to the fleet. Is that correct?"

"What are you suggesting?"

"That the city pays all the costs associated with re-fitting for war, and then charter me to send the ship to the fleet. It has the additional benefit of the city not owning a galley when the current crisis has passed."

"So, we save the cost of purchasing it back. What is your charter fee?"

"You pay the cost of the re-fit and I keep the galley. Something minimal in addition…say, five pounds and, of course, the Crown's payments for crew wages and victuals come to me."

The newly elected Mayor, Thomas de Howme, suddenly looks visibly relieved. "That would be most agreeable! Any estimate on the other costs?"

"Something around twenty-five pounds, plus the cost of the bows and sheaves of arrows. One hundred of each?"

"Eighty, how much do they cost?"

"The Crown pays one shilling for a bow and four p for a sheaf of arrows."

The mayor begins to do the math in his head. "So, five pounds six shillings and…eight pence."

"All told just over thirty-five pounds," the archbishop snaps impatiently. "More than we discussed, but we did not consider all of the costs we would have to bear after we bought it back. We still save money 'chartering' your galley. My Lord Mayor, we are agreed?"

"Yes, certainly, we are to have the ship in Sandwich as close to the first of March as possible."

"It is fortunate that the sails and ropes are already here, then. That is not much time."

James increased his offers for the houses on both sides of his to sixty pounds. The widowed owner of the house next to the alley accepts. The owner of the corner house on the other side declines and the offer is withdrawn. The widow purchases a smaller home on the west side of the River Ouse, and James' men help move her possessions. That is part of the agreement.

The house is fourteen feet wide with a single gable on the street side, about thirty-two feet deep with an open space behind. A cookhouse had been built at the back against the wall of the priory. An eight-foot-high wall runs the seventeen feet from the house on both sides to the cook house, which make it a private yard. The wall next to James' property is immediately removed to increase the size of his courtyard. The wall on the far side is then raised to twelve feet in height by utilizing the salvaged brick.

The façade of the house is renovated to match the front of Sir James' and the front door blocked over. The main entrance to the purchased house will now be from the courtyard. The wall between the second floor of the new house and the room over the alley arch is opened to create a doorway. A passage cannot be opened in the third floor because of all the roof trussing. The cellar had a dirt floor but seemed to stay dry, so a stone floor is laid to create a storeroom for foodstuffs. The front of the street level is turned into a warehouse space for high value goods. The back becomes a dining room for the staff. The second and third floors are turned into staff, and Companie, living quarters. James has agreed, under pressure, to have more Companie men present at the house at all times.

"I have already added a quarterdeck and raised the sides to a new deck amidships!" Swain is not a man that likes changes or short deadlines. His tone betrays his frustration.

"Keep all of that in place Master Swain. Just build a new fo'c'sle and replace the fighting tops with something smaller – of lighter weight."

"I'd like to put more rowing benches back in." Captain Carter points to where they have been removed.

"I can do that, Captain. Will fifteen on each side be adequate? We have thirty good oars."

"That should be fine. What's the crew size, Sir James?"

"I am thinking sixty in total."

"I have sixteen plus myself right now. That is a lot of mariners to find and we will need them if we are to board an enemy ship. We will be too small a crew to board a Castilian galley by ourselves."

"They just need to be men-at-arms and archers that can be trained to man an oar. Your crew can handle the sailing. I have already picked out another twenty-four men plus a cook and a purchasing agent, so we need to find another eighteen. Timing is not good."

"Not good because it is tight?"

"Not good because the spring planting starts soon and then the wool shearing. After the harvest is the best time to go to war if you are a landowner such as myself."

Carter shrugs. "If we have to sail undermanned, perhaps we can make a run back to Kingston after the planting. The purser is responsible for provisioning the ship?"

"Yes, and if any additional cargo is being carried."

"To Calais?"

"And maybe Antwerp or Bruges."

"Are you going to want me to get as far north as Kingston on regular timing?"

"That would be nice, but it will depend on the admiral and his expectations. A monthly run up to Kingston for provisions would save me a lot of money instead of buying food in Yarmouth or Sandwich."

"That's a day's run each way from Yarmouth. If we have independent patrols areas, I could ask for north of Yarmouth sometimes. Calais is just three hours from Sandwich with a good wind."

"Exactly," said James, smiling.

The sheriff's new bailiff arrives at James' home with a sealed parcel from the Prince of Wales. He is nervous after the events of the last few months and confides to Malcolm at the door, who has several men standing behind him, that Sheriff Bygod has left the city to attend to urgent matters on his own estates.

James is aghast at what he reads. Lancaster marched clear across France without ever bringing the French to battle. The campaign on which so much depended to restore the king's realm, and so much was spent from the treasury is a disaster. Over a third of the army is dead. The remaining starving and un-paid men have scattered to try and find their own ways back to England. The king and Prince Edward are furious.

"A barrel of salted herring works out to six meals for the ship. That is if each man gets two fish. I am figuring a barrel of salt pork to be about the same. Dried pease, hard tack, cheese, and ale – all in barrels. Your stewards are care-fully counting what they have left before letting me have anything. We can get fresh water in port each night, as Captain Carter says, it is mostly day cruis-ing, He wants five days water aboard at all times in case we are blown off our coast." Matthew has been promoted to managing the cargo and stores aboard the galley as 'purser' from his previous wool buying role.

"If you need help with the stewards, just let me know." James knew they might be over-cautious. "They are looking at low storerooms because Virgil doesn't make trips in January and February, but the *Marie* should be here this week with plenty of grain and pease, arrows, too. Make certain to buy sea coal in Kingston; you will need it for cooking. Where are you baking the biscuits?"

"Here in Yorke at the bakery. I've asked them to make five barrels a month and ship them to Kingston. I've got enough for the first month now. We have had to take bows and arrows from what is already on hand, Sir James."

"Tenebroides knows?"

"Yes, he has been a big help. Almost everything else will be brought aboard in Barmby. In the future everything will be taken to Kingston assuming *le Mare Majstro* can come north. If Carter can't, Master Tenebroides is talking about taking the *Christine* to Yarmouth to provision her. Have you thought about victualing other ships in the fleet?"

"One step at a time, but I like the way you are thinking." Matthew had been Justin's assistant buying wool, cutlery, and iron ingots in Sheffield. He was proving to be an excellent choice to manage purchasing for the ship. "If all the ships are trying to buy provisions in Sandwich or Yarmouth it will drive prices up. We will have plenty of salt from Barmby for the pork, salted herring, and cheese in a few months. I am loath to have to buy them now from the Hanse. Virgil will also be bringing in cloth and alum; we need to talk about that. The Crown pays ships based on three pence a day for each man plus two for food. With Captain Carter, his mates, and you and Ruddy our average daily wages are closer to four, so you need to balance the finances by using our own food supplies as much as possible."

The River Swale is frigid and swollen with snow melt as Virgil guides the *Marie* south and into the City of Yorke for the first time in the new year. Several months' production: cloth by the Flemish weavers, alum crystals from Clyde and his men on the eastern coast, and heavy lead pigs from Swaledale added to bushels of winnowed grains from the fall harvest make a full barge. The crew's own efforts have produced thirty sheaves of arrows for the galley. Owen the butcher and Oliver the fishmonger are now back selling in Yorke as a result of peacemaking by the mayor and the old archbishop, so fresh fish packed in snow from the village weirs and six sheep to be slaughtered round out the load. Demand for foodstuffs in late February at the Yorke market is sure to be high. Plenty of water under the hull but not as much bulwark above the water as he would like!

Master Tenebroides and his crew aboard the *Christine* arrive on the tide the following day. The new looms at Barmby produce a coarse woolen fabric from the poorest grade wool. It is quick to weave and gets no dye; just a cleaning in the fulling mill, a minimal trimming of the excess fuzz or nap and is sold at the market to make inexpensive clothing, which is all the poorest can afford. It is also used for sacks and rough blankets. It sells quickly and uses up wool that otherwise could not be sold but makes very little profit. Besides the fabric he brings barrels of salted herring, tuns of imported wine, kermes to dye the scarlets, cages full of chickens, and baskets of sea coal. They would have been able to sell all the sea coal they could buy, but instead, it is all used by the Companie at The Swan, the priory, at James' house, the workshops and by the smith. None is left to sell.

Le Mare Majstro emerges from the Humbre estuary into the heavier chop of the North Sea for her run down the eastern coast of England to join the fleet. The wind this early in March is frigid and vigorous. The seas are rough. They manage to make a fast passage. To Captain Carter's contempt, half the crew is seasick. He reminds himself that this has been true of the soldiers he has taken aboard on every voyage, and he is not feeling so good himself. The changes to the ship did not make her top-heavy as he feared and the deeper keel results in her making less leeway under sail. He is well-satisfied with her. They are one of the only ships to arrive at the walled port city of Yarmouth the first week of March.

Sir William Neville, Admiral of the North, is not here. Captain Carter reports to his lieutenant, Hugh Fastoff, and is sent to cruise the coast of Suffolk and Kent as far as Sandwich. They head down the coast and then slip across the channel to Calais. Matthew is able to get a good price for the scarlets woven in Richmond and dyed by Manser in Yorke. The alum is jumped at by the first house of dyers he visits. He also makes some contacts with members of the Staple Port of Calais that are licensed by the Crown to manage all wool exports, and make sure the king gets his customary duties and the hefty subsidy.

They return across the channel and anchor in "The Downs" off Sandwich. Several king's ships and the barges of the City of London are now anchored in this sheltered area where the "Northern Fleet" is to assemble. Six miles off the coast of England lay the Goodwin Sands. This ten-mile-long shallows running parallel with the shore is a peril to unwary mariners but also creates the enormous anchorage of The Downs off the coast. Twelve chickens are killed for dinner and cooked into a stew. Most of the crew have found their "sea-legs" now and have a hearty appetite. Sir William's other "lieutenant," John Brice, sends them down the coast to patrol as far as Ramsgate. As yet, there is no word of the Castilian fleet.

Carter keeps them within easy reach of the English shore. The deeper keel that Master Swain added over the winter has made the ship a good sailer. With the wind out of the northeast *le Mare Majstro* sails steady with her sails hard and firm off the coast of Romney Marsh.

"Ship ahead!"

"Where away?" Carter calls back to the masthead.

"Just off the starboard bow."

"Steady as we go." On this tack *le Mare Majstro* will continue to close the distance and cut off the quarry's escape away from the coast.

"It's a cogge. Flemish or Dutch built," the masthead hollers down.

"Archers aloft and to the fo'c'sle!"

The bigger ship is gradually being trapped against the coast. They suddenly turn southwest in an attempt to force a way out into the channel.

"Ease off a point to larboard. Run up the king's colors."

The distance closes to within hailing range, Carter cups his hands around his mouth and shouts, "Heave to in the name of the king!"

The cogge ignores the order and turns farther south threatening to collide with them.

"Turn with them!" Carter motions the man at the tiller below to turn parallel to the cogge. A collision with the heavily built ship would shatter *le Mare Majstro*. "Archers make ready! Loose arrows!" Thirty arrows fly across the short gap toward the cogge. The archers in the tops have an excellent firing angle down into the sailors aboard their quarry. "Again!"

"Bring us alongside, grapples! Boarders!" Lines with three-pronged grappling hooks are thrown across the narrowing gap between the ships as they came together. Archers in the fighting tops easily pick off the men trying to dislodge the hooks or cut the lines. By the time the men-at-arms climb up and aboard the higher ship the fight is over.

She is the eighty-tonne Flemish cogge *la Seynte Marie* out of Bruges and destined for Edinburgh, Scotland. Eight of the crew including her master lay dead and four others are wounded. As one of the first English ships out on patrol the surprise is total. The crew of the prize was completely unaware that an English fleet was putting to sea to control shipping in the channel. Matthew sits in the master's cabin and goes through the manifests. Captain Carter sorts through her charts, log, and at length finds her strongbox. She is a legitimate prize of war, after the king and admiral get their shares the rest belongs to Sir James, Carter, and his crew.

Matthew and the captain immediately remove most of the silver groats from the strongbox. The cargo includes silks from Italy, furs from Russia, and precious metals from Bohemia. Each of these items is transferred to *le Mare Majstro*. The ship has almost six hundred bolts of cloth aboard. The bolts of first quality Ghent broadcloth are culled from the cargo and re-stowed aboard their ship. Some provisions including biscuit, wine, and salt beef are also removed. When they return to the Downs, the king and admiral will have their shares calculated from what remains aboard *la Seynte Marie*.

"Matthew, you seemed keen to get that cloth aboard us. Is it really worth the risk and trouble?"

"Those 160 bolts of cloth are worth over nine hundred pounds, Captain."

Carter's mouthful of ale explodes across the cabin. After he stops coughing, he says, "How do we get it through Kingston without paying the import duty?"

"Leave that to me. I'd say those twenty-four bolts of silk are worth close to another three hundred pounds."

"I would say this has been a good day. How did you say the shares work?" Carter had not paid full attention when there was nothing to be paid out.

"One third to Sir James, one third to the officers: you, me, and your mates; one third to the crew."

"Let's keep any amounts to ourselves until after we leave Sandwich again. Otherwise someone will have a loose tongue and hang us all. I noticed you threw the cargo manifests and ship's log overboard."

"Aye, the king's representatives will be looking to make a comparison between what is supposed to be aboard and what is actually aboard – can't have that. What were they doing heading west off Romney Marsh if they were sailing for Edinburgh?" Matthew drummed his fingers against his temples in thought.

"They may have had another port-of-call first. The winds were against them for a run up the coast without some long tacks. If you think they were up to mischief, I mean that is possible, but it could have a perfectly innocent explanation."

"I'm not a sailor. What do you mean, 'long tacks'?"

"She is square rigged. One mast with one large sail on a spar mounted across the ship. Her best points of sail are with the wind behind her. Now that spar can be pulled around enough to sail across the wind and even a bit into the wind, but not directly into the wind. We can't sail directly into the wind, either, but we can sail much closer to the wind than she can. To make progress up the coast they would have had to sail across the wind to the east and then back across to the west. That would take a long time."

"So, what do you do?"

"Either tack or wait for the wind to change in your favor."

"So, why can we sail 'closer to the wind?'"

"We are fore-and-aft rigged not square rigged. If she was not so heavy and round, she could out sail us before the wind. How does Sir James know what his share is supposed to be?"

"My responsibility is to look after Sir James' and the Companie share. There are over twenty members of your crew that will make certain I do just that. Don't forget unless we try to sell the cloth and silk in Calais or Antwerp ourselves, we will be looking to Sir James to have it sold and trust him to see that we get our fair share not the other way around."

"Fair enough; I just wanted to see where you stood."

"Ruddy, Captain Carter asked if Sir James would see his full share. We need to keep an eye on him."

"Oh, I keep an eye on him. Did he suggest that Sir James be shorted?"

"No, he just asked."

"Seems like a reasonable question."

"What?"

"We just removed...what Matthew– 1,200 pounds worth of merchandise from the prize?"

"It's quite a bit more than that."

"Say, 1,600, then, so we are taking half of that – eight hundred pounds out of the pockets of the king and the admirals, right? Cheating them, but you're appalled when he asks if the owner gets his full share. He just wants to know how we play the game. Like I said, a reasonable question."

"When you put it that way…"

"Now that he knows how the game is to be played, we need to make certain he plays by our rules."

With the battle over, an effort is made to remove the arrows and stop the bleeding from the wounded mariners. In some instances, they just do not have the confidence to pull the arrow through without causing additional injury. They are made as comfortable as possible. Captain Carter assigns the first mate to sail the cogge and both ships sail in company to the nearby port of Dover to take the prisoners ashore.

Dover has had two ships put in recently with deserters from Lancaster's army in France. The English were in Bordeaux, a city in southwest France on the Bay of Biscay. The full scale of the disaster is now apparent. Hundreds of soldiers died on the march across France from injuries or disease. They travelled over three hundred miles south and west in an arc from Calais all the way to the Atlantic coast without a significant battle being fought, but the army was dogged by the enemy and there were continuous skirmishes particularly if the men left the main body in search of food. As a result, most were starving by the time they reached English duchy of Aquitaine.

Bordeaux could not have been a worse place to end up. The weak and surly men doubled the population of the city, which was suffering from another round of the plague. The harvest had been poor, and the price of food now became inflated and was unaffordable to men that had not received their pay. Many, weakened, succumbed to the ravages of the plague. They were reduced to refugees begging on the streets.

Matthew asks, "How many of Gaunt's army are here?"

Carter replies, "I'm not certain. The ones I saw look like hell."

"With the plague?"

"Starvation and worn out I'd say. If the plague was on them, they would be dead by now. Their voyage took several weeks due to adverse winds in the Bay of Biscay."

"We've got a ship with plenty of room besides our own."

"Matthew! Where would we take them?"

"Kingston and then it would be up to Sir James."

"Don't they have families and homes to return to? Why should they be our problem?" complains Carter.

"If they do, then they won't want our help. We can cook a meal for them, sound them out and make an offer. They all could use a free meal."

"Or we can leave them here and sail on to Sandwich with our prize."

"No, that is not an option for us," Matthew shakes his head.

"The hell it isn't!"

"Captain, we don't work that way. Our Companie takes in war veterans and puts them to work to grow our villages. Men are hard to find since the plagues."

A surprising number of the refugees in Dover are from Kent. The stew of salted pork and pease with biscuits was appreciated, as was the sack with a fish and biscuit for their travel, but the offer of a longer commitment is not taken. In the end, just twenty-two men with sunken eyes and taut skin join them aboard the cogge for whatever awaits them. Perhaps they just want to know that another meal will follow the one they had been given.

Their arrival back in The Downs is greeted with enthusiasm. The captured ship is surely a sign of good things to come for the fleet. There is currently a shortage of ships, and the king's agents settle quickly on a value of £210 for the ship and another £1100 for her cargo. Captain Carter turns over the cogge to the agents and they take £655 worth of the wine and cloth over to le Mare Majstro as their fifty-percent share of the prize. Matthew does not feel confident that an actual payment would be made promptly, if at all, but taking their share now in merchandise is gladly agreed to by all. The Crown's financial resources are stretched thin, so the arrangement is mutually beneficial. Certification that all the goods are exempt from import tariff is received in writing with the official seal of the Cinque port of Sandwich.

As long as they are back within ten days' time, John Brice, Lieutenant to the king's admiral, agrees to let them sail to Kingston to offload the spoils and the pathetic veterans of Lancaster's ill-fated campaign, and re-provision the ship. Brice became quite angry when someone termed the war refugees 'deserters' as he had seen the men and witnessed the obvious deprivation they had endured. Matthew warmed to him.

Captain Carter brings the ship up the Humbre at the end of two days sailing. The wind is strong out of the west, and the second day they are able to make the journey from Yarmouth all the way to Kingston.

"Tenebroides was here just over a week ago. I do not expect him back for at least another fortnight." Two fishing boats, Companie men, tie up to *le Mare Majstro* early the next morning.

Matthew nods. "Sounds right." He knew that the *Christine* usually made the trip monthly. "If we showed up for provisions, did he leave instructions?"

"He was planning to bring them next time. I've arranged for space in Master Quixley's warehouse. No one expected you back so soon."

"No reason to have thought otherwise, Piers." Piers is the leader among the small Companie community in Kingston. "Captain, I think we need to sail on to Barmby, and I would like to get word to Sir James."

"Agreed."

"There will not be any salt making yet. Can you buy any here?" He asks the fisherman.

"I can. We also catch the herring here but I've few barrels."

"We have empty barrels aboard. Piers, here is money for salt and sea coal. I'm sending two men ashore with you to ride for Yorke. I'd like three barrels of salted herring and three of sea coal, more if you can get it."

"When do you expect to be back?"

"A day to Barmby, one day there, and a day back; at least three days unless Sir James is delayed or has other plans for us."

James, Katherine, and a small escort arrive in Barmby the following morning. The war veterans look somewhat better for having had a week of steady meals, but those whose weakened state made them seasick on the voyage have not been able to keep anything down. They now look even worse if that is possible. Some simply could not keep any food down due to the level of their deprivation. In any case, they are ashore now. Lady Katherine and Malcolm attend them while James boards the ship.

"A good voyage, Captain!"

"Very good, indeed, Sir James, if Matthew's cargo valuation is accurate."

"It is fairly close. The cloth and other merchandise must be sold before it can be converted into shares. I am going to discount them one fifth. Full value on the coin, gold bar, and silver. The Companie share is 781 pounds, ten shillings. Your share, Captain, works out to three hundred ninety pounds fifteen shillings. Matthew, you and the other officers will receive ninety-seven pounds, thirteen shillings, nine pence each." James turns the ledger, so they can read the valuations and the division of the shares. It is an enormous sum. Most knights of the realm have an annual income of about one hundred pounds.

Captain Carter keeps trying to wipe the tears from his eyes until he blubbers out, "I can't read a thing right now! I've never even hoped to know such a fortune in my life." It came as a surprise to see a man so uncompromising stern displaying so much emotion.

"Let's go ahead and speak to the crew."

Everyone assembles on the main deck. James has the front row sit and the back row lean against the rail, so he can make eye contact with each and every man. "I am sure you are all aware that you have earned some prize money." The faces of the crew range from pure joy to distrust. The distrust seems to come from the members of Carter's original crew. "It is best to keep these things a bit quiet I find. The same man that could not be persuaded to leave his family and risk the perils of the sea will find it very unfair that you have enjoyed good fortune and he has not."

"After the king took his due, the share for each man of the crew works out to fourteen pounds four shillings tuppence. That's a bonus of over three years' daily wages!" There is some cheering of approval. "There is a bit of bad news, though – I need to sell the merchandise to pay all of you. That may take some time. I do not know how long you will be at sea in the service of the

Crown, but my intention is that you will be paid in full when that time is done. Matthew needs to know who should receive your share if something happens to you during your service – wife, child, relative. I'll take that list with me in the event that the entire ship is lost."

"This was providence and is unlikely to happen again. If you are fortunate enough to capture another prize it is unlikely she will have such a valuable cargo, and unlikely that you will be sailing alone; we would then have to share it with any other ships. You all know how prize money is distributed. One third to the owners represented by me, one third among the officers, and one third to all of you. I have here a full list of the cargo, the value of each item, and the distribution of the shares. You are welcome to scrutinize it now and ask any questions you may have. After that I will put it away. Master Tenebroides should be here by afternoon and we will transfer the cargo to the *Christine*. Well done!"

"Sir James, what does this say?"

"That says 160 bolts of the best quality Ghent broadcloth."

"And this one?"

"That is the bolts of second quality broadcloth."

"And this?"

"That is a bar of gold that was in her strongbox," James put his finger over his lips and gives them a conspiratorial wink. "And these are the bars of silver."

"Why would they have a gold bar?"

"My only guess is that the Scots have a mint in Edinburgh and that was its destination."

"And this is the Companie's share!"

"Quite right."

"So, eventually I get my share of that, too."

"Yes, you will."

Chapter 19

Faire Trade

The weather has been plenty wet, and it is clear to Clyde that more rain is on the way. The four Companie men depart Bollebi mid-morning. It is cold and drizzling until it becomes a downpour for the remaining fifteen miles of the trek southwest across the moors. By early evening, they hunker down, soaked to the skin, in a copse of trees to eat cold meat pies and wait for total darkness.

It does not take long for the overcast skies to blot out any remnants of a sunset. The remaining distance to Settrington is a soggy, miserable march. Clyde had marked the way clearly in his mind on his previous trip, and in the darkness and downpour they finally run into the beck, but they do not know if they are upstream or downstream of the manor. A crack of lightning illuminates the tower of All-Saints Church where generations of Bygods lay buried. They needed to head just a little way upstream.

No one is outside on such a dirty night. No dog begins barking. Clyde swings his pick into the corner of the earthen dam and the other three dug in, slipping and cussing under their breath, with the shovels. The storm, the sloshing and creaking of the waterwheel, and the volume of storm water rushing over the spillway cover all their noise. The mill pond is swollen over capacity as they dig a trench across the crown of the berm. Once the water has a path it quickly eats away the sides and bottom of their trench – ever widening and increasing in volume. Big chunks of earth break free and disappear in the rushing water.

"Time to go." Clyde leads them at a run south along the berm away from the manor and then east. They hear the dam breach behind them. At the edge of the woods they pause to see if they can discern the results of their mischief. The flood of water smashes into the barns, stables, and outbuildings. It shatters walls and timbers before hitting the side of the main house. The black forms of structures shift and collapse in the dark. There is screaming behind them as they get moving again. Dark, cold, wet, and tired, Clyde's steps have a mirthful spring in them.

In May, James goes with Harold, his steward at Gainsburgh, to the annual Lincoln Faire to sell cloth from the Flemish ship taken off Romney Marsh. Malcolm stays at the house, but Will and Geoffrey ride along as does the Lady Katherine. Kate also brings, Anne, her maid. He had not been to the city since securing the release of Companie men from the sheriff; it was hard to believe that had been over two years past. Though only half as large as Yorke, Lincoln is still one of the largest cities in England. The annual faire is the largest event in the city and attracts crowds from all over Lincolnshire and merchants from as far as London and even overseas. The Earninga Straete down from Yorke has more traffic than James could ever remember seeing on the old Roman road. He is glad to have the fishermen at Blaketofte ferry the bolts of cloth and Katherine safely dry across the Humbre estuary. The wagons and horses ford a bit later at low tide, but it is a wet mess. They had not been across long when the tidal bore surges in behind them. It is at least a three-foot wave and clearly a force with which to be reckoned. A loaded wagon behind them just makes it up the bank in time; the unknown driver white-faced with terror. "When the fishermen say it is time to get moving across do not delay!"

"Right you are, Sir James," agrees Will.

They have to pay a fee at the city gate to bring in their wagon of merchandise, and the two pack horses. Then also pay a stallage fee to the bailiff. The best stall locations naturally went to merchants from Lincoln. The next best locations went to vendors that had been at the fair for many years and 'reserved' their spot. Decent rooms are no longer available, but James has planned for that. The Companie men at Gainsburgh that escorted them on the road will take the horses back and then return three days later to bring them and the wagon back out. It is struggle to get through the mass of merchants, find a bailiff for a plot of ground, and get the wagon through. Large pavilions and canopies are going up. Vendors with push carts block access. Finally, they get through to their assigned spot on the outskirts and transform the wagon into a counter to display their wares under a tent of red and white striped sail canvas; bright colors are one thing they know how to do, and it will both attract attention and show off their merchandise. Colorful streamers flutter from the tent poles and the front is raised up each morning to create a shady awning. At night they stay in the tent and sample the abundance of food and drink available at the faire for their meals.

They sell four grades of cloth: scarlets woven in Richmond and dyed in Yorke; first and second quality broadcloth from the prize, and the poorer woven grade made in Barmby. Lady Katherine and Anne wear a different dress each morning and each afternoon. Kate's are not as form-fitting as usual. Valentine has cleverly draped fabric to allow for the child to come. She is showing some in the seventh month, but not too much. After this trip she will need to stay at home until the birth.

They are far from the only stall selling cloth. The weavers of Lincoln are known for good quality broadcloth, and merchants from the Flemish weaving center of Bruges have several booths. Nonetheless, they are able to do a brisk business on the first day selling out of the inexpensive cloth made in Barmby and much of the second quality broadcloth. In the afternoon word gets out, after Katherine and Anne promenade around the fair in their beautiful dresses, and the more expensive grades also begin to sell.

The faire is crowded with shoppers and many townspeople that have little money but enjoy the excitement of the performers and looking at the booths of food and goods. James wonders if the city or the monastic houses make the most profit, and if they squabble over it like they do in Yorke. He thinks it likely that they do; people are more the same than they are different when it comes to arguing over money. There is plenty to be made by all. He counts himself fortunate that Kate is not used to extravagance; there are plenty of fine things for sale at the faire designed to empty a man of his purse.

It begins raining steadily sometime after midnight and continues into the morning hours. The cloth is stacked high on one end of the wagon under a tarp and the men lean back against the pile and try to get some sleep. Katherine, Anne, and James sit on their cots as the water seeps in under the sides of the tent. Fortunately, the tent does not leak, everyone is above the wet ground, and the cloth is completely protected. By mid-morning, it is just a drizzle, but gusty, at times.

As they raise the front flap back into an awning it is apparent that everyone has not fared as well. Several tents have gone down and the main aisle between the stalls is a running stream. Geoffrey gets the cooking brazier going with the bit of sea coal they brought along while Will creates a little canal system to drain the water out of the tent. An enterprising vendor comes by with hot meat pies, and when the sun came out in the afternoon, so do the customers.

In June, James receives word that *le Mare Majstro* is no longer needed in the king's fleet. The Castilian armada that information indicated was going to threaten shipping in the channel has failed to materialize, and the treasury is out of money to support continued operation. According to Prince Edward, the Crown has spent £36,000 to protect shipping and the coast from raids or the invasion that never came; an enormous expenditure. Now plans are to mount a new invasion of their own in Brittany to regain lost territory. Ships are being assembled in Portsmouth, but the galley is deemed too small to transport troops.

Captain Carter sails up the coast into the Humbre estuary and anchors off Kingston. James meets them there riding down from Yorke, and Master Tenebroides heads down the River Ouse to join them with his crew in the *Christine*. He will be another day or two yet. Enough cloth from the prize has now been turned into cash from selling at the Lincoln Faire, plus a bulk sale to a Hanse ship here in Kingston to pay the crew their share of the spoils. The captain and his officers are paid half the amount due and will need to wait on the rest. The Companie men typically take a few shillings and add the rest to their ledger accounts signing the book with Malcolm and Sir James. The balance is counted into small pouches and labeled to be added to their sack in the cellar strong room. Neither Captain Carter nor any of his original crew opt to create an account. They take all the money they are due, as is their right.

"When you get to Stockton head up the River Tees as far as Yarm. Otto will be expecting you. Virgil has now been taking several wagonloads each month up from Richmond: wool sacks, cheese, candles, lead, as well as barrels of urine and some food supplies to take to Bollebi." James sails his finger down the coast chart and taps Bollebi. "Clyde will have a blue flag flying at the cliff top to guide you to the right spot. You will be able to offload onto the beach at low tide and take more wool and some barrels of 'natron' salt crystal from Clyde."

"He gets the piss?"

"He does. Clyde should be down on the beach when he sees you arrive. They have a crane at the top of the cliff to raise and lower cargo. Tenebroides will have shovels, empty barrels, and some salt for you to give Clyde. I am hoping Clyde has sea coal for you to load; he was not sure about that. Then sail to Calais."

"Nothing in Scarborough or here in Kingston?"

"Not as yet. Whatever Tenebroides has for you when he arrives tomorrow is what you will take this trip. After you sell the wool, candles, lead, cheese, and any surplus crystals in Calais you will come back here. Buy wine and spices in Calais, Matthew. I have arranged for space in Thomas Graa's warehouse. It is unlikely that Tenebroides will be in port at the same time you are; leave the wine, spices, and crystal in the warehouse and take whatever has been left for you."

"I need to make some notes. This is getting complicated."

James slides a leather-bound book across to Matthew. "It is all written down here including the price targets for buying and selling. Anything that is aboard here in Kingston will need to be declared with the customs officials. They will give you letters patent with a Cocket seal after you have paid the duty on items imported or exported. Those rates are listed here."

"Two barrels of natron salt end up here in Kingston; the rest is surplus to sell in Calais?" Matthew verifying what he reads in the book.

"Preferably in Bruges, you and I can go through all of this again in detail. The captain here is not interested in customs duties and the price of wool bags."

"So, the route is Kingston to Stockton, to Bollebi, then Calais, and back to Kingston – simple enough. Then do it again?" Captain Carter seems satisfied.

"Most likely. Eventually, I hope we can add more ports along the route. Avoid Dover and stay east of the Goodwin Sands. I suspect the Crown will have trouble gathering enough ships in Portsmouth and will try to pull you back into that mess. While they have so much of the fleet anchored there, prices will be good for us in Calais."

"I always try and stay clear of other ships at sea. You never know for sure what their intent may be."

"An excellent practice at the moment. There are a number of English ships accused of piracy operating from around Deal. Stay clear of them and the king's ships sent to catch them."

"I can out sail any cogge and stay far enough out to sea to prevent a galley dashing out to intercept me. I believe I can out sail any galley, too. How many men do you plan to leave me?"

"I thought a crew of twenty-four including yourself and Matthew would be adequate?"

"Agreed, that is gracious plenty to man the oars if necessary. The rest of the crew?"

"Tenebroides will take them." The wartime crew was over sixty men. "Back to Yorke or the manor they came from. They only agreed to join your crew for the season and should be well-satisfied with the result."

In Yorke Katherine does her best to contend with well-intended maids and mid-wives that insist on her going into seclusion in her own suite of rooms. This is a typical practice for women of noble birth, this 'lying in,' but certainly not for women that have daily work responsibilities. Her insistence on walking to the apothecary and compounding medicaments creates a good deal of consternation. With Sir James out of the city on a frequent basis, there is no one to contradict her wishes. Not that James would have. The appeals of Prior William and the mid-wife to him last week only resulted in an amused smile. She does have an escort everywhere she chooses to go, and he has succeeded in getting her to agree that she will not work in the herb garden.

"Coletta, do you stop by so frequently at the request of my husband?"

"I am happy to visit with you and see how you are doing."

"And give a report to Sir James."

"A reassurance that you are well and there is no danger to either the baby or yourself. Men know nothing of these things, and you must acknowledge that people are telling him that you should take to your chamber."

"Yes, they are telling him that."

"I asked him if he thought that noble women were healthier than peasant women! You do need to be cautious, however. Most women have had several children by the time they are your age. Concocting some pain-relieving ointment may mask a problem. It does not make the cause go away."

"I have not had any difficulties for several months now. Discomfort yes but not pain. Prior William is planning a mass to ask God to bless the birth."

"No harm in that and perhaps a great deal of good. I am certain that you are in the priory's daily prayers. You are in mine."

"Now we wait." Matthew gazes up to the blue pennant drooping at the masthead of the galley.

They do not have to wait long. Matthew's concern regarding how he would recognize and confirm Otto's identity vanish when he sees the stocky Fleming's blue hands and forearms. "Otto the dyer?"

"Matthew?" The burly Fleming replies. Matthew shows him the badge of John Chandos on his collar.

Le Mare Majstro's boat is already in the water. The trips to the wagons at the ford in the River Tees are short, but the boat is small, and it takes numerous trips to ferry the goods to the ship. The wool sacks are easy to tuck into a cargo net, raise up with tackle on the yardarm, and swing aboard. They do need to take care as the 364-pound sacks lift off that the boat does not become unbalanced and capsize.

"The barrel and the lead pans are for Clyde at Bollebi."

Matthew writes out the cargo list of wool, lead ingots, cheese rounds, cloth, candles, and the pans and barrel of urine for Clyde. "Eighty shillings is what I was told to pay you Otto; doesn't seem near enough."

"Joel buys the wool not me. I didn't pay for any of this merchandise. I built a new barn and just store what Joel sends me until you arrive.'

Matthew smiles. "Yorke charges a shilling for every sack of wool that enters the city and for every sack that leaves. We take it straight to Calais and avoid those fees."

"Give my best to Clyde. You know not to get on his bad side?"

"I have heard that."

The lookout up the foremast watches for shoals as the tide is beginning to head out and the captain is vocally nervous. Meanwhile the lookout in the main searches the top of the red cliffs for a blue flag atop a timber crane. They are again flying blue pennants from both masts to signal their identity to the shore. The wind is blowing towards them from the cliff tops, so Captain Carter reduces sail to stay close to the coast. The pennants at the mastheads stream out to sea but here on deck the cliffs block the wind almost entirely.

"Blue is not the best color against the sky."

Matthew shrugs. "Orange would be bad against the cliffs."

"Deck ahoy!"

"Where away?" The lookout points off the starboard bow. He can see what they cannot. Then they see some people at the foot of the cliff waving.

Matthew jumps out to help guide the boat in through the minimal surf and up onto the beach. "Clyde?"

"You must be Matthew."

Matthew again flips up his collar to show the badge of Sir John's Companie.

"I am Captain Robert Carter, how much bigger does this beach get?"

"Another hundred feet or so; then it drops off. You should be fine where you have anchored." A wagon is rolling down the steep incline towards them. Two men at the cliff base pull a rope left or right to keep it centered on the smoothed slope. A rope on the other end of the wagon runs to a timber arm high on the cliff. When the wagon reaches the beach, everyone begins to untie the secured wool sacks.

"There is a fourth sack coming down in the next wagon. Did you bring baskets?"

"We did, I also have some sacks of grain for you. Otto sends his regards with two lead pans and a barrel of piss. I've another piss barrel from Master Tenebroides plus shovels and salt," Matthew gives Clyde a quizzical look as he says this.

"Good, and you don't want to know."

The wagon is reloaded and starts its journey back up. "What is on the other end of the pulley?"

"Four big draft horses. You bound for Kingston?"

"Calais first and then probably Bruges; then Kingston."

"How long before you are back again?"

"About four weeks depending on the weather. I am supposed to give Sir James a firmer schedule after we complete this first voyage and get a better sense of time, but it is all dependent on wind and weather."

The wagon is heading back down the cliff. Matthew sees the barrels being rolled up the beach from the ship's boat, which has just returned. "I've got empty barrels for you."

"I'm giving you six barrels," Clyde replies pointing at the wagon. "I hope you have that many for me."

"Eight."

"I expected the barrels to be broken down. I'm glad they are still together."

"We had space aboard, so there was no point in knocking the hoops off."

"They should be filling those baskets with sea coal at the top now. If you bring more baskets, I can have them ready when you get here."

"Sir James did not know if you would have any coal for us. I'll get more baskets. Those barrels are the natron crystal?"

"They are. I was told to have fresh water for you, but I am out of barrels."

"We got fresh water yesterday in Stockton."

James sets up a cot in his study. No men are allowed Katherine's room – which had been their room. Pregnant women are only to be attended by women. Kate thought it nonsense and James agrees, but both are unwilling to take a chance on the health of the child, or her own, so they give in to the experts. 'I would prefer not to regret ignoring their instructions for the rest of my life should something tragic occur,' is James' only comment. That is hard to argue with.

As fabric is hung over the sealed windows James stands his ground, it is July for heaven's sake, and he insists that two windows be left partially open to get some fresh air passing through the room. This philosophy of creating a warm and dark womb-like chamber for the expectant mother can go too far.

The young Lady Mary is here to keep Katherine company. The midwife is now sleeping here full time, and so is Coletta. The midwife came highly recommended, but James wants someone he can trust implicitly in the room. It is more than annoying to be barred from seeing his wife in his own home. If there is ever another child, then he swears that things will be a bit different. There is no screaming or any of the other histrionics that he has been warned about. Coletta comes out and tells him that he has a daughter, and both the child and Lady Katherine are fine. 'No,' he cannot go into the room as yet.

They name the girl 'Philippa' after the recently departed queen of King Edward. Queen Philippa of Hainaut was, of course, also the mother of Prince Edward. James considered her to be kind, loyal, and generous – everything a woman should be. Kate is relieved that her husband shows no sign whatsoever of disappointment that the child is a girl. "No one will make a girl go to war," is his only remark.

The wind stays steady out of the west northwest, which is perfect to make good time heading south along the North Sea coast. Captain Carter heads deeper out to sea as they approach Scarborough to weather Flamborough Head. A cogge is heading to sea from the town and alters course to keep its distance. Trust at sea is low in these times and *le Mare Majstro's* lateen rig and galley build give every appearance of the predator. That is something that could work to their advantage under certain circumstances.

"Act like the aggressor and other ships will assume that is exactly who we are!"

"I once was ordered to charge a superior enemy when we were cornered – they broke and scattered!" Matthew replies. "Get into their heads and play on their fears."

"And at sea you have doubts about every ship you see. That certainly gets into your head," nods Carter. "If there is enough light tonight, I'll reduce sail and head southeast above 'The Wash.' If not, we'll anchor and wait until dawn."

"Out of sight of land?"

"By compass for seven or eight hours. If we don't see land at the end of that run, then I'll steer due south until we see the Norfolk coast. I intend to leave the coast again when we see Orford Castle; that is after we sail south past Yarmouth."

On even a just reasonably clear day, Calais is in sight across the channel from atop the cliffs at Dover, England. If the thought of boarding a ship and enduring the perils of the sea, and the channel can be treacherous at times, make you seasick before you finish crossing the gangplank, then Calais to Dover is the shortest place to make the crossing. It is also the Port of the Wool Staple. All wool exported from England must come to Calais to the staple merchants. These men have been granted a monopoly in exchange for collecting the subsidies due the king and funding the expense of defending the town. This includes maintaining the castle, the two walls and two ditches that surround the town and, of course, paying the garrison. The outer ditch can be flooded with sea water. The city is near the cloth-producing low countries where fine English wool is in high demand. When there is an oversupply of wool at the port it can drive prices down.

They spotted numerous vessels particularly when they passed by the broad estuary of the Thames in route but not nearly as many as expected. None come within hailing distance. Light rain showers reduce visibility. Two days later, Captain Carter stays east of Goodwin Sands, as he had been advised, and then pushes the tiller over to head southwest to Calais. A guard tower marks the end of the spit jutting east from the land to create the sheltered harbor. Under reduced sail they glide past and find a place opposite the castle to come about and drop anchor. If the port officers do not approve of their choice the captain feels certain they would be out in a boat before long to assert their authority.

"I suppose you'll be wanting the boat to head into the marketplace?"

Matthew clutches his leather valise with letters of introduction. "Time to find a buyer for all of this wool." They have thirty-six sacks of their own wool and forty that belong to John de Gisburn. Matthew does not have to find a buyer for de Gisburn's wool; he is a merchant of the staple, as well as a leading citizen of Yorke. The letter of introduction that he carries is from de Gisburn to his agent in the city. How Matthew wishes he could find out what price the merchant was getting for his own wool!

"I guess you will have to wait," Captain Carter points towards a small barge with the port's ensign flying from the bow and heading their way.

"We will need to up anchor and re-moor?"

"Asserting their authority as if one spot is not just as good as another," Carter replies with ill-humor.

A man in the boat hails, "*Le Mare Majstro?*"

"Welcome aboard." The captain helps the finely dressed man over the bulwark. "Captain Robert Carter."

"I am William de Gisburn; I have been expecting you. And you must be Matthew."

"Pleased to make your acquaintance, I have a letter of introduction to you."

"From my father no doubt. You have our wool and some of your own to sell me."

"I guess that depends on your price."

"Eight pounds ten shillings a sack up to fifty sacks. My father and Sir James negotiated the sale in Yorke. If you will come with me, we can go over the paperwork and letters of credit in my study."

"Sir James did tell me that he might be able to come to an agreement. He and your father worked together to have this ship constructed."

"When he was mayor; yes, I watched it being built. You've made some changes, but I still recognized her when you came in. Captain Carter, would you please raise anchor and tie-up at the second quay, just there, and you can begin unloading. My foreman is Tiddle and he is bringing the wagons now."

Matthew sits in the stern across from de Gisburn as they are rowed across the harbor. "That is a good price for Yorkshire wool."

"Demand is high here at the moment. The king has ordered the larger English ships to Portsmouth and the foreigners have bought evasions."

"Evasions?"

"They pay the king's subsidy and a fee in London to evade bringing the wool through Calais. It is a bad business. Bad for us and bad for Calais. The king's chamberlain fattens his own purse."

"Lord Latimer."

De Gisburn shakes his head in disgust. "Loans the king money and then repays himself double with the wool subsidy."

The next port is Bruges, which is just a few hours sailing east along the coast. Matthew knows he is not getting as low a price as a usual buyer might receive, but he is still able to negotiate below what Master Tenebroides buys wine, spices, and kermes for from Hanse ships in Kingston. Next time he will do better.

De Gisburn had suggested a Portuguese merchant, Pero da Silva, for spices in Bruges. Pero was able to find Matthew a source for the kermes – another Portuguese trader that was suspicious of doing business with them. Matthew's silver coin manages to make the purchase; the man's tone changed when he saw this was not to be a letter of credit. After Matthew inspected the kermes grain, he showed the man a sack of the 'natron' salt crystal with a wink. He recognizes it as alum, is highly interested, and a deal is made. It is clear to them that the other prefers to trade in the strictest confidence.

"You can get more of the crystals?" Pero asks.

"Sometimes," Matthew is cagey.

"At four pounds two shillings a bushel I will buy all you can bring me."

"Do you have a steady supply of kermes?"

"No, not steady. It can be hard to buy. I get maybe two barrels each month and sell it here in Bruges. You are taking this to England?"

Matthew nods. "You don't sell to anyone else taking the grains across the channel?"

"As far as I know this is the first time."

"If you would consider making me your exclusive buyer shipping to England, then every bushel of crystal I bring to Bruges I will bring to you first."

Pero nods. "Agreed."

There are several vintners competing to sell him the enormous tuns of wine. Captain Carter turns out to be well-versed in determining quality. Three of the barrels are rolled to the ship, up the gangway, and guided aboard. Tackle from the masts lower them slowly into the hold.

"We could have brought the wool here, gotten a better price, avoided paying the subsidy, and just made one stop."

"And not had letters of patent with the seal."

"Who would know?"

"Captain, we've been watched since we arrived. Everything we've unloaded and loaded has been noted by the port, that man over there – I've guessed him to be Hanse, and the sleepy old gent across the way."

"He spies for English customs?"

"Spies or enforces the law depending on your point of view!" laughs Matthew. "It is best to remember that Lord Latimer has authority over customs and is no friend of Sir James. We can't bring wool here to sell."

"The Hanse could sell here, and we could sell to the Hanse," Carter taps his nose with his fore-finger and smirks.

"Not if we've brought it through the customs house in Kingston. They will reconcile the shipments brought into Calais. We could sell the wool loaded at Yarm and Bollebi to the Hanse and avoid paying the subsidy, but we cannot be caught doing it!"

"He'd love to catch us cheating, then. He doesn't know what is in these barrels, though."

"They do know where I bought them, and they know I sold barrels there. They followed the wagons that picked them up on the quay. But no, I doubt they know about the kermes or the natron crystals in the barrels. I picked them up with some provisions for the crew and they just look like sacks of grain. The seller won't tell them anything. I don't think he trusts his own mother."

"Must be expensive. Those are the only items you stowed under my cabin floor."

"Very costly and I would like to avoid paying the poundage in Kingston. I think they mostly just watch the wool."

"How do you know they followed the wagons?"

"When I saw they were watching me I had them followed by members of the crew. At first, I thought they were watching to see if we were worth capturing at sea, but now I think they are just trying to make sure we don't cheat them out of the import and export duties."

Carter raises an eyebrow. "I'll wait for a good stiff wind to depart just the same."

The Archdeacon of Yorke sat quietly across from James at The Swan. "I am asking you to prayerfully reconsider, Sir James."

"Has the archbishop, prayerfully, reconsidered his position on the abbey's river tolls?"

"His Grace does not determine whom the abbot charges and whom he does not."

"I have heard, from what I consider to be a reliable source, that the archbishop specifically indicated that my barges should no longer be exempt from the abbey toll."

"Perhaps his Grace did not understand that your shipments of lead for the cathedral roof were on those barges."

"That was why the exception was negotiated in the first place; it was part of the price. It took a great deal of effort to come to an arrangement that was good for all parties concerned. Lead is not profitable cargo. The abbey toll makes it a loss. The benefit to me is from the exemption on the other goods I am shipping; it makes the lead ingots worth my inconvenience. I do have demand for the lead with the Hanse and in Bruges at a better price. In fact, I was told you were asked to find another source of supply for the cathedral roof."

"There has been some difficulty with that."

Inwardly, James smiles knowing that he now bought all sources of the lead being smelted in Swaledale. "Which is why you are here." The cathedral and other church constructions had demanded all the lead ingots over the past several years. Now, there was quite a demand locally because of that shortage for non-ecclesiastical customers, and they are willing to pay more.

"That is true."

"Perhaps the archbishop has the influence at court to get a steady supply from the king's mines."

"There seems to be a shortage at the moment, Sir James. Doubtless you already know that."

"Which brings us back to the abbey's toll."

"I am unable to get you preferential treatment on that."

"In that case I will need to charge seven shillings per lead pig delivered to the city wharf and no further, plus any river toll as a surcharge."

The archdeacon begins to calculate the number of lead pig ingots to the tonne. "That is an outrage! The price in London is much less."

"That is my *delivered* price. If you can buy it in London, I doubt you can best my price after shipping it here. Let me know what you decide."

The roofers at the cathedral site melt the lead ingots in a furnace, a fairly easy task because of the low melt temperature required, and then pour the molten lead onto a bed of wet sand to cast sheets for the roof. James had his smith observe the process earlier in the month, and after a few problems had been worked out, mostly using the wooden strickler bar to move the lead evenly over the sand, he is now casting the lead pigs into two-foot by four-foot sheets. One fifty-pound pig to a sheet and selling for eight shillings. The smith has enough roofing orders to use all the next three months of lead shipments coming into the city. James does not need the cathedral's business.

Saint Bartholomew Faire began, as it does every year, on August 24 – the feast day of Saint Bartholomew the apostle. The lord mayor of the City of London opens the faire on Saint Bartholomew eve by accepting a cup of sack, a dry white wine, from the governor of Newgate Prison and leads a procession of the Merchant Taylors' Guild to the faire with their standard silver yard stick to oversee the selling. Over time, the faire has grown to become the largest cloth sale in England and takes place in the precincts of the Priory of Saint Bartholomew at West Smithfield, just past Aldersgate, on the north side of London. James' intentions are to increase cloth production each year and use more and more of the wool himself, but the notion of selling in London seemed at best many years away. The taking of the cloth off the Flemish cogge changed that for this year. The annual London cloth faire is clearly the best opportunity to turn all that cloth into coin.

Janice the weaver travelled to Kingston to join *le Mare Majstro* for the voyage down the coast and then up the Thames to London. She is to help Matthew sell at their booth and help him learn everything he can about the faire and the cloth market with a mind to future years. After the late decision to go to Lincoln, and the resulting poor stall location, James corresponded, with the influential help of Prince Edward, to Prior Thomas Watford of Saint Bartholomew's to reserve premium booth placement for the three-day faire.

The faire is now a very important event for the cloth merchants of the kingdom. Yorke might be the second largest city in England, but it is a far distant second. The demand for all goods in London, especially expensive goods, is enormous. It is not just the population of the city but merchants from all over come to buy and sell. Flemings, Belgians, and Dutch weavers are well-known for high quality broadcloth and their merchants are here. The growth of the faire may be attributed to laws laid down by King Richard I, well over a century before, not only granting the Austin Canons all the event admittance and stallage fees, but also forbidding the taking of customs or tolls from merchants coming to buy and sell at the fair. Such an attractive proposition is not to be missed.

After working up the Thames, just past the Tower of London, they tie up long enough to unload to a hired carter at the quay, then re-anchor in mid-river. As they move through the narrow, crowded streets away from the river, the stench begins to dissipate, the buildings become smaller, and the streets less crowded. For Janice, Matthew, and the sailors walking with them the experience is an overwhelming sense of people squeezing in on them.

Thousands of people come not only to trade in cloth but to be a part of the excitement that is part of this spectacular occasion. Shows, entertainments, and all sorts of attractions come from far and wide to take advantage of the gathering. Spectacles of acrobats, competitions, puppet shows, and animals from far-away lands draw in the crowds. They consume from booths selling foods such as meat pies, sausages, and sweets. Many drink wine and ale with too much abandon. Things can certainly get rowdy and out-of-hand.

This is the place to sell the furs and imported silks taken off the cogge that can only be worn by the nobility due to the sumptuary laws. They have a hundred bolts of first quality Flemish broadcloth at twenty-eight pence an ell and almost two hundred of the second quality. Each evening the gates of the priory's walled precincts are closed for the night. Vendors are allowed to sleep in their booths. Matthew quickly ascertains the going rate for each type of cloth. Janice assesses the quality of their goods against the other sellers. As the cloth is war spoils, essentially without cost to them, there is no point in insisting on the highest prices with buyers. He knows what it is worth and asks a reasonable price. The cloth sells well.

Bertrand and the crew of the stone barge spent the past week collecting the wool purchased by Justin along the River Wharfe. Mooring the barge at the ford below Tatecastre the wagon's wheels are returned to the axles and the crane easily sets it on the bank. Using mules and the wagon they make numerous trips into the surrounding valleys to collect twenty-two sacks of wool representing the shearings of over five thousand sheep. Bertrand pays out eighty shillings a sack and is relieved to be free of responsibility for the money. Even if they only get £7 a sack, the wool cargo is worth over twenty years work by a master craftsman earning six pence a day. It is a fortune.

They make the short journey back down the Wharfe to the confluence with the River Ouse and anchor to wait for Master Tenebroides and the *Christine* to take the wool on downriver to Kingston. They should be here in the early hours of the morning. Then they will head back to Tatecastre and pick up a full load of stone for the cathedral construction in Yorke. In the meantime, since it is mid-afternoon and hot, two men stay aboard the barge, but the rest of the crew walks the half mile into Cawood to pass the time at the public house.

Chapter 20

Chase

The Merchant Adventurers' Hall in Yorke is not where the Florentine wool buyer wanted to be making his purchases. The wool merchants of the city aggressively bought up all the wool in the countryside, transported it to Yorke, and now are naturally looking to make a profit on the sale or arrange for shipment to Calais themselves. The Florentine thought he had agreements for wool from certain flocks around Tatecastre and all along the course of the River Ouse. If he wanted the wool this year, he would have to pay the higher price.

As high water floats his ship off the river bottom, the captain of *le Faucon Dieu* begins the journey downriver with his hold almost two hundred wool sacks below capacity. Five hours downstream later, the ship approaches the archbishop's palace at Cawood. Bertrand's barge is anchored along the bank piled high with wool sacks and just two men aboard. With all of the pent-up frustration, the urge is too much to resist. He backs the sail and throws the tiller over.

"Boarding axes!" he growls under his breath. "No witnesses!" The crew jumps down onto the barge and quickly overwhelm the surprised Samuel and the napping Tibb. Their axes make short work before any shout is made. Tackle swings down from the spar and the wool sacks are hauled up and over the high bulwarks of the cogge one by one. "Toss their oars in the river, so the crew can't follow us when they return."

Berus and Knute sit along the river edge, nursing pints of ale when an oar floats past and then another. "Looks just like one of our oars."

"There is a third one," Knute replies standing and looking upriver. "Cogge."

"Get Bertrand. I'm going to see what is going on!" Berus breaks into a run towards where they left the barge. It is not long before he sees a sack of wool rising up the cogge's side and he turns back towards the village.

The entire crew is now on the run back towards their barge. Too late as the cogge has pulled away and is heading on down the river. Berus recognizes the vessel that had been anchored upriver and shouts, "It is *le Faucon Dieu!*"

Samuel and Tibb are sprawled dead in the barge and the oars and the wool are gone. "They have to anchor soon; the tide is going to turn. Do we have a saddle for one of the mules?" Bertrand queries while running to grab the bridle of the nearest, be quick about it!"

The mules are along to pull the wagon. They do not have saddles. Shorter reins are improvised from cordage and Bertrand mounts bareback and splashes across the River Wharfe. "Try and recover any oars that you can!" They are moored on the wrong side of the Ouse to get ahead of the thieves at Barmby.

"Will do!"

Bertrand spurs through the Micklegate Bar just before it is secured for the night. It has taken just over an hour to ride the twelve miles north to Yorke. He gallops past Trinity Abbey down to the Ouse Bridge and across to Sir James' townhouse.

"Will! Saddle horses. Geoffrey! Find Master Tenebroides. Malcolm! Get Hugh." Sir James barks out orders, his carefully cultivated urbane demeanor absent.

"Tenebro get your crew together and head down the river immediately!"

"Sir James, I can't fight the tide."

"What! Oh of course, when can you leave, then?"

"High water is about midnight, but the moon doesn't rise until a few hours after that."

James is wild-eyed. "So, you'll have to just sit and wait?"

"Yes, but so does *le Faucon Dieu*."

"Bertrand says she is just below Cawood. Can you catch her?"

"They are a full tide ahead of me, but I can move faster down the river with my sweeps. I'll pull extra crew from the priory and here at the house. It will be close."

"Will I be able to get to Barmby before the Fleming?"

"Oh, yes, plenty of time for that, Sir James. Depending just how far below Cawood they have anchored, and when her captain is willing to start back down the river... He is unlikely to up anchor before first light. If he waits for sunrise, then it will be several hours after that. And, if he waits for that sunrise, I will be closer on his heels."

The mounted party departs through the Walmgate Bar and heads south. The gatekeeper easily rationalizes that letting Sir James out certainly does not put the city in any danger. A shilling is hard to come by.

James gallops into Barmby shortly past midnight after a three-hour ride and goes straight to the manor house to awaken Sigismund from his slumber. Paul, Geoffrey, and Will spread out across the cottages raising the call to arms. "Rouse yourselves, get your bow and a sheaf of arrows! Assemble at the warehouse!"

The men tumble out of bed and gather in the dark wondering what is going on. Brother Hugh, not wearing the white cassock of a Carmelite, kindles a small fire over which he gently heats a pot of pine tar. "Make fire arrows. Tie on a wad of wool with a strip of cloth and then dip the tip in the tar. C'mon get about it!" There are almost thirty Companie men at Barmby, but it is not long before the rest of the community join the gathering. That Sir James has just arrived in the middle of the night, and gotten everyone out of bed, has obviously created a stir.

"Listen while you work," James begins. "The crew of a Flemish ship attacked Bertrand's barge yesterday at Cawood. They killed two of our men and stole our sacks of wool. They are anchored upriver waiting on the turn of the tide. When they come by here, we will be ready."

"When will they get here, my Lord?"

"If their captain feels he can navigate the river by moonlight, then right about first light. If he waits for sunrise, then it will be another three hours. Master Tenebroides tells me he will be using his sail because he must go faster than the river to maintain steerage-way." The river heads mostly east and then turns almost due south just above Barmby where the Derwent joins and then turns east again another mile further south. "He will have to adjust his sail when they turn and that is the moment to let loose. Pick off the crew if you can. Put burning arrows into the sail and see if we can get it to catch fire. If the wool sacks are still on the deck, then light 'em up. Those of you that are not bowmen tend the fire or find a way to be helpful."

"Don't you worry about that, Sir James. Them Frenchies may have taken my thumb off, but I can still use this crossbow. When they expose themselves to douse the arrows..." He patted the stock of his weapon.

"Be sure to put some arrows into the hull that force them to do just that. If this west wind will get a bit of south in it, he will have a tough time on this stretch of the river sailing close hauled. Hopefully, we can create enough confusion to cause them to ground on a shallow spot. If they get by us at the lower turn, we won't catch them here."

Ben speaks up, "My barge is here." It is the barge that does the Derwent run. "We can attempt to board them, Sir James."

"I thought about that and decided you sit too low in the water. They will run you over and sink you if you are ahead of them, and if you try to come along side you will be too exposed on your approach and then have to climb up her high sides."

"So, if they get past us, then they get away?"

"No, Tenebroides is chasing them down the river and *le Mare Majstro* should be anchored in the Humbre. Paul Fitz-William is getting ready to ride on to Kingston now."

High water reaches the Flemings half an hour before it arrives in Yorke where Master Tenebroides is waiting aboard the *Christine*. The apparent advantage counts for nothing because they both must wait for the moon rise. The moon provides enough light to get underway simultaneously. "Sweeps in the water. Pull!" They need to pull hard against the river to take the strain off the windlass and ride out the anchor.

"Anchor's free!"

"Starboard oars reverse sweep." Once the bow is angled over, the current and the oarsmen pulling on the sweeps spin the barge within its own length to head down the river. "All oars pull forward. Easy and steady – we've got a long way to go."

Typically, the *Christine* rides the tide up and down the River Ouse. The lateen sails are used when the wind and river course made it more of an advantage than a nuisance as it curves this way and that. Tenebroides intends to use the sail at every opportunity no matter the effort required. The oars are normally more than adequate to maintain position around the river bends. They provide enough extra speed to allow steerage without strenuous effort with just six oarsmen on each side. The hull, however, is pierced with rowing stations for nine on each side, and Tenebroides gradually adds the novice oarsmen to let them get the feel of rowing.

A thicket of willow gives James just enough cover just above Barmby as he sits astride his horse at the river turn. Half the men are here, and the others have headed to the next turn a mile downriver. He will join them after the ship passes. Several men are hidden right on the banks of the Ouse and the rest are far enough back to arc their arrows down into the ship. The smoking braziers to light up the fire arrows are shielded from view. James himself needs to identify the ship as *le Faucon Dieu* in the early morning light and give the order to open fire.

He tries to picture the Flemish ship as he had seen her anchored in Yorke over the last week. As they were buying wool, he had paid her the attention due a competitor. Bertrand had assured him that she was the only cogge headed down river below Cawood but setting the wrong ship full of English wool on fire would be a mistake with severe consequences. As the sun begins to lighten the sky and illuminate the treetops on the far bank the round bow of a ship begins to emerge in the mist on the river heading towards them. He is looking for the blue and white striped square sail, but the ship is showing only a modest amount of canvas. Her captain has several reefs in the sail to prudently minimize its effect through the night.

"Make ready." The morning light hits the top of the mast and the upper edge of her crow's nest; it will not be long now. The sail is blue and white! "Wait, wait...light arrows! Release!"

A dozen arrows arc through the sky trailing black wisps of smoke. *Le Faucon Dieu* cannot retreat or veer to the right or left; she can only keep coming straight on down the river. The archers each light another arrow and release as a volley. The arrows that he can see seem to burn out shortly after they hit the target. Her crew is bringing the sail's spar around as far as it will go as she makes the turn. "Fire under the stern castle; get the man at the tiller!" Damn she is moving fast; once she completes the turn there is no longer an angle to get the man steering the ship.

"Aim for the sail and the crew." The Ouse is about three hundred feet wide here and the channel is on this side of the river – easy range. Flaming arrows are hitting the sail and smoldering in the hull. The men right on the river edge send arrows whizzing at any heads that appear above the bulwarks. The Flemish crew scampers back and forth under cover. As she goes past the men keep firing as long as the ship is in range. "Maybe she'll catch!" James shouts as he spurs away downstream frustrated with their lack of success but relieved that the ship is certainly *le Faucon Dieu*.

"I do not think we were able to catch her on fire."

Hugh nodded. "She is damp from the wet, night air."

"I am open to suggestions."

"If we can get these balls of pitch and wool on target, they should burn long enough to ignite her."

"Give the bastards credit. They never lost their nerve at the turn. Not much time now; make ready!" The archers are on the inside of the river bend, which allows them to stay in one place as the ship travels around them. "Release!" A scream comes from the ship, so at least one arrow found its mark. Wisps of smoke are coming from the sail and James can see some burn holes in it. The captain has let out another reef to increase speed as they make the turn.

Hugh launches a flaming ball the size of a man's head from the end of a pitchfork. It does not release cleanly and falls short. An arrow ignites the top of the sail and quickly burns a large hole up to the spar and starts the tarred rigging lines. Amidst the rain of arrows, a crewman leans over the edge of the crow's nest and throws down a bucket at the end of a rope. The bucket is filled with water and hauled back up. Some of the rigging is doused as the bucket tumbles back to the deck. Another arrow finds its mark.

The next flaming ball of wool and pitch flies over the side of the ship and disappears, either aboard or clear over and into the river on the other side. A man with a crossbow shows his head and ducks quickly back down as several arrows fly in his direction.

Hugh lofts another flaming ball in a high arc as the stern rides past. This one clearly lands aboard. Smoke trails from the ship as it heads out of range.

"Will, mount up and keep an eye on them. I want to know where they anchor when the tide turns, and anything else they do. Low water should be in just a few hours, so they will end up somewhere between here and Blaketofte. Take some others along to send me a message in Kingston and also back here to let Master Tenebroides know where they are and what is happening. Hugh, wait here for the *Christine* and have the men ready to board."

"Any notion when Tenebroides will get here?"

"In a couple of hours, if they can make a clean run. Then you will all need to wait as it will be low water and the tide will be coming back in. In the meantime, please break the sad news to Samuel's wife that she is a widow. I am heading on to Kingston."

"What will you do if Captain Carter is not there?"

"I don't know Hugh. If the Fleming bends on a new sail and the wind stays out of the west… I don't think Tenebroides will catch her before she gets out to sea."

"We have five fishing boats in Blaketofte."

"I'm listening."

"When they anchor in the Humbre we could attack them."

"I think the little boats would be at too much of a disadvantage in daylight. If Tenebroides believes he won't catch them and Carter is not in Kingston, then we may have to take more desperate measures. If it is dark enough, we should be able to do just that."

"You said they will need to anchor soon. We can march down along the river and catch them sitting there," Hugh offers.

"That is possible! Head to the bend below Goole to cut them off and then follow the river upstream until you find them." The Ouse makes several large loops that add miles of river here. Hugh's company can take a more direct route. You can be at the bend in about two hours, which is about the amount of time they have left until the tide turns against them. If you find them within the next hour after you reach the bend…" James thinks a moment. "You should have four hours with them at anchor. If they want to try and get away, they can only head back upriver, which is not the way they want to go. Be stealthy, Hugh… Catch them out splicing rigging or making other repairs. Afterwards make it to Blaketofte; there Tenebroides can take you aboard. I want big enough crews to overwhelm them in the Humbre."

Brother Hugh is in a foul mood. The contemplative life he had anticipated as a Carmelite friar is unraveling. His usual prayerful calm is displaced by fury as he thinks of Samuel and Tibb lying dead in the barge over sacks of wool. Both had been companions in battles and on the march. They were old friends. Samuel's wife had cried and hugged her little boy. At the head of the line were men that had been living in Barmby and occasionally traveled this path to Blaketofte. They know the bend in the river that Sir James had mentioned and the trail that leads there. The Ouse makes a large loop to the west, four miles in all, and they will cut across it to get ahead of *le Faucon Dieu*.

When the small column arrives at the bend in the Ouse there is no sight of the ship downstream towards Blaketofte. "Here it comes!" Tandy points down the river. At first Hugh could not understand what was coming because the cogge should be upriver from them and then he sees the wave speeding towards them as the tide pushed against the current and reversed it: the tidal bore. "And there is the Fleming!" Upriver about a mile the cogge came into view. "They will need to get their anchors out fast!"

"Alright, Tandy, take us to her. Keep out of sight – I want to surprise them."

James gallops into Kingston in the late morning, escorted by Malcolm and Will. "*Le Mare Majstro*," Will says as he points out to the ship at anchor in the estuary.

"That is a relief. Let's head down to the docks and find out if Captain Carter is ashore."

The captain is not, but Matthew is negotiating the price of baskets of sea coal and having them loaded into the ship's longboat. "Sir James! Paul has given us the hue and cry!"

The brush on the bank is thick enough to hide the anchored cogge from view as Hugh gives out assignments. There is a man with a crossbow at the bow and another at the stern. Two archers are designated to put each of these men under duress. The rest are tasked with killing the men bending on a new sail. In the steady breeze they are struggling to get the huge spread of canvas attached to the spar. Even though it is gathered into a long bundle, the big sail is heavy and catches the wind like a living, squirming thing.

"Nock an arrow, wait on my signal…release!"

Four men are working aloft. One falls and another slips to tangle in the footropes as the archers launch their second arrows. Hugh cannot tell if the crossbowmen were hit, but both are now out of sight. Additional crew members on the deck lose control of one side of the heavy sail that they had hauled up on block and tackle to the spar. Perhaps they let go of the line as the hail of arrows arced towards them and hopefully found the mark. Their captain is no fool, he has anchored on the far side of the channel; the ship is about 150 yards away. This is well within range but hardly point-blank distance.

Will rides up and points to the crow's nest. "They had an archer up there; he tried to pick me off a few times."

"I wondered where you were." Hugh nudges one of his archers. "Tandy, keep an eye on the crow's nest."

"We had to keep our distance."

As long as the crew show themselves the arrows fly. Each archer can casually aim and let fly three arrows each minute. There are a dozen archers in addition to Hugh who now gets busy kindling a fire. He wants to burn that new sail.

"Does anyone know how many men are on that ship?"

"Hugh, there is no way to know. It could be just twenty, or as many as eighty. As it should be just a trading vessel, I would guess mid-twenties. We are running low on arrows."

All four of the men that had been in the rigging were wounded if not dead. "Then he is short-handed now. Let's see if we can make things warm for them. Aim for the sail."

As a flight of flaming arrows strikes the ship her crew emerges. They scramble to get the sail back down under cover and haul buckets of water up on the far side of the ship to wet down the deck.

"Take your time; they aren't going anywhere."

From his vantage up high in the fighting top, James watches *le Faucon Dieu* ignore the hail from Sheriff Sir William Perciehay's boat and continue to sail past Kingston toward the North Sea as the sun sets. Bertrand had reported the murders to the sheriff after he saw Sir James yesterday evening, and they had gone to Cawood together the next morning. Sir James had reluctantly agreed to let Sir William take the Flemings into custody, but when they plowed on and would not let him come aboard…that meant James now had his acquiescence to take matters into his own hands.

The *Christine* has caught up and now follows the cogge just out of arrow range. Both ships sailed first along the southern side of the estuary to avoid the shallows along the north bank and then turned north past Kingston into the very northeast corner of the Humbre to skirt the enormous sand bars on the south before turning almost due south again. The Flemish captain knows his business in these waters and maneuvers his heavy cogge easily with the wind from the northwest. A mistake will leave him high and dry at low water.

Ahead of their quarry, Robert Carter stands at the helm of *le Mare Majstro* in the gathering darkness. At his shoulder is a fisherman, Stephen, from Kingston that is familiar with the lower Humbre estuary and will act as pilot in the night. Stephen's fishing boat is partially owned by James as are the boats of two other fishermen aboard. All three are Companie men. It is time to drop anchor; the tidal bore will be roaring up the estuary in minutes. "If they try to sail past in the dark, then bring us alongside and we will board them."

"I would not fancy fighting the tide in the darkness were I him, Sir James! These shoals don't leave much room for error."

"He may well perceive his situation as desperate, Captain. He just needs to slip past us far enough to make it a chase when the moon rises. If he stays at anchor, then we will board him at the slack. He can't help but know that."

"That will be about an hour before high water and also an hour after midnight," Carter offers.

"When does the moon rise?"

"A few hours after that."

"I expect him to try and sail past before moon rise, so be ready to bring up the anchor. In either case, we will board in the dark."

James felt, rather than saw, the cogge glide past in the blackness. "Malcolm, light an arrow! There!" He points towards the black bulk to starboard.

"Oarsmen ready!" Captain Carter hollers. "Pull!" And then, "Sails." It takes a bit of time to get some forward way on the vessel to ride over the anchor and give chase. "Windlass, you buggers!" They have been caught by surprise in spite of their preparations.

"Anchor is free and coming up!"

"Another arrow; higher arc this time. Tenebroides better be alert."

"Pull!" yells the captain.

"A bit more to starboard captain," guides Stephen. "How fast do you think we are moving through the water?"

"We are fighting this tide, and I can't see a thing!"

"Three miles from where we anchored, we have to turn to larboard."

"Just stay in his wake," James says calmly. "He draws more water than we do captain."

"Aye, Sir James."

"Don't ram him if he grounds. Stephen, what are his chances of staying in the channel in the dark?"

"Not good."

"Alright, then, take it easy captain. He will either run aground or anchor and wait for enough light to judge his position. We will run alongside when he does. Any sign of the *Christine*?"

"She is behind us a few lengths; I hear her oars."

Incredibly, two hours later, the cogge turns a few points east without striking a shoal. Stephen feels the wind on his cheek. "On this bearing, if it is right, they will be out into the sea in another three hours or less. Tide turns soon."

"Where the hell are we?"

"To your left is the Sonke Sand, a long shallow that is exposed at low water. To your right is a long narrow sand bar that divides the channel for the next two miles. He has timed it well – it is almost high water."

"Hail Tenebroides."

"They can't hear me over the oars."

"Stop rowing, then."

Soon the *Christine* catches up and comes alongside oars thrashing. James shouts, "Master Tenebroides! Catch them now before they get to sea!"

Tenebroides waves at his men and shouts, "Double men at the oars! Shake out a reef!"

"Launch arrows at the target and keep them flying." Tenebroides has another thirty men aboard in addition to his normal crew. *Le Mare Majstro* just has six more, including James, and is a bigger ship to row at speed and try to bring down the chase. "Just keep us close enough to join the fight."

Stephen notes, "Tide is turning; maybe another hour to Spurn Head."

"Moon coming up; full sail!" The last reef is shaken out and the ship surges forward.

Ahead in the moonlight a spit of land hooks almost two miles across the end of the estuary – the Spurn Head, beyond it is the sea. At one time the village of Ravenserodd stood at the end of the spit. A decade earlier a huge storm destroyed the village and drowned the occupants. There is not a single structure he can see as evidence it had ever been. The distance here narrows between the tip of the spit and the shallows on the Lincolnshire side to just under two miles.

"He has cut it too fine." Indeed the Fleming now has to steer further south to avoid the spit. Tenebroides had seen it coming and is heading to cut them off. A flight of arrows glint in the light of the rising sun as they arc down into the cogge.

"They are alongside! Dammit Carter get me there now!"

"Oars!"

It is a frightened crew awaiting their fate when James climbs up over the high bulwark and onto the deck of *le Faucon Dieu*. "They surrendered without a fight; most unfortunate, Sir James." Tenebroides and his men have blood lust in their eyes.

"Where is the vessel's master?"

"Il est mort Capitaine."

"Et qui est vous?"

"I am Thomas Besse. I have hired this ship."

"The ship captain's body is, indeed, lying dead on the quarterdeck. Took an arrow in the chest."

"Thank you, Hugh. His fate was quicker than all of yours," James menaces the crew, "But the outcome of your trial will have the same result; of that you can be sure."

"I was thinking it was a lovely morning for a trial right now, Sir James," Tenebroides' fury is running high.

"Um, well, I have an agreement with our sheriff about prisoners."

"I don't see where any of their crew survived the desperate fight to take their ship." The few remaining members of the crew do not understand English, but they clearly understood the nature of the debate.

"Same trial they gave Samuel and Tibb!" A growl of agreement rises up from the Companie men.

"Sir James, I beg you to have mercy. Twelve of our crew have died, or surely will, including the captain and several others are wounded," pleads Besse. "I have many connections high in the Royal Court."

"This is not war where I accept reasonable casualties. This was murder and theft."

"The captain is to blame. He thought he would not be seen taking your wool. These men are innocent of any crime, as am I."

"He personally killed both of my men? He loaded the wool aboard this ship unassisted? I think not Thomas Besse. The sheriff will try and sentence Flemings to death as quickly as Englishmen that commit murder. Your court connections be damned."

"No, he was not alone in committing the crime. The men followed his orders as sure as your men will follow yours if you tell them to kill me and these others. It will not restore your two men to life, and you have now recovered your property. Nothing is gained by further killing."

"It is a very good way to be sure that Flemish wool buyers obey the laws of England when they are here!"

"Actually, I am Florentine, but I do take your point. Perhaps we can reach an accommodation?"

"I am not in the habit of negotiating with individuals that have murdered my men. My only dilemma is whether to kill you now or turn you over to the sheriff."

"Would you consider a ransom for our lives?"

"Any monies that are aboard I intend to take. I will not be bought off for a few measly shillings." James draws his sword from the scabbard.

"I can offer a much more substantial ransom! Enough to make you a wealthy man!"

The Companie men began to snicker as James is already wealthy.

"Enough to make all of you satisfied! I have licenses aboard worth thousands of pounds."

"Well, what do you think?" The three ships lie at anchor in the lee of Spurn Head, waiting for the tide that will allow them to easily sail back up the estuary to Kingston. In the light of day, the cogge shows where some furious fires had burned aboard. Sections of the deck and fo'c'sle are blacken and charred. They must have fought desperately to put them out.

"Are these legal?"

"I believe so, Hugh."

"Worth over a thousand pounds?"

"Well over; they are licenses to ship five hundred sacks of wool free of additional customs and subsidies. The Cocket seal dangling there is from the customs house certifying that the goods have been recorded and all duties paid."

"How can they be allowed to ship without paying export duties?" Tenebroides holds his head. "This does not seem right."

"It is in repayment of a loan to the king."

"I do not understand."

"The king needed money quickly for the war, so he secured a loan from Florentine financiers. In repayment of the loan the Florentines receive the right to ship wool without paying customs duties in an amount that satisfies the term of the loan. The wool duties belong to the king and he sells them to get funding right away. It is perfectly legal, and I understand common practice. In a very real sense, they paid the customs duty in advance, although certainly at a discounted rate."

"How much did the king borrow?"

"Probably a lot less than these letters patent are worth. That is why the lenders agree to it. These also are licenses to ship to other ports than the Staple in Calais. We can get a higher price there."

"What prevents us from taking the licenses and killing the bastard?"

"The letters are made out to him. He needs to be our prisoner until we ship all one five hundred sacks. So, he is out well over two thousand pounds when you count the wool aboard that is not stolen from us, and at least a year as our prisoner; it will take us at least that long to use all the licenses. Almost certainly bankruptcy; that and his confinement are a substantial punishment."

"All that talk about 'connections at the Royal Court' is just buggery isn't it?"

"Perhaps not Hugh, did you take note of the signature on the licenses to evade the Staple? Our old friend Richard Lyons!"

"He must be lining his own pockets but good in some way."

"That is almost certainly true. Lord Latimer arranges the loan and the re-payment, but who keeps accounts as to when the loan is fully repaid?"

"Why Lord Latimer!"

"We will set aside money for the widows?" Hugh insists.

"Agreed. I'll explain what we are about to Captain Carter and our men. We will turn over the ship to the sheriff as the Crown's share of spoils and a third of the cash in the strong box. The ship is surely worth over 250 pounds and hopefully will delight him enough to not ask too many questions. Let's get all of the wool – how many sacks did you say?

"About 250 sacks. Twenty-two were stolen from us."

"That is more than I expected. Load *le Mare Majstro* to capacity for a run to Bruges. We will need to pay 80 pence per sack in Kingston; that is all. The sheriff agreed the ship and its cargo were forfeit if they ignored his hail and did not stop at the customs house. I will need to negotiate the spoils with Sir William and arrange storage for the rest of the wool in Kingston. At some point we may need to build a warehouse here."

Chapter 21

Love Letters

MAY-SEPT 1375

"You understand that you will be a prisoner aboard until I am able to acquire and transport all five hundred wool sacks."

"Sir James, surely we can craft a document that transfers ownership of my certificates to you or your agent?" Besse argues.

"Good idea, we will do that, too. You have given me good reason not to trust you and I don't. I imagine that if I were to release you...you would convince Lord Latimer to make trouble for me and nullify these pieces of paper."

"I would not do that, Sir James. I give you my word."

"Nonetheless, you will be our guest here aboard *le Mare Majstro* for the next eighteen months or however long it takes. Five hundred sacks are much more than I normally handle of my own wool. If you do anything to undermine our agreement or cause trouble, then I will consider my vow to release you unharmed cancelled. Make no mistakes Thomas Besse, or you will be accidentally lost overboard. You have my word on that!"

It was a long time and a great deal of money lost, but Besse had no doubt that Sir James would have preferred to kill him and satisfy his men that full justice had been done. Nor did he see where he had any choice in the matter. The time it would take to transport the wool was all that stayed his hand. "I understand."

The suggested document made Matthew agent to transport the wool using Besse's certificates. This should eliminate the need for Besse to come ashore and interact with the customs officials in Kingston. With these 'evasions' of the Calais

Staple they could take the wool to Bruges or any ports to the west where Matthew thought he could get a better price by not having to sell it all to an authorized merchant in Calais. Sir James has the customs agent in Kingston witness the agreement with his signature and seal in Thomas Besse's presence. Eighty wool sacks are stuffed into *le Mare Majstro's* hold and Captain Carter sets sail for Bruges.

"She did what?"

"Kate, as I said, in a dress made of cloth of gold Ales Perrers rode from the Tower to Smithfield."

"As the 'Lady of the Sun?'"

James smiled at her incredulity. "Yes, as the 'Lady of the Sun.' To a grand tournament in her honor with ladies leading knights by silver chains. It really has tongues wagging and they are not saying nice things."

"Well, it is hardly all her fault, James. The king must have approved."

"He certainly must have, and that is being taken as a sign that he has become a doddering old fool to have his mistress manipulating him so! Thankfully, Queen Philippa is in her grave."

"So, this means that I will be getting a dress made of gold?" she teases.

"Kate you are not the mistress of a senile old King; just the wife of a poor fishmonger."

Laughing, she says, "Last week you said you were a cloth merchant and the week before that you were a pirate!"

"I said I understood why piracy could be so tempting. Taking *le Faucon Dieu* was not piracy. It was the pursuit of murderers."

"That turned out to be very profitable."

"Yes, but that was a surprise. I was so angry that I really intended to burn her to the waterline with my wool aboard because I did not believe we would catch up to them. Tried damn hard to do it, too. We do still need to use the certificates to actually get much of the money."

"And you are getting along better with our new sheriff?"

"Better than the last, but we get a new one, Sir William Melton, next month. Oh, yes, Perciehay was absolutely pleased with his share and the ship.

He made enough for his commitment to the king and a handsome profit for himself. He had no interest in all the minor details. He signed off on the division of the spoils without really reading it – which was good."

"Did you do something underhanded James?"

"The certificates were a bit awkward to discuss and the whole of it could be umm… a bit difficult to explain to certain officials of the Crown. It was a big pile of coin and he just wanted to get his hands on it as fast as he could. Maybe he thought I made an error in his favor and wanted to get away before I realized it."

"May I ask just how tempting this…not piracy…pursuit of justice turned out to be?"

"The sheriff received the ship, which should be close to 250 pounds when sold and another two hundred pounds in coin from the strongbox aboard. Besse was expecting to buy much more wool than he was able to and had the money with him to do just that."

"And you just got certificates?"

"Certificates, all the wool aboard, and the balance from the strongbox. Those certificates alone are worth over half the total take of nearly three thousand pounds!"

"I heard your share is one third, my husband."

"Someone has been talking too much, but your source is generally correct. The *Companie's* share is a third. I usually pay myself last, which means I will not get my share until all the certificates have been redeemed."

"So, what does a dress made of 'cloth of gold' cost my sweet love?"

"Too much. Isn't that Philippa crying in the nursery?"

"Anne will see to the baby."

"Speaking of Anne, she and Miles are now living above your apothecary?"

"They are."

"He is still working out well?"

"He certainly does good work in the herb garden and takes good messages when I am not there. Now that Philippa can be with me at the store, business is getting a bit better. I'm afraid I will need to beg you for some help with the rent again, although he hasn't come by asking for it."

"No, he won't come asking anymore."

"Oh?"

"You have a new and more demanding landlord."

"And what sort of demands will this new landlord be making?"

"Come over here and we can discuss the new lease arrangements."

It looks as though a storm is coming towards them from the west. They are east of the Thames estuary, out of sight of land, and running north towards the Norfolk coast. A coastline Captain Carter hopes to sight before nightfall. This summer storm could push them farther out to sea this late afternoon leaving him in the dark, unsure of his location. It is a worrisome thought.

"Ship in sight!" hails the masthead lookout.

"Where away?"

"From the west and sailing northeast."

"I'm going aloft." It is probably nothing, but *le Mare Majstro* looks like a warship not like a merchant vessel. This ship is on a course that would intercept them – coincidence? English pirates are operating out of the Cinque Ports and the king has sent his ships to punish them. If he were one of the king's captains…he would suspect this galley. A big square sail running before the wind; she is closing the distance. One of the London city barges or one of Lord Latimer's ships – both seem like likely possibilities. Sir James told him not to take chances and that suits his own attitude perfectly.

Back down on the quarter-deck, he directs the helmsman, "Alter course a few points east." This will take him away from the pursuer but also farther out to sea. The triangular sails are trimmed to take the wind off the stern quarter instead of abeam.

"Won't they have the advantage of us on this bearing?"

"You're learning Matthew. Yes, with this wind they will close the gap now."

"You have a plan."

"I want them to alter course directly towards us. When they get near, we will turn back north as close to the wind as we can."

"Which they can't follow."

"Correct; they cannot sail as close to the wind as we can, and we will then soon be to windward."

"What if he holds his current course?"

"Then we will change our heading when that rain squall hits him and blinds him. He sees the storm too, and I believe he will want to close with us as much as he can before it does."

"Deck thar," the lookout shouts. "She has turned toward us."

"Let me know when the squall hits them," Carter shouts back. "Well, that answers that question."

Matthew shrugs. "We've got nothing aboard that could be called contraband."

"We've got a lot of money in the strongbox from this trip into Bruges. We also have Thomas Besse aboard."

"So?"

"What if that ship belongs to Lord Latimer?" Carter points out.

"So, Besse could ask them to free him and take him back to London. Make us come, too. The situation could get difficult," posits Matthew.

"That's how I see it."

Before long, the top of the ship's sail is visible from the deck. "How severe is that storm?"

"You are full of questions Matthew. We shall just have to see. In another moment, both of us will be needing to give our attention to that storm and forget about each other!"

"I think I will go below and try to stay dry."

The storm suddenly reaches their pursuers and entirely hides them from view. "A few points back to the north! Be ready to shorten sail just before that squall hits us; it will not be long."

The storm lasted just over an hour. Under reduced sail *le Mare Majstro* ran before the wind when it blew hard and cheated back towards the north when it seemed to abate. There was no sign of the other ship when the rain cleared from either the deck or the masthead. "Due north helmsman. As close to the wind as we can. I want to close with the coast. Shake out another reef!"

"Where are they?"

"Your guess is as good as mine Matthew. With any luck they were dismasted in the storm. The masthead thinks they were still carrying full sail when it hit them. That can make bad things happen."

"Early nightfall?" It is still overcast.

"Likely to be unless it clears. I am hoping to catch sight of the coast before then."

They did not. Captain Carter sets a course to run parallel to the coast for the night under reduced sail to prevent the chance of running ashore in the darkness. In the cloudy, wet morning, the wind is still out of the west and gusty.

"Where are we?"

"I would guess east of Yarmouth. We'll sail north as close to west as we can for a few hours. If we do not sight the English coast, we'll turn back south and tack until we do."

After several hours they did turn south trying to gain as much sea to the west as they could. In a short while, the grey outlines of the Norfolk coast are made out by the masthead lookout.

"Were you worried?"

"Naw, well, maybe a little." Carter laughs. "Bring her about!"

"Err, Master Matthew?" Ruddy leans against the rail. "Cuzzin here told me something you might need to know."

"You have my full attention."

"Master Thomas gave me a message for his wife when we were last in Kingston."

"From Besse? Where did you take it?"

"He asked me to give it to the customs house; said they had post to London every week."

Matthew shows alarm. "What did it say on the cover?"

"I don't know. I think it was the name of the customs man."

It could be a harmless letter to a worried spouse. That was natural enough. "Besse should have asked me if he could send that letter."

"He said you probably would not let him, and his poor wife must think him dead."

"Odd that he has never mentioned having a wife, though. If he gives you another letter to take ashore first bring it to me. He is using you, Cuzz. Do you understand that?"

"So, this is a message that was waiting for Besse in Kingston?"

"Yes, Sir James, the customs man slipped it to Cuzz on the street in Kingston yesterday, and this is the letter that Besse was passing to the customs officer to send on to London," the messenger fidgets nervously as James considers the information. James decides to travel by horse to the port after receiving Matthew's message. He brings a large escort with the intention of bringing the wool profits back to Yorke with him.

"Then they would each have to be in response to previous correspondence. The question is are these affectionate letters between a man and his wife, sent without your permission, or are they messages disguised as such?" James laid out both letters on the table before him. The letters to Besse were in a beautiful round hand. Those from him looked like they were scribbled in the dark. That made sense as he obviously couldn't be seen writing them.

"Does Thomas Besse actually have a wife in London?"

"He never mentioned a wife or family when we first captured him, but at the time he was concerned for his own skin and with good reason. If we start with the assumption that he is writing to someone other than his wife...who would that be and what does he want?"

Matthew suggests, "Probably asking Lyons to free him from confinement with us. He said he had connections at court."

"He did, and he cannot be caught asking because that would violate his agreement with me and put his life in danger."

"I told you that we were pursued off the Isle of Thanet."

"Yes, we need to be careful of seeing the devil in every shadow, though. It could have been a king's ship believing you might be engaged in piracy. Piracy is a real problem for the king, Matthew. Do you write love letters to Trina?"

"No, I guess I should. Justin could read them to her."

"She would treasure them I am sure, but I've never sent affectionate poetry to Katherine, either. What about this 'mea, dulcis amor nisi certa scientia periculum liberabo te in mare?'"

"'Only the sure knowledge of my sweet love will free you from peril on the sea'? I think I am going to be sick!"

"Not a romantic Matthew? How about 'tis better to die brilliantly in love than never to have loved at all?' Or this from Besse to his wife: 'The beauty of the setting sun over the spires upon the headland make my heart ache for you.'"

"I think he is lovesick, and I'm about to be seasick."

"Copy them both out for me exactly as they are written. Then reseal the originals and have Cuzzin pass them along, as intended. Make sure I see every future message passed on or off the ship. He may try and pass messages in Bruges, too."

"So, we are free to kill him once we have used all of his wool certificates."

James leans back in his chair in his Yorke study. "Easy, Paul, if his wife or whomever he is corresponding with knows we have him prisoner, and he goes missing... Well, we could be accused of foul play."

"He could cause us no end of trouble after we release him!"

"Perhaps he could. I intend to highly suggest he return to Florence and not to England, but yes, he could. What do you think of these?"

"I find the verses awkward. It seems to me she would be telling him about any children and news of the Florentine community in London."

"'You are as Horatius holding the bridge to my heart' does nothing for you Paul?"

"I don't know much about Italian women, but I just cannot imagine any woman I know writing such drivel. Mary would never write something like that to me and she is very much a romantic at heart."

James laughs. "Paul, perhaps you need to polish your courting skills to win the Lady Mary, then!"

"Do you two want anything?"

"I am as Horatius holding the bridge to your heart, my darling Kate!"

"I did not know you were already drinking."

Laughing, he says, "Not quite the response I was expecting."

"Of course, you are my hero, James. What on earth are you reading?"

Handing one over, he says, "Love letters…or maybe coded messages to Lord Latimer."

"'Atop the scarlet cliffs north of Scarborough' is where you told me Clyde's little village lies."

"The ship passes there heading to Stockton. What about 'die brilliantly in love?'"

"Like Manser?"

"Very funny. No, not dye brilliantly like cloth; die brilliantly like death."

"Unless you are talking about using alum to dye brilliantly. The alum you kindly supply me for my shop is an excellent antiseptic and, indeed, has many other medical uses my dear, but that is not why you are importing it. Haven't you been trying to keep you source of supply a secret?"

"I have."

"And didn't you suspect Lord Latimer of intimidating Bygod into searching your barges and even this house for alum when he was sheriff?"

"I did."

Kate smiles. "Does Clyde have anything to do with your alum imports?"

"Have I told you, Paul, what a brilliant woman I married? The spires upon the headland could be Whitby Abbey. That is just five miles south of Bollebi."

Paul looks concerned. "Is this saying, 'identify the source of their alum if you expect to be rescued'?"

"It could be interpreted that way," nods James.

"We've passed these letters along."

"We need to make some preparations."

How much Thomas Besse knew is unclear to James. The letter writers seem to be playing a game as to who could be the more cute and clever, which made deciphering the actual communication difficult. It was unlikely they had established a code because they just would not have had an opportunity once Besse was aboard and no reason to have one before he was captured. That was unless they had been up to some kind of clandestine activity all along. It did seem certain that Besse knew they were selling alum in Bruges and taking it aboard at Bollebi. The ride to see Clyde made for a long day.

"Sir James, this is a surprise!"

"We may have trouble on its way Clyde. Our passenger aboard *le Mare Majstro* may have been sending messages about your work here."

"What sort of trouble?" his eyes gleam with anticipation.

"Has anyone aboard *le Mare Majstro* been up the cliff?"

"No. In fact they were here just yesterday. I go down to the beach; they never come up."

"Show me around. How many of your people here know you are refining alum from the shale?"

"I imagine everyone here knows what is going on. This is a small community, but they are careful to call the crystals 'natron salt.'"

"If I asked them what natron salt is used for would they know?"

"They would know what I told them and that's not much. I just know what you told me. It is used to make glass; lowers the melting temperature of the sand when the natron is mixed in. Otherwise it requires too much heat."

"And that it is a particular kind of salt that is hard to find and therefore expensive."

"They know that, too. Matthew always refers to the barrels as natron crystals on the beach. Nobody says 'alum' here."

"No visitors?"

"No one comes up here. The shepherds keep an eye out for me in all directions."

"All your wool is gone for the year."

"It is. Natron, cheese, and skins are all that we are lowering to the beach right now."

"I need you to dis-assemble the crane and meet Matthew at Whitby to trade cargo for the next few months. The crane may be what searchers are seeking to find Bollebi. Maybe they can signal to you as they sail past and then wait for you at the village."

"I forgot to mention the sea coal. We use the crane and wagon to bring it up and lower it down to le Mare Majstro."

"Just leave it at the base of the cliff and they can load it there."

"It doesn't go that way. The sea coal is collected at low tide and has to be hauled up before the tide comes in over the beach to the cliff base. If we left the coal there it would be washed away."

"I forgot that it floats."

"Seems counter to logic doesn't it."

"Better leave the crane, then. You need the coal to cook and heat your lead pans."

"We can take of ourselves here if need be, Sir James."

"I know you can. I never had any doubts of that. The problem is that they can always send a larger force and that is a game we cannot win forever. If someone comes by, I want you to be very defensive but finally confess to growing crystals of natron salt that are sold in Bruges. You need to be convincing enough, so that they do not return."

"They won't ever return to nowhere if you give me the word."

"If you doubt that you have convinced them, then make certain none live to return, but then we will have to be on our guard forever."

"When will they be here?"

"No way to know; a few weeks at the earliest. If they cross the Humbre we'll be watching and try to send you warning. I do think that is most likely. If they take a ship up the coast, we won't know."

"Likely put in at Whitby and need to get horses. We can keep a watch there."

"Good idea. Even if they come across the Humbre they will come through Whitby. A good chance they will overnight at the abbey. Now Clyde," James put his arm around his shoulders. "The barrels I've brought you have actual natron salt in them. If you need show them the result of what you are making…"

Clyde smiles and then starts laughing.

The following month, Matthew found Sir James waiting for him on the beach with Clyde below the hamlet of Bollebi. As the sea coal came down the cliff and the grain and empty barrels went back up, he received his instructions. Then they sailed on to Kingston.

La Rodecogge sat at anchor in the offing at Kingston, just as they had been warned. The *Christine* is also riding easily at her mooring just a bit farther up the estuary. That was like Sir James to have plenty of force on hand. Sure enough, their own anchor had just splashed down when a boat began rowing towards them from Lord Latimer's ship.

"Stand your archers down captain; I board in the name of the king!"

"The hell you do! Hook on and you'll be dead at your oars!" Carter roars back.

The men in the boat stop rowing and the man standing with the grappling hook sets it down on a thwart. The two men stand glaring at each other. *La Rodecogge* clearly has a large crew and they are lined up along the rails with keen interest. "If she starts to raise anchor to close with us let me know," Carter whispers to his mate.

"You are suspected of carrying illegal cargo. I am a lawful customs officer of the king."

"We have not even presented our manifest to the customs house as yet and you well know it. I remember your ship. You chased us several months back and had no cause then, either."

The man spreads his hands out in a show of innocence. "I'm doing what I've been ordered to do, Captain. Customs has the right to board ships in any English port."

"I count twenty-four armed men in your boat. That is hardly a customs inspection, and don't you try to tell me different. This is a legal merchant vessel owned by Sir James d'Arzhon. A man in good standing with the king and you would do well to be mindful of that!"

"And I am the lord chamberlain's representative appointed to see that customs duties are properly and fully paid!"

"Then you should know that we do not pay the poundage on imports until we present our manifest to the customs house!"

"I am required to match your manifest to an inspection of your cargo."

"Then you may come aboard and do just that – only you. If someone else starts climbing up the side, I'll drop a gift that will smash your boat's bottom clean through." A seaman sets a lead pig up on the rail to emphasize the point.

"Alright, then, I am coming aboard." The boat hooks on, and the custom agent climbs warily up the side.

Carter points to Matthew. "He handles the manifests and cargo."

"There isn't much here," the agent notes scanning down the list.

"We off-loaded cargo from Bruges and Calais here on our way north ten days ago. Right now, we have sea coal to unload – which we do not pay fees on as it is not imported," Matthew says pointedly. "We will pick up export cargo here and add that to the cheese and hides and such aboard. It is all listed here as are the fees to be paid."

"I'm going below."

"As you wish." Matthew follows him through the small ship end-to-end. In the captain's cabin the rug was rolled back and the trap door to the hidden hold is wide open.

"What is in the barrels?"

"Natron salt."

"Open one up."

"Which one would you like me to open?" Eventually all six barrels are opened, and the man tastes the salt from each. It clearly did not taste very good.

"I was told it is not for food."

"No, it is not." Then he emptied most of a barrel onto the deck, but it was natron all the way down. "What is in the locked chest?"

"Money, my ledgers."

"No proof of customs fees paid on past shipments?"

"I turned those over to Sir James on the way north. He doesn't want to me to keep too much money or documents aboard because of piracy and risk of shipwreck."

"Open it."

Inside are canvas sacks of coin, Matthew's ledgers, and another chest. "Open the small chest."

"That is Captain Carter's; you will need to ask him to open it."

"Every man aboard is on deck?"

"I believe so."

He gives each man a hard look; all of whom stare back threateningly. None is Thomas Besse. "A rather large crew for a merchant vessel." Fourteen men that had been with James had come aboard at Bollebi.

"In these times it is hard to know whom to trust."

"Indeed, it is captain. I will need to inspect you again before you leave."

"I don't like this at all. Tonight, when the tide turns, they will be able to drift down on us before we know it. Jasper, rig a buoy in the event we have to cut the anchor cable and have an ax at the ready. At least then Tenebroides will be able to salvage our anchor."

"He is working his way to us now, Captain."

"Prepare to take the *Christine* alongside!"

"I've been told to stay here until either you depart or *la Rodecogge* does. I've got forty men aboard."

"How many do they have, Master Tenebroides?"

"We've been counting the last few days; it is hard to tell. At least eighty but maybe a hundred. I can stay lashed right here; that will give them pause." Tenebroides made every effort to display the size and armament of his own crew while the sea coal is brought aboard and the wool off-loaded.

"That is a large crew!"

"They have been sent to suppress the English pirates in the channel, so they need it. Sir James does not trust Latimer, but the king does, and we need to be mindful of that fact."

"Expensive to pay such a large crew."

"I have no doubt that Lord Latimer is rewarding himself handsomely from the king's coffers for any and all expenditures!"

"Let's get your cargo aboard and see if Matthew can settle up ashore. I may be able to catch the last of ebb and get a few miles south before the turn."

"Wind favors you if it holds." Tenebroides turns to Matthew. "Here is my list; you can prepare your manifest now."

"Just fifty wool sacks?"

"End of the season," Tenebroides explains. "They belong to Thomas Graa and need to be taken to Calais not Bruges."

"The manifest will only take a moment. Captain, I'll need a boat."

"Getting it in the water now. Bosun lower a boat! Master Tenebroides, how heavy is your anchor?"

While Matthew is ashore at the customs house, Tenebroides anchors the *Christine* and Carter pulls up his own anchor. The *Christine's* anchor now moors both. This will save time as they merely have to untie to depart. Far better than chopping through their anchor hawser in an emergency.

"What are the cogge's options now?" Tenebroides ponders aloud. "They can send men up the coast searching for Clyde. If so, we can watch them here to see if they do."

"They could first sail up to Scarborough or Whitby and then send their men ashore."

"They could; Clyde is watching those ports. They can chase you at sea."

Carter smirks. "Never catch me in that fat tub, and they know it. They might board you after I sail."

"To what purpose? They saw everything aboard here that could have been transferred to me. What about wait for you off Bruges or Calais?"

"I'll keep a lookout when I put to sea."

"They were nervous as thieves in a confessional ashore, but I've got my Cocket seal!" Matthew is triumphant.

Tenebroides asked, "What about the agent aboard *la Rodecogge*?"

"He was there too; tried to delay the approval. I reminded the Kingston agent that he and I did business every month and *la Rodecogge* would not always be here."

"Careful threatening an agent of the Crown..."

"He has been warned before; back when they were boarding you every month Tenebro. You should have been there when Sir James enlightened him."

"I would have enjoyed that. You said they wanted to come back aboard before we sailed."

"I told him if he wanted to inspect us again, he needed to do it within the hour."

"Where is your guest?"

Carter smiles. "Sitting in a fishing boat off Spurn Head."

After an hour, they cast off lines from the *Christine*. Carter is able to pilot down the Humbre towards the North Sea several miles before the tide surges back in. *La Rodecogge* stayed at anchor off Kingston. In the late morning, Thomas Besse is back aboard along with several barrels that had been left with a pair of fishing boats. Latimer's ship is still several miles back when they began to shoulder into the waves of the sea, but they are also headed out of port.

Chapter 22

In the Smoke

September 1375

"Not in late September!"

"Why the hell not?" James responds to Master Tenebroides in frustration.

"The weather is too rough, and the wind is vigorous and steady from the north. I cannot make progress against that with mere sideboards and no keel! She is not built for that."

La Rodecogge had turned north as she left the Humbre into the North Sea. Piers, James' tithe-man in Kingston had immediately dispatched a rider to Yorke with the news. James then rode down to Barmby to meet the *Christine* and all the men aboard to get Tenebroides to follow her up the coast. And, using their oars, beat her to Clyde's settlement. If he could not get there in time with enough men, then Clyde would be easily overwhelmed, and everything lost. Now Tenebroides is being difficult.

Alum production has yielded seventy-five bushels this year. Even a modest increase next year would exceed £300 in value and this is just a small clandestine operation. The potential of full-scale manufacturing funded by Lord Latimer, or the crown, is enormous. Latimer may believe he is breaking up smuggling of alum by James into the country, but once he found out what was really going on... The secret production of alum, at the very least, everyone here would be in danger. The irony is that Latimer thinks he is pursuing the illegal importing of alum. The only thing illegal going on is a modest amount of alum exporting. Control of the only alum production in England could be akin to a gold rush!

"They will be in Bollebi long before we will be ready to meet her, then."

"I don't think so," Tenebro said, smiling. "With that square rig she will have to sail many miles tacking back and forth to make any progress at all. It would take a most fortuitous change in normal conditions for them to sail up the coast in a reasonable time. If we make haste, we will beat them there on the march."

"In that case, wagons with provisions will meet you in Elfwynton. I need you there by noon tomorrow!" James nearly sprang up onto his courser. "Every man aboard and any Sig can spare. You can leave the *Christine* here." Even a modest numerical advantage can be leveraged to overwhelm an enemy and reduce James' casualties dramatically. His problem is time.

La Rodecogge has eighty to a hundred men aboard, or so Tenebroides believes. James' challenge is to get enough men to Bollebi to meet, no defeat, that threat. Tenebroides should have at least fifty Companie men still aboard from everyone loaded on to meet the threat of *la Rodecogge* in Kingston, his own crew, and men from Barmby. Between The Swan, the priory, shipyard, shops, and his house in Yorke, James hopes to muster another thirty-five. Clyde should have another ten or twelve. If he can locate Virgil and his barge crew that will be nine more plus any men he can pull from their villages along the Swale. There will not be time to get more men from Richmond. Once in Yorke, James sends a rider up the Swale to find Virgil. He sends Paul Fitz-William ahead with a dozen horsemen to warn Clyde and then watch up and down the coast for their enemy.

Two days later, the little army camps outside Wharram Percy at the edge of the North Yorkshire moors. James now has eighty-six Companie men with him. Virgil has been located near Brecken-on-the-Swale, and left the *Marie* pulled up the side beck near the village. He is marching to meet them in Bollebi with ten men beside himself. As yet, there is no word from Paul. The next evening, they are still ten miles southwest of Whitby Abbey having moved just over twenty miles. James is antic with the slow pace, but the men are still getting used to being back on the march. His sense of urgency is shared by all.

Just before dark two riders arrive from Paul. *La Rodecogge* was spotted struggling to get into the harbor below Scarborough Castle early that afternoon. The scouts would have been here sooner, but James had been too optimistic and expected to be just north of the abbey tonight. They started there and then had ridden southwest along the anticipated line of march until they found them. The good news is that they are closer to Bollebi than the men aboard *la Rodecogge*.

"Why land men in Scarborough, and not further up the coast? If we were right about the letters, then surely they know we are putting cargo aboard north of Whitby."

"I'm telling ya, Sir James, this steady wind out of north wore 'em out." Tenebro gave an 'I told you so' look and continued, "Likely figured they could make more progress ashore."

The next day, Paul meets them on the march, and rides along with James. Paul shares that between ninety and a hundred men came ashore the previous day from *la Rodecogge*; he feels certain it is a good count. They had, indeed, started north up the coast this morning. By early afternoon, the Companie crosses the beck and reaches Bollebi. An anxious Clyde is waiting for him as James rides up out of the creek bed towards the semi-circle of cottages built into the hill. His worry changes to glee as he sees the size of James' little force.

"We are goin' to have us a nice little fight!"

"Clyde, find a mount and show me the lay of the land," James responds. "You'll have word for me tonight on their progress, Paul?" It was more statement than question.

"Yes, as soon as they stop today, we will get word."

The little beck runs south, parallel to the coast, for less than a mile before turning east again to empty into the North Sea. Between the wide gully, that holds the beck, and the sea cliffs is about a half mile. Where the beck flows east, the ground climbs steeply out of the gully to the north and the cliffs get steadily higher as you head up the coast. Where the beck meets the sea is a small collection of ramshackle shelters for fishing and collecting sea coal. A cart path climbs back and forth up the side of the gully here, and then runs along the brink of the coastal cliffs. Those cliffs are already well over a hundred feet high less than a quarter mile away from the huts. By the time they are opposite Bollebi, which is on the back side, the cliffs have reached two hundred feet. Here Clyde shows James the smoldering piles of alum shale. There are over a dozen in various states of burning depending upon how long they have been there. Most are about thirty feet long and just over a head tall. The wind blows hard here at the top of the cliffs. It dissipates the smoke immediately, except between the piles where it swirls, but you can feel the warmth just the same. James turns the wrong direction just once and gets the smoke into his eyes and mouth.

James rides south and then back north several times in an attempt to discern the most probable line of march for his enemy. Assuming they are trying to locate a smuggling operation near the cliff edge, based on information in Thomas Besse's letters, they should hug the coast. While it is only half a mile between the beck gully and the cliff that is still far too wide a battle front for his hundred-plus men. James wants to entice the men from *la Rodecogge* and then trap them if possible, along the cliff edge. That is also safely away from the little village and Clyde's refining operation.

Virgil marches in that evening with sixteen men. It is obvious that they have pushed themselves hard. "Joel is coming with more men and wagons of provisions from Richmond, but he may be a few days." His eyes are bright with anticipation and he continues with a growl, "Where are the mangy curs?"

"Nice to see you too," Clyde retorts with a laugh.

"One of Paul's scouts just came in; they are south of Robin Hoode's Baye. Tucking in for the night." James smiled. "You made good time."

"Thanks! Where is Robin Hoode Baye?"

Clyde grins. "Jest below Sherwood Forest, of course!"

"You two are picking up right where you left off ten years ago," James shakes his head. "About fifteen miles south of here. I do not expect them until late afternoon tomorrow at their current rate of march." James adds, "We have some time to prepare. Clyde, have your shepherds move the flocks away from the coast."

"Already done."

"Any notion of their numbers, Sir James?"

"A little confusion on that," Paul chimes in. "We counted almost a hundred when they landed, but now we count less than ninety."

"Deserters?"

"Or a bad count, Virgil. With you we now have a 110. More if Joel gets here on time."

"We will fight won't we, Sir James?"

"Oh, yes, Clyde, my preference is no survivors to tell their story. I want to lure them into a trap against the cliff."

Tenebroides had been quiet until now. "I'll make certain everyone knows what we are about then."

The next morning is overcast as James divides his men. Clyde's group is to wait among the burn piles to block their further progress north. Tenebro will have most of the archers just southwest of Clyde. Virgil will lead the main force from the west to drive them to the cliffs. Paul's mounted party will sweep in from behind to prevent any escape back the way they came. Will leads the 'bait' group where the beck meets the sea. The key is to lure them in, deeper and deeper, before they realize what is happening. Then spring the trap at just the right time. James worries that Clyde will not wait patiently until their enemy reaches the burn piles; he promises over and over that he will. "Keep hidden in the smoke until they are upon you! Then let the smoke be in their face when you pounce," he admonishes. At mid-day Joel arrives with another twenty-two men; they are worn out having covered over sixteen miles since daybreak. James holds them back as a reserve.

Allan was able to buy a horse in Scarborough; hardly a fine steed, but it would have to do. Lord Yarburgh's frustrations continue to mount when a dozen men disappear the second day. A gnawing suspicion, because the deserters include Roger Elford, is that this was planned all along. Elford is a long-time liegeman of his brother-in-law, Lord Latimer. Allan's wife, Latimer's much younger sister, died in childbirth quite a few years back but he supposes they are still brothers-in-law. The man is still uncle to his three children. All he shares with Elford is a dislike of d'Arzhon. Elford's hatred seems to come from a manor, Appleton Rabek, that he had control of...his future made until d'Arzhon interfered.

Most of his men are Flemish mercenaries. Allan thought this meant experienced, professional soldiers when he agreed to lead this expedition. Nothing could be further from the truth; the men are simply weavers and dyers that lacked enough work to earn a living. They drag on the march and complain constantly, "Where is the plunder we were promised?" The slow pace meant that they consumed all their food before getting as far up the coast as he hoped. As a result, he had needed to buy provisions in Whitby. Not only was he out of money now, but he may have lost any element of surprise on the smugglers.

Yarburgh's scouts spy the huts at the mouth of the beck in the early afternoon. Men are working there and have fires going. He pushes the main force to hurry forward to catch them, particularly when they receive reports that the men are vacating in panic as they approach. They must have had a watcher keeping an eye out. Why would they take such a precaution? Perhaps because they were up to something illegal! The men on the shore have two horse drawn carts. They have headed up the beck and then up the steep incline on the north side. They left so quickly that their fires are still burning.

As they splash across the beck in chase, the men and their carts are about three hundred yards ahead and nearing the top of the rise. Lord Yarburgh, mounted, urges them on up the steep incline in pursuit. When they are halfway up, archers show themselves at the top and begin loosing broadheads down the slope with lethal accuracy; his men are not carrying shields. "Get after them!" Yarburgh demands, "They are few!" He acts like a sheepdog behind his men pushing them up the rising ground, whacking the laggards with the flat of his sword and cursing them. The men bunch up on the narrow cart path as they puff along. It is a long steep climb that winds the men long before they reach the top.

The archers keep moving back as they shoot their arrows down the incline. There are half a dozen of them now and the groups of his men make easy marks. Gasps and screams of pain and fury fill the air as the shafts find targets. Finally, they reach the top of the ravine to catch their breath and the arrows still come at them. Some of his men sit down or hide behind any cover they can find while they rest. Just six archers. "Rush them!" Yarburgh screams in rage. This has got to be the smugglers' nest. Even though they have reached the crest of the ravine, the way forward is still uphill. Always the bow men are just out of reach; now less than a hundred feet ahead.

Several of his crossbow men stop to put a bolt to their bows to reply to the tormentors. Putting a foot into the stirrup and cranking back to load the bolt. They immediately become the focus of the archers up the hill. What was first just an annoyance, a few men dropping, is now a serious threat. His men are falling and too winded to close on the archers. More are crouching down to hide from the arrows behind any clump of grass or shrub. No, they are not cowardly! Arrow shafts protrude from them where they lie! Where are all these archers coming from?

Virgil waits and waits as he peers through a gap in the heath where he crouches in hiding. The captain is cutting it too close, he gasps to himself, but he dare not advance until he gets Sir James' signal. Now, there it is! He stands and waves his halberd left and right and then starts forward at a soundless trot. He almost gives a yell from habit, but Sir James wants them to close the gap before the enemy is aware they are coming and can form a fighting line.

Still they cannot get to the archers. The men farthest up the hill, closest to closing on the archers, become the targets, which causes the others to lag behind. In desperation a group charges ahead in a sprint, falling to the arrows at point-blank range, but some few just getting there, gasping for breath. The archers still retreating behind some grey mounds. They are on them now! Finally!

Suddenly men-at-arms leap from behind the smoking mounds with a screaming battle cry and chop his exhausted men down. Then Yarburgh sees the line of men closing rapidly from his left. Where did they come from? To his right is the cliff. "Form a battle line," he yells as he points towards the new threat. They try to do as he asks in little clusters facing the onslaught. More damn archers, that little red-bearded man looks familiar. Tired and outnumbered, the axes and halberds fall on them with a vengeance. They retreat towards the cliff and attempt to re-group. Their backs are now almost to the edge of the cliff, and now they have no room to maneuver. The pounding of the surf is in their ears from far below.

A man swings a long ax wildly and Virgil steps in to block it below the blade. He slams the butt end of his halberd between the man's legs and then thrusts the blade to split his face and shoves him aside. One of Virgil's men has slipped down to the ground and is set upon by two of the Flemings. Virgil swings his weapon and catches the nearest just below the ear spinning him in a spray of blood as he keeps moving towards the second man. He turns to run, but straight into the swinging mace of another big oarsman. The few that still stand throw down their weapons in surrender, but there is no quarter.

Lord Yarburgh pulls his mount around to save himself but sees a mounted force cutting off any retreat back down the slope. Spurring forward he races for a gap between the smoldering mounds and the cliff edge. Almost through! Then his way is blocked by a horseman in full breastplate and helmet emerging from the smoke. Allan quickly wheels his horse left around a mound only to find the horseman has blocked him again. Smoke blows into his face blinding him and he swings his sword wildly towards his closing foe. The sword is swept contemptuously aside by a war hammer. His horse is knocked sideways by the bigger warhorse of his opponent as they collide. His shield, too slow to rise, as he tries to maintain his seat on the stumbling horse; a mace crashes against the side of his helmet and tumbles him from the saddle.

The knight stands over him as he struggles to regain his senses; the war hammer pushing back his chin. "Cousin James," he gasps, "as I should have expected." Suddenly it is all clear to him: he is just a diversion to get James and his men well away from Yorke. Yarburgh starts to laugh uncontrollably in pain, in misery, in frustration, and in his own stupidity at being so used before blacking out.

It is market day in Yorke. Lady Mary of Rabuk shops with her maid among the stalls. She really does not need anything in particular, but it is an enjoyable diversion to spend the day in the city. Some of her men brought in a wagon load from the manor with her goods to sell. A man ahead looks familiar moving through the crowd. He reminds her of Roger Elford, with a chill, the man that took over her manor and treated her so badly when she was just a child. No, it cannot be, he would not show himself here in Yorke.

For James' shops and vendors still here in the city, nothing new has arrived this week on barges, but some has come in from the priory villages to the east and there is stock on hand. Lady Katherine is upstairs with the baby and her maid. Some servants, Malcolm and a few Companie men are the only ones left at the residence.

Malcolm opens the tiny wicket door to see who has knocked so insistently; the whole of the front door remains secure as he peers out. "What is your business?"

"Is this the house of Sir James d'Arzhon?" The man asks showing both hands to either side of his face open in innocence. His left hand is missing the thumb. He was an archer caught by the French and rendered unable to draw the bow against them again. Malcolm unbolts the door and the Companie men behind him relax and start to move back into the house.

The blade catches Malcolm in the belly as he reveals himself in the open door. He lashes out at the man's face with a fist and puts his shoulder to the door to force it closed again. "Help me!"

The guards rush back as more men from the outside force the door. "Secure the house!" Malcolm shouts back towards the inner door. A knee between the door and the jamb to prevent their closing it is chopped with a hand ax but quickly replaced with an iron bar that helps the attackers force it open. The small space limits full swings, so small axes and daggers are employed to work their deadly menace. The doorway confines entry for the more numerous attackers mitigating their advantage, as the men behind push forward they force their comrades unwillingly into the blades of Malcolm and his men, but eventually the numbers tell.

Upstairs, Katherine secures the door to the bedroom when she hears the shouting. She sends Anne to carry Philippa down the back staircase to the priory to get help and looks for a way to defend herself. She is supposed to retreat down the hidden staircase, as well, but cannot bring herself to do so.

Swain steps over the fallen bodies, carefully avoiding the growing pools of blood. One man sits holding his slit belly as his life bleeds away. Four others are already dead.

"Get out to the courtyard; they have an alarm bell," Elford barks at two men. "Move!"

Under the staircase going upstairs is a door. Swain opens it to reveal a staircase going down. Two of the men with him thrust him aside and hurry down to the cellar. He follows at a more measured pace borrowing a lit candle from the wall sconce before he descends with their leader, Roger Elford, behind him. It is dark and his companions immediately came back to him, and his light. Another candle holder is at the foot of the stairs and they put the wick to the flame to get more illumination.

It is a storeroom with an arched ceiling and goods on shelves. It is well-organized and appears to be used regularly. Flour, grains, sausages, and other smoked meats hanging from the ceiling. Boxes hold carrots and turnips packed in sawdust or straw. The walls seem solid to the touch. Surely the cellar is much larger than this. "I do not think we are in the right place."

"You said the cellar Swain!" Elford growls threateningly.

The wall behind him appears to be of more recent construction than the others. "I think we want to be on the other side of this wall."

"This is solid," he says, rapping it with the pommel of his dagger. More recent it might be, but it was not new, and it was made of heavy stone blocks. "You keep looking Swain, I will try and find the answer upstairs. Son, you keep an eye on the boat-builder."

Swain heads back up the staircase. The rear wall of the room, opposite the dead men, is wood paneled. The middle panel has a doorknob. Behind the panel is a small room or closet in front of an enormous fireplace; the opening is as high as his shoulders. The fireplace was clearly no longer in use but had once been for roasting great haunches of meat. It had been closed off in some previous remodel. Swain mused out loud, "He said, 'I've been down the chimney,' so this may be the place."

Three large spits nearly span the entire opening. A chain engages the gears mounted on the right of each spit. Outside the fireplace is a large cast-iron wheel, Swain releases the catch and the wheel began to slowly turn, the escapement rocking back and forth to allow the cable to unwind and turn the spits. He stops the wheel and pulls up on the cable. "There is a weight on the end of this, down in a cellar." Clever mechanism he thinks, wind it up once and then it slowly turns on its own.

"I did not see any weight."

"No," Swain replied. "I did not, either." He steps around the left side of the spit rack and ducks into the fireplace. It is very clean for an unused room, not even any dust. He brings the candle towards the rear and taps the cast iron back plate. It gives a deep solid tone. On his left are stone shelves with iron cooking pots of various sizes. He opens the lid of one. Oddly, it is filled with sand. He sets it down on the floor of the fireplace. The next one is also filled, as are they all.

"We need to hurry!"

"Do you see a way to get into the chimney?" His head brushes something. It is an iron lever to open the flue. Swain pushes it up, but it doesn't not budge. Then he pulls it down. The entire floor of the fireplace suddenly drops slowly with him in it into the cellar. He looks up and sees only the iron flue and lever still just above his head. The cast iron fire-back is still next to him, too. He hears the boots of his companions stomping above him and looks around, thankful that his candle did not go out. He steps out of the fireplace and sees an iron gate reveal itself in the light. He grabs one of the bars and shakes it; not much movement at all. There are locks at the gate top, bottom, and in the middle that each secure rods that go into the stone ceiling, floor, and wall.

Swain reaches his candle through the iron bars and into the room beyond. There are wooden chests with iron strap-work of various sizes on shelves. A table with candles and ledgers – all beyond his reach. A noise behind makes him jump in fright. He turns in time to see a massive counterweight descend as the fireplace disappears back up into the ceiling.

Above, the men stand in a fireplace that descended from the chimney. It has a stone floor and metal basket to hold logs behind the spits. If they had not seen him disappear, Swain might have never been here. "What the hell?" They step back around the spits and back out into the small room. Immediately the floor rises behind them to reveal the previous firelay, but Swain is gone.

The two go back into the fireplace again. "It's the flue lever he was pushin' on." They drop very rapidly down and stagger when they hit the bottom.

"Wait!" Swain yells too late as the men tumbled out into the room. The counterweight comes back down, and the fireplace goes back up. "Crap!"

"The treasure!" One finds his candle on the floor and re-lights it from Swain's.

"How do we get out of here is what I want to know!" Swain begins to inspect the lead counterweight and its thick chain that disappears into the dark shaft above. "At the moment, we are trapped."

"We need to find the key to these locks," they say, trying to shake the gate. Their eyes are locked on the chests beyond it.

"Help me lift this weight." They reluctantly do, slightly moving the heavy counterweight, but the fireplace does not come back down. "I hope the flue lever does not keep it from moving. We need to remove the counterweight." There is a torch sitting in a bracket mounted to the wall. It appears to have been here a long time unused; perhaps it is for emergencies. Swain gets it down and sets his candle to the pine pitch to get more light on the mechanism.

The torch lights immediately and illuminates the entire chamber. "Pig farts! What's that smell?"

"Brimstone! Put it out!" The pitch will not extinguish, but only burns more furiously and releases its toxic fumes into the chamber. The men begin coughing and their eyes burn. Swain's last thought, oddly, is that the pots filled with sand on the stone shelves must be to adjust the weight in the fireplace versus the counter.

Elford reaches the second floor. He can hear a bell ringing behind the house and then it goes silent. The first door is locked, the second leads to an empty dining room looking out over the street. He returns to the first door and slams his shoulder into it. Gawd that hurt. The hinges are on the other side; he will have to focus on the latch. He looks around and finds a heavy iron firedog in the dining room.

It takes some heavy blows, but finally the jamb breaks, and he shoves the door open breathing hard. Katherine icily returns his stare from where she sits in the bedroom and serenely adjusts the skirt of her fine dress. He looks around but she is alone.

"Where is the treasure?"

She only smiles slightly in response. "I know of no treasure."

"I warn you, you will tell me what I want to know, or you will be very sorry!"

"Lady Mary has told me of your despicable cruelty and depravity, Roger Elford, but I cannot tell you what I do not know."

"You must know something." His eyes linger over her. "And I intend to enjoy finding out." He begins to cross the room towards her.

Katherine glances at James' jeweled sword leaning against the wall. Elford follows her glance and quickly moves to block her path. "I think I'll take that, too. Your scheming husband will not be needing it again!" He admires the gems in the pommel and laughs.

The cup of lye catches him full in the face as he turns back towards her. "Whore-spawned witch!" he screams in pain as the acid burns his eyes and face. He yanks the jeweled sword from its scabbard and slashes blindly at her striking the empty chair. "Ah, God, it burns!"

Katherine is out the door as he stumbles to his knees.

Friar Hugh sprints across the priory courtyard and through Prior William's study with two brothers behind him. An ax is in the hidden stairwell, and he grabs it on the way up. He emerges through the wardrobe and into the bedroom.

"Hugh."

The house is unexpectedly quiet, and he looks around. Lady Katherine sits calmly in a beautiful midnight blue dress that shimmers in the firelight.

James' naked sword lays across her lap and at her feet is a man in a puddle of blood. A fire-dog lays next to his smashed-in head.

"Roger Elford," she says in response to his raised eyebrow. "Would you please look downstairs and then out by the stable?"

Hugh nods. "Yes, my Lady, and he motions to the two other friars that have just made it up the stairs. At the bottom of the staircase, he finds the bodies. They are all dead. As he stands up, the sheriff, Sir William Melton, hurries in the open front door, his men behind.

"I need to check the stable," Hugh says and leads the way out the back door into the courtyard behind the house; Sir William is close behind.

A stable boy sits holding his head next to the bell. Two men lie, apparently dead, nearby. Judd the fellmonger comes out of the stable with a bucket of water and a towel. "He'll ba-ba-be alright, Hugh." Then, nodding at the dead men, he says, "Not ours."

"I would assume the others are in the cellar, Sir William."

"Lady Katherine, will you please have someone to show us the way?"

Brother Hugh speaks up, "That would not be wise."

"There have been seven, no eight, men killed here and maybe more. I am the sheriff here! Do not presume to tell me what would be wise!"

Katherine replies softly, "Sir William, I believe you misunderstand Brother Hugh. The cellar air may be filled with deadly poison. It is unsafe for anyone to enter the cellar without Malcom or my husband...and Malcolm is dead."

Chapter 23

Westminster

January 1376

On the eve of Epiphany, Sir William Melton, Sheriff of Yorkshire, knocks at the door of Sir James' house.

"Won't you come in out of the cold? My men can take your horses around to the stable." Sir William had inherited many estates in Yorkshire and was in high standing with the Crown having served with Lancaster on the continent. James intended to do everything possible to build a good relationship.

"Thank you, Sir James." Sir William leaves his men on the street to go with their mounts through the arched gate and into the courtyard and stable while he follows his host upstairs.

"May I introduce my wife Katherine and offer you a warm glass of mulled wine?"

"Yes, thank you. Lady Katherine and I have met under most unfortunate circumstances. I have brought you correspondence from Prince Edward. It arrived at the castle this morning."

James was torn between being furious with Katherine for staying in the house rather than escaping into the priory as she had been told or being proud of her for standing her ground. In the end he decided he was both. They did mutually agree that if there was a next time, she would take the hidden stairs and get out. James took the offered canvas envelope and set it down on the table next to him. "I wondered what would coax you out into this bitter cold." The day was overcast and cheerless.

Will brought in the glasses of wine. "I have sent warm mugs out to your men in the courtyard, Sir William. There is a brazier burning there, as well."

"Oh, yes, thank you for that." He seemed to have forgotten about them and kept glancing at the letter sitting next to James.

"May I take a moment to glance through this to satisfy myself that it is nothing urgent?"

"Please do." The sheriff relaxed a bit into his chair and took a sip from his glass.

"I have been asked to attend a parliament at Westminster."

"London? When, my dear?"

"It is summoned for February 12."

"Well, that makes sense, then."

"How so, Sir William?"

"I had similar packets for the archbishop and abbot of Saint Mary's. Also, one for Ralphe de Hornby; the town council will need to elect someone to attend."

"I find it somewhat surprising," James ponders aloud, "as the king is surely asking the commons to grant more taxes."

"And the clergy, as well. Why do you find it surprising?"

"Because the king will want to continue the wool subsidy on exports and the other tariffs that cost merchants such as myself so much money. If I were in his place, I would choose men that did not stand to lose so much and were more likely to support his request."

"You will oppose the request?"

"No, I will not. I do not want to risk the king's disfavor. Although I wish the money would be spent to better purpose."

"How long will you be gone?" Katherine asks.

"A few weeks. I have never attended one, but I understand they do not last long. It does say that I will be reimbursed for my expenses at four shillings per day."

"I am not pleased to be left alone in Yorke again."

"That is understandable; I will take the necessary precautions."

It is not until April 28 that the parliament actually opens in the Painted Chamber of the Palace of Westminster. The previous day they had assembled, but there were too many men missing. In the presence of the king, the Prince of Wales, and all the great nobles of the land, Sir Thomas Knyvet, the Chancellor, delivers the 'pronunciation.' This charges the assemblage with three purposes. These center on defending the realm and a request for taxes to support that effort: a tenth from the clergy, a fifteenth from laymen, and an extension of the wool subsidy and the other customs for two years. James winces at the mention of the wool subsidy, even though he was expecting it. The fragile Prince Edward is carried in on a litter, so that he can be present.

There are about three hundred men assembled for the parliament. This includes about seventy knights, such as James, and about 160 representatives from the towns to make up the 'Commons.' The 'Lords' include the archbishops and bishops of the Church, twenty-five priors and abbots, as well as almost fifty lords, including the Duke of Lancaster – John of Gaunt. James does see his cousin Lord Yarburgh, but they are careful to ignore each other.

James knew most of those from Yorkshire including Archbishop Alexander Neville. Every time he saw the man, he thought back fondly of John de Thoresby who had died several years past. Also present were Abbot William of Saint Mary's with whom he had a mixed relationship after the peasant rebellion, the elected representatives of the city and some of the outlying towns. James made the acquaintance of Sir Robert de Boynton who held three manors in east Yorkshire on and near the North Sea coast. The leaders of the Church paid him no mind other than the aging Bishop of Durham, Thomas Hatfield, who greeted him warmly.

James travelled to London in the company of Thomas Graa and another merchant, John de Eshton, both representatives for the city. Together they made a large party and shared one wagon for the baggage. Thomas had rented a house and is pleased to share it and the rent expense. The stench of crowded London is overwhelming. James had thought Yorke bad enough, but many more people are living packed in between the River Thames and the city wall here. Animal droppings are left in the street where they fall, and human waste is dumped from the homes to join it.

"I for one am not looking forward to another two years of the wool subsidy," de Eshton expresses a common sentiment among the wool merchants.

"None of us are," James agrees.

Graa is stoic. "As long as this endless war continues, there will be the subsidy."

"This war was going on when I was born, Thomas. I spent too many years fighting it, and it will continue long after I am dead and buried!"

"But adding on a fifteenth again; it is too much, James."

"It does add up and is a hardship on those that work the land and see very little coin cross their palms. For me it amounts to a pittance compared to the wool subsidy, the wine tariff, and the rest of my import and export customs."

"You have no idea," Graa laments.

"Actually, since I handle a great deal of your wool, and you ship ten sacks for every one of mine, I have a very good idea how much the subsidy must be costing you, Thomas."

"And I say it is too much."

"And I agree, but I see no other course of action."

"We will just have to see what tomorrow brings."

"I see the misguided fools of Yorke have sent you to represent them."

"My Lord Latimer." No surprise that the king's chamberlain would be present in his ermine trimmed scarlet robe and gold chain of office. "It is Prince Edward that appointed me to a seat."

"He always held you in greater esteem than you merit."

"And I am thankful for that. I bid you good day."

"Do not be so hasty. I have come to understand that you have a steady source of alum, James."

"I am in the cloth trade; that is rather essential."

"But your source does not seem to come from the usual places or at the usual prices."

James smiles. "I am told it typically originates in the Mediterranean region."

"But that is not where you get it."

"Obviously, I do not personally have contacts there, but I do not consider it to be of your concern."

"Ah, but it is of concern to the Crown and therefore of interest to me. You are not as clever as you think, and I believe a court of inquiry will loosen your tongue." He smiles in an irritating manner.

"Doubtful."

"Do you believe you will get away with the murder of Edmond de Poule?"

"Never heard of him."

"Murdered in Yorke at your direction a few years back. I have ways of insuring that the king's justice is properly enforced. I have witnesses."

"Men paid to lie." James turns and walks away.

"I'll see you hung, then; don't think I won't! Your choice. You got away easy last time."

With that James turns back to face him. "I am not a youth of seventeen now, and I assure you I have not forgotten. Your time will come."

Latimer laughs with scorn. "And I suppose you will see that it does. One of your criminals in the dark? Or do you plan to kill me personally? The protection of the prince will not last forever..."

"Nor the king's!" He will need to ask Hugh if he has any idea who Edmund de Poule might be. "At least I won't need someone pinning your arms for me if I do!"

The following morning, the lords meet in the White Chamber and the commons in the abbey chapter house. The prelates of the Church also meet in convocation at Saint Peter's to consider the king's request for a tenth. A tenth from the Church will bring £18,000 in revenue to the Crown and can be collected much more quickly than the tax on the laity.

James settles into a corner seat on the bench wondering exactly how the proceedings will unfold. Do we start by approving the fifteenth and then the subsidy? It starts very differently. It is proposed that they all take an oath of loyalty to each other, so that they will be free to speak openly. Then a knight that James does not know, speaks out, "This heavy taxation upon the commons and the king's lack of funds is only because I have heard that there are some people that have taken gold and silver belonging to our lord the king for themselves."

Another stands. "The Staple at Calais used to be profitable to the realm because English merchants maintained the expense of soldiers there, but now Latimer and Lyons make money selling evasions and the king has to spend eight thousand pounds each year to defend the town." More rise to express similar sentiments.

Sir Peter de la Mare then sums up the sense of the body in such a clear manner that all present cheer him.

For the next ten days, the commons continue to debate the matter without much apparent progress or definitive purpose. It is exactly why James had declined membership on the Yorke town council – such a waste of time. He believes that regardless of wrongdoing, which he knew was rife and detestable, the king needs the money to defend the realm and continue the war. Surely all of this talk is pointless, and perhaps even dangerous. On Friday, May 9, Sir Alan Buxhill, Constable of the Tower, delivers a message from the king asking for an answer. By consensus it is decided to go the lords and present their case. Sir Peter is chosen as the spokesman.

Upon their arrival, they are informed that only a small delegation will be allowed to enter. Lancaster, presiding, demands the delegation state their business. Sir Peter replies that they have all come to put their case before the lords, "What one of us says all say and agree to." He refuses to say more until all of the commons have been admitted to the chamber. When this is done, he states that they have considered the king's requests and now beg the consultation of four bishops, four earls, and four barons. The request is granted and the next day this committee of lords joins them.

There are clearly two camps: those that want reforms in the government supported by the crown prince against those led by Lancaster seeking to preserve the status quo. In the commons the distrust of Lancaster is clear as is the fear that he will succeed his father as king. Wittingly or not, the duke has enabled corruption to surround the king and the financial administration of the crown. The bold talk makes James nervous, though he heartily agrees with them. Prince Edward must have encouraged them to speak out so against those so close to the king.

With the support of the committee of lords, Peter de la Mare presents to the whole parliament 140 petitions demanding reforms: against excessive taxation, mismanagement of the war, and charging Lord Latimer, Lord John Neville, Sir Richard Sturry, Richard Lyons, and others of faults that must be put to right for the good of the kingdom and demanding an account of public expenditures.

"Lords and magnates of the realm, by whose efforts the government of the kingdom is conducted, I wish to express how weighed down the common people have been by the burden of taxes, now paying a fifteenth, or a tenth, or even providing a ninth to the king's use. All of which they would bear graciously if the king should gain any advantage or profit from it. It would also have been tolerable to the people if all that money had been spent in advancing our military difficulties, even if unsuccessful. Instead, it is obvious that the king has not been so advantaged. Because the commoners have never been told how such great sums of money are spent, we are demanding a statement of accounts from those who received the money, for it is not reasonable that the king needs such an enormous sum if his ministers serve him with faith and loyalty."

Further that they will consider no grant of taxation until these matters have been addressed. The lords refuse to impeach those accused without a trial, but an agitated Lancaster rules that the accounts of the Crown be turned over.

"Well?"

"Sir Peter, if my clerks and business partners kept such ledgers, they would need to find other work." James has the books of the Exchequer laid out before him.

"So, they are stealing!"

"Possibly, but the accounting is poorly done and incomplete in places. If you want to obscure misdoings, I don't suppose you would record them. For example, it appears that a loan of 20,000 marks required a re-payment of 30,000!" One mark equals two-thirds of a pound or 160 pence.

"Quite a premium."

"We need to speak with the royal treasurers and get an explanation of these entries."

"Scrope and Exeter?"

"Sir Peter, those men are here in London, and we should be full in our understanding before making accusations."

"Indeed, we should. You will help me with your knowledge of finances when we meet with them."

"Are you not the steward of the Earl of March?"

"Indeed, I am James, but these accounts are insensible to me."

"They tell me you have gone from running river barges to trading wool and now to weaving cloth."

"Your Royal Highness is well-informed, as always," James replies softly. The prince's room at the Palace of Westminster is dark and soothing. "I appreciate your help at Saint Bartholomew's."

"Speak out, or are you alarmed at my sickly pallor?" Prince Edward's long illness has left him weak and bedridden.

"I am most distressed to see you this way; I fear for the realm."

"Honestly said. A booth location at the cloth faire is nothing I assure you. You would be dumbfounded at the favors asked of me!"

The prince's steward rolls in a barrel. "What is this?" demands the prince.

"It is a gift from Richard Lyons, my Lord. It is not sturgeon as marked." He reaches in and pulls up a handful of gold coins and lets them spill back into the barrel making a lovely tinkling sound. "Must be a thousand pounds here."

"You see James they appeal to my greed to buy their way out of the trouble that their own craving for wealth has bought upon them! But I am beyond the need of earthly treasure now. Send it back and tell him he will reap the fruit of his wages and drink what he has brewed."

"After speaking with the Bishop of Exeter and Scrope, I believe we have the evidence to convict Lord Latimer and Richard Lyons of abusing the trust of the king to their own profit, my Lord."

"Well done! I have always suspected it was so. You need be careful of your own safety here in London James."

"Yes, I have been warned. There is also much resentment against Ales Perrers, my prince. Her intimidation of justices, and thousands upon thousands of pounds taken from the royal accounts and into her own..."

"I thank God my mother is no longer alive to endure my father's mistress and their bastard children. Come closer to me James." As James leans close against the bed the prince is racked with a brief coughing spell. "The future of the realm depends upon you ridding my father of these leaches that take advantage of his age and trust and gorge themselves upon the life-blood of England to their own selfish maws!"

James nods and realizes that this may be the opportunity to deal with Latimer once and for all.

"Sir James d'Arzhon!" A well-dressed gentleman hurries to catch up with James as he heads back to his lodgings.

James slips his hand unobtrusively to the hilt of his dagger. "You have the advantage of me, sir."

"William Canynges of Bristol," he says, catching his breath. "I believe I owe you a glass."

"How so?" James replies thoughtfully. "I do not believe we have met."

"I am the owner of *la Petur!*" When James still looks befuddled, he says, "Grounded for over a month in the River Ouse."

"Oh, yes, of course! Forgive me I have been consumed by other matters. A delicate operation getting your ship floated off."

William steers James into a fine establishment babbling non-stop about the ingenious method used to float his ship off the river bottom. "You are sitting with the parliament, are you not?"

"A difficult business."

"Personally, I have wondered whether you are all very brave or very foolish, if you will forgive my speaking plainly."

"I wonder the same. If Lord Latimer remains in his office the consequences could be grave, indeed."

"He is no friend of mine, nor of Bristol!" William pours them each another glass. "Charged us an exorbitant fee for the safeguarding of the city liberties."

"I saw an entry for that in the King's Chamber ledger, two thousand marks, if I remember correctly."

"You are mistaken. We paid *ten* thousand marks!"

"No, I would have remembered that large a sum," James asserts.

"I delivered the payment myself."

"You have a receipt for ten thousand marks?"

"Signed by the chamberlain himself. It is still in my possession!"

"I would very much appreciate seeing that receipt William." If James can prove that Lord Latimer took eight thousand marks for himself and only put two in the king's accounts, then that may be enough more evidence to incriminate him beyond even Lancaster's tolerance.

"And so you shall, Sir James," he says, refilling their glasses, "and so you shall."

Peter de la Mare reports to the whole parliament that he has received the king's approval for the royal treasurers to give evidence. Richard Scopes confirms that Latimer and Lyons made the loan of 20,000 marks at the expensive premium of 10,000 marks. A man named John Pyle is in the parliament from London and under oath is directly questioned by Lancaster himself. He, too, incriminates Latimer and Lyons.

Lyons asserts that he was acting with the king's warrant when questioned before the body. When ordered to present that warrant, he cannot, as 'it is from the king's words' and not a document. Testimony is given that the king states that he has not entered into such an office with a Richard Lyons and further does not recognize him as his officer. It appears that any authority he has been exercising comes solely from the king's chamberlain – Latimer.

Lord Latimer answers questions fully while insisting that he has no obligation to do so. To de la Mare's questions, provided by James, he answers with arrogance; he clearly believes any charges have no teeth. He must presume that Lancaster, representing the king, will sweep them away with a wave of his hand. He says that the commons have no authority as they are not his peers; only the lords may bring him to trial. This assertion is dismissed as the lords are in fact also hearing the case and stand in judgment. The missing balance paid by the City of Bristol is augmented by charges that Lord Latimer similarly stole much of the fine paid by a Robert Knolles to settle with the king for the failure of his military foray into France. The charges are judged to have been proven. The assembled parliament now loudly demands his arrest.

On Saturday, May 24, after meeting separately, the parliament meets as a whole once again. Peter de la Mare speaks again to express the will of the commons that they will not discuss the matter of taxes and subsidies until the king has removed those impeached including the treasurer and chamberlain. In addition, Ales Perrers is accused of improper behavior to the detriment of the king's honor and reputation. She has taken thousands of pounds of gold and silver each year from the royal treasury. For the good of the kingdom, she should be removed from his presence. The lords support the ultimatum.

"Lancaster is in a rage. I have a source in their confidence."

"So, I have heard James. What is less clear is the object of that anger."

"Frustration with any and all Peter, including us, but also with himself and Lord Latimer. He spares no one in his rants. This could be dangerous."

De la Mare paces uneasily back and forth. "Prince Edward called the king and Lancaster to his bedside today. He asked them to affirm his son Richard as the rightful heir to the throne after his death."

"He believes his time is very soon now."

"Sir James?" A valet has appeared at the door. "A message from Prince Edward asking you to attend him."

It is nearly dark as James leaves de la Mare's lodgings. Where are Paul and Will? The valet indicated they were waiting for him here in the garden courtyard. A sudden movement catches the corner of his eye, and he springs back as a dagger lunges towards him from behind a potted tree. A sharp pain runs up his arm, and he throws his cloak in the face of his assailant.

As he spins away, a cudgel hits him hard on the side of the head staggering him but not knocking him down. James stumbles back away from the door to give himself time and space to clear his head. He gets across the yard as they close in, draws his own dagger, and puts his back to the garden wall. Blood is running down from his ear.

"Treasonous bastard," one of them growls, raising the cudgel for another blow. James launches himself off the wall forward as the club begins its decent, stabs for the man's belly, and rams his shoulder into him. The cudgel flails harmlessly over his back. James spins away, twisting and ripping the dagger sideways and free. Then dazed, he stumbles and staggers out into the street as the other man advances again.

He can hear Paul shouting for him as he slides in the filth of the gutter in the narrow street. It had rained earlier, and the little light that came from the moon reflects off the dark puddles and disorients him. The side of his head is pounding, and his dagger hand is sticky with blood. James runs and shouts, "Paul! Will!" The footfalls of his assailants are right behind him. He turns the corner into a side street, but it is a dead end. In spite of his situation the foul stench of the alley still manages to assault his senses. His back is to a wall.

"Get him!" They inch forward warily having seen what happened to their comrade.

James can still hear Paul and Will, their voices desperate and the echo of feet running, but he does not know where they are, or where he is, for that matter. Which will attack first? The three edge closer, but each seems to wait for another to engage.

"Oh, there you are finally, Will!" James looks up the alley. As they hesitate and glance back, he kicks a pile of excrement up into the face of the boldest and then slashes under his blocking arm for the neck, resulting in a scream until his blood chokes off the outburst and he falls back, clutching his severed throat. The other two will not fall for that trick, but at least there are now just two. He thinks it is two, but his vision is blurring.

A party of men now arrive at the end of the street. "Lay down your weapons!" their leader demands forcefully.

"It appears that you are in need of assistance."

The voice sounds like his cousin. "Allan?"

Paul sews up the gash on his arm. A dressing has finally stopped the bleeding on his head. Why do head wounds always bleed so damn much? The slash on his leg is bound tight but seems minor.

"Where the hell were you?"

"Will and I got a message to meet you in the front hall."

"Any sign of the man that gave you that message or the one to me?"

"Gone."

"I am thankful for your help, my Lord."

Yarburgh replies, "I caught wind of this ambush just an hour ago. It appears we were just in time, although you were not completely undone yet. One is still in the garden lying with his guts spilled next to him; another is dead in the alley."

"I was dazed and could not see them clearly. I am indebted to you."

"James, I have thought poorly of you for a long time. I thought you left childishly sore at losing Marjorie's hand to me. I did not know Latimer beat you almost to death and whipped the skin off your back. I thought I was only going to honor our agreement that spared me your sword up north, but I..."

"He made it clear that I was not a suitable match for his younger sister. I continued to pursue her affection. It was a mistake."

"He bragged about that last night; said he was going to finish what he started. I just did not quite understand exactly what he meant."

James nodded. "I'm glad you didn't help him. I was never fully certain you would honor our agreement."

"James..." Allan paused thoughtfully. "Do you think Marjorie ever knew why you left?"

"I do not know. I spent a lot of years wondering just that."

"I guess it doesn't matter now."

"She has been gone for almost what – five years?"

"About that," Lord Yarburgh said. "I had a tough time in France. I thought I would never get out. I blamed you that I was there."

"I deserve that blame. Everything I've heard about that campaign is beyond my understanding. Was Lancaster unwilling to engage the French?"

"Afraid to risk it all in a pitched battle? I have not heard it put that way, but it makes more sense than any other explanation. Not like your days with Prince Edward and Chandos."

"No, it was always the French king that played for time. This time that worked very well for them. I'm relieved that you made it back, Allan; honest, I am."

"I am not the same man that left for Calais, James."

"Sir James, we have received a response from Hugh." Paul holds a letter.

"On the identity of Edmond de Poule?"

"Hugh believes he was Latimer's man. The one murdered in the room of a prostitute shortly after Sheriff Bygod forced entry into our house."

"I remember now; while Katherine and I were in Barmby. Any notion as to who Latimer's 'witnesses' might be?"

"Paul says that the murder has never been solved and that part of the reason is that no one ever came forward as a witness."

"I believe Lord Latimer has direr concerns at the moment; at least I hope so."

Two days later, the king agrees to the parliament's demands removing Ales Perrers, Latimer, and the others from his council and names new councilors. Emboldened further, de la Mare attacks Latimer for taking payment from the French for the surrender of two castles in France, Becherel, and Saint-Sauveur, for which he was the warden and demands that he and Lyons be imprisoned. Witnesses come forward to support the charges. When Latimer requests time to prepare a defense, the king's new counselors refuse and make him respond to the charges now. Further charges continue to be leveled, including defrauding the king of fines paid and taking them for himself.

Eventually, Lancaster gives in to the pressure of the proven charges. The Commons having the power to grant, or not grant, a tax assessment have established themselves as a force in the governing of the realm. Lord Latimer and Richard Lyons are imprisoned and fined. Latimer alone is fined 20,000 marks. Ales Perrers is banished from the king's councils and ordered to forfeit many of her possessions.

On June 8, the proceedings are interrupted with the news of Prince Edward's death. The business of the parliament is brought to conclusion in the next few weeks in a melancholy mood. The jubilation over their success is tempered by the feeling of despair over the prince's passing. While he lived, there was the feeling of invincibility; he had never been defeated in battle, but now who will command the armies of England to victory? Surely not the Duke of Lancaster who marched an army all the way across France without ever bringing the enemy to battle!

Before departure a celebratory dinner is held. The king pays for the venison and the wine. Lancaster is noticeably absent.

"Well, James, you must be pleased," Thomas Graa says admiringly as they ride north. "Sir Peter and our king's younger sons, Cambridge and Woodstock, seemed most appreciative of your efforts."

"The earls were most kind. The question is Lancaster. Will he honor his vow to Prince Edward to ensure young Richard is our next king or seize the throne for himself?"

"He will be tempted. He must know that he is not admired or trusted but he has that Plantagenet arrogance and temper. At least Latimer is in prison; that is highly satisfactory to us all."

"Yes, it is. Let us pray that the king is now better served."

Epilogue

It is an easy run down the coast to Scarborough. Carter stays far enough out to sea for *le Mare Majstro* to weather the headland dominated by the castle and then brings the tiller over to head into South Bay. The Hanse trader *Neuchâtel* rides gently to her anchor, and they glide to spot just beyond her and drop their own.

It is now late afternoon, and Matthew is rowed across for a social call. "Have you been waiting long?"

"We got in late yesterday. Not a problem as I had a full day ashore. Have you brought me wool?"

"Just twelve sacks again this month Master Schiffer."

"I am prepared to pay seven pounds twelve shillings a sack as agreed."

Not paying the customs subsidy makes that an excellent price and with Latimer in prison they are avoiding it on every sack accumulated north of Yorke. "It will be dark soon enough for transfer."

Thomas tries to climb again. Waves crash against the base of the cliff far below. Matthew had let him go ashore for some exercise while *le Mare Majstro* took on cargo lowered down from the rim. It was not the first time he had been allowed to stroll the sand because he could not go far, and the beach disappears into the sea at high tide. Besse knew Matthew had very few of his wool certificates left now. They soon would no longer need him aboard, and he had fears that he would not be released. He had learned too much about their cargo and evasions of customs duties.

He slipped away from the crew ashore as far down the coast as he could. Then saw the last of the wool sacks go aboard while he clung close behind an outcropping of the steep, red cliff wall. Nervously he waited for the alarm to be sounded and the beach to be searched. Instead, he watched the ship weigh anchor and set sail to the south. He is climbing in a ravine where the water run-off has cut a gully in the side of the cliff. The beach below is now gone to the sea. His footholds keep giving way and crumbling down into the surf below. Several times he almost tumbles down too.

Exhausted, he finally reaches the top to see the last of the day disappear beyond the horizon. It is dusk, and the cliff behind dark. He is covered from head to toe in red clay.

"I would guess that was a difficult climb."

Startled, the last of the light behind the man, he blurts out, "Who might you be?"

The bear of a man smiles and says, "They call me Clyde." The club strikes Thomas full in the face, and he tumbles over back into the abyss.

Virgil watches Matilda sitting up in the bow as the *Marie* sails down the Ouse towards Yorke. They are passing Popeltone now, so it will not be much longer, and they will see Saint Mary's Abbey and the spire of Saint Peter's. The crew tends the sail and the light breeze is steady from the west; no need to use the oars. Plenty of water under her keel in the Spring as usual. She brushes the hair back from her face where it had slipped out of her cap and looks back towards him with a smile. No, he has never had a more pleasant run down the river.

"Well, yes, he could deny us permission to marry but that is unlikely," he had told her. "Nothing to worry about. Getting his approval is not even needed. I am a freeman." She had badgered him continuously on that possibility ever since.

"But he does own my brewery, and he does own your barge! He may not be our lord, but he might as well be." She thought Sir James might be angry that they had not gotten his permission before staying together and now, when told, would show his pique.

Virgil assured her that Sir James surely had known for some time and if he had disapproved would have already let him know. "No, a dowry is quite unnecessary, Matilda!" She had brought two kegs of ale just to be sure. Explaining that Sir James 'owns' the brewery and the *Marie* only behalf of the Companie seemed like it might be confusing.

Laughing at her struggle, Joel had suggested Matilda meet with Lady Katherine and secure her as an advocate. He was kidding, of course, but that was now Matty's plan! How do women go from complaining that you are gone too much to be in a committed relationship to becoming so fiercely determined to make it absolutely official?

"I expect to sell a full wool sack to you this year, James!"

The Lady Mary is no longer a little girl, almost eighteen now. "You have 240 mature sheep already, then. You have done well."

"More than enough to pay you back for the original flock of one hundred."

"I hope we can still count on you as a wool supplier, Mary."

"Yes, you can. We had some buyers try and buy our wool last month, not that we would have sold it to them, but they offered less than what you have been paying us. My reeve was surprised. I was not."

"A Yorkshire buyer or someone from overseas?"

"I will find out if you want to know."

"Please do, I like to know whom I am competing with for wool. We are having a dinner this afternoon at The Swan, a marriage celebration; we would be delighted if you will join us."

"I think Katherine has already invited me. We are going to The Swan after our fittings with Valentine. I believe the bride is coming with us, too."

"Now I understand what is going on. Kate mentioned that we are buying Matilda a dress as a wedding gift, but now I see that each of you are getting one."

"We know some people in the cloth trade," Mary confides in a pretense of confidentiality.

"I do not want to sign the ledger with Paul and take more money to pay my wages again this week. It is starting to add up!"

Janice grimaces. "Sir James does not like it when you do not show a profit." Elias squirms all the more on his stool. "You've brought your ledger?" It has been a long time since the morning, when the woodworker showed up to learn how to use a loom at her shop.

"I've only been responsible for the boatyard for a month. Help me, Janice! Sir James is going to dismiss me!"

"Swain needed help with his accounting, too." She runs her finger down the expenses of the boatyard. "Where is your income?"

"I won't complete the repairs to the fishing boat in the yard until next week; payment is due, then."

"You may want to collect a deposit when the boat arrives in your yard and another when you are at the half-way point. What else have you been working on?"

"We finished two looms. One for you and one to send down to Barmby-on-the-marsh. They are not due until next week. Plus, they are really for Sir James, right? So, we don't get paid for them."

"Oh, yes, you do! I pay for mine and Sigismund has to pay for his. Your accounts show the sale as income and our accounts must show the expense. Sir James will have all the ledgers open on his table when he audits them. Bring my loom over today, and I when I pay you it will more than cover your wages for the week."

April is when the plow teams begin turning over the fields to put in a new crop. Nothing to harvest, but it is also when tender shoots of borage, cress, nettles, and saxifrage can be gathered from the edges of the woods and bogs to create an excellent salad. By the time summer arrives, and these plants begin to flower, the leaves and stems will turn bitter. Michael, the chef at The Swan, dresses them simply, first with oil and then vinegar and a sprinkle of salt.

James reaches for his mug of ale and realizes that all eyes are on him and that conversation has ceased as he takes a drink. Something is afoot. The ale has a different taste and darker color – quite nice. "This is not from Tatecastre, is it?"

"Do you like it?" Diane asks with a sly smile.

"Tufty did not make this at the priory, either." It was very good, indeed, as he took another, more analytical sip. "The barley has been caramelized."

"Not the barley. What do you think of it?"

"It is excellent. Matilda, did you make this?"

Everyone begins laughing and nodding as Matilda beams with happiness and relief."

She reveals, "It has rye malt and some caramelized rye malt added."

"We need to find you an apprentice. Someone you can teach your craft."

Michael now arrives leading a procession of additional dishes. There is a pastry filled with a mixture of spiced dried fruits sauced with white wine and mixed with salted herring. The cloves, ginger, mustard, and pepper create a sweet dish with the fruit that balances the fishes' lingering salty taste. The main dish is spit roasted venison basted with red wine and ground ginger. It is still sizzling as it is set on the table.

Kate nudges James' elbow and guides his gaze to where the Lady Mary sits with Paul Fitz-William. They are clearly enjoying each other's company this afternoon.

"You seemed a bit distracted at dinner, my love, in spite of the occasion."

"I hope it was not noticeable to any besides you, Kate."

"Likely not. Everyone was having a marvelous time."

"I received a letter from my cousin in London."

"Lord Yarburgh? I thought you were not on the best of terms."

"We weren't for a long time. Perhaps each of us found a bit of empathy for the other as time went by. He writes that the new parliament has granted a full pardon to William Latimer."

"Why would they back down?"

"I near as I can tell, not a single knight called to serve last year was called back again to the new parliament!"

"Surely he will not serve the king as chamberlain!"

"It does not say. If Lancaster needs financing for a new campaign, he may well go back to those that can get it for him. He also writes that our parliament's speaker, Sir Peter de la Mare, has been imprisoned in Nottingham Castle. It appears that loyalty to England is not the same as loyalty to the Crown!"

Historical Notes

This is a work of fiction and so, of course, are the main characters. King Edward III, Prince Edward, John of Gaunt (Lancaster), Ales Perrers, William Latimer, Richard Lyons and many others are actual historical individuals. I did not want the facts to get in the way of a good story, but I also wanted to convey what was really happening at the end of Edward III's reign. Times of societal change are interesting to me. The combination of the Hundred Years' War, the emergence of a merchant class, and the impact of the plagues make this a time of upheaval. *The Time Traveler's Guide to Medieval England* by Ian Mortimer and *England in the reign of Edward III* by Scott L. Waugh were helpful to me and give a good factual understanding of those times. Much of what I thought I knew before I started working on this book, from movies and literature, was not correct!

In general, the more historical information I was able to uncover, the happier I was, and I have tried not to contradict known facts. Even the smallest facts, at times, were able to inspire part of the tale; the actuals events are more interesting than I could possibly conjure. Considering this story takes place in late medieval England, about 650 years ago, I find it astonishing how much information exists, if you are willing to keep digging. I have often used the older spellings for places when I could discover them, as in Gainsburgh instead of the modern Gainsborough, in an effort to help the reader distance themselves from the world of today.

Many streets in the City of York are still called 'gates' as in St. Andrewgate after the Norse 'gata,' meaning street. The city gates are called 'bars' and so you end up with the 'Micklegate Bar' for example. Perhaps because it 'bars' your way as you travel down Micklegate 'street?' I hope this was not too confusing. I do have a fascination with how things were made in the fourteenth century. I have indulged it in this book and fully realize that you may not share my intrigue; I apologize if you found it distracting.

You may find it interesting that alum was actually discovered in Bollebi (now Boulby) in the North Yorkshire moors in the reign of Henry VIII. By that time, the pope had created a monopoly on alum, which was obviously a problem for Henry, but it took many years to make the venture commercially viable. There are places in the world where alum crystals form naturally, clearly Clyde and Sir James were able to keep their accidental discovery a secret. In general, the refining process in the book resembles the actual one employed. I am sure an expert chemist on the subject would dispute that assertion, but I did not want to spend an entire chapter detailing the refining of alum from shale and you would not want to read it. Swaledale, west of Richmond, was indeed a source of lead mining, even in those times.

All the monasteries in England were dissolved by Henry VIII around 1536 and that includes Saint Mary's Abbey and the Carmelites, or Whitefriars, in York, but both actually did exist in the locations described. The foundations of Saint Mary's are now the museum gardens, and the Whitefriars were near Carmelite Street in the city today. They did have a quay on the Foss, they did own five shops on St. Andrewgate, and they did charge a young man named Richard with being apostate after he left the order and returned to his father, John de Thornton, a spicer in the city. The prior, in those years, was in fact named William. So, yes, I chose William to be the name of the prior in this book. Other than his first name, I could discover nothing about the actual man.

You may well have gotten tired of hearing about wool. It would be impossible to overstate the importance of wool to the English economy and finances of the crown in that time. To this day, the seat of the Lord Speaker in the House of Lords Chamber is "The Woolsack," a large, wool-stuffed seat covered with red cloth. It was introduced by King Edward as a reminder of England's source of wealth. The customs subsidies paid on wool, the Staple of Calais, and Latimer's selling of evasions are as accurate as my research allowed me to be.

A Flemish cogge was taken by 'a city barge' off Romney Marsh in March 1375. That writer is probably referring to one of the City of London barges, but I stole the prize for the City of Yorke's galley to fit my story line. The individuals that appear as mayors, sheriffs, archbishops, and abbots are almost always the actual historic names of the persons that held the office at that time. In general, other than the name like Prior William, I do not know anything about their character: if they were mean-spirited or warm and generous. What they say and do in the book is fiction. I did repeat words attributed by medieval chroniclers to Prince Edward, but those words are likely only the gist of what may actually have been said. It seems that many writers in those times were spinning their words in admiration or hatred to forward their own agenda – imagine that! For example, I seriously doubt that Ales Perrers, King Edward's mistress, was a witch or ugly as written by the chronicler Thomas Walsingham. Beautiful and charming women have always been able to enchant men, and kings usually do rather well in that game.

Edward, the heroic son and heir of King Edward III, is always referred to today as the 'Black Prince,' and there are differing views as to whether he was called as such in his lifetime. Most historians believe not, and I've followed that opinion. He is believed to have encouraged the knights of the commons to present their charges and he did die before parliament concluded. That final chapter leans the heaviest on the history books. The parliament of 1376 is known today as 'The Good Parliament,' and more is written about it than any previous parliament or parliaments after for the next hundred years. It was the first to elect a speaker, Peter de la Mare, and the first to impeach officers of the Crown. Latimer, Lyons, and Ales Perrers were charged and punished just about as written here, depending upon whose account you believe. My main source, if you want to learn more, was *The Good Parliament* by George Holmes.

Lord Latimer is described as having a loose morality, being greedy, proud, cruel, deceitful, and lacking wisdom by the Saint Albans Chronicler. The description may be somewhat unfair, but it does reflect what many must have thought of him at the time. I decided these were excellent characteristics for the antagonist in my story.

King Edward III dies the next year and is succeeded by his ten-year-old grandson, Richard II. The convicted courtiers are pardoned as John of Gaunt, Duke of Lancaster, regains his hold of the government. William Latimer signs as witness to the king's last will and testament in October 1377. His return to favor took less than a year. The Flemish financier Richard Lyons is murdered by a mob led by Wat Tyler during the 'Peasants Revolt' on the streets of London in 1381. Perhaps all that is the grist for another story…

Frank Macaulay

February 5, 2019

CPSIA information can be obtained
at www.ICGtesting.com
Printed in the USA
FSHW020726040420
68803FS